ANDREW KN
Leeds. His shot
widely published. As a write.
forty fantasy and science fiction novels ...
names for independent publishers.

He is active in the British SFF community and can often be found on convention panels.

Follow Andrew on Instagram @knightonandy and Bluesky @aknighton.bsky.social

THE
EXECUTIONER'S BLADE

ANDREW KNIGHTON

NORTHODOX PRESS

Northodox Press Ltd
Maiden Greve, Malton,
North Yorkshire, YO17 7BE

This edition 2024

1
First published in Great Britain by
Northodox Press Ltd 2024

ISBN: 9781915179265

This book is set in Caslon Pro Std

To Milena, who strives for truth
and justice with words instead of blades.

CHAPTER ONE

An Executioner's Duty

Lena swung the axe in steady, constant strokes, each blow sure and strong. Splinters of dragon bone flew from her blade across the cavern floor, disappearing into the shadows. She didn't bother keeping track of them. One of the sgeir could sweep up those fragments and sell them to an alchemist in town. Lena earned enough as an executioner to buy bread and meat, enough from chopping bones to buy ale and spirits. Others could grub around in the dirt for the sake of a few pennies. One way or another, she was probably damned, but she wouldn't let herself be pathetic too.

The caverns were busy. Spring had come early, and with it mating battles among the monsters that wintered in the mountains. The winners would have their pick of mates, while the worst of the losers would come here to die in the caves above Unteholz, following instincts no scholar could explain. And with the campaign season starting, there would soon be war beasts too, battered, bleeding, and weighed down with broken battle harnesses, strong and beautiful creatures sacrificed for human folly, come to breathe their last beside their kin.

That brought them to the sgeir, these outcast scavengers and dwellers in the dark. People Lena could tolerate.

Across the cavern, a family were butchering the remains of a wyvern. Two adults took old but well-honed knives to the scale-covered skin while their children drained blood into clay pots. The meat would come next, then the high value parts like bile and brains and balls. They would carry off the smaller bones in their rickety hand cart, leaving only the most unwieldy for the likes of Lena. Some of the axe sgeir teamed up with families to work a body together, combining brute force with the butcher's art, but Lena preferred to work alone.

The caverns were vast. They had to be to hold all the creatures that came here, sick or wounded, looking for comfort from the cold stone. Their breath filled the cavern: the rattling of diseased lungs, the whimpers of bleeding beasts, the snorting and snuffling of those that were simply too old to live. Sad sounds that brought back memories of the beasts Lena had ridden and fought when she was young. She and those creatures had been proud and powerful together, strong of body and will. She missed that, though she didn't deserve it anymore. She hoped that some of her beasts, at least, had missed her for a while. That much, perhaps, she deserved.

The ball joint cracked off beneath her axe and rolled across the floor. Lena stopped it with her boot and kicked it into a heap of scraps, then added the rest of the bone to those piled up on her hand cart, pale cylinders stacked as neatly as firewood. Dragon bone was light, strong, and virtually immune to fire, useful in construction projects as well as alchemy. Every year, the city council earned a tidy sum selling the monopoly to trade in these bones, and every year the merchant who bought it did well. They could afford to pay Lena a good price.

As she reached for another bone, a man approached. He looked out of place in the dying caves, and not just because he wore bonded plate armour instead of rags and dirt. The sgeir skittered nervously between the dying beasts; Soren Baumer swaggered.

Lena scowled and hefted her axe. She didn't like to be reminded that she lived at the city's beck and call.

'Headsman Sturm,' Baumer said. Two steel-clad fingers tapped the spot beneath his eye, warding off the bad luck that hung around an executioner like crows around a battlefield. He only did it briefly, a gesture of habit rather than fear, and the nod that followed was no less civil than it would have been for anyone else.

That was one of the reasons Lena didn't dislike Baumer. He could do social niceties when he must, but he preferred getting to the point, like a good soldier, and he didn't pretend to be more than he was. If she'd been twenty years younger, then she might have got him drunk, and given him a tumble just to see what lay under that armour. But she had too many grey hairs to attract men under forty, and too little patience to teach them how a woman's body worked.

'What brings you down here, Captain?' Lena asked.

'The only thing that ever would,' Baumer said. 'You're needed for an execution.'

Lena rolled her shoulders. There was a click as something shifted awkwardly, but no more pain than she ever felt after a morning's work. She hefted her axe and lined it up over the bone.

'I'm busy today.' The axe fell. Splinters flew.

'You know that's not how it works.' Baumer kicked the bone away. 'You don't get three florins a month and a free house for skulking in the dark.'

'I know what I'm paid for.' Lena shifted a bone along and set her foot to hold it still. 'You don't like the way I work; you can go find a different executioner. Or don't you want to risk another Artzny?'

Lena had seen her predecessor at work when she arrived in Unteholz and had been left baffled at how he got the job. Artzny had once taken five blows to complete a beheading, and the condemned had gurgled in pain up to the fourth stroke. There was a skill to swinging a sword, whether it was a duelist's rapier or an executioner's weighty blade, and in ten years of service to the city he had never mastered his own craft. There should have been someone else willing to take his pay, but maybe those strong enough didn't think they deserved to be shunned.

Lena knew better. She accepted the scorn as easily as the

isolation. Like every man or woman she'd set her sword to since she came here, and unlike many of those she'd set it to before, she was getting what she deserved. Of course, she knew how to cleanly chop off a head, or a hand, or a tongue when the crime was libel. The council had been so grateful to find her, she had almost set her own terms.

Baumer narrowed his eyes and moved closer. Around them, the dying breaths of a dozen vast creatures filled the air, a rasping reminder that nothing lived forever, no matter how strong it was.

'You forget, I was there when you made your deal,' Baumer said. 'I know what concessions you got. No breaking on the wheel. No part in the torture of suspects. You see the evidence before you do the deed. But working to Maier's timetable was never negotiable, so put your axe away and come with me.'

'Fine.' Lena had known she wouldn't win this argument, but sometimes you fought for the sake of fighting. 'Let me get my things.'

She set her axe down on the hand cart with its burden of bone, fetched her tunic, and gathered up her lanterns.

'Who am I killing this time?' she asked.

'Blessed Beatrice Saimon.'

'The high priest of Mother Sky?'

'She stabbed her husband to death.'

'Isn't she married to a councillor?'

'She was.'

'No wonder the judges want her dead.'

Lena snuffed out the wicks on three of the four lamps, then hung the last from the side of the cart. It would be enough to light their way out of the caves.

'Her congregation won't like it,' she said.

'Fuck 'em. Bunch of heretics and rabble rousers, with their talk of new saints and holy storms.'

'That's half the city you're talking about.'

'And if they came back to the old faith, then we'd all be living in peace.'

Lena wasn't going down this path. War had made her many things-proud, powerful, a killer-and she regretted them just as much as she missed them. When Baumer talked with such casual certainty about the blood-stained business of faith, he reminded her too much of her old self.

'Hanging?' she asked.

'Maier's granted Blessed Saimon a beheading.'

'How merciful.' Lena's voice was barbed with disdain. Renate Maier, Unteholz's richest merchant and head councillor, only gave to others when it let her show her power, and when it lost her nothing in return. If she wasn't giving Saimon a drawn out hanging, then she had something to gain in return.

'Can't go around hanging priests,' Baumer said, his own sneer showing what he thought of the legal nicety. 'Even if they worship Mother Sky.'

'Mother Sky or Father Earth, it doesn't matter. We all die the same.'

'Careful, you're starting to sound like a Moon cultist.'

She snorted. 'Do I look like I eat babies?'

Baumer looked her up and down in an exaggerated way, and she was pleased to see he took his time. Then he shook his head.

'You look like you eat swords and spit bullets, just like always. Still, I want to know now, which way do you pray, Earth or Sky?'

Lena wasn't getting drawn into that debate. She'd cared about how people prayed once, had spent years fighting the bitter wars that still raged over faith, but that was the past. There was a reason she had come to a neutral city, one of the few places left in the Principalities of Stone where you wouldn't be taxed or jailed or dragged to the gallows because of which god you thought set the rules, or which books of scripture you read. A place where the authorities tried not to open that wound any wider. A place where she could find peace.

She gripped the worn wooden handles of the cart, lifted its back end, and set it trundling towards the tunnels, wobbling as the crudely made wheel crossed the uneven floor.

A commotion broke out towards the mouth of the cave. Her head shot around, and muscles tensed, ready for danger.

With a roar like the rending of mountains, a manticore staggered down the cave. Feline eyes wept blood and rot oozed from sores at its furred joints. Feathers fell, dirty and frayed, with each flap of its wings. Its voice was ragged, its movements made ferocious by pain.

Sgeir ran from the beast, tools abandoned as terror took hold. A few might be brave enough to finish off a beast on its last breath, but none of them were warriors.

A family cowered behind a wyvern's cadaver. Too slow to run, they had become trapped between the half-butchered corpse and the granite wall. The manticore screeched and twisted its head, leonine mane flying as it caught some scent over the death and decay. It bared its teeth as it turned on the trapped sgeir.

Lena picked up her axe and looked to Baumer, who shrugged.

'The beast will die soon anyway,' he said. 'I'm not risking my life for it.'

'And for them?'

'They're just sgeir.'

The manticore advanced with a feline prowl, a predator closing in on its prey. Its growl shook the air in Lena's chest.

She set her jaw and strode towards the manticore. Beneath the tragedy and the terror of the dying beast, she saw the magnificent creature it had once been, a battle steed for a drachenritter, the elite of any army. A collar lay around its neck, gilded leather tarnished and stained, raising sores where it was too tight. Her heart had no place for pity, which demeaned the noble and gave mercy to the vile, but she mourned for the beast and for its lost rider even as she hefted her axe.

The manticore had almost reached the family. One forepaw planted on the wyvern's corpse, the other raised with claws bared. It loomed over them, taller than any bull, mane wild around its head. The poison barb of its tail swayed as it prepared to strike.

Lena's axe was made for butchery, not fighting, and its weight was all in the head. At least she had sharpened it well. That was one thing in her favour. She adjusted her grip, shifted her hip back, and swung.

The manticore screeched as the blade bit the base of its tail. Blood streamed across matted fur, severed muscles twitched, and the tail flopped uselessly to one side. The creature twisted and lunged at Lena; teeth bared.

She stepped back, avoiding a swipe of the creature's claw. Her heel hit a lump in the ground, her ankle twisted, and she fell, landing on her arse. She gritted her teeth as she slammed against the stone, but kept hold of her axe despite the jarring pain.

The manticore advanced faster than she could scramble back. Its hot breath stank of decay, and she could see the frenzy in its bloodshot eyes. The beast had poison in its blood. Soon it would be dead. That was little comfort if it tore her open first.

Jaws opened wide, and jagged teeth descended. Lena rolled left, dodged the bite, and slammed into the creature's leg. As it lifted its paw, she swept the axe around. There wasn't enough force in the blow to pierce its hide, but it knocked the beast off balance.

In that moment, Lena came to her feet again. She brought the head of the axe back behind her shoulder, then swung with all her strength, striking the manticore's leg just above the knee. There was a crunch, a spray of blood, and the creature crashed to the floor, howling and gnashing its teeth.

Lena darted back and readied her axe.

The manticore strained with its remaining foreleg, trying to lift itself. It huffed and wheezed, mouth flecked with foam, before finally collapsing, its flank trembling as it heaved ragged breaths in and out.

With a heavy heart, Lena stepped up to the fallen beast. She unfastened the rusted buckle at the back of its neck and let the frayed collar fall to the floor. She stroked its mane, ran her hand along its neck, and felt their spirits connect.

It had been a long time, too long, for her to control the sensations that flowed from the beast. Loss, frustration, bewilderment, the inexorable draw of the bone caves, and now the intense pain in its leg and tail. Her heart raced as if the pain were her own.

With a great effort of will, she forced herself to think soothing thoughts. She remembered meadows in the mountains, a summer breeze, the contentment of a full stomach. Those memories flowed from her into the beast, calming its spirit and easing its final moments.

The manticore closed its eyes and tilted its head to let her scratch under its chin. Rasping breaths became a purr. The pain and panic became a memory of contentment, a reminder of closer connections between rider and beast, something they had both lost. It had taken all the strength Lena had to leave such bonds behind, and the feeling rushed back now, like the memory of a lost lover, swinging her heart between joy and bitterness on every beat. She couldn't allow herself to give in to this longing. If she did, she might never let go again.

She took a deep breath, stepped back, and raised her axe. Mercifully, the manticore's eyes remained closed as she brought the blade down.

Baumer was waiting when she got back to the cart.

'Don't you need to mark your territory?' he asked. 'Stop some other lowlife stealing your kill?'

The sgeir family were emerging from behind the wyvern, knives and hatchets at the ready. They looked at Lena with gratitude and confusion.

She took a rag off the back of her cart and wiped blood from the axe blade. Her shoulders were aching from the impact of that final blow. Later, she would drink the pain away, but later had to wait. She had a duty to fulfill, however ignominious.

'Come on,' she said, grasping the handles of the cart, careful not to look as the butchery began. 'Councillor Maier will be waiting.'

Councillor Maier's mansion was in the Hochfel district, where the homes of noble merchants sat like eagle's nests on a rocky outcrop running from Steel Peak. To the east and south, the warehouses of those same merchants gathered around trading halls and wagon parks, while to the north, across the city walls, the River Seltwasser tumbled out of the mountains and raced down the valley into the heartland of the Principalities of Stone. Hochfel wasn't the sort of place Lena often went. The liveried guards frowned upon anyone dressed in labourers' clothes, even those hired to maintain the mansions. But with Captain Baumer at her side, no one stopped her.

They entered the Maier mansion through a side gate in its stone walls, crossed a compact courtyard, and went into the main house through the servants' quarters. They strode through the bustle of cleaning, mending, and cooking, bored eyes looking up as they passed. Lena knew the way by now and all the servants recognised her. Most tapped the skin beneath one of their eyes as she walked past.

She ignored them. Why meet anyone's gaze when all they saw in her was death? Even if she had wanted a confrontation, it wasn't as if they were wrong. One way or another, death was all she had brought anyone for a long time, and if people thought that a soldier's killing was purer than that of an executioner, that just showed what fools they were. What she did now wasn't a curse, it was a penance.

Baumer opened a sturdy pine door and let them into Maier's wood-panelled antechamber. The walls were stained a warm brown and polished to a shine, the floor decorated with black and white tiles like the grid of a counting board.

Lena flung herself down on the bench that ran along one

wall and stretched her legs.

'She's going to make us wait, isn't she?' Lena asked, staring at the closed door of Maier's office.

'She's a busy lady.'

'And you spend your time just sitting around?'

'I wish.' Baumer grinned. 'Every idiot in this town wants my constables settling disputes. Who stole whose pig? Why some wall shouldn't have been built? What really happened to the Saint Colved's Day pudding? At least on campaign you got to rest after a day's march.'

'Apart from the foraging, cooking, standing watch, digging latrine pits…'

Baumer laughed. 'In a city, I can pay someone to take away my shit.'

There was a fruit bowl on a pedestal by the door, a reminder to visitors of Renate Maier's wealth. Among local apples and pears there were oranges from the Salt Cities, mangoes from the groves of Imperial Vacaros, and strange yellow fingers from over the eastern seas. How many other merchants could fetch fresh fruit from across the Saved Lands and beyond? And how many could afford to leave it out for visitors?

'You want something?' Baumer asked, pointing at the fruit. 'She'll never notice.'

Lena shook her head. She wasn't taking anything that would make her more obliged to Councillor Maier. A clear head wasn't enough where executions were concerned. She had to be sure that she wasn't being influenced.

'Most people I know, they'll take a good feed wherever they can find it,' Baumer said, looking at her thoughtfully. 'You take those opportunities when you might have a long, hungry march ahead.'

'I'm used to getting by with what I have,' Lena said. 'Though if it was a bowl of ale, that would be different.'

Baumer laughed and picked up an orange. He peeled it as easily as if he weren't wearing his gauntlets, bonded armour turning the metal into a second skin. The sweet smell of citrus filled the air.

'They friends of yours, that sgeir family?' he asked.

Lena frowned. 'What sgeir family?'

'The ones you saved from the monster. They must mean something to take that risk.'

'I don't like to see innocents hurt.'

Baumer tossed a piece of orange into his mouth and chewed thoughtfully.

'You must have friends, though.'

'I have people I'll tolerate.'

Baumer laughed and bit into another segment of the fruit. Juice dribbled down his chin and onto his breastplate. He pulled a cloth from his belt to wipe the armour clean, then polished the offending spot until it shone.

'Everyone has friends,' he said, like it was an ordinary fact. 'Colleagues, folks you drink with, old comrades in arms.'

'Friendships are like marriage: I've tried, but it just made me weak.'

'I'd call that horse shit if it weren't for your job. Who chooses to be an executioner?'

The door behind Baumer opened, and a tall, elegant woman emerged. She was dressed in the simple green robes of a bishop of Father Earth, with a gold disk pendant as big as Lena's hand. She smiled smugly.

'Holy Kunder.' Baumer bowed his head respectfully. 'It's an honour.'

Lena pushed herself resentfully to her feet and gave the smallest of bows. She might not have a mouse's turd's worth of interest in gods and prayers, but she wasn't idiot enough to offend the Keeper of the Cage Cathedral.

'Headsman Sturm,' Kunder said, fingers touching beneath her eye, and her smile sent a shiver up Lena's spine. 'You'll be earning your keep today and defending the true faith in the process. May Father Earth guide your arm to a swift and judicious end.'

'Years of practice will make more difference,' Lena said.

Bishop Kunder paused. Her eyes narrowed.

'Your status grants you some leeway, Headsman,' she said. 'A space for incivility. But take care. These are dangerous times for all our souls, when heretics steal our Father's temples and rewrite our most holy scripture. I would be a poor guide to the people of Unteholz if I let careless words undermine their faith.'

Lena bit back a response. She needed the acceptance of the city's high and mighty to keep her job, and it was a job that suited her well. Better to eat the dirt they fed her than to be left at an empty table.

With a swish of her robes, Kunder departed through the outer door. Once she was gone, Baumer nudged Lena.

'Come on, it's our turn.'

They entered the office of Renate Maier, merchant, councillor, and judge. It was a well-lit room, its large windows lined with leaded glass. A sturdy desk of darkly stained pine stood next to a fireplace carved in the shape of fruiting trees. Behind the desk, shelves were lined with ledgers and scrolls, and above them leather-bound books of history, philosophy, and law. A series of sturdy locked boxes sat opposite the window, each one covered in fine leather, iron bands and heavy locks guarding hidden wealth.

Maier sat behind the desk, watching them with an expression as blank as the parchment in front of her. She was perhaps ten years younger than Lena and took time to hide the years she had. Someone with less experience around wealth and power might have missed the powders hiding small wrinkles or the grey strands at the roots of chestnut hair. Some might even have been impressed with her gold rings and fitted velvet doublet.

'Take a seat,' Maier said without pleasantries.

Lena sank into one of the armchairs across the desk from Maier. It was comfortably padded and solidly made. The legs didn't wobble under her weight, unlike her own furniture.

'The Blood Court met today,' Maier said, tapping the red and black stole draped across the desk. 'We have condemned Beatrice Saimon for the murder of Fiete Saimon. Given the nature of the case, with a priest killing a council member, I want this put behind us as swiftly as possible. I therefore order you, in my role as judge of the Blood Court, to behead Beatrice Saimon today.'

It made sense. Murder between spouses made good scandal for the pamphleteers, but the murder of a councillor threatened the social order, while the execution of a priest, whether of Father Earth or Mother Sky, risked igniting an inferno of religious resentments. Some people would still compare this with the killings of Sky priests in Alvard and Gothersrech, but swift action would cut off the spread of such voices, and perhaps preempt the raging of the mob. These were the judgements by which Maier held Unteholz together, and with it all her profits and prestige.

'Short notice,' Lena said, 'but I can do it. I just need to hear the evidence.'

Maier scowled.

'If this is your condition for killing someone, then you should attend court.'

'You knew my conditions when you hired me. I'm not sitting through the petty squabbles and bickering lawyers.'

'Then you need to put your trust in the judges.' Maier tapped her stole again.

'I'll take your word for it that some criminal deserves to lose a hand or a tongue, but I draw the line at a life.'

'I could find another executioner.'

'Not one who can do the job cleanly. You want this done with some dignity; give me my evidence.'

Maier sat looking at Lena for a long moment, then drew a sheet of paper from the shelf behind her.

'Very well,' she said, running a finger down neatly penned text. 'Councillor Fiete Saimon was found dead in an alley outside his home three nights ago. He had been stabbed repeatedly in the chest and left face down in a pool of his own blood. His wife, Holy Beatrice Saimon, was found roaming the taverns in a wild and disoriented state. Neighbours stated that the Saimons had been arguing loudly and repeatedly. Other witnesses attest that Beatrice had taken to drinking heavily around the city's taverns, where she complained about her husband to any who would listen.'

It was an all too familiar story. A marriage gone wrong, and a temper lost. Hot words turned to hard blows, fists to blades. The only surprise was that the other spouse had emerged uninjured.

'Who found them?' Lena asked. 'The body and the wife?'

'Me and my men,' Baumer said. 'One of the neighbours heard shouting in the street and sent for us to calm things down. I found him dead, got my men together, and went looking for her. We didn't have to look far.'

'Anything else worth mentioning?' Lena asked.

'A knife found among Holy Saimon's belongings. It was blood-stained and matched the wounds.'

'Show me.'

Baumer looked at Maier and raised an eyebrow.

'You insist?' Maier asked.

'You know I do,' Lena replied.

'Very well.'

At Maier's nod, Baumer got up from his seat and headed to one of the chests along the wall. He took a brass key from a ring on his belt, opened the lock, and retrieved a bundle of woollen cloth, which he laid on the table. When he pulled the cloth back, it revealed the curved dragon's tooth blade and engraved steel guard of an Illora dagger.

'That's a distinctive knife,' Lena said, looking from Baumer to Maier.

Baumer gave a small nod of acknowledgement. He knew what he was looking at, and how unusual it was. The merchant monarchs of the Salt Cities gave these blades to their favourite priests, a sign

14

of faith and of fidelity to the princes' cause. With the Salt Cities at peace for several years, and war still raging in the Principalities of Stone, it was rare for such a priest to risk the journey north.

'A pretty weapon, I'm sure,' Maier said. 'Now, are you ready to do your duty?'

Lena considered telling Maier about the knife, to remind her that she was more than hired muscle, but she didn't want the other woman's pomposity to get a rise out of her. Let the mighty head of the council stay ignorant on this one small thing.

'It seems damning,' Lena said, looking from the Illora dagger to Baumer and then down at Maier's notes. 'Give me two hours to sharpen my blade and ready the Weeping Stone, then you can bring Blessed Saimon to meet the gods.'

CHAPTER TWO

FOOD FOR WYVERNS

Even with less than a day's notice to prepare, a large crowd gathered for the execution. Thousands of people poured out of Unteholz's shops and workshops to watch the procession march from the citadel, down through steep and winding streets, to the execution ground outside the city walls. From merchant lords to miners to beggars, each became one more body jostling for a view. If Mother Sky's scripture was true and anyone could be destined for greatness, then this was the perfect chance for their strength to shine. In a crowd there was no order, no hierarchy, just the flexing of voices and muscles and will.

Lena would have preferred to send her victims on their way without an audience, all those damned eyes watching her, demanding that she perform, waiting to judge her if she failed. She would allow that it was good for someone to see her skill in action, but few of them appreciated her work. They were too swept up in the spectacle, their blood pumping in anticipation of seeing someone else's blood spilt, a sentiment that risked boiling over from grotesque absurdity into real danger. This was how cities came to be sacked, not though careful calculation but a failure of control. The mob was like a dragon; the stronger it grew, the harder it was to control, and without perfect discipline, one day it would break loose and devour everyone in sight.

For now, the crowd's chatter was harmless, a soft sound that drifted out to Lena as she waited by the Weeping Stone. The Stone had stood on this site for longer than records recalled, probably longer than Unteholz itself. A wide, dark slab of rock, it stood out from the slope above, creating a natural platform from which to view the flat ground around its base, or to be seen from below.

Even in the height of summer, water dripped from the stone's flat underside. Tradition said that Father Earth had set the mountain to weeping for the victims of the criminals executed here. Some priests said the story was a reminder that no one could escape divine justice. City leaders used it to assert Unteholz's unique importance among the Principalities of Stone. To Lena, it was proof that people would believe anything if you said it often enough.

While the sound of the crowd grew, she washed vulture shit and muddy claw marks from the stone, then saw to the rotting flesh that hung from gallows frames to either side. She had cut some of these grotesque decorations from living criminals: hands of thieves, tongues of slanderers, ears of a notorious swindler. Others were the corpses of murderers and robbers, left to dangle long after the rope choked off their last breath. All were left as warnings against a life of crime, reminders that whatever the gods did to a soul, humanity could do worse to a body. They hung until the flesh had been devoured by scavengers, or stolen by alchemists if the darker rumours were true. Only then were the bones taken up to the funeral plateau.

That was one more way in which Blessed Beatrice Saimon's fate would be different from an ordinary criminal. Too many dead priests had become martyrs to one side or the other, with pilgrims whipping themselves into a fervour where the bodies hung. Sky worshippers, looking for fresh saints to herald the reforming storm, strung skeletons together with gold wire over their altars or hung them from banner poles. The last thing the council wanted was a martyr cult adding to the city's tensions.

Saimon's body would be disposed of quickly and quietly once the bloody business was done.

The sound of the crowd was growing louder as it approached the Manden Gate. Lena set aside the bucket of bones she had gathered for the graveyard, laid her tunic over a rock, and retrieved her executioner's sword from the gallows post.

Taking the grip in one hand and the red leather sheath in the other, Lena drew the blade she had named Brute. It was a hefty two-handed weapon only a head shorter than her, with a blunted tip and edges she had sharpened until they sliced flesh at a touch. For all its bulk, it weighed little more than a babe in arms, but that weight was poorly balanced, not good for the back and forth of a fight, only for a single swing. It was a weapon designed for one purpose only, the bloody art of justice.

The crowd spilt out through the Manden Gate, a jostling throng of bodies, as noisy as any carnival day. Some were laughing and chattering, flirting in the face of death. Others, many in the bright colours of Mother Sky, were in a more sombre mood, and angry words flew as the two groups crossed. City constables in blue and grey livery stepped in to keep the peace.

Traders had come before the spectators, selling food from hand carts along the route, and the smells of smoked sausage and fermented cabbage drifted through the lingering reek of rotting flesh. A faith that singled out wealth as a sign of virtue appealed to such men and women, and many of them were dressed as brightly as the mourners. Perhaps they would grieve later, when they had sold all their wares. For now, it would be a sin not to profit off such a festive affair.

The forerunners of the crowd ignored the traders. They hurried to the base of the Weeping Stone or to the raised ground to left and right, eager to get the best views. They pointed and shouted, waved at Lena or stared at her sword, indifferent to the disdain with which she watched them.

Then came the procession.

Councillor Maier led the way in her role as head judge of the Blood Court. She was mounted on a black stallion, wearing the judge's red and black stole over black velvet tunic and hose, her head bared in solemnity.

Behind her came the condemned. Beatrice Saimon was dressed in the bright yellow robes of a Sky priest, though hers were torn and stained. Her elaborate god medallion had been taken from her, though out of respect for her holy profession it had been replaced by a clay lightning bolt on a piece of rough twine. Her hands were cuffed, and her ankles shackled so that her bare feet moved in small, shuffling steps. Fingers clutched a small book of saints' lives, pages falling from its cheap binding, and the crowd snatched them up, relics or souvenirs. As was traditional, the jailer had shaved the prisoner's head for the execution, his crude razor work leaving her scalp raw and bleeding.

Beside and behind the condemned came a column of liveried constables, fifty men and women with the grizzled look of veteran soldiers, the city's law officers in times of peace and its military officers in times of war. Each one rang a bell to draw the crowd's attention and carried a hefty cudgel in case that crowd drew too close. Baumer stood out among them, his tabard cleaner and less faded than the rest, his armour gleaming on arms and legs.

It wasn't uncommon for the procession to be followed by a few friends and family of the condemned. What surprised Lena this time was the sheer number of them. At least a hundred of the Blessed Saimon's congregants followed in a mournful column, heads bowed over lightning bolt medallions and books of saints. The faithful on both sides were numerous in Unteholz, but Lena hadn't expected this many to weep for a murderer, however pious she had been.

The sound of the constables' bells rang clear through the crowd, echoing off the city walls and the mountain slopes, then down across the terraced fields to the edge of the pine forest. To the east, distant smoke rose above the trees, the thin trails of a hundred campfires. That was the surest sign that spring had come to the principalities, the smoke trails of an army on the march.

The procession made its way along the short track from the gate to the execution ground, while the crowd churned around it, some people pushing for a closer look at the condemned, others jostling for position around the base of the Weeping Stone. At last, Maier reached the base of the Stone, dismounted, and handed her reins to a page. She paused for a moment, while the crowd watched her watching them, a reminder of who held power. Then a hush swept across the execution ground as she led Saimon, flanked by a pair of constables, up the steps to the rear of the Weeping Stone.

Lena met them there, her sword over her shoulder. By tradition, she should have been part of the procession. Tradition could go piss in a dragon's mouth for all she cared.

'Beatrice Saimon?' Lena intoned, beginning the formalities of her work.

The woman looked up, as if surprised to hear her name. She seemed dazed, her mouth hanging open, eyes wide and vacant. Lena had seen the shock of this moment leave people aghast or hysterical, but she had never seen one as bad as this. The rush of the past few days-slaying her husband, being arrested, a swift trial and now her death march-had clearly broken Saimon. She was so pitiful, Lena felt a welling up of sympathy, despite what the woman had done. She wanted to lay a hand on her shoulder and tell her that everything would be alright.

Except that it wouldn't.

'You are Beatrice Saimon?' she asked again.

'I… Yes. Yes, that's me.'

Saimon's brow furrowed as she looked down at her hands. Heavy manacles had bitten into her flesh, leaving crusted blood around her wrists.

'Why am I here?' she asked distantly.

'Beatrice Saimon, you have been found guilty of the murder

of Fiete Saimon,' Lena declared, raising her voice so that the whole crowd could hear. 'By the judgement of the Blood Court of Unteholz, you are to die this day. Do you wish the consolation of a priest that your soul might find mercy in the beyond?'

Saimon gave a wide, childish grin. 'I am a priest!'

That look on her face, that bright tone of voice, gave Lena pause. Was something wrong with the woman? She had been the city's leading Sky priest, so she couldn't be a simpleton. Perhaps she had been beaten around the head, though there was no bruising on her face or beneath the stubble of her scalp.

Lena glanced at Maier and raised an eyebrow. The councillor nodded curtly towards the expectant crowd.

There was a job to be done. Swallowing her doubts, Lena took Saimon by the arm and led her to the front of the stone. A murmur of excitement ran through the crowd, interspersed by wails of grief and cries of 'shame!'

Lena pressed down on Saimon's shoulder and the woman sank unresisting to her knees. Lena had expected her to pray in this final moment, to acknowledge her guilt to Mother Sky and all her saints, to seek forgiveness and grace. Instead, she looked in puzzlement at her surroundings.

Lena stepped around to stand a pace behind Saimon's right shoulder. She took a firm grip on Brute's handle and drew the sword back over her shoulder.

Saimon looked around, and those wide eyes seemed to stare into Lena's soul.

'They say I killed Fiete,' Beatrice Saimon said, tears running down her cheeks. 'I would never do that. I love him.'

For a moment, doubt stirred in Lena's heart. Then she thought of the evidence, of the trial, of this woman's poor husband and victim. She wouldn't be the first murderer to go to the grave proclaiming her innocence, desperately hoping to avoid the consequences of her crime.

'Face forward,' Lena said sternly. 'It's better not to see it coming.'

Saimon nodded, smiled sadly, and turned her head.

Lena shifted her foot back, found her point of perfect balance, and swung the sword.

The hand cart rattled as Lena pushed it up the winding trail to the funeral plateau above Unteholz. The route was so familiar that she could have followed it by the feel of the ground through her shoes. She'd been up here so many times in the past five years. It was a journey she always made alone, without the religious processions of friends and family that accompanied an honest corpse. Her victims were not granted the ringing of gongs and the lighting of lanterns during daylight, to ward off Brother Moon, the bringer of death, and keep him from taking more souls. Executees had a swift, silent funeral, with only Lena to mark their end.

She had known honest people who had died since she came to the city, and might even have paid her respects to one or two, but no one wanted to see an executioner at a funeral, any more than they wanted them at a fair or a public dance. Her profession hung around her like the miasma of rot around a gallows post, and there was no place for that stench in decent society. She didn't really mind; it was just the price she paid to be left in peace.

A pebble rolled from under Lena's foot and bounced away down the mountainside. She listened to the clack as it rebounded off rocks and trees, past the mouths of the caves where the monsters went to die, and down towards the city.

Unteholz spread out below her, as impressive as the day she had first seen it. From up here on the lower slopes of Steel Peak, she could spot the brightly painted houses of merchants and artisans, the pale canvas of stalls in the market, and the crowded web of paupers' streets where wooden buildings rose in rickety heaps. There was the dark and forbidding central keep; the vast rib bones, leathery walls, and spinal spire of the Cage Cathedral; the smoking chimneys of the foundry district. Around it all was the thick ring of the city walls, a smooth semicircle of cut stone that ended at the impassable rock face against which the city stood.

Outside those walls, mine working dotted the mountain side, their debris littering the slopes beneath them. Between lay the terraced fields of upland farms, and beyond that the forests where the city's hunters and herders roamed, heading towards Green Mountain and the Heights of Chelmek in the south, or down along the banks of the Seltwasser to the lowlands of the northeast. From up here among the dead, the whole place seemed blessedly still and peaceful, but down there it was a swarming, chattering, cheating mass of humanity.

At the top of the trail, the plateau opened up in front of her, acres of flat ground cupped between the brooding mass of Steal Peak and the dizzying slopes of the Needle. The short grass and dark dirt was littered with the white of bones. Older ones cracked beneath the wheel of Lena's cart as she pushed its grisly load towards another rise at the southwest corner.

Vultures looked up as Lena passed, a whole wake of them, hundreds strong, scattered across the plateau. Everyone who died in Unteholz came here, so there was plenty for the birds to feed on. Bodies laid out in honour by their families were torn away in strips of shredded flesh, so that they might return swiftly to the womb of Mother Sky, while their bones took the slow path down into Father Earth. Only two types of people were granted places on the higher plateaus, where the wyverns crunched even bone to dust, ensuring that no remains were left for morbid souvenir hunters or dark alchemists. One high plateau was for the rich; the other was for Lena's victims.

Pushing the cart across the plateau was an awkward business.

Lena had to keep moving or the wheel might become stuck on old bones protruding from the dirt of the funeral ground, protrusions over which she might trip in her haste. If she had an apprentice, then she could fob this task off onto them, but apprentices came with a heap of burdens, not least the need to constantly explain herself. Instead, she brought every body up alone.

The air here was clear and refreshing. No living humans lingered with their stink of sweat and smoke. Unlike the bodies at the Weeping Stone, the ones on the plateau were never left long enough to rot and stink: scavengers devoured them long before that time could come. It was good to find somewhere clean and at peace.

At the corner of the plateau, she pushed the cart up another, narrower trail, to a patch of flat ground in front of a cave mouth. A low, rasping hiss emerged from the cave and there was movement in the deep dark of its shadows.

A wyvern emerged, forked tongue flickering from a long scaly face, fifteen feet of lizard stretching out from nose to tail. Both feet clawed at the ground, and it spread its wings wide, a warning to rivals of its prowess. It opened its mouth, revealing three rows of jagged teeth, and roared.

There was a great beating of wings as vultures took flight. Even Lena, who had spent decades around such beasts, froze for a moment at the sound.

She snatched a bone from the bucket hanging off the back of her cart, the skull of a notorious highwayman, and flung it into the air. The wyvern snatched the skull between its jaws and bit down with a crunch.

'There's more where that came from,' Lena said, tipping the rest of the bones out.

The wyvern sank onto its belly, still chewing the skull, and let out a contented rumble. Lena strode forward, careful not to show the sort of skittishness that might trigger its predatory instincts, and laid a hand on the creature's nose.

'It's good to see you,' she said. 'You look well.'

The wyvern's breath was hot and earthy. Its tongue flickered out, brushed the back of Lena's hand, and drew back in.

She smiled. This was what she missed about soldiering. Not the people or the orders or the hunt for glory, whatever the piss glory really was. She missed the creatures, those she'd killed and those she'd cared for. She missed having a connection to something magnificent.

She had never allowed herself to find a bond with the wyvern before. Beasts were her past, people her present, a way of atoning for her sins. But her encounter with the dying manticore had shaken her, and she needed a reminder of what else this bond could be. Needed to feel the good of it, just once more.

Slowly, tenderly, she reached into the wyvern's mind. She tasted bone between her teeth and felt a surge of vitality. The ground pressed against her body and a warm hand rested on her snout. For a moment, she caught an acrid scent beneath the blood and flesh of a fresh body. Most of all, she felt a connection, tentative but touching, a joining of two spirits.

The wyvern looked into her eyes, and she looked back. It recognised her as one of its own.

Lena relaxed, long-held tensions easing from her muscles. She smiled at the wyvern and took a deep, contented breath.

'I brought you something special today,' she said. 'Not just the usual bones.'

Reluctantly, she took her hand from the scaly skin and let the connection fade. It was too fresh, too little practised to continue without that touch. She wanted to linger there, to hold them both in that moment of joining, a closer connection than human beings could provide. But she didn't deserve that, and the wyvern deserved better than to be dragged down into human life, where they killed for money or power or which god had come first, out of desires that they dressed up as needs.

She grabbed the cart, wheeled it over to the wyvern, and

tipped out Beatrice Saimon's mortal remains. The severed head rolled away from the body and came to rest against the wyvern's claw, dead eyes staring up at the monster that would make a meal of them.

Normally, Lena had no trouble facing the people she had killed. No one could stay sane in this life without becoming inured to the corpses they made, and unlike the people she'd killed in war, she could be sure that those she executed deserved it. But something about Beatrice Saimon's eyes made the hairs stand up along Lena's forearms. The sadness and bewilderment the priest had worn at the Weeping Stone was still there, an expression Lena had never before seen on a killer.

That was the problem with people. Even when they were dead, they could get their claws into you. The joy wasn't worth the pain.

The wyvern sniffed at the body, nudged it away with its snout, and settled down with its eyes closed.

'Not hungry?' Lena asked. She looked again at Saimon's face. 'Can't blame you.'

She patted the wyvern's claw but kept clear of its mind. She didn't want to feel that bond only to abandon it again.

'Time for me to get back to the dead.'

Wheeling the bloodstained cart before her, she headed across the funeral field and down the mountain side, back to the noise and mess of humanity, where a bottle could distract her from the insistent tug of memory.

Beyond Unteholz, out across the forest, smoke still rose from the camp of an unknown army. War was stirring once more across the Principalities of Stone, generals gathering their forces to fight for faith, power, and wealth. Old princes and nervous peasants would guard Father Earth's traditions from the reforming storm of Mother Sky, all those merchants and mercenaries looking to prove a scripture in which the world worked by their rules, to throw off the shackles of tradition and let each person follow their destiny. There would be blood in the valleys and fire in the city streets, noble deaths and dreadful atrocities. Perhaps this year they would eclipse the infamous Slaughter of Saints, proving that the Principalities could match the Salt Cities in even the worst ways.

The wyverns would eat well.

CHAPTER THREE

SEEDS OF DOUBT

Lena walked down the dirt street from her home towards Othagate, an accumulation of ramshackle dwellings just inside the Manden Gate. As she got closer, the buildings looming over her changed from stone walls and tiled roofs to timber and thatch. Newer, cheaper, and more vulnerable to fire in the summer months. If she'd had to hold Unteholz against invaders, she would have started by tearing down Othagate, to remove a liability and have its timbers ready for repairs. She would have felt bad, because Othagate was where she was most at home, a place where poverty over-rode social niceties and even the taboo against executioners was only half observed. Good thing then that a hundred disasters would have to fall, both on her and on the city, before she became Unteholz's defender.

A scrawny cat with ginger fur peered out at Lena from the mouth of an alleyway. She stopped, crouched, and faced the cat, slowly closing her eyes and then opening them again. The creature watched her with suspicion, eyes wide and nose twitching, tail raised and ready to run.

Lena rummaged in her pouches and found a strip of dried beef. 'You look hungry,' she said. 'Can't have that.'

The cat looked nervously to left and right, then stalked out of the alley and snatched the offered meat from Lena's hand. It chewed at it frantically, like it was afraid the morsel might vanish if it paused to take breath. Lena crouched motionless, watching its skin-on-bones frame heave.

She thought again about Beatrice Saimon. A wealthy woman, a senior priest married to a leading merchant, Saimon could have lived her final days in comfort, paying to have cushions and fine food brought to her cell. But according to Eljvet the jailer, she hadn't asked for any of that. She had simply lain on a bare cot between her arrest, trial, and execution, eating the gruel she was given, and some stew brought by her parishioners. Fasting was a tenet of Father Earth, not Mother Sky, who encouraged her followers to enjoy everything they had earned, so these days of abstinence weren't an act of faith. Lena would have taken it all for signs of remorse, a guilty conscious eating up a murderer, if not for the way Saimon had spoken at the Weeping Stone, denying her guilt to the last.

Slowly, gently, Lena lowered her hand onto the cat's head. It flinched, shoulders tightening, and for a moment stood frozen in place. Then it started chewing again and even let out a small purr as Lena stroked its back. Lena's heart lifted at the feeling of that tiny, warm body, with its soft, dirt-streaked fur. It didn't judge her, and for as long as she could feel its heartbeat, she forgot to judge herself. If this sharp, suspicious creature thought that she was a good person, then maybe it was true.

Voices emerged from down the street. A band of men and women in hard-wearing, soot-stained smocks appeared around the corner, labourers let out of the foundries at the end of the day. They were in boisterous spirits, laughing and chattering and waving at people through their windows.

The cat's head shot up. It stared for a second and then ran off down the alley, half-chewed meat hanging between its jaws.

Lena followed the cat into the shadows, where no one would make the sign of the eye. She dressed plain enough not to stand out, but there was someone in every crowd who had stood close to the Weeping Stone, who had memorised her features in the moment before the noose tightened or the sword fell. Someone whose fascination and fear would spread like a whisper through the rest.

There was a way to her destination through the alleys, around the closely crammed backs of homes and workshops, stepping over midden heaps and around outhouses. Lena took that path with shallow breaths and swift strides, stalking through shadows made longer by the dusk.

Pamphlets peeled from the walls of the alleys, crudely printed sheets showing images of people at prayer, at war, or on their death beds. These were the work of evangelists, a sign of the ongoing struggle for the souls of Unteholz. Most carried slogans praising the salvation brought by Father Earth or the reforming wind that Mother Sky blew in. A few even bore the sinister messages of the Moon Cult, proclaiming the imminence of a great levelling. Lena had heard it all a hundred times. Once, she had taken a side. She wouldn't make that mistake again.

There were people here, but they walked alone, and none caught her eye. Whether they were going to relieve themselves or sneaking around the city, no one in these back streets wanted to make conversation.

The cat had vanished into the mass of streets, but Lena didn't mind. It would find her again when she came this way, as it had a score of times before. Cats were smarter than people; they knew when they were onto a good thing.

Voices emerged from one of the dingiest alleys. Lena frowned and glanced toward them, struck by the strangeness of sounds in a place of skulking silence.

'Say it,' a young woman's voice said. 'Say it or I'll hit you again.'

A mumble followed, too quiet for Lena to catch.

'Louder.'

Mumbling again.

'Louder!'

'I'm a turd.' That was the mumbler, having found his words.

They came low and slow, thick with misery.

'What sort of turd?'

The casual cruelty of the young woman's voice was a spur pricking the flanks of an angry beast that lived in Lena's heart. Hand on the dagger at her hip, she walked as silent as a shadow down the alley.

'I'm a fat turd,' the victim said. 'A fat, ridiculous turd.'

'You forgot greedy, holding out on us like this.'

The alley opened into a yard between a bakery and a potter's workshop. Four youths stood in the yard, all dressed in frayed tunics. A portly boy with scraggly shoulder length hair had been shoved against a kiln by a girl a hand and a half taller than him, while two others watched and smirked. Like the girl, they held stout, dented cudgels of polished pine.

'It's all I have,' the portly boy said. 'Please, Tild, I need to eat.'

'You can eat back at the Warrens,' the girl said, and held out two measly pennies for her accomplices to take. 'If she'll let a failure like you eat.'

'Please,' the boy whimpered. 'I can't-'

The girl's hand whipped out, knocking the boy's head back against the kiln and leaving his cheek red.

'I decide what you can and can't do, you snivelling little turd.'

'I thought he was fat,' Lena said, stepping into the yard. 'Can't be little and fat.'

The boy's eyes lit up with hope. Those of his tormentors narrowed and a slim, vicious smile slid up the leader's face. She tossed back her grubby blond hair, took a step away from her victim, and raised her cudgel.

'Seems someone doesn't know what's their business and what isn't. Would be a shame if that got you hurt, old lady.'

Lena patted the dagger at her belt.

'I won't need this to show you what an old lady can do.'

The girl ran her gaze up and down Lena, brow furrowed in calculation. She snorted derisively.

'I don't think so,' she said. 'Deppel, you move an inch and I'll beat you until you bleed.'

The boy shrank back against the kiln, more terrified than ever.

Lena matched the girl's predatory grin. Her senses became sharper as she sidestepped around the yard, keeping her back to the buildings and her eyes on the girl but her attention on the other two. They thought she was a stupid old lady, that she had forgotten about them, and now they were flanking her, cudgels raised. It wasn't a bad plan. She probably would have done the same, if she had been stupid enough to get into their position.

One of them suddenly swung his cudgel, trying to catch her by surprise.

Lena jerked back and grabbed his arm as it swung past. She wrenched his wrist. He grunted in pain, and the cudgel clattered to the ground. She could have snapped that arm, but these were just petty kids, and where would the justice be in that? Instead, she flung him at his companion, knocking them both to the ground.

Another cudgel swung as the gang's leader joined the fray. Lena blocked the blow, forearm to forearm, and slammed her knee between the girl's legs. The girl gasped and curled over, then sank to the floor amid a litter of old pottery shards.

One of the boys started pushing himself to his feet, but stopped when he saw Lena looking his way.

'Please,' he said. 'We didn't mean-'

'I know what you meant.' Lena picked up the two pennies from the dirt. 'I've cut the hand from enough robbers to hear their tales. You're young, you can learn better, but if I catch you at it again, I'll drag you bruised and bloody in front of a judge.'

She pressed the pennies into the palm of the portly boy.

'You should get out of here,' she said. 'Before they get back up.'

She strode away, arms swinging, a smile on her face. That hadn't been much of a challenge, but it was at least an imitation of the action she missed. No point in lingering, though, or gloating over such an easy win. The day was almost over, the shadow of the narrow peak known as the Needle stretching out across the city's slums. The alehouse had been calling to her for hours and fighting added to her thirst.

Footsteps scurried after her. The boy appeared, clutching his pennies and smiling widely.

'You're her, ain't you?' he said. 'You're Headsman Sturm!'

Lena nodded. It might not be the name she had been born with, but it was the only name anyone in Unteholz needed to know.

'I seen you take the hand off Fat Janny, and when you hung Tomas the Black.' The boy almost poked his own eye out in his rush to make a warding sign, but if he was afraid of being cursed, then his face didn't show it. 'Is it true you once chopped a man's feet off and left him standing on the stumps?'

Lena quickened her pace, using long strides to leave the youth behind. All she wanted was some peace.

He hurried after her, panting as he tried to talk and keep up.

'I was there today as well, when you done for Blessed Saimon. That was amazing how you took her head off like that, one swing and then thud.' The boy stuck his tongue out and crossed his eyes, an impression like no corpse Lena had ever seen. 'I can hardly even hit a hanging sack with two swings straight. How'd you learn to do that?'

'Practise. Go try it.'

'It's a shame, though. Blessed Saimon was nice, her husband too. They was always good for a bowl of stew or a few pennies from the poor box on holy day mornings. Talked nice about it too, smiled and everything, talked to me like I was a person. Most people don't do that, even when they're giving alms, but they would ask about where you lived and what you was doing and did you want to find someone to apprentice to. Can't imagine her stabbing no one, never mind him.'

Lena slowed her pace and looked at the boy. He couldn't have been more than thirteen years old, softer and rounder in the face than most of the ragged urchins who lived like vermin in the city's streets. How had he kept that guileless grin while living in the gutter?

And what else had he noticed?

'What's your name?' she asked.

'Deppel.'

'Deppel what?'

He shrugged. 'Just Deppel.'

'You hungry, just Deppel?'

'Always,' he said eagerly, but then his expression turned, and he flinched as she moved her hand. 'Why?'

'Because I'm going to buy you dinner.'

Toblur kept one of the least disreputable alehouses in Othagate. It wasn't well lit, the rushes on the floor weren't changed often, and its inhabitants included as many vagabonds and cutpurses as poor, honest craftsmen. But Toblur kept the swindlers from working his room and stopped most arguments before they turned into fights. There were hardly any brawls except on feast days and no one had been stabbed there in over a year. It was far from good enough to earn the title of inn, but it drew the sort of customers who wanted to drink in peace, and who helped Toblur keep it that way. People like Lena.

This sort of place was why she liked the city, and the isolated life she had carved out for herself. Most people didn't want to talk to an executioner, and she didn't want to talk to most people. In a place like Toblur's, that meant they left her alone rather than deliver threats and insults. Unteholz had space for an executioner who kept to herself, and for an old soldier who wanted solitude.

She sat on a stool with her back to the wall, a pot of third brew ale on the table in front of her. It was weak, bitter stuff, and normally she would have drunk better, but she wanted to keep her senses. Across the table, Deppel was devouring the blackened bread trencher on which he'd been served a stew of offal and swede. His fingers and chin were slick with gravy, and he looked as happy as a hired sword on a pillage. It reminded her of when her own Jekob had been young, though his table manners had been better than this, as had the food. She wasn't going to admit that she missed those days, but the thought did make her smile, at least until more bitter memories threatened to follow. She took a long drink to wash them away.

It was just one more evening in Unteholz, so the alehouse wasn't busy. A dozen men and women sat around the room, weary and wary of the world. A set of knucklebones rattled on a table and quiet words were mumbled around pots of drink. The smell of tallow candles and a dried dung fire almost drowned out the smell of humanity.

'You knew Blessed Saimon,' Lena said, leaning forward over her drink. 'Tell me about her.'

Deppel chewed, swallowed, and wiped his chin with the back of his hand. Some of his lank hair had dangled into the stew and now it dripped down the shoulder of his tunic.

'What do you want to know?' he asked.

There was the question that vexed Lena. Something about the priest and her death didn't sit right, like a meal that left her stomach churning. It couldn't just be the plea of innocence: those were two-a-penny among the desperate and the damned who came to pay their price at the Weeping Stone. But she couldn't grasp the reins of this misgiving, and she didn't like to be bucked by her own thoughts.

'Was there something wrong in her head?' It was the obvious answer. If a person didn't understand their loss, then they could hardly grieve.

'Like that woman what drowned her sister in the spring,'

Deppel said, spraying crumbs across the table. 'The one you hanged last month.'

'She wasn't mad. She just wanted to convince the priests she was possessed.'

'Why?' Deppel leaned forward to listen, the last of his bread clutched forgotten in his hand.

'If they did an exorcism, she could claim that they had driven out a spirit that used her body for murder. That would make her innocent. It was a way to avoid the noose.'

'And you worked that out?'

'Yes.'

'How?'

'I'm not here to tell you stories. Answer my question. Was Holy Saimon mad?'

Deppel shrank back a little, watching her from behind the shelter of his hair. After a moment, he started chewing his bread again, and a thoughtful expression emerged. At last, he shook his head.

'Don't reckon so. She acted odd sometimes, pulling faces and saying strange things, but it didn't seem mad. It was all jokes between her and her husband, you know? Stuff to make them both laugh while they were handing out alms.'

'So they seemed happy together?'

'Oh yeah. I seen them kissing in the temple and everything. Don't reckon you're meant to kiss in temple. You can probably be flogged for that, can't you?'

Lena shook her head. She'd flogged a few people found guilty of sacrilege, but this wasn't Gothersrech, where the slightest transgression could be treated as a sign of sin. It took more than a quick grope between the pews to put you in front of an Unteholz judge, and she was glad of that. It never seemed like much of a crime to act in a human way around holy things. If Mother Sky or Father Earth cared, then they could leave it to divine justice and let Brother Moon take the guilty soul.

What interested Lena more was that the Saimons had shared happy times as well as the arguments witnesses had talked about. It didn't matter to her if other people had their cosy little lives together, their shared secrets and their held hands, but it mattered that she had only been shown half the truth. That was how battles were lost. Sometimes, it was why towns burned. You couldn't blame a person for what they didn't know, but she had sworn she would never make mistakes like that again. Had she made a liar of herself?

She waved a barmaid over to pour her more ale.

'What's the most horrible murder you ever hung someone for?' Deppel asked.

'We're not here to talk about that.'

'Why not? It's interesting. I heard about this woman once, she caught her wife hugging a strange woman, and she thought they was cheating and gutted them both and hung their guts up round the house. Only it turned out the other woman was her wife's long-lost sister. Imagine that, all them guts everywhere, and the constables coming in, and then she found out what she done. They said she stabbed herself and pulled her own guts out in her cell.'

Deppel mimed slicing his stomach open with a crust of bread.

'That's a stupid story,' Lena said. 'She wouldn't have a knife in her cell, and she would have fainted before she pulled her own guts out.'

Deppel shrugged. 'Tell me a better one then.'

'No, tell me about Holy Saimon.' This was exasperating. She wanted rid of the boy, but not until she had something useful from him, and that was proving hard to find.

'I don't get it,' Deppel said. 'You don't want to talk about murders, but you keep going on about this priest what you chopped.'

'Did you see her arguing with anyone else?'

'You think she killed some other people? Like there's bodies they're gonna find, all rotting and full of maggots, like when no-one knew old Master Wurzbreg had been killed and he just lied there in his tannery for a week and the tanning vats hid the smell and-'

'Stop talking about old murders and answer the thundering question!'

Deppel curled in on himself like a whipped dog, his shoulder blades rising around his ears.

'What was the question again?' he whispered.

'Did Saimon argue with anyone else?'

'Oh, yeah.'

'Who?'

'Bishop Kunder mostly. They was always arguing. You must have seen it.'

'Why would I have seen it?'

Deppel leaned back and looked at her, his head on one side and his brow furrowed, like he had discovered some incomprehensible new creature and was trying to understand how it could live.

'They was arguing in public all the time. In front of their temples. In the market square. In council meetings. Everyone seen it.'

'Clearly not everyone,' Lena said through gritted teeth. 'What did they argue about?'

'Religion, of course.'

Now it was Lena's turn to sit back and contemplate her own idiocy. Of course, the city's most senior Earth and Sky priests had argued. People fought wars over the petty details of how they prayed and who they prayed to; over whether they should build statues of saints, which books counted as scripture, how priests should dress, even whether to wash on the way into temple. They fought like salvation hung from every detail. She'd fought those wars herself, though her reasons had never really been about faith. Saimon and Kunder fought over souls for a living.

It wasn't what she'd been looking for. She'd been probing for personal grudges, for evidence of violence or a short temper, something to reassure her that the woman she'd executed, so passive and meek, could have turned around and slain her husband. Instead, her thoughts headed in a darker direction.

Sound reason and strong evidence had led Baumer to blame Saimon, but the woman who killed her wife in Deppel's story had reason and evidence, too. Baumer's reason had been stronger, of course, but it might mean he hadn't considered other suspects.

Religion was all the motive some people needed to kill. If Natalia Kunder had argued with Holy Saimon, then she might have argued with Fiete Saimon too. He'd led Mother Sky's faction on the city council, defending the rights of heterodoxy in the face of Kunder's fiery faith. That gave the bishop good reason to kill Fiete, either for his own sake or to lash out at his wife. Kunder didn't look the sort to do the deed herself, but thousands of souls came to hear her preach at the cathedral each day, and every congregation had its fanatics. It would be easy enough to provide a knife and a target.

Lena dismissed the idea with a shake of her head. Beatrice Saimon had owned the knife that killed her husband. She'd been wild drunk on the night of the murder, ranting and raving, as she'd ranted so often about her husband's failings. They had the murderer. They didn't need to find another.

'What happened to your face?' Deppel asked.

'What do you mean, what happened to my face?'

Deppel shrank into himself again, his head sinking turtle-like between his shoulders.

'The scar,' he whispered. 'I was just wondering about your scar.'

Lena sighed and rubbed her eyes, briefly blocking out his sad, hurt expression. What was wrong with her today, that she suddenly cared how the world reacted?

'It's an old war wound,' she said.

'Looks like something clawed you.'

'It did.' She ran her fingers across the ravaged flesh and shuddered at the memory of the pain, of her own blood streaming across her armour.

'What done it? Was it a dragon?' His eyes were wide, his tone hushed with awe. 'Did you kill it back?'

'You think I'd have lived through a dragon doing that?' She shook her head.

'Did you ever fight a dragon?'

'Only drachenritter fight dragons.' It was an evasion, not an answer, and still said more than she wanted to.

'Were you a drachenritter?'

'I didn't want to talk about executions. What makes you think I want to talk about this?'

Deppel turned his eyes down to the table. The boy had a gentleness at odds with the streets where she'd found him, something almost civilised. Was he really the street rat she'd taken him for, or some craftsman's son who'd gone wandering and landed in the gutter?

'Have you got family, boy?'

Deppel hesitated, then shook his head.

'No.' He looked at her. 'Have you?'

'Not worth talking of.'

'What's that mean?'

'It means you're too inquisitive for a boy your age.'

'You still just want to talk about Holy Saimon?'

Lena waved a server over. He poured more ale for her and, at her signal, a cup for the boy. It was weak stuff, the sort a craftsman would give his apprentices with dinner, and Deppel had earned it. A touch more comfort before he went back on the streets. A moment more of sharing a table, before she went back to drinking alone. Not that she preferred this, but there was a warmth to it she found briefly comforting, like throwing an old blanket over her shoulders while she looked for a cloak.

Deppel grinned, grabbed the cup, and took a long gulp. He licked his lips, looked down at the half-drained cup, and then back up at Lena with a calculating expression.

'You want to know who Councillor Saimon argued with?' he

asked.

Lena leaned forward, twisting her own cup in her hand. 'Who?'

'Councillor Maier. Her what done the trial.'

Lena hesitated. It was an obvious gambit, portraying councillors from different faiths as rivals. Was the boy just telling her what she wanted to hear, for the sake of an evening in a warm alehouse? Or was there something real here, slicing away the story she'd been told like cutting fingers from a thief?

'Go on.'

Deppel looked around the room with exaggerated care, then leaned forward conspiratorially.

'They was both merchants, yeah? Both trading metal and monster bones down to the towns in the valleys. Sometimes one of them got something the other one wanted, and they argued in the trading halls.'

'How would you know that?'

'Lots of rich folks at the trading halls. I go begging there on days when caravans have come home, and the purses are fat. You'd be amazed what people will say in front of a beggar.'

'Go on.' She kept looking at the boy, her drink all but forgotten.

'One time, she said he stole a contract off her to sell wyvern hides to the armourers down in Kveld. Another time, she brought a wagon full of foreign fruit in two days before he did, meant there was no-one left wanting to buy his. He said how she had a spy in his house, then they done that thing where rich folks grab their swords, but you know they ain't really gonna fight, like it's just a way of decorating their words.'

The judge of the Blood Court had almost tried to kill the victim herself. It didn't paint a pretty picture of justice-as if justice was ever anything but ugly. This wasn't proof of a crime of course, but it could be enough to make Councillor Maier squirm, and that made Lena smile.

Except that Maier had nothing to worry about, as the case

was already closed. Besides, she was too straight-laced to do her opponents harm.

Wasn't she?

The councillor had gone to great lengths to keep Unteholz out of the war. Unlike the merchants of many cities, she hadn't turned to Mother Sky and called out for reform, perhaps because, in Unteholz, the merchants already ruled. Maier had stuck not just with the faith of Father Earth but with the stability his priests claimed to love, for which some of them seemed willing to let the world burn. Belligerent citizens of both sides had been driven out and ambassadors from Stromrotter and Alvard exiled for stirring trouble. Several citizens had left bruised and battered after they pushed their luck. Maybe Maier would take steps like that for profit as well as for peace.

Lena looked down at her cup. Was this ale stronger than she thought? She kept losing track of the thing that really mattered. There were no suspects, no accusations to make Maier squirm. The judges had found the truth, and Lena had acted on it. For five years, she had only ever drawn a sword to bring justice, and she'd done it again today. The alternative was that she'd killed an innocent woman, and that didn't happen.

'You want to know a secret?' Deppel whispered.

Lena nodded, intrigued despite herself.

Deppel looked pointedly at his empty cup.

'Sometimes I have trouble talking,' he said. 'Mouth gets all dry. Might need something to help it.'

'Gods, you're bad at this.'

Lena laughed and waved the server over. Once their cups were refilled, Deppel leaned in close.

'Councillor Saimon didn't just trade at the halls or out of his house,' he said. 'He went to the Blade Market.'

'The Blade Market.'

Lena had heard that name, spoken softly at the edges of conversations she wanted no part of. Anyone who spent their nights in places like Toblur's heard it from time to time. She'd brushed the idea aside as a metaphor or more trouble than it was worth, but either the ale or the story of the Saimons had done something to her mind and now curiosity had its hook in her.

'Want to see?' Deppel asked, looking up at her uncertainly. 'Because tonight's the night.'

Chapter Four

The Blade Market

The moon cast stark shadows across the mountainside, deep pools of gloom amid the pale light. Distorted by the darkness, objects shifted and merged, became more than they were in the day: a skull instead of a boulder, a bristling giant where trees had once stood. The danger of the wild was doubled when night held the world in its all-encompassing grasp.

Lena followed Deppel up a wide but neglected track, past the mouths of the beasts' caves and across narrow icy streams, towards an old mine opening. The ground was scattered with broken chunks of rock, the detritus of those delving for ore and coal. The path itself was made of rubble, rough edges pushing into the soles of her shoes.

Other people were on the track. They moved alone or in small groups, silent and furtive. They walked together and yet apart, sharing only the steps they took and the biting cold of the air.

Crossed swords were suspended above the entrance to the mine. One was an ancient drachenritter's blade, simple and clumsy by modern standards, with notches along the edge. The other was a duellist's weapon, the sort favoured by wealthy young posers and the killers who preyed on their arrogance. Neither was a fit tool for a real fight.

As they approached the cave mouth, Lena pulled her hood forward. She had picked up a cloak from home before coming here, not because she feared the cold, but because she couldn't be seen. Too many people knew her face. Too many here would have lost hands or fingers at the Weeping Stone, or have seen her send their friends to the hells where Brother Moon ruled.

Her mouth was dry and her hands twitchy. She blamed it on bad ale, but she still would have taken another cup for courage.

At the back of the cave, where its light would not be seen from the town below, a torch was flickering, the first of many leading down into the old mine. Deppel followed that light and Lena followed Deppel, joining a flow of people that swept them along like rainwater through the gutter, washing the city's filth into the depths. In another place and time, a raised hood might have caused questions, but half the people here hid their faces; hoods, scarves, even masks let them shed their identities and enter the blackest of markets without fear.

Noise drifted out of the tunnel ahead, a hubbub of voices, clattering of pots, jingle of coin. The mine shaft opened up, and they emerged into the bustle of the market.

It was a wide, man-made cavern where rich ore had been carved from the rock. The ground was uneven, with peaks and troughs large and small, for no miner dug more stone than they had to. Some stalls were reached by ramps and ladders, while others seemed piled on top of each other. Some had crude canvas awnings covering their wares, others were little more than rickety tables, while the largest were brightly coloured tents tethered to the rock walls.

Deppel tugged on Lena's arm, then nodded to a platform at the side of the cavern where rows of barrels waited to slake the shoppers' thirst.

'I've fed you enough,' she said.

'Ain't what I mean. Best views from there.'

She cast an appraising eye across the rest of the market. He was right. A drink would give them an excuse to watch the ebb and flow of humanity, and that platform the best view of it all.

'Fine,' she said. 'Lead the way.'

Deppel wove a path through the crowd, surprisingly nimble on his feet for a lad as round as an apple. Lena, following with a purposeful stride, bumped into one man, then another, then a masked woman with a fistful of pamphlets.

'Watch where you're going,' the woman said with a glare.

Lena clenched her fist and readied a retort, but held both back. She needed to stay calm and slip by unnoticed.

'Do I know you?' the woman asked, peering under Lena's cowl.

'Not likely,' Lena said, then pointed to the pamphlets by way of distraction. 'What's that?'

'This here's the truth.' The woman thrust one of the sheets into Lena's hands. 'But be careful: truth, like a moth, is too fragile for the light.'

She winked and walked away, handing out more pamphlets as she went.

Lena squinted at the sheet of cheap paper. 'NONE HIGH, NONE LOW' it said in crude, blocky print. 'LET THE LEVELLING COME.'

Messages from the cult of Brother Moon: lunatics, fanatics, outcasts. It was said that they had brought the plague to Drescheim and murdered the Count of Arlsbach. Whenever a baby went missing, the finger of blame pointed their way. Earth and Sky followers might brawl on feast days or war against each other in the valleys, but faced with the terrible shadow of Brother Moon they would become family again, united behind the gods of life. Lena had executed a pair of Moon cultists for blasphemy over the winter, left them swinging by the neck while an angry crowd pelted them with stones. They'd mouthed heretical prayers around swollen tongues, standing by their faith even as it killed them. That took a dangerous sort of courage.

She dropped the pamphlet and looked around for the pamphleteer. If she could hand those out unhindered, then the rule of law really did stop where the market's blades met. The woman was nowhere to be seen.

Lena started walking again, but people kept getting in her way. She snarled and almost snapped before she realised what was happening. She had got so used to crowds parting before her, fearful of everything she represented, that she now took it for granted. With her face hidden, she had to work her way through the crowd, the same as anyone else.

Once she accepted the awkward effort of manoeuvring around others' paths, she settled readily into the crowd. The space that usually surrounded her was gone, replaced by the press of bodies, the closeness of laughter, the bustling, shoving, chattering sense of humanity. Not quite the camaraderie of an army, with its shared purpose, but a taste of what that had meant. It was like drinking third ale in place of imported Vacaran wine, not as rich but a better substitute than ditch water.

Wooden steps bound with old rope took her up to the bustling platform. Some of the customers there were already drunk and sloshing their tankards around. Others had the glassy eyes and vacant smiles of silver dream users. Tiny, stoppered pots sat in a row next to the big casks of ale.

'I know you, don't I?' asked the man in front of the barrels.

Lena froze with one hand halfway to her purse. With the other, she eased her dagger from its scabbard, keeping it hidden beneath her cloak.

'I don't think so,' she said. 'I've never been here before.'

'Still…' He started pouring her drink. 'I've seen you around the city.'

Lena tensed.

'You're one of Jager's hunters aren't you? You've all got that weatherbeaten look. Bring anything good down off the mountain this time?'

Lena let out a held breath and slid the dagger back into its sheath.

'Only my apprentice,' she said. 'Give me two cups and make

his something weak.'

Deppel was waiting for her at the edge of the platform, smiling with nervous excitement.

'Tell me what I'm looking at,' Lena said. 'And for Moon's sake don't point.'

The lad lowered his half-raised hand and nodded to the right.

'That's where the main action is. Thugs for hire, fences, gang leaders looking for recruits.'

It was hard to make out faces through the tarry smoke of burning brands and cheap oil lamps, but Lena still recognised some of them, people she'd flogged, branded, or taken fingers from on the orders of the court. Some of the men had the look of veterans, wearing scraps of old uniforms and scars on their cheeks, carrying the sort of serviceable, inexpensive weapons that were churned out by industrial armouries. Others had civilian clothes with knives and clubs hidden in their folds. Taken together, they were as guilty a band as she'd ever seen.

'Down in front of us is the arena. They don't start the entertainment for a while, gives people time to get business done first.'

Sure enough, a patch of ground in front of the platform stood empty, fenced off with iron bars and guarded by surly, muscular women and men. If there was going to be combat, that might be worth sticking around for. It was a while since Lena had seen anyone fight with any skill, and she missed the art of it, as well as the raw thrill.

'The back of the market's mostly smugglers. They've got banned books, untaxed spirits and spices, artefacts from across the Midnight Ocean, anything what can't be sold in a proper shop.'

Familiar figures, lean and raggedly dressed, stood around laden handcarts next to the smugglers' goods.

'Why are there so many sgeir here?' Lena asked. She wasn't used to seeing the scavengers outside of the monster caves and the city's slums.

'The merchant house monopolies keep prices on monster parts down. It ain't safe to work against them, but no one's gonna notice if a few bits and pieces ain't there. Buyers get them cheap, sgeir keep all the cash. Once in a while, someone gets caught taking them out of the city, but otherwise it works out fine.'

That explained the handful of smugglers Lena flogged every spring. She'd assumed that they came into the caves themselves, that she'd just never seen them, but it would be safer and easier to rely on the sgeir. The taint of their presence bothered no one down here.

That pleased her. Good people were usually rough around the edges, and the sgeir were no exception. Beneath their odd customs and accents, most of them were a cursed sight kinder than the merchants who ran the city.

'How do you know so much about this place?' she asked.

'Been here before,' Deppel replied.

'That's obvious, but how come you've been here?'

He tensed for a moment, then raised his cup and drank slowly. She could almost hear his mind grinding away like broken clockwork, trying to find an excuse.

'Friend brought me,' he said.

It wasn't an answer that spoke to innocence, but she didn't really care. Plenty of people lived at the fringes of the law: beggars, tinkers, guildless craftsmen scraping by on odd jobs. As long as Deppel had never hurt anyone, that was between him, the constables, and the gods. If he slipped into real crime, then she'd do her duty and chop off whatever the judge ordered, but until then, he was just another kid.

'Why would Fiete Saimon come down here?' Lena asked. 'He owned the monopoly on selling dragon bone to seven cities and manticore sinew to five. He didn't need secret deals to make his money.'

Deppel shrugged.

'All I know is I saw him one time. He was wearing a mask and hood, but he had these fancy boots I'd seen him wear the same day. Wyvern skin with gold lion spurs.'

Lena rolled her eyes. Boots were a waste of wyvern hide. It made good, flexible armour, but if you kept scuffing it against the ground, then the scales would fall off. Add gold fixings and you had a piece of pointless, showy nonsense.

Somebody bumped Lena from behind. The platform was increasingly crowded, people jostling for a view of the arena. A lean man with tattoos down his cheek muttered an apology in a thick Dunvari accent.

'Is a pretty lady under there, yes?' he said, reaching for the edge of her hood.

Lena grabbed his wrist and twisted. Breath hissed between the man's teeth, and he dropped his cup. His companions turned to them, but Lena had a knife in her hand as she pushed the man away, and she shifted into a fighting stance before she even realised what she had done.

The man looked at her, his hand resting on the axe at his belt, and she could see the calculation going on behind his eyes, working out if this was a fight he could win. It wasn't-she knew that by the way he held himself-but a fight would bring attention. She grabbed hold of Deppel and dragged him back through the throng.

'We need to get out,' she said.

'Don't you want to see the man Saimon met?'

Lena hesitated at the top of the steps. What was she doing? A sad expression on a murderer's face, one too many beers, and here she was, following some sick strand of curiosity about the husband of a woman she'd slain. The law's bloody-handed killer, wandering a cave full of criminals in search of clues to nothing. Yet she couldn't stop. An uneasy feeling had settled in her gut, and she couldn't rest until it was gone.

'Who did he meet?' she asked.

'He runs a stall near the back.'

'Show me.'

Once again, Deppel led the way, down the steps and through the crowd around the arena. Lena couldn't find comfort in the bustle any more, too aware of the people pressing in, of the danger they represented. A sense of excitement was growing around them, a hubbub of voices and a swarm of expectant faces. Deppel couldn't simply slide through the gaps anymore. Both he and Lena had to push their way through, and more than once she had to tug at her hood to keep it from being swept back.

'Hold!' A row of men and women blocked their way, all wearing leather tunics and carrying cudgels. They had cleared a corridor through the crowd, and a cage was being dragged through on squealing wheels.

Inside the cage was a gryphon. It wasn't yet full grown, its body only the size of a plough horse. It clawed at the base of its cage with lion-like paws and rattled its beak against the bars. Wings hung loose by its sides, golden feathers trailing through the gaps of the cage. Green eyes darted back and forth in obvious agitation.

'What the hells are they doing?' Lena asked. 'It'll lose its mind trapped like that.'

'It ain't for long,' Deppel said. 'Just to get it to the arena.'

'They're going to make it fight?'

'What else would they do with it?'

Lena laughed. 'It'll take to the air, kill everyone in reach. These idiots are going to get what they deserve.'

'I've been down here a few times, and I ain't never seen nothing fly out.'

As the cage passed in front of them, Lena realised why. Blood was crusted around the joint where the wing met the gryphon's shoulder. The sight made her feel sick.

'They clipped its wings,' she said.

'Stops it getting away, don't it?' Deppel said. 'Clever, right?'

'Barbaric. Those creatures are born to fly. Only the worst streak of dung would do a thing like that.'

Too late, she realised that the nearest guard was listening. He prodded her chest with his truncheon.

'You got a problem with this?' he growled. 'Cause I'm here to make problems go away.'

'No problem,' Deppel said. 'We're just here to watch the fight, ain't we auntie?' He flashed Lena a warning look. 'Come to see what all the fuss is about.'

Lena stared after the gryphon. By the bald patches in its fur, it had been sick long before these monsters got hold of it, but the wounds they had inflicted were adding to its torment. She ought to put it out of its misery.

Her hand slid down to her dagger.

'Auntie?' Deppel said. 'We should go see that man now, yeah?'

Lena looked down at him, then across at the guard, who was peering into the shadows of her hood.

'Sorry, sir,' she said, suppressing the anger in her voice. 'I didn't mean anything by it.'

The guard stood a moment longer, hefting his cudgel and eyeing her up. But the cage had reached the arena, and he was being called over. He grunted and turned away.

Deppel led Lena on across the cave. Behind them came a roar and then a cheer. Glancing back, she saw the gryphon emerge into the arena and another cage draw up, some other dying beast to be goaded into fighting for the crowd. Anyone treating beasts like that in her army would have suffered the lash for their cruelty and wastefulness. Here, they gained riches and applause.

This was why the world needed executioners. Only fear kept some people from a slide into savagery.

They approached a row of trestle tables where smugglers and fences laid out their wares. Stolen jewellery and clockwork devices sat alongside the innards of monsters-hearts, livers, brains, those parts that would fetch the highest price from the most exclusive buyers. Three human hands, each coated with wax and clutching a wick between the fingers, sat on a strip of moth-eaten velvet, next to a box claiming to hold the tongues of liars. She had heard stories of people stealing body parts from battlefields, to use them in forbidden potions and enchantments. Despite everything she had ever seen of humanity, she had assumed it was a myth. Apparently she had been very wrong.

A woman could fight and die for her city, her family, her faith, only for her body to be sold like so much meat on a butcher's block. Yes, it was just a body, the soul long since passed away, but there should be dignity in death, if not for those passing on then for those they left behind. There were parts of the world where men and women were sold as slaves, but nowhere this grisly trade would be allowed.

'Why the hells did you bring me here, Deppel?' she hissed. 'I kill people for acting like this.'

He looked away, shame-faced and cringing.

'Dunno,' he muttered. 'Just thought you'd want to see.'

'I'm sure Captain Baumer would. And once he was done, there'd be nothing left.'

Was that really true? Would the authorities stamp down on a place like this, or was it easier to let it slide as long as it stayed out of sight, not unsettling the sensibilities of upright citizens? Hells, this place was probably packed with the city's richest and most reputable, hiding their faces the same way she did. Everyone had their vices, and a place like this made it easier to hide them.

Near the end of the row sat a cluster of stalls laden with small bottles and boxes, each one scored with angular and esoteric sigils.

'Down there,' Deppel said with a nod of his head. 'Bald bloke in the middle.'

The man looked like a skeleton had been draped in the thinnest layer of skin then covered with a leather apron. His eyes were sunken and bloodshot, his shaved head shining in the gangrenous light of a green lamp. Long, stained fingers held out a bottle to a customer.

'Fiete Saimon had business with him?' Lena asked, watching

the man from the corner of her eye.

'Saw them meet down here. Saimon made straight for that stall, though he was pretending to look at others along the way. Whatever he was buying, he'd done it before, 'cause they knew each other. Stood talking a long time before he bought anything.'

Lena made her way along the stalls, pretending to pay attention to pouches, packages, and parcels while she crept closer to her prey. His fingers seemed to dance through the air as he talked, forming abstract patterns or pointing out potions of interest to his customers. He talked constantly, pausing only briefly to listen to their requests. More than one customer was on the verge of turning away before he offered up a bottle for coin.

'You gonna buy that?' asked the woman behind a stall.

Lena looked at the small jar she'd picked up. A nutty aroma emerged despite the wax seal, a scent that might have been sweetly appealing if not for the skull and dagger on the front. She put it down and took a step back.

'I know you, don't I?' the woman said, tilting her head as she peered beneath Lena's hood.

'I don't think so.'

'Yeah, I do.' The woman held up her left hand. Two fingers were missing, pale scar tissue grown over the knuckle joint. The other two tapped her face slowly, just below the eye.

'I don't know what you mean.'

Lena turned in haste and bumped into a customer at the next stall. A bottle slid from his hands and shattered, spattering his feet with thick liquid. He yelped and fell back as his shoes started to smoke.

'Hey!' said the seller behind that stall. 'Who's paying for that?'

'Never mind paying, do you know who she is?'

Lena stepped across the fallen man and shoved her way through the throng. People turned to scowl and swear as she barged them out of the way. The noise of the crowd grew, even as the outraged alchemists shouted after her. Faces turned to watch, among them a group of arena guards. Lena gripped the handle of her dagger. At least she would know what she was doing in a fight.

A soft hand took hold of hers.

'This way,' Deppel said.

He pulled her along a line of sgeir stalls, then into a cluster of food carts. His path wound around and about, Lena seething with frustration at the time they were wasting while voices cried out behind. Yet those voices were fading, lost in the hubbub of the Blade Market.

Deppel stopped so suddenly that Lena almost knocked him over.

In front of them, the guards had opened a way through the crowd. They were followed by a gang dragging a heavy chain, and on its end the dead body of the gryphon, caught on a pair of butchers' hooks. Blood, fur, and feathers smeared the cold stone. A trailing paw seemed to twitch as it bumped across rough ground, making a final, pitiful grasp at life.

Lena felt the weight of that body descend upon her. The breath caught in her throat as she looked from the gryphon to the men and women dragging the chains, each of them spattered with the creature's blood. Not the killers, but still stained by the crime.

In that moment, she stopped seeing the people around her and instead imagined Holy Beatrice Saimon, a knife in her hand, blood flying as she stabbed her husband over and over.

A terrible realisation dawned.

Behind them, voices rose once more. Were the alchemists still pursuing them, or had someone else started a fight? Was doom or distraction on their tail?

'Come on,' Deppel said as the corpse slid past. 'We're almost out.'

They reached the mine shaft leading out of the cave. Lena let her hood slide back as she hurried up the passage and out into the night, desperate for fresh air. Her pulse was pounding like a drumbeat in her ears. She wanted to howl in rage, to tear the truth from the raw rocks of the earth. The terrible truth that she had not wanted to see.

At last she stood on the cold mountainside, trying to steady the spinning of her head.

'Are you alright?' Deppel asked, his face crumpled with concern.

'Blood,' Lena hissed. 'There was no blood.'

'What?'

She grabbed him by the sleeve and dragged him down the trail. 'You ever stab someone to death, Deppel?'

'No!'

'Well I have. Scores of them. Hundreds even. It makes a thundering red mess, the sort of thing no one can miss. So how come Beatrice Saimon was found wandering the taverns, drunk and rambling, without anyone stopping her? If she'd been covered in blood, she'd have been dragged to the constables long before the body was found. And if she'd changed out of the bloody clothes, then Baumer would have found them, like he did the knife. No way she was smart enough to get rid of the clothes but not the blade.'

'So what happened?'

'Someone else happened. Some pig-prodder killed Fiete Saimon and dropped the crime at his wife's feet. They set it up so I'd kill her and cover the trail.'

'Are you sure?'

She remembered Beatrice Saimon's wide eyes, tears running down her cheeks as she spoke her last words. 'I love him.' Not loved, love. Not the words of a murderer who had seen her husband's death, but of a poor bewildered soul who couldn't bear to face the reality of her loss.

'I'm sure,' Lena said, her hand clenching around the handle of her knife. 'Someone made me into a murderer, and I'm going to make them pay.'

CHAPTER FIVE

THE CALL OF JUSTICE

The wood panels of Councillor Maier's antechamber had been polished since the previous morning. A scent of nut oils and beeswax filled the room, close enough to food to make Lena's stomach rumble. The last thing she'd eaten was the dried beef she'd shared with a street cat, and lack of sleep only made her more hungry. When the servants had brought her in, she had hoped to raid the councillor's ostentatious fruit bowl, but apparently that was only filled during the day. Now she'd been sitting for hours, staring at its empty pedestal in the candlelight.

She needed a drink, but the servants refused, so instead she distracted herself by whittling patterns into a wyvern scale, using a small knife she kept in her boot. It scratched back and forth across the chitinous surface, while scrapings formed a patch of pale dust on the chequered tiles at her feet.

Calm. She needed to be calm. Raised emotions led to poor decisions, and she was here to fix a mistake, not make more of them.

Dawn broke through the leaded glass of the window, sending fingers of sunlight questing through the room. A glance outside showed the sun entirely risen above the Heights of Chelmek, yet she was still waiting like she'd been for half the night. She had told the servants it was important, so why hadn't they fetched Maier yet?

The outer door of the antechamber opened. Lena leapt to her

feet, eager to get this done and lift the weight of responsibility from her shoulders. But instead of Renate Maier, Soren Baumer walked in, plate armour gleaming and metal boots clanking against the floor. He made the sign of the eye, then looked at the knife in Lena's hand and snorted with laughter.

'If this is an ambush, it's shit,' he said. 'That won't even scratch me.'

His gauntleted fist clanged against his chest.

'I could stab you in the neck or the ear,' Lena said, raising the knife to head height before sliding it into her boot sheath.

'You could try. Hells, I think you should. I've been woken at dawn for your bullshit. I'd love an excuse to punch you right now.'

They both laughed.

'So what is this about?' Baumer asked, sitting down on the bench next to her.

'Easier if I tell you both at once.'

'Sounds ominous.'

Lena shrugged. 'It's not good.'

'Then let's have something that is first.'

Baumer glanced at the empty pedestal, then shouted at someone in the corridor. A moment later, a liveried servant appeared with a bowl full of fruit: apples, oranges, pears, and figs. Lena's mouth watered, and she reached for the bowl, but at that moment the inner door swung noiselessly open, and another servant appeared.

'Councillor Maier will see you now.'

Inside the office, Maier stood behind her desk, dressed in a loose velvet robe and none of her usual rings, but with the wrinkle-concealing powders that pretended to be her skin. Her arms were folded, and her face set in a scowl. The only object on the desk was an empty coin purse, limp strings dangling over the edge. Someone had removed most of the chairs, leaving Lena with no choice but to stand.

'I don't appreciate drunkards hammering on my gates in

the middle of the night,' Maier said, her voice flat and cold as a frozen river. 'Waking my husband. Scaring my children. Sending my staff into a flurry of fruitless activity.'

'I wasn't drunk,' Lena snapped. 'I'd just had an ale or two.'

'Well that makes everything better.'

They glared at each other while Baumer leaned against the fireplace, seemingly indifferent to the tension.

'What do you want, Sturm?' Maier said.

'It's the Saimon murder,' Lena said. 'We executed the wrong woman.'

Maier took a deep breath and looked at Baumer, who simply shrugged.

'You think Holy Saimon somehow switched places with an impostor?' Maier asked, her voice thick with disdain. 'Perhaps she found a changeling like in a children's tale and tricked it into dying for her?'

'I mean she didn't do the killing.'

Maier narrowed her eyes.

'You're serious?'

'No, I came here in the middle of the night for a joke. Wasn't it hilarious? Ha ha thundering ha.'

'Headsman Sturm, you are on thin ice already. Don't make the mistake of forgetting who pays your wage.'

Lena took a deep breath. Her whole body was tense, her thoughts skipping off the surface of exhaustion, twitching and twisting as they went. It would be all too easy to let the wrong words slip out, ill-informed and ill-shaped, jagged things set on starting a fight.

'I'm serious,' she said. 'I killed an innocent woman.'

Killed her on your orders, she added inside her head. *Killed her because of your mistake. Killed her because, like so many of us in this frightened age, you rushed to judgement.*

Maier settled into the only seat, straightened her robe, and steepled her fingers in front of her.

'Explain.'

Lena kept her gaze firmly on the councillor as she set out her case: the knife, the lack of blood, Saimon's behaviour at her execution. How she'd come to this conclusion she kept to herself-the city's highest judge didn't need to know about Deppel or the Blade Market. But all the facts about the case were there, as clear as the blue sky above the mountaintops.

When Lena had finished, Maier looked to Baumer.

'What do you think?' she asked.

The captain shrugged and smiled unconvincingly.

'Piss poor luck for the Saimons if it's true,' he said. 'But I'm not sold.'

'Nor am I.' Maier leaned forwards, her attention back on Lena. 'This whole thing seems driven by little more than misplaced feelings, some pang of remorse ill-fitting an executioner. Are you weakening in your resolve, Headsman Sturm? Have you lost what it takes to do the job we pay you for?'

'I've lost nothing,' Lena growled, her hand closing around the pommel of her dagger. 'You want to test my resolve; I'll show either of you what it takes to live through this.' She pointed to the scar on her cheek. 'It isn't just about how Saimon behaved, it's about evidence that doesn't add up.'

'It adds up perfectly for me. The woman committed the crime outside her own home. It was simple enough for her to clean up and to dispose of her blood-stained clothes, probably burnt or given to a beggar.'

'Then why keep the knife? That makes no sense.'

'Killers don't always make sense, Sturm, you should know that by now. Beatrice Saimon had a wild temper and a taste for drink, as evidenced by witnesses at her trial. The woman was barely coherent from the moment of arrest to the moment you delivered justice upon her.'

'If it had been justice, then I wouldn't be here.'

'No, you would be in some rat-infested tavern on the cheap side of the city, or passed out from drink in a bed we bought for you.'

'How I spend my time is none of your cursed business.'

'When you get drunk and disturb my family on a fasting day, it is very much my business.'

Lena stood stiff-backed, staring at Maier. Her mouth was dry, her pulse pounding.

'This is important,' she said.

Maier sighed and gestured to Baumer.

'You're both soldiers, Soren, why don't you talk some sense into her?'

Baumer held out his hands, gauntlets gleaming, and gave Lena a sheepish smile. The swaggering confidence with which he policed the streets was no substitute for real wits. Lena almost pitied him. He might be a soldier, but he wasn't the sort that she had been. There was too much of the thug about him, the air of a mercenary used to answering orders, not questions.

'You want the truth?' he said. 'Holy Saimon was a shit. She was always causing trouble, going down the market and stirring people up.'

'You mean preaching?'

'Preaching the worship of Mother Sky.'

'The last I heard, that was legal in this city.'

'As long as they don't cause trouble, sure. But between us...' He gestured from himself to Lena in her simple, undecorated clothes. '...we all know what Sky priests are like. Preaching about the coming storm, stirring people up against order and tradition. They take temples from god-fearing priests and cover them in statues of their thundering new saints. Saimon, she was the ring-leader.'

'You mean the high priest?'

'Come off that, it's not like Bishop Kunder, anointed by the Herarch himself. Their priests just got together and said she was in charge. You wouldn't run an army like that, and it's no way to run a church.'

Lena shook her head. 'You might not like it, but she was important to a lot of people.'

'Of course she was, the noisiest one always is. You should have seen her shouting at people on their way to the cathedral, saying it was a place of sin.'

'You think that she was a murderer because she preached things half the people in this city believe?'

'I'm saying that me and my constables ended up in fights with her congregation a dozen times this year, and that never happens with the followers of Father Earth.'

'Got into fights with...' Lena turned her attention back to Maier, who sat watching them with pinched lips. 'You send the constables to break up Sky faith meetings?'

There was a drawn out silence. Baumer, his eyes wide and mouth clammed shut, took a step back.

'The safety of this city relies upon maintaining an equilibrium,' Maier said, her voice carefully controlled. 'Steps must sometimes be taken to avoid a dangerous imbalance. That is why the Moon Cult is illegal, because they are brutal fanatics with no respect for the social order. And it is why we must sometimes deal with other rabble rousers.'

'Rabble rousers whose religion you disagree with.'

'My duty is the stability of Unteholz. I disagree with all rabble rousers.'

Maier's gaze was an accusation levelled at Lena. It seemed like 'rabble rouser' could mean anyone the judge disagreed with, and that it was a label that could bring real trouble.

Lena rolled her shoulders. Something clicked, and she felt a brief tug of pain, followed by relief as tension eased from a muscle. With measured steps, she walked to the window and looked out across the city, over tiles and thatch, towers and terraces, the looming ribs of the cathedral and the imposing black stone of the keep. Smoke was already swirling from the foundries, and she could hear the rattle of cartwheels as wagons full of miners headed for the pits. Somewhere beneath all the architecture and industry there were criminals and cultists, agents of foreign powers and of unholy creeds, the tinder that could ignite a conflagration like those she had seen in other lands. How much of a spark would it take to set the city blaze? And was it better to risk a candle flame than to live in the dark?

'It's not just about Holy Saimon,' Baumer said. 'It's about Councillor Saimon too. He was a good citizen and a good councillor. Made sure my boys and girls got their pay on time. Passed sensible laws to stop cheats and trouble-makers. He didn't deserve what that crazy arsehole of a wife did to him.'

A wyvern soared over the terraced fields outside the city, wings spread wide to catch the wind coming up the valley. Its head was tilted down on its long neck, watching for wild beasts out of the forest or stray goats that had roamed from their flock. Looking for something vulnerable to pick off.

'You're right,' Lena said. 'This is about getting real justice for Fiete Saimon, but apparently that doesn't interest you.'

'Enough.' Maier's voice was hard as a blade. 'You may not believe in anything, Executioner Sturm, but I do. I believe in order. I believe in tradition. I believe in this city and its citizens and the difficult peace we have achieved. I will not have you tear that down in some self-pitying fit of pique.'

Lena stared at her, speechless. Just because she had stopped fighting over religion, that didn't mean she'd given up on her principles, did it? Sure, she spent her days hiding in work or in a bottle, trying not to think about things like war and faith and family, and she couldn't remember the last time she'd stepped inside a temple. But she had a code. She had a purpose.

She remembered her younger self, so full of steel and certainty. That Lena would have had none of these arguments. She would have looked through them and seen excuses not to fight in a war for the salvation of the world. Was Lena really arguing with Maier for what was right, or was she arguing with herself, trying to get that ghost off her back?

'Justice has been done,' Maier said. 'The law has been upheld. If you go throwing accusations at innocent people, casting doubt on the firm and righteous hand of the law, then you will shake faith in the system that holds our society together. On the basis of nothing more than a whim, you will embolden criminals and create fear in the hearts of the innocent, fear that they might suffer for someone else's crimes, that you might be coming for them.'

'If we got this wrong, then they have reason to fear.'

'We didn't. They don't.'

Maier got out of her seat, took the empty pouch off the table, and went to a chest at the back of the room. A ring of hefty keys emerged from within her robes and a moment later the chest swung open. There was a clink as the councillor counted coins into the pouch.

'The law must be upheld,' she said. 'You play a vital part in that, Lena, and we often forget what a strain it puts on you. The isolation, the bloodshed, dealing with all the worst people in our city. I step into court and face criminals for a few days each month, but you do it every time you go to work.

'Perhaps it's time you found an apprentice, to share the burden and prepare for your retirement. I'm sure that I can talk the council into paying their wage. And until then…'

She walked around the table, took Lena's hand in one of her own, and pressed the pouch of coins into it. The leather of the pouch was soft, and Lena could feel the size of the coins through it. Ten silver shillings, a generous sum by any standard except those of the wealthy.

'A long-overdue bonus,' Maier said, 'in recognition of your good work. Yesterday clearly took a strain on you. We'll hold the other prisoners awaiting your ministrations while you take some time off. Relax, drink a good wine for once, maybe go watch a play. A few days seeing the lighter side of life will put all of this into perspective.'

'So you won't investigate the Saimon crime again?'

Maier squeezed Lena's hand tight around the pouch of coins. 'There's no need. For any of us.'

Lena emerged from the side gate of Maier's mansion and stared down the streets of the Hochfel district, with their paving stones, raised beds of fragrant flowers, and fountains fed by mountain streams. Up here, no-one smelled the stench of the city, that mix of gutters, animal sweat, and furnace smoke. They didn't even have to get the dirt of the streets on their boots. What greater value could there be than stability, when stability kept you like this? Who here would give a dead man's breath for something as disruptive as justice?

'How'd it go?' said a small, nervous voice.

Deppel was sitting where a buttress met the outer wall of Maier's grounds, hidden by shadows and the indifference of those who never looked down.

'What are you still doing here?' Lena asked.

'Waiting for you.'

'Why?'

Deppel stood but stayed where he was, the scuffed toes of his shoes pressed together, one hand pressed to his stomach while the other scratched the back of his neck.

'I thought maybe I could help. You know, with the investigation.'

'There isn't going to be an investigation.'

'You think Holy Saimon done it?' His mouth hung open.

'No.'

Lena turned and strode off down the road, stamping her

frustration out on those clean, straight cut stones. Footsteps pattered after her.

'That don't make sense. If she didn't do it-'

'If she didn't do it then we killed the wrong woman, and how could the great and noble councillors of Unteholz ever admit that they might be wrong?' Lena kicked a pebble, which went bouncing along the street ahead of them, rattling down to the town below.

'Does this happen a lot?' Deppel asked.

'It had better not.'

Lena's hand closed around the hilt of her dagger. Life had been so much easier when she was a soldier. If you had a problem, then you could fight it; even insubordinate soldiers could be knocked into line with a few good blows. But you couldn't use fists to settle this issue, any more than you could in a marriage. She felt as trapped and frustrated now as she had when she and Jahann were together.

'So the killer's gonna get away with it?' Deppel asked.

'Like hells they are. They made me a murderer. I'm not letting that rest.'

There was the younger self she had felt looking over her shoulder. She might not be fighting for faith any more, but she could fight for what was right, could find the satisfaction that came from struggle. She felt as though she were bonded to a dragon, a wild and blazing spirit running through her, forcing her feet ever faster, rushing towards the city and…

And what? What could she possibly do about this?

'I can help!' Deppel said brightly.

'You?' Lena sneered. 'You're just a child.'

'I'm fourteen years old,' he said sharply. 'I could be an apprentice by now.'

'Like I said, a child.'

'That don't mean I can't help. I led you to the Blade Market, helped you see something weren't right. I can take you more places, tell you about the Saimons and their lives.'

'You got lucky, saw something by chance. I've got everything I need from you.'

The patter of Deppel's footsteps stopped. To her relief, Lena found herself walking alone again, out of Hochfel and onto The Shucks.

While Hochfel had been a place of watchful silence, The Shucks was filled with the gentle chatter of crafters. Some were already at work: a silversmith pumping the bellows of her forge, a potter rocking a pedal back and forth to drive his wheel. Others were setting out their wares, laying them on bright tablecloths to attract the wealthy patrons who descended here like richly feathered birds. It was nothing to the bustle of a real working district, but it was a sign that the day had truly begun.

The Shucks had always done well out Unteholz's merchant elite, but it had grown further in recent years, as religious loyalties shifted. To Father Earth, ostentation was a regrettable excess, but to Mother Sky it was a virtue, a way of showing who she had blessed. Congregants came here for jewellery, doublets, perfume, and enamelled washing bowls. For those who stuck with the old faith, there were simple but well-made tunics in black and brown, with hints of holy green. With every year that passed, the factions grew more visibly apart. Maier and her allies would have to fight tooth and claw to hold them together.

At one end of the street, a servant was tearing down handbills that had been plastered up in the night, crudely printed sheets showing broken chains and the words 'NONE HIGH, NONE LOW'. The Moon Cult might be small, but its members were never short on zeal. Lena admired their courage; putting up those posters could get a person hanged. But she had no patience for zealots or foreign theology. If the gods touched everyone equally, then why were there beggars and lepers? It was a faith that said the whole world was unjust.

She turned right and headed uphill, around the backs of the

foundries and down towards her home. But before she was even out of The Shucks, hurried footsteps caught up with her.

'I know something else,' Deppel said, panting as he tried to keep up. Lena lengthened her stride, but he persisted, practically running along beside her. 'Something you'll want to know.'

'Something you just made up.'

'No!'

'But you didn't tell me just now because you were feeling shy, like a precious little prince on his wedding day.'

'What? No, I just…'

He sounded strained, like he was speaking under pressure, but no-one was asking him to talk.

'I could get in trouble for telling you,' he said. 'Big trouble.'

Something about the certainty of those words made Lena stop. This wasn't the burbling desperation of a man blagging for what he wanted. It was the tight voice of genuine fear.

They hadn't yet reached the foundry smokestacks, but labourers were bustling past on their way to work. She drew Deppel off to one side, between the workshops of two crafters who weren't good enough for The Shucks.

'Tell me,' she said.

Deppel glanced back and forth, shifting nervously from one foot to another while he caught his breath.

'You know who Jagusia Brodbeck is?' he asked.

Lena nodded. How could she not know that name, when so many criminals passed through her care? She might not attend trials or interrogations, but she heard the rumours that hung like spectres beyond the light of proof. The infamous highwaymen who left town two steps ahead of the constables. The smugglers who only appeared on moonless nights. The handful of bosses who oversaw the city's crime gangs. Bosses like Jagusia Brodbeck.

'You know what she looks like?' Deppel asked.

Lena shook her head.

Deppel looked up at the sun, then gave a small nod. 'You want to see?'

She wasn't sure where this was going, but he had her attention. Half the severed hands lying around the Weeping Stone had been lost for crimes that Brodbeck ordered, though no-one had ever proven it. If she had some connection to the Saimon murder, then Lena could bring justice for more than just one dead priest. She could prove to Maier and herself that she stood for something.

She bit back a smile.

'Show me.'

Rustbeck was a busy street, full of the homes and businesses of moderate merchants, those constantly hustling to keep themselves from slipping down the social ladder while hunting for that one deal that would raise them into the great trade houses. There was a bustling tumult of wagons, messengers, and men and women bartering outside their own gates, trying to shave a few shillings off the price of a delivery. These were the sort of people who had embraced the Sky priests' religious reforms, and this was reflected in the edifice that towered over the end of the street, the Temple of the Sundered Rose.

A decade before, the Sundered Rose had simply been the Rustbeck Parish Temple, one more shrine to the glory of Father Earth. Then its priests had switched to the new faith. Mother Sky's lightning bolt had been lifted from halfway up the altar to hang above the Father's disk. Pedestals had been raised and niches carved into the walls, to hold the statues of saints. Copies of reformed scripture, containing those disputed new-old chapters that scholars had supposedly rediscovered and restored, arrived fresh from the printing presses of Kirkstat, to replace illuminated tomes passed down from priest to priest. Those ancient and revered books were locked away, relics of an age and an order this new wave of believers wanted to leave behind.

The temple had already been impressive, its walls made from slabs of smoothly carved granite gouged from the flanks of Steel Peak, except for the entranceway, which was a proud arch of imported marble. Holy Saimon's congregation had gone further, gathering enough wealth to hire an architect of the new school, who had capped the building with a broad dome and tall tower that spiralled to a tapering pinnacle. A grand tableau was added to the upper reaches of the front wall, bearing carvings of blank-faced holy men, victims of the Slaughter of Saints. An old building laden with dust and abstraction had been re-energised along with its congregation, a shining example of religious reform.

On a balcony above the entrance, a priest was banging a gong, calling the righteous to worship. Lena's breath caught at the sudden closeness of that sound, moved by a heady mixture of anger and shame, and by a memory of more noble feelings. She was tempted to follow its ringing inside, but who would she pray to any more, and why would they listen? She had fought against the followers of one faith, then she had abandoned the other, and throughout she had felt distant from it all. People around her had screamed for salvation and damnation, while she lived for the thrill of the fight and the satisfaction of a duty well served. Even if she wanted salvation, even if she deserved it, no god was going to listen to her.

She sat with Deppel on the edge of a fountain across from the temple, watching the congregants arrive. As each new arrival reached the top of the steps they paused, dipped their hands into a newly installed marble font, and cleansed themselves before they walked in. A junior priest stood with a towel in his hand and a bright chain around his neck, welcoming all comers to a purer form of faith.

Deppel chattered away, talking about the people who lived here, the things he'd seen them do, the ones who had risen higher and those who had sunk from view. Lena tried to block the noise out, but lack of sleep had weakened her defences. She splashed her face with the icy cold water of the fountain, channelled from one of the mountain's meltwater streams, and rubbed her eyes. She needed food and sleep, and before that she needed a drink to settle her thoughts. But first she wanted to see Brodbeck.

'That's her,' Deppel said with a nudge.

Lena followed his gaze to a woman ascending the temple steps.

At first glance, she might have mistaken the woman for a member of a merchant house. She was dressed in a red velvet doublet with black silk beneath the slashed sleeves, matching hose, and shiny black riding boots with viciously barbed spurs. Gold chains hung around her neck and gemstones sparkled on ear studs and bracelets. It was the sort of ostentatious wealth beloved by Mother Sky's faithful, and characteristic of those who had made their money in business.

But other details gave Jagusia Brodbeck away. She wore her blond hair cut short, unlike the members of the merchant houses, whose long braids were often oiled and decorated with lockets and flowers. Her hands were bare of the rings that even an Earth worshipper like Maier wore, and that would have got in the way of hauling stolen goods or wielding a weapon. It was those weapons that told Lena the most about this woman, not because it was technically illegal to wear them, a point that didn't matter to those who could afford the fines, but because of how the weapons looked. Yes, they were flashy, the sword resting in an ornamented scabbard, the pistol covered in enamelled decoration. But it was a shortsword rather than a rapier, good for fighting at close quarters, and the mouth of the gun, which protruded through the end of a quick release holster, was blackened from repeated firing.

Lena hadn't known what to expect of Brodbeck, but this fitted.

The gang leader reached the top of the steps and walked into the temple, followed by an entourage of thugs and two pretty young men wearing silk robes and simpering smiles.

'How often does she come here?' Lena asked.

'Once a week, at least,' Deppel replied. 'This is the service she comes to regular, but she goes to others too, and brings presents on holy days.'

Lena stroked her chin and kept watching the door. The gong had stopped ringing and now voices emerged, raised together in song. It was an old hymn, a good one for marching to. Lena hadn't sung it in a long time.

Criminals were as superstitious as anyone. Most carried lucky charms or religious icons when they came to the Weeping Stone. Many sought consolation in prayer right up to the moment that the noose tightened around their neck. There was nothing suspicious about a crime boss going to temple.

But it was a connection, one that no one had told her about. If Brodbeck came regularly to Holy Saimon's temple then the priest must have known who she was preaching to. She would have seen the wealth that Brodbeck wore and learnt where it came from. Was that as far as it went, or had their relationship gone deeper? Saimon's followers often got into fights with the worshippers of Father Earth, so perhaps she'd tried other criminal activities in the furtherance of her faith. The devout seldom respected boundaries that weren't granted by their gods.

Of course, the opposite story was possible as well. The priest who died trying to stop a criminal was a story as old as faith. Opposing Brodbeck could have bought the Saimons a brutal end just as easily as allying with her.

And if it did turn out that Brodbeck was involved, if Lena could prove her part in a murder, then there was a chance to cut a cancer from the flesh of Unteholz. To fight a good fight again.

She stood and stretched. The rumbling of her stomach was a distraction from thinking through her next steps. Fortunately, Councillor Maier had given her enough money for a hundred hearty breakfasts. That bribe to stay silent would fuel her first steps towards justice, and to hells with Maier if she complained.

'Where do we go now?' Deppel asked.

'I'm going back to Toblur's,' Lena said. 'You go do whatever it is you do with your days. Begging at the temple door, maybe?'

'What about catching the murderer?'

'I'll do that later.'

'I want to help!'

'And I want to be left alone.'

'But I've been helpful. I told you things. Showed you things.'

His look of disappointment made Lena sag even further on her weary bones. Jahann had been the one to say no when it was needed, not her. She could dish out discipline, but disappointing children was another matter.

'It's not you, boy,' she said. 'I just don't like having people around. I prize my peace.'

'I can be quiet. You won't even know I'm there.'

Lena doubted that very much indeed. His chatter was already tiring her out.

'What's the point in having you around if I won't know it?' she asked.

'I'll keep out of your way until you need me, and then I'll be there. I can carry messages and fetch things and tell you about the people and places I know. And I can get where you can't cause everybody knows Headsman Sturm and nobody knows Deppel the street rat. Please, please let me help!'

The worst of it was that he was right, he really could be useful. And perhaps, if he could learn to keep his mouth shut, that usefulness might outweigh the annoyance.

'Fine. You can help. And you can start by shutting up until I've eaten. Clear?'

'Yes! I'll be as quiet as–'

He froze beneath her glare, clammed his mouth shut, and nodded vigorously.

'Come on then,' Lena said. 'Let's go look for clues in a heap of bread and sausages.'

CHAPTER SIX

THE ALCHEMIST'S LAIR

Most of the alchemists' shops stood in the same street, between Unteholz's considerable foundry district and its smaller cluster of tanneries. With billowing chimneys on one side and vats of piss treating leather on the other, the place stank like a plague corpse on fire. It wasn't the worst stench Lena had ever had to tolerate, but she was glad she hadn't come here until her breakfast settled. Chucking her guts up in front of a suspect would have made her a lot less intimidating.

The signs hanging over the alchemists' doors all followed the same theme-either a bubbling crucible or a pestle and mortar. Outside the third shop the pestle was green, the mortar blue, and they appeared to be crushing a tiny phoenix, flames fluttering from its feathers. It was an ambitious sign. In all her years, Lena had only encountered a phoenix twice, and no army in the Principalities of Stone had ever tamed one for battle.

Inside, the shop was filled with the same things she had seen in the previous two, mostly boxes and pots sealed with intricate sigils. A few glass jars showed off more striking ingredients: slabs of bright red fungus, piles of long pointed teeth, liquids that shimmered in the light from the open windows. A thin trickle of smoke emerged through the curtain from an inner room, bringing with it a smell at once both sweet and acrid.

Deppel entered the shop two paces behind Lena and stared wide-eyed around him.

'Are they the same as the ones what was in that last shop?' he asked, pointing at a row of jars.

The curtain twitched, and an apprentice emerged blinking from the back room. She was about Deppel's age, blond and well-built with a face that was either freckled or scarred by the spattering of potions. She smiled at them and wiped her hands on a cloth hanging from her leather apron.

'Can I help you?' she asked in the soft, lilting accent of the Duchies of the Loom.

'I'm here to speak with your master,' Lena said.

'What is it you're looking for? We may have it prepared already.' The apprentice's eyes flicked up and down Lena, across Deppel, and back again. 'A charm against bullets, perhaps, or a blade poison-purely for killing rats, of course.'

There was only one reason to want a poisoned blade, and it wasn't rats.

'You think I'm a street thug?' Lena folded her arms across her chest.

'Not at all! But you would be amazed at what people seek. A healing draft then? An ointment for some itch? A potion to help your lover last?'

'Your master. I want to speak with them.'

The smile never left the girl's face, but it tightened at the edges. Her tone lost a little of its warmth.

'Of course.' She raised her voice. 'Master Pawlitzki, a customer wants to see you.'

'You deal with it,' said a sharp voice.

'She insists.'

There was a clang and a muttering. The curtain was flung back, and a man emerged. Tall and thin with a bald head and pale skin dappled with coloured stains, he was instantly recognisable from the Blade Market. Lena suppressed a smile at having so quickly tracked down her prey.

'You're Master Pawlitzki?' Lena asked.

'Doctor Waclaw Cornelius Pawlitzki, master of the seven arts and thirteen base principles.' Pawlitzki intoned the words to a steady rhythm that imbued them with some significance Lena didn't know. Then his eyes narrowed, and he stared at Lena without shame or self-awareness. 'I know you, don't I?'

'I'm Lena Sturm, the city's executioner. Most people have seen my work.'

'Headsman Sturm.' Pawlitzki's face lit up, and he made a cursory sign of the eye. 'Are you here to sell? I can offer you an exceptional price for eyes, tongues, or reproductive organs. Hands have value, and I would happily take them off you, but the coarseness of the work they go into means that it is of less interest to me, and frankly, the customers for a hand of glory often provide their own, such is the nature of the criminal confraternity. Remuneration would depend upon the particulars of the offence. Murderers and thieves provide the best hands, but the tongue of a blasphemer could be worth its weight in gold.'

His fingers waved enthusiastically through the air, then snatched up a quill from a lectern in the corner of the room. He started scribbling away in time to the figures he spouted; it seemed that almost every part of the human body had its price, if it came from the right human. Lena stood and let him talk, filled with loathing at the trade he was suggesting, while Deppel wandered the room, peering into jars and bottles. He gave a small cough and pointed discreetly to a box decorated with a picture of a hand, palm out, candle flames flickering from the tips of the fingers.

The apprentice watched Lena for a while, a frown falling across her face. At last she reached out to touch her master on the arm. The torrent of words stopped, and he blinked at her in surprise.

'Master, I don't think she's here to sell you ingredients.'

Pawlitzki frowned.

'Then why is she here?'

Lena let a predatory smile slide up her face. It was an

expression that had once been a warning to her soldiers that they were crossing a line, then later to her young son when his antics had gone too far. Whether turned upon a mud-stained Jekob or a dozen surly soldiers, it was a smile carefully crafted to instil fear and uncertainty.

'You knew Fiete Saimon,' she said.

Pawlitzki stepped back from the lectern, one hand clutching the quill, the other rubbing at his apron.

'That is a private business matter.'

'Questions hang over Saimon's murder. You've just admitted to an interest in body parts and connections to criminals. Do you want to tell me about your business, or do you want to take it in front of the Blood Court?'

'Surely that case has been resolved? Further investigatory efforts would be the height of futility.'

'I'm not saying the Blood Court would care about that.' Lena opened the box with the hand on the front. 'This, though…'

Three human hands stood inside the box, stiff and waxy with an oily gleam. A candle wick emerged from the tip of each finger.

'How dare you!' Pawlitzki slammed the lid shut. 'All of my ingredients have been bought from legitimate sources.'

He was so close now Lena could smell the mess of chemicals that stained his apron. Sulphur, vinegar, saffron, saltpetre, piss, a mess of the appealing and the appalling, that blend of allure and aversion that put her on edge whenever she met an alchemist. They were good for healing salves and gunpowder recipes, but she wouldn't trust them any more than she would trust a wyvern with a flock of sheep.

'What's a legitimate source for a human body part?'

'Certain merchants who negotiate fair fees with grieving families or those dying without relatives.'

'Really? So if I bring in Fat Janny and show him what's in that box, he won't recognise the birthmark on the middle hand? The one I took off him and left hanging by the Weeping Stone?'

Pawlitzki glanced down at the box and cleared his throat.

'I can hardly be held accountable if my suppliers sometimes take shortcuts in their search for-'

'You say you have suppliers; I say you sent your girl to the Weeping Stone at night with a shuttered lantern and a sack.' Lena pointed at the apprentice, who went pale and pressed herself back against the shelves. 'How do you think the court will see it?'

Drops of sweat were forming on Pawlitzki's brow, tiny, treacherous points that gleamed in the light.

'What harm does it do?' he asked, his voice rising in pitch. 'These things were going to waste. Now instead of being left to corruption's grasp, they'll generate fresh matter of good use.'

'Good use?'

'A hand of glory helps people sleep.'

'Helps them sleep while burglars break in. Remember, I spend time with criminals, I hear their tales.'

'Please,' Pawlitzki said, 'let's come to some arrangement. What can I do for you?'

'Tell me your business with Fiete Saimon.'

'Yes, yes, of course.' Pawlitzki pulled the curtain aside and looked over at his apprentice. 'Lotta, look after the shop. I'll be with our guest.'

Lena followed Pawlitzki into the rear of his shop. It was shrouded in the deep red glow from a fireplace full of throbbing embers, and in one corner the sickly yellow light of a single tallow candle. A book was open on a desk next to the candle. Over the fire, a cauldron bubbled steadily away, and to one side something was burning in a small black pot, sending smoke down an elaborate array of twisting glass pipework. Whatever it was, it made Lena's eyes water and the back of her throat sting.

Pawlitzki strode to the back of the room and started rummaging through a set of heavy chests.

'This was my business with Saimon,' he said, handing a bundle to Lena.

It was heavier than she expected. She unwrapped the cloth to reveal three daggers, all rusty and with a crust of bark and lichen flaking away around the hilts.

'Old weapons?' she asked, frowning in confusion. What use were these to anyone?

'Rare ingredients.' Pawlitzki opened a jar full of sweet smelling water and another holding tiny, dried black toadstools. 'These may seem like mundane matter to you, but to a master of the seven alchemical arts they are more precious than gold. Fiete had a knack for finding such things.'

'These are worth a lot?'

Lena peered at the toadstools. Hadn't she seen those growing on a grave once, during the Highwater Vale campaign? And what was going on with the daggers?

'Do you even understand what those blades are?' Pawlitzki asked. 'Those are greenwood knives, embedded in the trunk of an oak for a generation while bark grew over them, the elements of wood and iron intertwining to stimulate the forces within. Their rust, flaked away and carefully powdered, provides the fundamental union underlying some of the most potent-'

'How much do they cost?'

Pawlitzki shook his head. 'I offer an education and you reduce it to base commerce. Such is the way of the world.'

'Answer the question.'

'Those each cost me a ducat, and I had to argue Fiete down from two.'

Lena stared in disbelief at the rusted, useless weapons. When she started out as a soldier she had barely earned a florin a month, never mind a whole Salt City ducat. The bag of silver shillings Maier had given her, which at the time had seemed an extravagant boon, would buy a quarter of one of these sorry things.

'Was everything you bought off him this expensive?' she asked, carefully setting the blades down on the desk.

'At least.'

'And you argued over prices?'

'Of course! What sort of business would I be running if I didn't?'

'Arguments can get heated when there's a lot of money at stake.'

Pawlitzki gaped at her, open-mouthed.

'Are you saying that I stabbed Fiete? That's absurd.'

'He brought you blades. Easy to get carried away when they're around.'

'His wife killed him. Everyone knows that.'

Pawlitzki's voice had become shrill. He turned away from Lena, grabbed a poker, and stabbed at the fire. Hot coals rasped across each other, and sparks flew through the room. Lena, who had tensed the moment he grabbed the iron rod, now watched his back. Was it a trick of the light or was he trembling?

'Holy Saimon didn't kill her husband,' Lena said. 'Whoever did, I will find them.'

Pawlitzki went still. After a moment, he turned to face her, the red hot poker in his hand. His eyes, which had been staring into the smoke and heat, were more bloodshot than before.

'If you're looking for a killer, there was already one close to Fiete Saimon,' he said. 'Jagusia Brodbeck.'

'Brodbeck was part of his wife's congregation. If you want to distract me, then you'll have to do better.'

'They shared more than a priest in common.'

Pawlitzki stepped away from the fire, his expression feverish, the poker still raised. Lena's hand slid to her dagger.

'I saw them talking,' he said. 'Whispered words born in dark corners. I tried to warn him that only danger could come of that woman, that her blood generates its own poison, and he just laughed me off, said that the chemicals were making me paranoid. But my mind is not addled yet, Headsman Sturm, for all that my gift will one day be my ruin. I see the world in all its glory, and soon I will open others' eyes too. They will taste the sweet elixir of truth and they will feel the touch of the gods.'

His jaw was clenched, the poker trembling in his hand. As he spoke he had crossed the room, so that he stood a bare two paces from Lena. She could see the spittle on his lips and the fever in his eyes, an armed madman bearing down on her. Old instincts rose and muscles tensed, while her grip tightened around her dagger.

'You bring that poker one step closer, and I'll gut you where you stand,' she said, drawing the blade.

Pawlitzki blinked.

'There's no need for threats, Headsman. You have already forced my cooperation.'

He walked to the fireplace, laid the poker down, and peered into the bubbling cauldron as if nothing had happened. Still watching him warily, Lena slid her dagger back into its sheath.

'You sound as if you know a lot about Brodbeck,' she said.

'Be careful, Headsman. Asking questions about her has cost many an honest citizen their life.'

'But not you?'

'I don't ask questions. I just notice things about some of my customers.'

'She's one of your customers?'

'Really, Headsman? Do you want to get us both killed?'

'No one needs to know what you tell me, as long as you tell me right now.'

Pawlitzki stared into the fire, its light giving his face an unholy glow. His eyes flitted back and forth, as if he were examining and assessing the options lying ahead of him. Lena found herself curious, wanting to know what went on inside the mind of this strange and unsettled man.

'Fine,' he said at last. 'I do a great deal of business for Jagusia Brodbeck, have done since she was a lieutenant to Old Man Rochus. I don't discriminate in my customers, and I don't ask what they want my creations for. The art of generating fresh matter is rewarding, and payment a necessity I will not scorn. But I can tell you, Brodbeck buys more silver dream than anyone else I know, and unless I'm mistaken, she takes some of it herself. Half her waking hours, she's barely in our world, never mind in a clear state of mind.

'You want to know what I know about Jagusia Brodbeck? I know that she could have killed Fiete and barely even remembered a moment of it. Whatever they say, I am not the one whose mind is addled, and I am certainly not the citizen you should harangue.'

He glared at Lena again, but she didn't flinch. Perhaps he really was distressed by this whole business, grieving for someone he had lost and angry at the people who had endangered his friend. Or perhaps a guilty conscience pushed him onto the defensive.

'Have you heard of the Slaughter of Saints?' Lena asked.

Pawlitzki waved a hand as if summoning memories from the air.

'A massacre of priests down in the Salt Cities, if I recall correctly. Are you going to threaten me with the same terrible fate, Headsman?'

She took a step closer and lowered her voice.

'Do you know who General Torresto was?'

'Not one of my customers, I can tell you that at least.'

'Torresto hired the soldiers who committed the Slaughter of Saints. When people heard what had happened, a great mob went to him, demanding to know where the murderers could be found. Torresto believed in loyalty, and he wouldn't betray those men and women to the mob. So instead, the mob beat him to death and flung his body in the swamp.

'I'm not going to threaten you, Doctor Pawlitzki. But remember, people get upset when priests die, and they don't like folk who cover for the killer. Better to tell me what you know now than to wait for the mob.'

'I have told you,' he snapped, turning away from her. 'Now if you're quite done here, Headsman, I have work to do.'

'I'm done.' Lena pulled back the curtain and relished the fresher air outside the alchemist's lair. 'Good day, Doctor.'

CHAPTER SEVEN

SINNERS AND SAINTS

The Cage Cathedral of Saint Lukara was one of the most amazing sights in Unteholz, if not the whole Principalities of Stone. Its main chamber was a ribcage a hundred feet high, covered in leather a foot thick and set with stained glass panels. A spiral staircase ran up the spinal column that was its macabre steeple, with the topmost bone forming an arch that held the city's greatest gong. The altar was a calcified scale the size of a farmer's wagon. Father Earth's priests sought to inspire awe wherever they preached, and in the Cage Cathedral they had excelled themselves.

For Lena, it held a particular sense of the uncanny. In her years as a drachenritter, she had lived and fought close to all manner of monsters, from wyverns to manticores, gorgons to gryphons. She had ridden them into battle, feeling the powerful pulse of their muscles and the red rush of their killer instincts. She had stood against them, sword in hand, and seen the light fade from radiant eyes as she delivered a killing blow. She had fed them and watered them, brushed the knots from their fur and cleaned the dirt from their wounds. Through the bonds they shared, the longings of these monsters had become as vital to her as the feelings that stirred in her own heart. She could never love people like she loved those beasts.

And now she had to step inside one of their bodies.

She touched one of the bones that flanked the cathedral's looming doors. It was staggering in its size, unlike anything that stalked even the wildest parts of the Saved Lands. If she hadn't seen it for herself, she would never have believed it, and unsettled as she was to be walking into a corpse, she was curious too, longing to learn what this creature had been. Was it really the vast dragon that the legendary Saint Lukara had slain, or was it something else, something older than humanity? Was it truly a creation of Brother Moon, sent to destroy all that was good, or had Father Earth and Mother Sky created it, as they had created all other beasts?

'Do you think it was all covered in scales?' Deppel asked, breaking into her reverie. 'They must have been enormous. Bigger than me. Bigger than you even. Could have used one as a sledge, ridden all the way down the mountain in winter on a piece of a dragon.'

He made a swooping movement with his hand, accompanied by a whooshing sound.

Lena gritted her teeth. Her own Jekob had never been as talkative when she had been at home, but she had still struggled with his chatter, seeking conversation whenever she craved a moment's peace. It was what the young did.

'Come on,' she said. 'We won't find answers out here.'

'Sorry,' Deppel mumbled, flinching from her gaze.

Others were walking in and out of the cathedral. It was the largest temple to Father Earth in a hundred leagues, with a reputation made grander by the myth of Saint Lukara and the beast he had slain. There were pilgrims from across the Principalities, all of them wearing disk amulets and clutching prayer beads, come seeking miraculous cures to ailments no surgeon or alchemist could mend. Every spring, a fresh trickle of pilgrims began their progress through the mountains to Unteholz, and every autumn a handful remained, unable to drag themselves from a city that had seemingly saved their lives. They hung around the square, listened to sermons and watched the burnings of heretical books, prayed through the night and begged for alms while they waited for their god to touch them again.

She might not feel the fierce faith that was ripping the principalities apart like a butcher's blade, but when she saw a woman walk on legs that had been ruined, Lena could understand the power this place held. Perhaps these pilgrims deserved to be healed, in a way that she didn't. They were naive believers, innocents in a world stained red with guilt, while she was a ghost of failed dreams and other people's nightmares, walking proof that humanity would not succeed when left to its own devices.

Gods, but she wanted a drink. Mother Sky allowed brewers and pie makers to sell their goods outside her temple, because there was nothing wrong with sating bodily desire. Father Earth, if his priests were to be believed, took a very different view, and there was nothing to slake Lena's thirst within sight of the cathedral. No point delaying then. Time to get the business done.

Walking through the doors of the cathedral was like walking into another world. The city air, thick with sweat and rot, was drowned out by the sweet scent of incense from burners in elaborate brass stands. The coloured light spilling in through stained glass mingled with the flickering flare of burning brands, and at first Lena had to strain to make out shapes in this shifting light, where the face of a priest might be red one moment and blue the next, depending upon which window they passed. The fixed points that made the world comprehensible, the clear shapes and patterns of human life, came to her in pieces, broken by shadows and the swirling of smoke.

A choir was singing in front of the raised altar at the far end of the cathedral. Their voices echoed from the high ceiling, reverberating around the room so that they seemed to mount upon each other and become something louder, larger, and still exquisitely beautiful. Those wandering the chamber, priests and pilgrims alike, trod softly and spoke quietly, but it wasn't enough to stop their every sound being amplified and echoed, forming an irregular percussion that threatened the flow of the hymn.

Her own thoughts became discordant in the face of faith.

Priestly robes and religious icons brought back memories she would rather not face, their features still sharp despite the battering of time. Among them was a version of her who had once been certain, who had believed that the world could be made right. She knew better now. All that could be done was to stop it getting worse, to shore up the broken walls of her own home instead of trying to raise a palace.

Lena approached the nearest priest, a stout man in simple green robes who was collecting donations from visitors in a worn wooden bowl.

'Holy one,' Lena said, forcing a tone that could almost have been respectful. Deppel imitated her, down to the slight bow of her head.

'Have you travelled far?' the priest asked, holding the bowl out expectantly. Deppel's fingers twitched as he looked at the coins, but he stayed a step to Lena's side, waiting and watching.

'Just down the street,' Lena said. 'I'm here to speak with Bishop Kunder.'

The priest looked her up and down and his smile stiffened.

'If you are seeking a blessing, you could join the pilgrims waiting for the afternoon service.' He gestured towards a line of dusty travellers who stood expectantly at the side of the church, near the base of the longest ribs. 'Or if you have a message from your employer, then I can take it.'

Lena wasn't going to be fobbed off by some functionary, even one who carried the blessings and the wisdom of the church.

'Please tell the bishop that Headsman Sturm is here to see her.'

The priest took a swift step back, as though he had touched something rotten and feared the stink might stick. The coins rattled in his bowl as he raised his fingers to touch beneath his eye.

'Holy Kunder is busy with Father Earth's work,' he said with a curl of his lip. 'I'm sure she will not have time to speak with an executioner.'

'Tell her I've listened to her concerns about the souls of the people,' Lena said, voice low as she forced herself to play a part. 'I need her help in protecting them.'

'Why should I tell her anything from you?'

What patience Lena had for priests was already spent. She advanced, and the man backed away, until he was pressed against one of the ribs of the cathedral, his hood askew around his shoulders, eyes wide and shoulders tensed.

'Because I'm going up there either way,' Lena said, pointing towards the episcopal throne that sat to the right of the high altar. 'And I expect your boss will want some warning.'

The priest twisted out from in front of her and hurried away, his sandals slapping against flagstones, coins bouncing in his bowl. Lena followed at a more measured pace, looking up at the ceiling as she went.

She had wondered if the skin of this place was manufactured, a series of hides stitched together to create the impression of a single whole. It was easier to believe in that than to believe that it really was a single layer of skin, preserved by dessication, enduring the centuries of mountain weather. But there was no sign of stitching, no splits caused by the ageing of hides, as happened with even the best taxidermy. It seemed that the legends were true. This beast really had lived, and eventually died. Might others like it still be out there in the world, hidden from the eyes of humanity? That would give her more faith in the gods than any amount of prayer and incense.

The priest knelt in front of the episcopal throne, grovelling before Bishop Kunder. As Lena approached, Kunder waved the unfortunate man away, and he scurried into the shadows at the foot of a wall where scribes and attendants waited on Her Holiness.

The throne sat on a granite podium; a grand seat of obsidian decorated with a web of gold lines that radiated from the bishop herself. Father Earth's priests might decry the Sky worshippers' ostentatious displays of wealth and power, but the church had never been humble.

Kunder was regal as ever, sitting straight-backed and with her chin lifted, a plain golden disk medallion gleaming upon immaculately tailored green robes. Everyone around her made the sign of the eye, and Lena's chest tightened at that barrier raised against her, but the bishop's hands lay motionless in her lap. Why should she fear evil, when god himself had marked her out?

'Headsman Sturm,' the bishop said, her voice carrying despite its seemingly soft tone. It held a hint of a southern accent, a trace of something soft in the way she pronounced her vowels. 'I'm told that you've come on a mission of salvation. Have my words finally raised your mind from base matters?'

'Scripture teaches that our world is a reflection of the holy,' Lena said. 'Doesn't that make everything blessed?'

'So you do know the holy books.' Kunder's tone was approving, but she raised a questioning eyebrow. It was rare for followers of Father Earth to read religious texts for themselves, rarer still for them to answer back to a priest. 'Yet you show the shallowness of your learning. My reflection in the mirror is not as substantial as my face, Father Earth's reflection in this world not as glorious as his divine reality.'

'Injustice in this world endangers souls, doesn't it?'

'Indeed.' Kunder leaned forward; hands clasped together in her lap. 'As I explained in my Meditations Upon Jurisprudence, any crime corrupts, and one that goes unpunished becomes a chain that weighs a soul down, forever keeping it from the peace it deserves.'

'Then you need to know that a murder goes unpunished.'

'A murder?' Kunder's eyes narrowed. 'Why bring this to me? You're the executioner.'

'And I executed an innocent person for murder.'

'As long as you did the will of the court then you were living a life of obedience, as our father demands. You need not fear for your soul.'

'It's good of you to be concerned for me, your grace, but it's not my soul I'm interested in. It's the real killer's.'

'And who would that be?'

'Given the tensions between your churches, I wondered if it might be one of your priests.'

I wondered if it might be you, she thought, but kept the words to herself.

The flunkies lurking in the shadows gasped, but Lena kept her focus on the bishop, watching her reactions, looking for signs of a guilty conscience or fear of getting caught.

If the bishop gave herself away, then it was hidden by the poor light.

'A ridiculous accusation,' she said, glaring at Lena with cold eyes.

'Not an accusation, just speculation,' Lena said. She too had tensed, responding to the other woman's demeanour and the burly priests moving to flank her. 'Someone framed Holy Saimon for killing her husband. It would be foolish not to consider religious motives.'

'This conversation is absurd. We are priests of the holy church, not common street thugs.'

'Anyone can kill.'

'Only the sinful can murder.'

'And yet I've executed priests in my time.'

'Priests or heretics?'

'The conflict between your congregation and Holy Saimon's went beyond just words. Did the two of you ever fight?'

'More ridiculous implications!' Kunder was on her feet, her face red, pointing at Lena. 'You're nothing but a lowlife and a heretic, a woman soaked in blood and sin. I should have you thrown out of here.'

'I'm just looking for answers, Holy Kunder.'

'I owe you no answers.'

But the ones she had given told Lena a lot. Defensive people normally had something to hide.

Deppel tugged at Lena's sleeve. His gaze was darting

frantically between the priests closing in from all sides. Other people were also paying attention, women and men turning from their prayers to watch, pilgrims creeping out of their corner to hear the bishop's words. The harmony of the choir faltered as the choristers' attention wavered.

Still Lena paid them no attention. She could deal with any priest who tried to manhandle her, and she couldn't see Kunder triggering a lynching in her own temple.

'Tell me,' Lena said, arms folded across her chest, eyes locked on Kunder's. 'How was your relationship with the Saimons?'

'By what authority do you ask these questions?' Kunder asked, her calm poise returning. 'If the court was concerned with this, then they would have sent a constable.'

'I know how to look at evidence as well as any liveried thug.'

'It is not your place. Does Captain Baumer even know that you're here flinging baseless accusations at honest priests? Does the council?'

'I don't need the court's blessing to ask questions.'

'And without it I don't need to answer them.'

The priests and pilgrims were crowding in, surrounding Lena, blocking her path to the episcopal throne. She heard the muttering of their anger, but kept her own in its place. She took a step back and bumped into the priest she had met on the way in.

'I see what this is.' Kunder stood tall on the steps of her throne, chest out, smiling triumphantly. 'It's a Sky worshipper's plot to slander the true church and drag souls off the path of righteousness. Have you adopted that foul faith, Headsman Sturm, or are you just their tool, nothing more than a hired blade sent to kill that which is pure?'

The crowd grew closer, muttering about killers and heretics. For the first time, Lena wondered if she had made a mistake. She could take any three of these fat priests and weary pilgrims in a fight, but not a whole mob. She held her hands loose and turned slowly on the spot, watching as they shuffled closer.

Deppel, his hands at his chest, pressed in close to her side.

'You've made your point,' Lena said, her throat tight. 'We'll leave.'

The doors of the cathedral suddenly seemed a long way off. Lena took a step forward, towards the men and women standing between her and those doors. A red-faced woman in loose green priestly robes blocked her path, one fist balled in her other hand, an angry sneer on her lips.

Lena stepped closer, until her face was inches from the priest's. She raised an eyebrow and the muscles in the side of her face tightened, accentuating her scar.

'You want to try me?' she hissed, one hand settling on her dagger.

The crowd was rumbling with excitement, but it was one thing to cheer on a fight, another to risk the first punch. The priest's confidence faltered. She swallowed, lowered her fist, and stepped out of the way.

Lena advanced down the nave of the cathedral, Deppel scurrying along behind her. Every step of the way, the crowd stood strong until the very last moment, then parted. She heard their chanting and muttering, anonymous cries calling out for a beating or worse. More than once, a sudden movement made her tense and turn her head, arms moving to defend herself from a blow that never quite came.

At last, they reached the doors. Here stood a final line of priests silhouetted against the daylight, some carrying stout sticks or heavy tools. One held a ceremonial Illora dagger, with its distinct dragon tooth blade. None of them faltered in their resolve as she approached.

Lena licked her lips and set her hand on the pommel of her dagger. She wondered about reaching down into her boot for the whittling knife, but the risk of a moment's crouched vulnerability outweighed the benefit it could give.

'The moment I make a gap, you run,' she whispered to Deppel.

The boy nodded.

One of the priests raised his stick.

Lena drew her dagger.

'Let them pass,' Holy Kunder called from her throne. 'And let them remind others, I will not tolerate heretics here.'

The priests parted. Lena and Deppel stepped out into the light.

Lena shook her head and sheathed her dagger.

'Next time, I'll tackle Kunder differently,' she said.

'Surely you ain't gonna try that again?' Deppel asked, wide-eyed.

'Of course I am. Holy Kunder just reached the top of my suspect list.'

Chapter Eight

A House in Mourning

The Saimon mansion was in the Hochfel district, just one road over from Councillor Maier's home. The front was built from herringbone rows of red bricks, a rare and precious commodity compared with the mountain's plentiful stone. The gates of the walled courtyard were open, allowing Lena and Deppel to march straight to the front door, past a carriage house, stables, and small storage barn. Smoke drifted from the tall square chimneys at the south end of the house, and on the slope behind, a diminutive figure in a yellow jerkin was tending a terraced garden in which rose bushes, herbs, and fruit trees grew like tiny miracles from the stony ground of a mountain spur.

Gravel crunched beneath their feet, drawing the attention of a stable girl and a snort from the horse she was grooming. The girl watched in surly silence as Lena approached the front door and banged the heavy brass knocker.

Lena had considered approaching the servants' entrance, as she did when summoned by Councillor Maier. The Saimon household had troubles enough, and no one wanted a headsman at their door. But coming through the servants' entrance would have meant acknowledging her social inferiority, and right now she needed to be someone servants answered to, not someone they sneered at. So here she was for the first time in years, at the front door of a grand mansion.

The door opened on smoothly oiled hinges and a man stared

out at them. He wore a smart yellow doublet with a steward's brass chain of office and a strip of black mourning cloth bound around his left arm. A pair of bright, inquisitive eyes assessed her from behind a mask of stony seriousness.

'I don't know what you've heard,' he said, 'but we are not offering funerary alms.'

'And we're not beggars or opportunists,' Lena said. 'I am Headsman Sturm, and this is my assistant, Deppel.'

Behind his neat black beard, the steward's frown deepened.

'You have some nerve coming here, with the blood of my mistress on your blade.'

'According to the judge, the blood of your master was on hers.'

'Unless you've come to take another head, we have no time to spare for you.'

He started closing the door, but Lena shot out a hand and help it open despite the steward's efforts. Twenty years ago she would have knocked the man down and strode straight in, but many things had been different twenty years ago, not all of them for the better.

In the present, the Saimons' steward pressed his shoulder to the door.

'You don't think she did it, do you?' Lena asked. If she was right, then this might be easier than she had expected.

'I said that I have no time to spare.' The steward leaned in, and the door inched towards its frame.

'I don't think she did it either. I want your help to set things right.'

The steward stopped straining. His eyes narrowed as he looked at Lena.

'What sort of trap is this?' he asked.

'No trap. I've been used in an injustice, and I don't mean to let that stand. Will you help?'

He hesitated, hope and cynicism warring in a weary face, but hope was always a hard lure to resist. At last he took a step back and opened the door wide.

The great hall was well lit, with afternoon sunlight streaming in through generous windows of leaded glass. The floor was tiled, the walls whitewashed, and the wood of the door frames varnished to a rich hue. A map hung from the wall to one side of the fireplace and on the other side was a portrait of a man and a woman dressed in black and yellow robes. The man, round-faced and jovial, was holding a small set of balance scales, while the woman clutched a book and an amulet in the shape of a lightning bolt. Her face was achingly familiar, for all that it was smiling instead of mournful and lost.

Fiete and Beatrice Saimon, their spirits preserved in oils while their bodies became food for carrion. Without moving an inch, they twisted the knife of guilt in Lena's guts.

'What's your name?' she asked, tearing her eyes away from the painting.

'Jonatan Ottmor,' the steward replied. 'I've been with the household since I was an apprentice clerk. I never in my worst nightmares imagined it might end like this.'

He led them through a door at one end of the room, into a well-appointed parlour. Benches and stools were gathered around a table with ornately carved legs, at the head of which were a pair of matching oak chairs. The fireplace was empty, as were the shelves of a dresser at the side of the room.

'We've started packing things away,' Ottmor said, settling onto one of the benches and gesturing for them to sit. 'Don't know what will happen to any of it, but we needed to keep busy.'

Another servant poked her head around the door and shot Ottmor an uncertain look.

'It's alright, Bessa,' he said. 'Tell everyone to carry on with what they were doing.'

She nodded and disappeared.

'What will happen to all of this?' Lena asked, waving at the fine furniture, the locked trunks, the expensively glaze windows in the walls of an impressive mansion.

'We don't know.' Ottmor sagged. 'They didn't have any children, though they often talked about it, so there are no easy heirs. The mistress said she had relatives in Gautenveld, so maybe it'll all go to them. But given the way she died…'

The city council could confiscate the belongings of any murderer or traitor. Usually, that meant a few shillings to be dished out to the alms houses, but this wasn't the usual sort of case. The councillors would be tussling for control of that wealth while they waited to hear back from Gautenveld. Maybe one already had a plan to get hold of it all, a plan that gave a motive for murder.

Or perhaps they would leave it be. After all, this had been the victim's home too. Seizing it would look less than righteous.

'Tell me about the night of the murder,' Lena said. 'Did your master and mistress leave the house together?'

Ottmor looked away.

'Their plans for the evening changed,' he said. 'They were going to the theatre together, but the mistress decided against it.'

His tone was tight, formal, too stiff for a man discussing sad memories.

'Did they argue?' Lena asked.

Ottmor glared at her.

'So you've heard the gossip,' he said. 'What did the neighbours' servants tell you? Some wild story about a marriage breaking down, about bitterness and blows exchanged?'

'I'm not asking the neighbours' servants. I'm asking you.'

He sighed and rubbed his eyes.

'Yes, they argued. Theirs was a passionate relationship, one full of ups and downs. More downs lately, but it's not the first time, and it won't be the last. Or wouldn't have been if not for…'

He took a deep breath, then continued.

'They argued. The mistress left for the tavern and sent the coachman home after he dropped her off. The master decided to go to the theatre without her. He said he wanted to walk and to be by himself, to clear his head, so I didn't send a boy with him.'

His breaths became ragged, his hand curling and uncurling in his lap.

'If I'd just sent someone with him, maybe they could have stopped it. Maybe none of this would have happened.'

Silence descended on the room. From elsewhere in the house came the thud of moving furniture.

'Tell me about the dagger,' Lena said. 'The one he was killed with.'

'It wasn't hers,' Ottmor said, some of his previous steel returning. 'The mistress liked to display fine things, and that would have been hanging on a wall for all to see. I never set eyes on it before the constables pulled it out from under the bed.'

'Whoever used it, they had to bring it into the house after the murder. Did you see anyone coming or going?'

'No, but…' Ottmor looked away, embarrassed. 'On nights like that, when they both went out angry, we knew we wouldn't be needed for hours. Some of the staff found the arguments upsetting, so I gave everybody the evening off. Most of them went to see family or have a drink. Bessa and I stayed, just in case we were needed, and we spent the evening reading to each other in the kitchen. Someone could have crept in without us seeing.'

'Reading, eh?' Deppel sniggered.

'Yes, reading,' Ottmor snapped. 'Bessa is an honest woman, and I do not take kindly to your insinuation.'

'Could Holy Saimon herself have brought the dagger back in?' Lena asked.

'I thought you believed her?' Ottmor's anger was rising, his face turning red.

'I do, but others might ask that question, so I need to know the answer.'

'Absolutely not. The mistress didn't sneak in and out of her own house, she had no need. If she wanted to bring something in concealed, she could have wrapped it in her cloak and walked openly through the door. We waited all evening, but she never returned. The next time I saw her, the constables had her in their cells.'

The sounds of moving furniture had stopped. In their place, footsteps approached down the hall.

The servant Bessa came into the room again, holding a painting on wooden board a foot across. She held it up for Ottmor to see.

'What do we do with this one?' she asked.

It was a portrait, head and shoulders only this time, done without the finesse of the painting in the hallway but clearly with more love. The warmth of Fiete Saimon's personality shone through in his wide, full-lipped smile and the twinkling of his blue eyes.

Though the painting drew Lena's gaze, it repelled Ottmor. He rose from his seat and stalked over to the window, as far as he could get from the image.

'We should burn it,' he said with forced steadiness. 'It has no financial value, and I dread to think what sort of villain will want it.'

'It don't seem that bad to me,' Deppel said, tilting his head on one side.

'A painting of a dead man by his supposed murderer?' Ottmor said. 'Nothing good can come from that.'

'Holy Saimon painted?' Lena asked.

'Mostly stories from scripture, but she said painting real people was good practice.'

'She made me look like an angel,' Bessa said softly. 'And the master...'

She sniffed, laid the painting on the table, and brushed imagined dust from it with a cloth. Her undisguised grief brought a lump to Lena's throat.

'Seems a shame, burning that,' Deppel said, peering at the picture. 'Can we have it?'

Ottmor turned upon him, red-faced and teeth bared.

'Of all the impudent, presumptuous, wrong-headed-'

'Jonatan,' Bessa said, and her sad voice soothed his rage.

'What else will we do with it? Do you really think the mistress would want his image burned?'

Ottmor scowled and clenched his fists.

Lena looked at the painting again. Now she had a face to go with the other one in her mind, the whole business seemed more real. Remembering what had happened to this man drove a spike of anger into her heart, cold and hard as the mountain side. It was a feeling she needed, a feeling to drive her on.

Could she admit that? Could she say that she needed this painting to remind her of what was at stake, to be the spur to her flank as she charged towards justice? That she craved a partner for the ghostly face that haunted her when she closed her eyes?

Those weren't thoughts she would share with her closest comrades, never mind a pair of strangers.

'The painting could be helpful,' she said. 'To show to witnesses.'

Ottmor stared at her like he was peering through fog, trying to find an enemy concealed in the swirling mist. Then he shook his head and flung his hands in the air.

'Take it,' he said. 'And anything else you think might help. It's not as if the mistress can use it any more.'

A sudden hammering on the door made them all look around.

'Someone else with you?' Ottmor asked.

'No.'

'Then I'd best see to it.'

As he left the room, Bessa picked up the painting and wrapped it in a wide strip of cloth.

'Here,' she said, handing it to Lena. 'You might not want people to see you carrying that. They'll think you nicked it.'

A familiar voice drifted in from the great hall, draped in layers of echo. Then came the clank of metal footsteps and Soren Baumer strode into the room.

As usual, the captain of the city constables was dressed from head to toe in plate metal armour. A helmet hung from his right hip and a longsword from the left. Behind him came a pair of constables wearing the city's blue and silver livery over tarnished chain mail, and then Jonatan Ottmor, his expression grim.

Baumer groaned when he saw Lena.

'You're doing it, aren't you?' he asked. 'Exactly what you were told not to.'

Lena turned in her seat, stretched her legs out in front of her, and leaned back.

'I don't know what you mean, Captain Baumer,' she said.

'Like hells you don't. You were told to leave this alone, yet here you are at the Saimon house.'

'We're just visiting,' Deppel piped up. 'Ain't we, Mistress Sturm?'

'Who the hells are you?' Baumer towered over Deppel, gauntleted hands planted on his hips. 'No, don't answer. You're clearly a moron, so keep your gob shut while the grown-ups talk.'

Deppel shrank back, eyes downcast. Lena felt a tightening in her chest, an impulse to comfort him that caught her by surprise, but she kept her calm and kept her seat.

'Sorry, Captain,' Deppel mumbled.

'You will be, you little snot.'

'I thought you were here for me, Soren,' Lena said.

'That I am. You know what the councillor said.'

'She said that she wouldn't investigate the Saimon murder again.'

'Yet here you are.'

'Just because you're not investigating doesn't mean that I can't.'

'That's not a thread you want to untwine.'

'Seems like two different threads to me.'

'You know full well what's expected of you. You've got the coin purse to prove it.'

'I thought that was a bonus for my good work.'

'Don't play the idiot. That's this kid's job.'

He kicked the leg of Deppel's stool, making the boy wobble and almost fall. Lena jerked to her feet.

'Is this really needed?' she asked. 'Tracking me down here just to stop me talking with these people.'

'Like I give a cursed turd for these people.' Baumer jerked a thumb toward Ottmor, who stood in the doorway, Bessa huddled beside him. 'But you pissed off the bishop. Then the bishop summoned Councillor Maier, who doesn't like being summoned. Now she's pissed off, so she summons me. And guess what? Now I'm pissed off too.'

He kicked the stool again and Deppel fell to the floor with a whimper.

Without thinking, Lena grabbed Baumer's arm and pulled him back.

Anger flashed across Baumer's face. He grabbed her arm and yanked her up with all the strength his bonded armour gave him, swinging her through the air and slamming her into the table. Before she could get her breath back, Baumer leapt into the air. He landed on the table with a thud, one foot each side of her, a gleam in his eyes.

She looked up at him, a shining statue in engraved steel. Part of her was itching to fight back, to vent her frustrations with her fists and feet, to show the world that she was still a fighter. But a smarter part of her recognised the truth. Even in her prime, she couldn't have matched the strength and agility of an armour-bonded warrior, and even if she could win, Soren Baumer wasn't really the problem.

She moved one hand off her dagger and held both up in surrender.

Baumer jumped off the table, hitting the floor with a clang. The others watched, Ottmor and Bessa backed up against the wall, the constables grinning with pride. Deppel lay where he had fallen, eyes wide.

'Get back to your drinking, Headsman,' Baumer said. 'We'll all be happier that way.'

Lena climbed off the table. Slowly, stiffly, never taking her eyes off Baumer, she picked up the cloth-wrapped painting.

'You know this business isn't right, Soren,' she said.

'I know my orders. This time, you get a telling off. Next time, things get serious.'

Her hand tightened on the edge of the picture. If she wanted, she could swing it now, catch him in the face before he even moved, break his nose then leap on him before his sword was drawn. His bonded armour would count for nothing with a dagger through his neck.

She took a deep breath and two steps back. She didn't want to hurt Baumer, but her pride wouldn't quite let it go.

'You think you can take me?' she asked.

'Hells yes,' Baumer said. 'But I'd be sorry to do it. You're one of the few people in this town worth half a dead dog.'

'Please, I'm worth two dead cats at least.'

'That won't stop me doing my job, it just might mean I need a bigger drink after.'

Lena smiled and shook her head. If she was going to have her plans frustrated, it might as well be by him.

'We'll leave,' she said.

'And you'll drop this shit.'

It wasn't a question. Baumer took orders, and he gave orders, without leaving space for doubt. Besides, Lena would have had to lie to give an answer, and she didn't want to waste her breath on that.

'Thank you for your time, Master Ottmor,' she said.

'Thank you for your visit.' Ottmor shot a hostile glance at Baumer. 'It's good that someone cares.'

He led Lena and Deppel to the front door. Outside, dusk was closing in on the city, steel grey sky above a patchwork of stone and shadow.

Gravel crunched beneath Lena's feet as she crossed the courtyard.

'What you gonna do now?' Deppel asked. 'Back to the cathedral? Talk to someone new?'

'I'm going home,' Lena said with a yawn.

'You're giving up?' Deppel's face fell.

'You don't pick a fight after a forced march. We've been awake for two days and I'm inches away from doing something stupid. I'm going to eat, then drink until my brain slows down enough to sleep. Maybe when that's done I'll have a clue what to do next.'

CHAPTER NINE

CRIMINAL CONNECTIONS

The sound of raised voices woke Lena. Her neighbours were arguing again. Not the ones next door-walls carved into the mountainside didn't let much noise through-but the couple across the street. She had been tempted more than once to go over and shut them up, but that would mean getting involved in someone else's life. Better to lose the odd hour's sleep than take on that burden. Besides, what wisdom could she offer a struggling couple? If they were arguing, at least they were saying something to each other, instead of letting the silence become so uncomfortable that war looked like a better option than home.

A blade of light came through a gap in the shutters, slicing across the room. It illuminated the back wall, where her old armour and sword hung, reminders of her glories and her mistakes. The armour was wyvern hide, joined together with strips of sturdy leather, a few of the scales missing and most of them scorched or scratched. They had been through a lot together, Lena and her armour. The same went for the longsword that hung beside it in a scabbard stripped of its ostentatious ornaments. Tools of war reduced to mementos; reminders of memories she shouldn't let go.

She had done good work with that sword once upon a time, and that thought let her keep a little of her pride. Not just pride in herself, but in the women and men who had marched with her, a family forged in muddy camps and training grounds.

She missed what they had been. What she had been, or at least pretended to be.

She still didn't know when she had crossed the line, when fighting for justice had gone from a guiding principle to a comforting lie. Some time before the Siege of Alvard, when she had woken up with ash on her hands and seen her people laughing over charred bones. Probably years before that, though the innocent monsters she rode had kept her from seeing what lay in human hearts. Perhaps she had known from the start, but had lied to herself. She had to be good at something, so why not that?

It was just one of the reasons why she deserved days like this, her head throbbing and her skin sticky with sweat despite the cold mountain morning. She flung off the blankets, swung her legs over the edge of the bed, kicked away the empty ale jug, and stood. The chill of the stone floor chased away the cobwebs of sleep.

Within two minutes she was dressed and down in the main room, with its fireplace, cooking pans, and well-worn table and chair. Her hand cart sat in an alcove with Brute hanging from a hook beside it, where the sword would catch the attention of anyone coming in. An executioner's blade was enough to put off most callers.

There was a new addition to the room today. Fiete Saimon's portrait hung from a nail that normally held a frying pan. The warmth of his smile, captured by his wife's brush strokes, was an unsettling reminder of a double injustice. Lena had thought herself inured to death, but those deaths had been war, or they had been justice, society doing what it needed to do. This time the world was turned on its head, execution made into murder. The idea was a fire that raged inside her, threatening to consume every other thought. This time, she knew when the line had been crossed, and she would not rest until she had crossed back.

She headed into the pantry at the back of the room. Its cool, soothing, cave-like darkness was lined with shelves of food, firewood, and candles. Hidden in the deepest darkness at the back, a two-foot slab of stone covered another opening, where she kept memories best left alone.

She found a length of sausage, a hard end of bread, and a pitcher of ale. She downed the ale, took a bite of the sausage, and headed for the door, feeling her vitality return. Daylight was waiting, and she had a murderer to catch.

When Lena opened the door, Deppel tumbled in at her feet. She blinked in confusion as he looked up with a sleepy smile.

'How long have you been on my doorstep?' she asked.

'Dunno.' Deppel got to his feet. 'Little bit.'

'Don't you have a home to sleep in?'

'Got here early.' Deppel looked down. 'Didn't want to wake you, so I… I must have dozed off.'

The boy hunched over, shoulders by his ears, one hand rubbing the back of his neck. He was pale and twitchy, as pathetic as a new-born pup.

Against her better judgement, Lena pointed to the pantry.

'There's bread on the second shelf,' she said. 'Get yourself a chunk.'

'Really?' Deppel looked up at her, eyes wide and smile beaming.

'Yes, really,' she snapped. 'And while you're about it, tell me why you're here at all.'

Deppel headed into the pantry.

'You said I could help you investigate, remember,' he said. 'I know you're gonna find the person what killed Councillor Saimon, and I want to see how you do it. I bet when you find them they'll be so scared it'll all just come pouring out. They'll see you've got them, and they won't be able to stop from talking. And then you'll take them up to the Weeping Stone and then…'

He emerged from the pantry, holding a chunk of bread like it was a sword. He swung it through the air and made the sound of a head coming off. It was surprisingly convincing.

'It's going to be brilliant.'

'Death is terrible, even if it's earned. Forget that and you lose yourself.'

'Oh.' Deppel nodded solemnly. 'See, this is what I need to learn.'

He bit a chunk out of the bread and looked at her expectantly, just like those half-forgotten faces around the campfire, waiting for her to tell them the battle plan. She didn't deserve that life any more, but this was different. What was she going to do, turn away a starving child?

'Come on, then,' Lena said. 'To work.'

'What are we doing here?' Deppel asked, looking up nervously at the sign above the alehouse door. It was a pair of giant dice, one a neat cube and the other misshapen, both with their six spots showing.

'I thought you knew about criminals,' Lena said. 'This is the Lucky Dice, haven to half the low rent thugs and swindlers in this city.'

'And we're going in?' Deppel tugged his collar up and pulled his hair down around the sides of his face. 'Is that a good idea?'

'I've been wanting to see inside this place for years,' Lena said. 'Do you know how many crimes I've punished that started with a conversation here?'

She rubbed her hands together.

'That don't make it sound good.'

'Do you have a better idea for how to learn about Jagusia Brodbeck?'

'Why would I have an idea for that?' Deppel shrank back as if he had been slapped.

'Then we're going in.'

Andrew Knighton

The door to the Lucky Dice hung open, letting light in and smoke out. Lena stepped through the doorway and paused just inside, waiting for her eyes to adjust to the gloom.

The inside of the Lucky Dice made Toblur's alehouse look like a royal palace. The rushes were spread thin on the floor and clearly hadn't been changed in weeks. Smoke billowed from a fireplace with a clogged chimney, accompanied by the smell of a distinctly unappetising stew. Half the people in the place, and there were plenty of them, even this early in the day, were puffing pipes, creating a mix of tobacco, cannabis, and craydragon fumes that contributed to the grey fug.

No silence fell as Lena entered the room, but there was a change in the tone of the noise. Some voices became higher and sharper, others faded away. Recognition had been inevitable, and it was satisfying to hear these wretches respond to seeing her in their midst. For once, she didn't mind seeing everyone reach for their eye.

She strode over to the bar, a pair of planks laid across empty barrels. The barmaid, a skinny woman in a worn woollen tunic, didn't look up from washing tankards in a half barrel.

'Are you going to serve me?' Lena asked.

'If you've got money, we've got ale.'

Lena dropped a couple of coins on the rough counter, more than the beer here would be worth and enough to make sure they got served.

'Make his small and weak,' she said, gesturing at Deppel.

'A drink to match the boy.' The barmaid shrugged. 'Why not.'

She plunged two tankards into another barrel. Both were dripping when she handed them over, one full and the other halfway there.

Lena took a sip of her ale. It was exactly as rough and watery as she'd expected. Anywhere else, she might have complained, but here it would help keep her head straight.

She turned and looked around the room.

113

There were plenty of familiar faces, and judging by the number of missing ears, fingers, and even hands, she had met others at the Weeping Stone. But she didn't just want familiar. She wanted someone whose story she could remember, someone with connections.

While the rest of the room's denizens watched Lena and her drink, an adolescent girl got up from her seat and slid out the door. Lena recognised her thin face and grubby blond hair.

'That was your friend, wasn't it?' she asked.

'Tild,' Deppel said, the name practically a groan.

'Can't say I'm surprised.'

At last, Lena found what she was looking for. She walked across the room, navigating the islands of malevolence centred on each table, and approached a bearded man in a grey cloak. He was sitting on a bench beside a window, a tankard in his hand and a tiny pot with a broken wax seal sitting next to him. The stump of his other wrist rested on his knee.

He scowled at Lena and clumsily tapped his face, almost poking his own eye.

'Goadrik Harn,' she said. 'I thought you were going home to Vor Yasgrik. That's what you told the judge when you were pleading to keep your hand.'

'Moon eat your heart,' Harn said in a guttural accent. 'I've no words for you.'

'Really?' Lena sat down next to him, stretched her legs out, and laid an arm around his shoulders. She pulled him close and leaned in conspiratorially, lowering her voice. 'Because I remember you being very talkative once. A dozen others were arrested thanks to you. Do you want me to tell all your friends about it?'

Harn tried to shift away from her. His leg knocked the pot next to him and a tiny measure of oily blue liquid trickled out.

'Silver dream?' Lena shook her head. 'I didn't take you for a man who'd hide from reality.'

'Fuck you, you cur.'

'Oh, Goadrik, I wouldn't fuck you with my worst enemy's hole. Now, think carefully. Do you want this conversation to drag on, while I drag up the past and take a look at my handiwork? Or do you want me to piss off before more people hear about our little chat?'

Malevolent glee added its barbs to her voice. Questioning criminals could be a lot of fun, when you weren't doing it under Councillor Maier's stern gaze, and when you had the right pressure to apply. It was a form of justice in its own way, making the guilty squirm.

Harn stiffened. Most of the alehouse's denizens were pretending to carry on their conversations, but he must know that he was being watched. Every moment she lingered here brought him closer to trouble from the people he worked with.

On her other side, Deppel also sat tense, not even sipping the ale Lena had bought him. She had thought he would be comfortable with places like this, but apparently she'd misjudged the lad. Perhaps she could raise his spirits by bringing him in on the questioning, a comrade helping her fight the good fight.

'What do you think, Deppel?' she asked, then paused for a moment to drink her ale. 'Do you think this is going to go well for Master Harn?'

Deppel sat chewing on his thumb nail. His eyes darted back and forth, constantly looking around the room.

So much for his help.

'What do you want from me?' Harn growled.

'You're a man in the know. That's how you were able to drop so many other lowlifes in shit and keep your punishment down.' She tapped his stump with one finger, and he flinched, drawing it back into the darkness of his cloak. She'd known veterans who bore such wounds with pride, for all the grief that came with them, but those were battle scars whereas Harn's was nothing to be proud of. 'So tell me, what was going on between Brodbeck and Fiete Saimon?'

Harn snorted.

'You think I'm close enough to know Brodbeck's comings and goings?'

'I think you're a good listener. That was how you knew when Kajet Bronislew would be on the south road with a fat purse and not many guards. It's how you almost slipped through Baumer's fingers. You're like a privy sponge, Harn, soaking up all the shit around you. Now tell me something before I have to squeeze it out.'

Harn looked around, taking in the people watching them and the ones pretending not to. He took a deep drink from his tankard, ale dribbling into his ragged beard.

'I know nothing about Fiete Saimon,' he said. 'But I know that Brodbeck was profiting off his wife.'

'Go on.'

Harn leaned in close.

'Holy Saimon was stirring her congregation up against the Earth priests, saying how the old ways were corrupt and only Mother Sky could make things right.'

'Of course she did, that's her job.'

'But it was causing trouble, see. Fights between Sky and Earth worshippers. Mina Arwin's workshop got burnt down, because she argued with her Sky worshipping neighbours. Her Earth friends beat up Detlev Volgod and Helge Kamedge in revenge, only they beat Kamedge too hard and he died. Then his family got a mob together, and they-'

'People fight over religion. Next you'll tell me that stones are hard. What does it have to do with Brodbeck?'

'Her and her people are profiting off it. If a house is getting ransacked, they'll get in with the crowd and carry things off. If a mob's getting together, then they'll sell them weapons. You remember that brawl in the marketplace on St Anasta's Eve?'

'I flogged eight people for it.'

'But you missed the ones who stirred them up, made sure the

city constables would be busy with that instead of watching the gates.'

'And then they smuggled something out.'

'In, out, I don't know the details, I just know some people who were very happy afterwards.'

Lena sat back and took a sip from her tankard. The story was a vague and obvious one, with all the strength of the Lucky Dice's ale, but it made sense. Brodbeck might be a believer, but plenty of self-confessed believers put profit before principle, and using the city's religious divisions was a natural move for one of its leading criminals.

Did that make Brodbeck more or less of a suspect for framing Holy Saimon? The priest had been stoking discontent like a blacksmith stoked his fire, raising the heat that would forge her congregation into a weapon of faith, while Kunder did the same on Father Earth's side. Take either woman out and the blaze could falter, robbing Brodbeck of her opportunity. On the other hand, watching the authorities kill their beloved priest might stir fresh flames among the faithful, turning the whole city into an inferno.

Lena scowled and took a gulp of her ale. Weren't clues meant to bring her closer to an answer?

A long shadow passed across her through the window. A moment later, the girl Tild walked in, followed by half a dozen heavy-set men and women. Most of them wore sleeveless leather doublets that showed off the muscles of their tattooed arms. They all carried cudgels.

'Told you,' Tild said, pointing at Lena. 'And Deppel brought her here.'

Lena took a deep breath, got to her feet, and stood facing the thugs. She knew herself well enough to admit that she'd been looking forward to this. If they thought that she would be intimidated then they were fools. She might have grey hairs, but she had more experience of violence than all of them put together.

'Deppel did no such thing,' she said. 'I knew where I needed to go.'

'Deppel, Deppel, Deppel.' The leader of the group, a woman with a broad smile and a missing earlobe, shook her shaved head as she looked at the boy. 'I thought you was one of us.'

Lena shot Deppel a suspicious glance. How stupid had she been, not to wonder who the boy had been before she found him? Here she was, playing the amateur constable while ignoring the criminal at her side. For all she knew, he was as deep in with the gangs at Tild or Harn. That was how it always worked, the people close to her were the ones who hurt her most.

Or the ones she hurt.

'One of them?' she asked, her voice flat as the skin of a drum.

'I wouldn't… I wasn't…' Deppel's tankard clattered on the floor. 'I didn't mean it!'

'Didn't mean what?' Lena growled. 'Helping me or helping them?'

With surprising speed, Deppel leapt onto the bench and flung himself through the open window.

'Come back here, you fat turd,' Tild yelled and ran out the door after him.

Racing footsteps disappeared into the noise of the city.

With a snort, Lena turned her attention to the thugs facing her. The occupants of the nearby tables backed away. Harn was sidling along the bench into a darkened corner.

The woman pointed at Lena with her cudgel.

'I hear you've been asking questions about Mistress Brodbeck,' she said.

'And you've brought me the answers?'

'The only answers you'll get.'

'Let me guess-stop asking questions or I get a beating?'

'You think you can leave this place untouched, Headsman?' The woman spat the final word like it was a curse. 'You'll take your beating, and then you'll stop asking questions, else there'll be worse to come.'

The woman stepped forward and her companions spread out around her, closing off Lena's escape routes. She could try to follow Deppel out the window, but this lot looked young and fast, able to reach her as she climbed out. There would be no stopping a blow if she had her back to them.

'You've made your point,' Lena said. 'Just let me past and I'll get out. No more visits here, no more questions. I get back to my own business and you get back to yours.'

'You are my business now, Headsman.'

The leader wasn't the first to come at Lena. Instead it was two of the men, both with their cudgels raised, their expressions as ugly as a boar's arse.

Lena flung her tankard into the first man's face. He stepped back blinking, more surprised than hurt, and she took his moment of blindness to grab the cudgel and twist it from his hand.

Lena grinned.

Then the other one was on her. She blocked his cudgel with hers, heard the sharp crack of wood against wood and felt the blow judder down her arm. Then she was striking back, lunging left and right in a string of blows that flung him off balance. He tried to parry, stepped back, stumbled over a stool, and almost lost his balance. A quick kick to his knee and he was on the floor.

By then the rest had closed in and Lena's excitement gave way to well-trained instincts. She slammed her shoulder into someone's chest, smashed her cudgel into a face, and stamped down hard on a foot. A blow bounced off her shoulder and someone tried to grab her arm, but she wrenched it free and punched them in the face.

Another blow came in, too low and fast for her to block, a fist slamming into her side. She staggered, winded, hit the wall, bounced back and lashed out. There was a crunch, a spray of blood, and a groan of pain as someone's nose gave way.

She couldn't fight properly pressed against the wall, so she took a wide, ungoverned swing that forced them all to back off, then used the moment to step out into the room. Most of the alehouse's other inhabitants had retreated to the corners, so they could watch the fight in safety. Of course, no one went to fetch the constables.

Lena parried a cudgel blow, ducked under another, and came up swinging. One of her attackers crashed into a table, which collapsed beneath her. A kick collided with Lena's thigh, and she was forced towards the bar, but she was still standing, and that was what counted.

'You're tough for a wrinkled old goat,' the leader of the gang said.

'Like leather,' Lena replied. 'I've hardened with age.'

'Don't stop you being outnumbered.'

'Doesn't matter when I can outfight any ten of you.'

Her thigh was aching from a kick. That never would have happened in the old days. She took another step back, shifting her weight, and felt the planks of the bar press against her spine.

'Come on, then,' she said as the thugs prowled towards her. 'Let's get this done so I can get back to drinking.'

There was a glug. Something heavy hit the back of her head, shattered, and covered her in ale. The blow pushed her forward, her head spinning, shards of pottery tumbling to the floor. Sharp pain said that one of those pieces had sliced her scalp.

She raised her head just in time to see a fist. The blow caught her square on the jaw, and she fell against a table, a sharp pain in her lip and blood in her mouth. She tried to raise her cudgel, but it was knocked from her hand.

The blows fell like hail on a rooftop, a thundering of fists and feet. She stumbled through them, heading for the light of the doorway. They didn't try to stop her, just kept beating her as she went, until she staggered out of the alehouse.

Passers-by stared at Lena as she stood in the middle of the street, bruised and dripping with ale, blood oozing through the hair on the back of her head. She straightened and turned to face the Lucky Dice, where the leader of the thugs stood in the doorway, cudgel in hand and cruel laughter in her eyes.

'That answer your questions?' the woman asked. 'Or do you want to nose around the boss some more?'

Lena spat blood into the dirt. The embarrassment was worse than the pain, caught out by a barmaid in a tavern brawl. She was better than this.

She wanted to finish it off with some witty comeback, to win back some sliver of pride. But her head was pounding and the words she thought of sounded stupid even to her. Some days you got what you wanted, and some days you got what you deserved. Now she knew which sort this day was.

With aching steps, she trudged off up the street, seeking a physician for her wounds and a drink for her soul.

CHAPTER TEN

FURY IN THE FOREST

The manticore bone snapped beneath Lena's axe. A few white shards fell away, leaving two jagged ends of a piece that had broken too easily.

She frowned, set the axe aside, and picked up the pieces of bone. They were lighter than they should have been and riddled with holes. She ran a finger across one of the broken ends and the inner bone crumbled to dust.

She peered into the ribcage. A family of sgeir had stripped the skeleton clean, taking the hide, organs, and every inch of flesh. But the scavengers didn't have saws or axes strong enough for bone work, so they had left that to her: a sad skeleton painted in a last layer of blood, not dry and white like old bone but pink and sticky and stinking of death.

There was a lump growing across three of the ribs, something the sgeir hadn't known how to butcher and so had left. No wonder this creature had died. Something had been growing inside it, eating it away. An old warrior's worst enemy, their own body.

So much for satisfying work to settle her mood and distract her from her pains. Instead she was left imagining the poor beast's pain and confusion as cancer sapped its strength. Better to go down fighting than to have death creep up on you like that.

''Scuse me, Headsman Sturm,' said a voice behind her.

Lena looked around to see a nervously stooped sgeir. She didn't know his name, didn't know any of the sgeir that way.

Knowing names meant knowing people, and she had come here to be alone-to the city, to the caves, to her dual lives as butcher and killer. But she had seen this man around often enough, usually with his extended family, all as ragged and hungry looking as he was. She knew him as an archetype of the people she worked alongside, among whom she was accepted.

'What do you want?' she asked.

'Something's wrong with the beasts.' He glanced over his shoulder at a small crowd of expectant sgeir. 'We hoped you might know what's happening, seeing as you live out in the streets.'

Lena frowned. She hadn't known that they saw her as a figure of authority, but it made a twisted sense. If your clan lived in caves, then you might look up to the visitor from the land of houses.

'Tell me what you know,' she said.

A mass of growling, snapping, and hissing reached Lena as she approached a low ridge west of Unteholz. It was an unremarkable place, just one more line of rock rising through the edge of the pine forest, where the green wild and the grey wild met. But those fierce sounds told Lena that she was in the right place. She hefted her axe and marched on up the slope, pine needles crunching underfoot.

The sgeir had been right. Not a single monster had entered the caves all day and none were coming. This sort of quiet happened some days in winter, when the passes were blocked with snow and half the beasts were hibernating. But it didn't happen in spring, and it definitely didn't happen while there was war on. Something was drawing away the dying monsters that were Unteholz's lifeblood. Now she knew where, but not how or why.

She smelled the beasts before she saw them. The stench of

wet fur and rotting flesh, of blood and piss and dying things, overwhelmed the sweet scent of the trees and the trampled flowers amid their roots. But there was something else too, a smell halfway between a fine stew and a tanner's vat, somehow both mouth-watering and nauseating.

What the hells was going on?

The trees grew thinner as the ground grew stonier and at last she saw the beasts. There were a dozen of them, fierce bodies covered in fur and scales, with rending talons and snapping jaws. A wyvern spread a tattered pair of wings that tangled in the branches above. A gryphon reared up, shedding feathers as it went, and battered with its front paws at the rock, even as it cried out like the mother of all eagles. Between them, a unicorn raised its splintered horn.

Some of those creatures could have been saved. They needed splints for broken bones, salves for their wounds, somewhere they could rest and be fed, all the things that made it worth their while living around humans. Lena had none of those things, however much she wished for them, and the leaders of Unteholz were too ignorant to see the point. To them, wounded beasts meant sinew, bones, and scales, they meant goods for gold. They paid for butchers, not stable hands, and so that was what she had become. Sometimes mercy was as close to justice as life got.

In the centre of the beasts was a stone column with spiral stairs carved around its side, one of the ancient watch places left behind by the Laugerin Empire. Legionaries, uniformed and disciplined, had supposedly surveyed the land from these commanding pillars, a thousand years before Lena was born. But the figures up there now had none of the legions' discipline and dignity.

Waclaw Pawlitzki stood on the top of the pillar, high enough among the treetops for the sun to shine off his bald head. Beside the alchemist, a large cauldron stood over the remains of a fire, blue smoke drifting from its rim, while the alchemist's apprentice stood behind him, peering out nervously at the roaring, scrabbling creatures below. Pawlitzki shifted nervously from one leg to the other while his fingers drummed against his scalp.

Pawlitski was too high up for the monsters to reach, but that didn't stop them trying. They shoved and scratched at each other to get closest to the pillar, then tried to scramble up its sides. But the steps were too narrow for them, and the trees kept the winged creatures from flying. Instead they scraped and slathered and screeched with a desperation Lena had seldom seen.

Nausea tipped her impatience over into anger. Clearly, the alchemist had done something to attract these beasts, some idiot trick that drove them wild and got him trapped up there with the girl. If he kept drawing the creatures this way, then they wouldn't go to the caves, which would mean no corpses for the sgeir to butcher, no coin to buy food for their gaunt and restless children. These beautiful beasts would still die for lack of care, and no one would be the better for it.

Someone had to fix this, and that someone wasn't going to be the idiot alchemist.

Lena hooked a leather strap around her axe and slung it across her shoulder, then walked slowly, carefully towards the beasts. The closest was a unicorn, half again as tall as any warhorse, with a tangled grey mane and the tip of its horn broken off. It had clearly been a war beast, as its flank was striped with pale scars as well as recent wounds. Whoever it had fought for, they had taken off its collar before letting it run off to die, but they hadn't taken the spear tip from its flank, and fresh blood ran free each time it rose on its hind legs. What sort of rider left their mount to suffer like that, when they had lived and fought together?

The unicorn didn't notice her presence until she laid a hand on its side. It was soft and smooth as silk, warm as sunset on a summer's day, and it reminded her of her first lessons in beast handling, back with Grey Tancred at the Eschart stables. Her heart reached out to forge a bond before she'd even stopped to think.

The unicorn's emotions thundered across her. Longing blazed

like a beacon, so fierce it almost burned away the beast's pain and exhaustion. Lena found herself desperately hungry and desperately horny and utterly certain that both feelings could be quenched at the top of the pillar, by whatever made that wonderful and terrible smell. She wanted to run up the face of the rock, her hooves hammering at its surface until she reached the pinnacle and then-

She broke away. Her heart was hammering, her mouth dry, her head spinning with desire. In that moment, she would have jumped Pawlitzki himself if he'd been down there with her, would have flung him to the ground and banged him senseless. Then the feeling passed, leaving only the image of the naked alchemist with his pale skinny limbs and his stained fingers, and she shuddered at the thought.

Desire shifted to anger. These poor beasts were already on their way to death, now Pawlitzki was driving them mad, making them fight each other to get to him. Her lip curled as she strode past the unicorn to the base of the pillar.

The unicorn's hooves hammered against the base of the steps, a battery of blows that threatened to split those hooves and would certainly split Lena's skull. She took a deep breath and laid her hand against its flank again.

Once more, their minds joined, but this time Lena was ready. Instead of letting the unicorn's passion overrun her, she pushed back, sending in the most soothing thoughts she could form. It wasn't easy to gather calm when the air was full of howls and hisses, but she had done it amid the clamour of battle, and she could do it here. Peace pulled at the wild beast's heart. Hooves stopped beating at the stone and it turned its head to be stroked.

The creature's muzzle was flecked with foam, its eyes bloodshot, but still there was something soothing about the feel of its coat beneath her hand, the warmth of an animal's body and the simplicity of its thoughts.

'There you go,' Lena said softly. 'Isn't that better?'

With one hand still on the unicorn, she climbed the first few steps. Her arm stretched out to keep the contact, but she had to move on, however reluctantly. She let go and swiftly strode up the spiralling stairs, as the unicorn whinnied and pawed restlessly at the ground.

As she ascended, she ran the gamut of wild monsters, dodging claws and teeth, soothing any creature she could touch, racing past others in a desperate rush. Hot breath and the smell of fur pursued her until she was out of their reach and rising up the last turn to the top of the pillar.

'Headsman Sturm!' Pawlitzki said as she approached. 'What are you doing here?'

'Me? What the flame are you doing?'

The pain and frustration of the beasts below swirled through her mind, drowning out any sense of calm or reason. She grabbed Pawlitzki by his apron and swung him out over the monsters, one heel teetering on the edge of the pillar.

'Please stop!' he whimpered, clutching her wrist. 'Don't feed me to them!'

'Feed you to them? I ought to butcher you myself and offer them the prime cuts.'

'But I didn't do it!'

'Didn't do what?'

'Whatever you're angry about.'

'You didn't drive these creatures mad?'

'Why do you care about that?'

She pushed him further, so that only his toes were on the pillar top, only her strength keeping him from a fall into rending claws.

'Why don't you?'

Tears ran down Pawlitzki's cheeks.

'I'm just trying to bring peace, I swear.'

'You call this peace?'

'I'm working on a potion!'

'A potion? A thundering potion?'

'A potion to end these foolish wars.'

'This is meant to bring peace?' Lena pointed at the smoking cauldron. 'I think you got it very wrong.'

'Not this one!' His foot slipped off the edge and his eyes went wide. He stared down at the ravening beasts in unutterable, unadulterated panic. 'Please, please let me explain.'

It was hard to maintain a righteous rage against such a pathetic figure. As her first fury faded, Lena found that her arm, battered in the Lucky Dice, was aching, her grip on Pawlitzki weakening. A little longer like this and he would slip through her fingers. Much as she loathed him, she didn't want his blood on her hands.

Not yet.

She pulled him back in and dumped him next to his cauldron. On the far side, his apprentice stood pale-faced and staring.

Lena peered into the cauldron. The smell made her gag. Inside was something like a thick soup, pieces of plant and animal bobbing about in a dark, oily liquid.

'I've been working with an ancient recipe,' Pawlitzki said, looking up from where he lay huddled. 'One from imperial tablets. According to contemporary chronicles, it would generate a sense of unity and closeness between those who consume it, a counterbalance to the ructions from which disharmony stems. What better way to bring some semblance of peace, to fend off the disaster bearing down upon us?'

'The only feeling this is giving me is nausea,' Lena said.

'There are uncertainties about the recipe of the peace potion, methodologies and components that are at odds with the modern alchemical arts. I have been experimenting with substitutions, attempting to understand the underlying principles and revive a lost creation.'

'And this is what your experiments made.'

She pointed down at the raging beasts.

'No! I thought that perhaps fresher ingredients would work better, and so I made a potion to summon monsters.'

He pointed at a crossbow lying by the fire.

'You think you can fight monsters?' She picked up the crossbow and turned it over in her hands. It was a fancy-looking piece, highly polished and decorated, but with lousy draw power. The idiot had bought an aristocrat's toy, not a real weapon.

'I had to try,' Pawlitzki said sullenly. 'People need this potion I'm crafting. Look at the wars in the other valleys. Look at the fights outside the temples. Look at your own bruises. We need peace.'

'Peace through violence.' She flung the crossbow at his feet. 'Good thing we've got smart people like you to dream that up.'

Except that she had believed it herself once. She had never been like the mercenaries, always looking for their next war. For her, combat had not been the goal, despite the rush it gave. Her purpose had been a better world, and victory was a means to an end. As the struggle grew more desperate, and that end seemed more distant, she had fought all the harder to reach it. By the end, she was tearing the world apart because she didn't know how else to save it.

Then she had woken up to ashes and the truth.

She pointed at the cauldron. 'How long is this crap going to keep drawing them in?'

'I don't have extensive experience with this concoction, but if De La Porcente is correct, then it will keep luring suitable targets here for several days.'

'Days. Days of that lot down there while we're stuck up here?'

'Well, yes, and any other monsters that pass. This is a puissant potion.'

There was a flap of wings as a gryphon tried to take flight. It still didn't have the space and its feathers were malting, tumbling away as it battered against the branches. Screeching in frustration, it sank back down and clawed at the stone. The sound grated at Lena's heart, but a more practical consideration helped her set sympathy aside. How long before one of these creatures made it into the air?

'Can you cancel it out?' Lena asked. 'Make a potion to calm

them down or drive them away?'

'Perhaps, yes.' Pawlitzki peered thoughtfully into the cauldron. 'We know that De La Porcente's recipe affects the beasts, so with the right substitutions it might affect them in different ways. Ox rust, perhaps, or feller's root…'

He fell silent.

'Well then,' Lena said. 'Get on with it.'

'I don't have those things here! Besides, it would take days of experiments to even come close to-'

'You can't undo this?'

'I didn't say that, just that it would take time and ingredients and-'

'And we're stuck up here without them. Gods, you're as much use as an infant in a siege.'

'Actually, during the siege of-'

'Shut up.' She turned her glare on the apprentice. 'What about you, any ideas?'

The girl shook her head.

Lena took a deep breath. She couldn't afford to make this about her anger. Give in to that, and you were as bad as any mob.

An agonised howl rose from the ground below. The unicorn's injured leg had finally given way, and it had fallen. Now other beasts were trampling it. The sounds of its pain tore at Lena's heart. It was one thing to give these creatures a swift and merciful death in the caves, another to watch this carnage.

'What happens if we throw this down to them?' she asked, pointing at the cauldron.

'Oh, that would be interesting,' Pawlitzki said. 'I think they'll attempt to eat it, and whatever else it falls on. I imagine that they'll fight each other for access to the greatest concentrations. Should it land on the creatures themselves, things could get incredibly messy.'

Lena sighed as she looked down at the beasts. The unicorn was dead now, its mane ground into the dirt, an elderly, grey-scaled wyvern standing on its chest, trying to reach up the pillar.

Some of the others were faltering as the strength that had brought them to Unteholz faded. They were all dying, and she had no way to heal them.

Reluctantly, she unslung her axe and went to the top of the steps.

'Throw it over the side,' she said. 'All of it. I'll deal with what's left.'

Lena walked, blood-stained and weary, along the trail back to Unteholz. She stank of the beasts she had slaughtered, and their screams echoed in her ears. Any time she closed her eyes, she saw them tearing at each other, a frenzied mass of fur, feathers, and scales. She had seen humans do worse than that before, but never animals. It wasn't their blood lust that made her sick. It was the fact that she had been part of it.

Pawlitzki walked behind her, carrying his empty cauldron, and then his apprentice with her sack of ingredients and the pathetic crossbow.

'Don't you want to harvest the parts?' Pawlitzki asked. 'I mean, that's what you do isn't it, you and the sgeir?'

Lena kept walking. She couldn't even begin to explain what she had felt as she strode into the chaos at the base of the pillar. The frenzied air of death and desire. The passion of the beasts so intense that it burned at her mind just from standing close to them. Walking into that tangled carnage to finish off each beast in turn. Every stroke of her axe a death. After that, she had no heart for butchery.

Gods, but she needed a drink. A drink and to be left alone.

'You know, it was the peace potion that brought me to Saimon,' Pawlitzki said. 'He promised the rarest, freshest ingredients. Hearts from mighty dragons. Sinews from young wyverns. The finest unicorn horn. Quality is critical if this endeavour is to fulfil its potential.'

Lena turned, teeth bared, ready to tell him what she thought of his endeavour.

Something else caught her eye. A man stood beneath one of the trees, watching them. He wore a leather tunic, and a faded woollen hood pulled over his head. From his belt hung a shortsword, a quiver, and a piece of cloth stitched with a red tree against a black background. She didn't remember which lord that sign belonged to, but she knew when she saw a war scout.

Her mouth went dry. She had come to Unteholz to leave that life behind, but here it was, creeping out of the wilderness to watch her.

'What is it?' Pawlitzki asked, turning too slowly to see the scout disappear into the trees.

'Trouble,' Lena said.

Chapter Eleven

An Army at the Gates

Lena strode up Needletip Street, the widest thoroughfare through Othagate and the labourers' districts beyond. A crowd was gathering outside a parish temple on the north side of the street, gawking at some drama on the temple steps. Getting through the crowd was like trudging through a swamp, shoving and sidestepping her way through a mass of bodies that threatened to bog her down. Lena cursed under her breath as she pushed a protesting woman aside. What was so thundering special that it deserved all this?

On the steps of the temple stood a priest, clad in the traditional green robes but clutching a clean new printed book that could only be the revised scripture. He wore amulets showing both the disk of the world and the lightning bolt. A man trying to tread a middle way, but Lena had seen too many others to think that could last. He was standing his ground, but his body betrayed him, hunching away from the dully clothed, red-faced parishioner bearing down on him.

'You can't put that here,' the parishioner shouted. 'You've got no right.'

He pointed past the priest to where a pair of masons were setting up a wash bowl on a plinth of heavy grey granite. The sides were carved with images, and Lena would have bet her left hand that they depicted the lives of saints.

'Nobody has to use it,' the priest said.

'Yeah, right. That's what they said at Rustbeck, now a man can't step inside that place without committing heresy.'

'It's just for those who want it.'

'And I suppose this is just for those who want it too?' The man snatched the book of scripture out of the priest's hands and held it up for the crowd to see. 'This book of lies.'

He tore out a fistful of pages, then flung them in the priest's face. The priest's expression changed; fear swept away by outrage.

'You filthy, ignorant, ash-blackened-'

The priest grabbed at the book, and his parishioner used it to hit him in the face. The crowd surged forward with cries of outrage for both sides, and Lena had to shove and strain not to be carried along. She pushed her way out the far side and hurried on up the road, leaving the brawl behind. Of everyone in this city, she had the least right to tell people not to fight over religion, but while this might seem like the most important thing to the crowd now, something was coming that would soon change their minds.

Dodging around wagons and side-stepping pedestrians, she rushed along the tangle of streets through the heart of the city. This place was never truly quiet, even in the depths of night, and in the middle of the day it was a teeming mass of humanity, a chattering, bargaining, squabbling, celebrating mess, a place that was brilliantly, obstructively alive. Some days Lena loved it and some days she hated it. Today she just wanted it to get out of her way.

The citadel was different, a bastion of grim black stone towering over Unteholz, a shadow cast into the air. As she strode past a token sentry, through the heavy oak gates, and along the tunnel that pierced the outer walls, Lena felt a chill that didn't just come from within. This place was designed for strength, not for comfort.

Half a dozen shackled prisoners were emerging from the dungeons into the courtyard. Eljvet the jailer led the way, tall and buck-toothed, with a cudgel in his hand and a whip coiled at his side. He grinned at Lena, but she didn't smile back. She had no time for a man whose career was built on casual cruelty and squeezing his captives for cash. When Eljvet beat a prisoner for breaking his rules, it wasn't a fair fight, or a sentence handed down by the court, it was opportunistic malice under the cover of law. She couldn't bring herself to despise him, not when she was part of the same machine, taking broken people and spitting them out in bits. Not when the two of them were both scorned for work that others needed them to do. But she had taken on this work to atone, while he embraced it with a dark delight. There was a deep valley of difference between tolerating a man and sparing him a smile.

'Come to join us for the walk to the stone, headsman?' Eljvet asked. 'You could at least have brought the lash with you, add to the parade a bit.'

Lena cursed under her breath. She had forgotten that she had work today, whipping thieves and cutting the tongue from a Moon cultist. She should be at the Weeping Stone already, clearing the ground.

It would have to wait.

'Where's Baumer?' she asked.

'He'll be out in a minute.' Eljvet left his miserable charges and ambled over with a smile that set Lena's teeth on edge. 'Said he needs to talk to you. Don't reckon it's a good talk neither. What have you been up to, eh?'

'I don't have time for gossip,' Lena said. 'Where is he?'

'There.'

Baumer appeared on the steps to the keep. His armour shone in the sunlight, a bright contrast to the shadowy stonework. He had an apple in his hand and a scowl on his face.

'Sturm,' he bellowed. 'We need words.'

'Told you,' Eljvet whispered, then giggled as he backed away.

Baumer descended the steps, metal clanging against

stonework, and strode up to Lena.

'You couldn't resist, could you?' he said.

'Whatever this is, it can wait,' Lena said. 'I've just seen-'

'No excuses.' Baumer raised his voice to cut her off. 'You were told to stop that Saimon business. Instead, you picked a fight about it at the Lucky Dice.'

Lena smiled sheepishly and held her hands wide.

'I'm sorry, alright?' she said. 'You know what it's like. Sometimes you've just got to scratch an itch.'

Baumer stared at her for a long moment, and she waited for the response that discipline demanded, the one that she probably deserved. Instead, he burst out laughing.

'Moon's sake, Lena, I've heard that excuse for one drink too many or fucking the wrong person, but not for fighting lowlifes in a cheap tavern.'

Lena unclenched and let her smile widen. She didn't want to be that soldier, the one every officer hated, the one who set a bad example for the rest. Discipline mattered, obedience mattered, and if you were going to buck against the system, then it had cursed well better be for a good reason. But it was nice, just once, for someone to find her amusing. It was good to be more than a figure of fear. If she could share a smile over the prospect of a bar brawl, then maybe she wasn't alone.

'What can I say? Sometimes a whore and a pot of ale just aren't enough.'

'I got another earful from Maier because of you.'

'I'll buy you a drink or two, make up for it, but right now-'

Hoof beats came hammering down the tunnel from the gateway and a rider appeared. He was finely dressed, his fitted black tunic emblazoned with a red tree, and his horse was a sleek black mare. He held himself with a herald's pride, the confidence of a man who didn't need to wear a sword because he had an army at his back. When he pulled the reins, his horse stopped on the spot.

Two constables ran in behind him.

'Gate,' one of them panted. 'Come from… East Gate… message for…'

'I come from Lord Everhart,' the herald proclaimed. 'General of the Third Host of the Righteous. I bear a message for the rulers of Unteholz.'

'What the flame is this?' Baumer asked, staring at the herald with disdain.

'It's what I came to tell you,' Lena said. 'There's an army coming.'

By dusk, the so-called Third Host of the Righteous had arrived outside Unteholz. The wind whipped at Lena's face as she watched from the walls, assessing just how damned the city was.

Like most armies, it was mostly infantry, professionals armed with arquebuses and polearms followed by a rabble bearing a jumble of spears, axes, and bows. Matching uniforms said there were mercenary bands and household guards in there, not just rough levies, and there were armour bonded knights, their plate mail gleaming in the last rays of the sun.

Light cavalry rode around the flanks, scouting the edges of the woods and the slopes behind Unteholz. Judging by their speed and skill, some were horse bonded, but probably not all of them. Most of the riders with that gift would be coming up behind, with the war beasts.

What beasts they were. A dozen gryphons, a score of manticores, two flights of wyverns soaring over the city while their riders judged the lie of the land. And towering over the rest, slow and stately, their wings folded in as they walked up the mountain, were a pack of dragons.

Lena had grown so used to dead and dying beasts that she had almost forgotten the predatory beauty of those creatures. Seeing them now, with their scaled flanks rippling and their bright eyes blazing, it took her breath away. She remembered how it felt to have such a beast beneath her, to soar through the air with a lance in her hand and no concern except where she would strike. She remembered the terror of facing them too, of waiting for that single moment when the beast was close enough to strike but hadn't killed you yet. Her hand tightened on her dagger hilt and her heart beat faster as she remembered standing on the walls of Kirkstat, greatsword in hand, watching a dragon hurtle towards her, flame blazing from its maw, and knowing that only her skill stood between her and death.

Glorious, terrible days.

Footsteps clanked along the walkway. Baumer stopped a foot from her and stood, staring out at the army.

'Artillery's not here yet,' he said.

'Of course not. Can you imagine hauling that shit up a mountain? Their siege train's probably days behind.'

'How many do you reckon there are?'

Lena scanned the assembled horde, doing some rough, instinctive maths.

'Fifteen thousand here already,' she said. 'Add in stragglers and those guarding the baggage, I'd call it twenty.'

'Sounds about right.'

Baumer drummed his gauntleted fingers against the battlements. He stood stiff, his easy swagger swept away by the face of war. Lena found herself a little surprised. She'd always seen Baumer as the sort of man who took war in his stride. He'd clearly lived through it.

'What did the herald say?' she asked.

'They're here for you.'

Now it was her turn to stiffen as cold fingers clawed up her spine. There had always been a risk that the world would catch up with her one day, but she had never imagined it would come like this. Was it better to know that the gears of righteousness turned and the guilty would pay for their past, or was it better to think that you could hide away and somehow make amends? Justice was a slippery thing, especially when you were on the receiving end.

'Well, sort of.' Baumer chuckled mirthlessly. 'They're here because of Saimon's execution. This Everhart is some big Sky general. He heard that Unteholz's Earth-worshippers killed one of their priests. Says it's a murder and they're here for justice.'

Relieved as she was to hear that this wasn't just for her, Lena still found herself gripped by tension. She knew how this game played out.

'Let me guess,' she said. 'We hand over the people responsible or the army will be forced to seize the city.'

'You've got it.'

'Who do they say is responsible?'

'They're being vague. Buys them time to bring up the cannons. But the herald talked about Earth worshippers on the city council and the undue influence of Bishop Kunder.'

'They're aiming big.'

'Big enough to make sure the answer's no.'

So there it was. Someone else had come seeking justice for Saimon, but what they really wanted was an excuse to seize Unteholz. Maier's policy of neutrality had reached its limit.

'You think we can trust the Sky worshippers in the city?' Baumer asked. 'If I wanted to tear down the old faith, I might take this chance.'

'They're still citizens of Unteholz. Their loyalty's to the city first.'

'And yours?'

'I've seen too many cities burn. I'm not going to be responsible for one more.'

Seen it, heard it, smelled it, tasted the ashes on her tongue and felt the charred stones radiate their heat. No, she wouldn't listen to another city's screams, or sit through excuses about taking lives because it saved souls. Those screams haunted her in the moments when the world was still. They drove her to action and to drink, anything to blot out the past. They were the accusing voice from which she had come here to hide.

'Isn't this going to be fun?' Baumer said, stony-faced, his gauntlet grating against the stonework.

'Full of honour and glory, I'm sure.' Lena sighed and stared out across the army, counting the monsters again.

A dragon raised its head and blew fire into the gathering darkness. By its blazing red light, Lena watched her fears closing in.

CHAPTER TWELVE

TO SAVE THE CITY

Lena was sitting in Maier's antechamber when a girl came in, no more than seven years old, with blond hair hanging loose over a blue woollen tunic, carrying a wooden ladle. She planted her feet shoulder width apart and pointed the ladle straight at Lena.

'You! What are you doing here?' she demanded. 'Are you a Sky spy?'

Lena laughed and shook her head.

'I'm waiting to talk with the councillor,' she said.

'Hm.' The girl strode over to examine Lena more closely, the ladle raised like a sword. 'What are you doing then?'

'Whittling.' Lena held up the piece of carved wood, no bigger than the palm of her hand. She kept her whittling knife back, out of the child's reach.

'Is it a cat?'

'That's right.'

'I like cats, but daddy says we can't have one.'

'What does your mother say?'

'Don't know. Mummy's too busy for things like cats.'

'That's a shame.' Lena knew how it was to be that parent, to be torn between home and work, to feel guilty even when you did the right thing and to constantly wish you could do more. She hesitated, then pressed the carving into the girl's hands. 'Why don't you have this cat? It's a lot easier to look after.'

'Really?'

The girl flung herself at Lena, who jerked the knife out of the way. For a moment, she felt awkward and embarrassed, then the simple affection of the hug melted something inside her. She patted the girl's back and smiled.

'You're welcome,' she said.

The door of the office creaked open, and Maier looked out.

'Mummy!' The girl rushed to her. 'Look what the nice lady gave me.'

'That's lovely, Heida,' Maier said, beaming down at her daughter. 'Did you say thank you?'

'Thank you!' Heida said.

'Not to me.'

'Oh.' The girl turned, cleared her throat, and spoke with careful intonation. 'Thank you very much for my present. I will take good care of it.'

'Now run along,' Maier said. 'The headsman and I need to talk.'

They both watched, laughing, as the girl walked out of the room, whispering into her new cat's ear as she went. As soon as it was just the two of them, Maier's expression hardened.

'Come on in.'

Lena followed the councillor into her office. It was more crowded than before, with a row of trestle tables set up beneath the windows. They were littered with maps, lists, and counting boards. Scribes sat at the tables, busy with their work. The scratching of quills and clatter of counters gave voice to minds hard at work. She recognised some of this paperwork: tallies of soldiers, contracts to hire mercenaries, food bills and calculations of water supplies. Unteholz was going onto a war footing. The problem was that it was too late.

'You should let them in,' she said.

Maier sat down behind her desk, where a half-empty coin bag lay next to another counting board. Salt City ducats sat in neat stacks next to the board, coins any merchant in the Saved Lands would accept. She waved to the chair across from her, rings flashing in the candlelight.

'Let who in?'

'Everhart's army.'

'And lose our independence? Never.'

'I don't think it's independence you're worried about. I think it's your head.'

Maier shot Lena a look of cold fury.

'How dare you?' she asked. 'I've dedicated my life to this city, Sturm. Do you think I would let it burn just to save my own skin?'

'You're a merchant. You've dedicated your life to gold.' Lena sat, hands gripping the arms of the chair. 'That tells me what sort of person you are.'

The scribes scribbled faster, as if their pens could draw a protective line through the stony silence hanging above their master's desk.

Maier's face was red with fury.

'You saw that little girl,' she said at last, pointing out the door. 'You think I would let anyone hurt her? I've built somewhere precious and safe for my family, and I'm not handing it over to a band of thugs with delusions of salvation.'

Lena raised an eyebrow. This was a way only civilians talked about soldiers, casually dismissive of everything they did except destroy. An army could be many things, but it was never just stupidity and violence, there was skill and dedication there, passion for the work and for the cause. Yes, there was always some selfishness and hate in the ranks, but there was always nobility and camaraderie too.

And none of that mattered now, because Lena wasn't here to defend her old life. For once, she meant to save lives, not end them.

'Have you ever been through a siege, councillor?' she asked, her voice as cold and flat as Maier's. 'It's an ugly business, and what comes after you lose is worse. When a city surrenders, there's a little light looting, then the commanders apologise, and everyone gets back to work. When a city's stormed, the streets run red with fire and blood, a punishment for resistance and a message to the next town.

'If you want to keep your family safe, you'll stop this madness before it starts.'

Maier pointed out the window.

'You think any incoming army, whoever they worship, will leave the leaders of this city in place? Or that they'll let us quietly get out of their way? That's not how this works. If we let them in, then I make my children orphans at best, and they won't be the only ones.'

'How are you planning on keeping them out?'

'The same way any city would, by rallying our militia bands. There are men and women across Unteholz who have trained for this moment.'

'How many?'

'Enough.'

'How many?'

Maier glared, then turned her attention to one of the clerks. 'Patka, how many do we have on the rolls?'

'Nearly five thousand,' the clerk replied. 'And the constables.'

'Five thousand amateurs and fifty professionals,' Lena said with a sneer. 'Against twenty thousand, all hardened from the campaign trail. You want to pick that fight.'

'I don't want to pick any fight, but I have a duty to defend what belongs to us.'

'It all comes down to who you include in 'us', doesn't it?' Lena said, knuckles whitening as her hand tightened on the arm of the chair. 'After all your talk of neutrality, you're siding with the Earth priests.'

'I'm not siding with anyone. I'm trying to keep us safe.'

'You're failing.'

'The past ten years of peace say otherwise.'

'What's outside our gates agrees with me.'

Maier stared at Lena, who stared straight back. She could

keep this up all day if she had to, would keep it up if it saved them from the things she'd seen.

'The people of this city will not stand for surrender,' Maier said.

'Tell that to our Sky priests. You let that army in, and they'll bang the gongs to celebrate our liberators.'

'Anyone who thinks that way is a fool, and you know it. It's our duty to protect the citizens of this city, whether or not they appreciate it. You of all people should see that.'

'You won't be protecting anyone by starting a war.'

'I didn't start it.'

'But you won't stop it?'

'I thought you were a soldier,' Maier hissed, eyes blazing.

'I was. That's why I hate war.'

Maier took a deep breath, then let it out slowly between her teeth. Rings clacked softly against each other as she folded her hands in her lap.

'Neither of us wants this siege, Sturm,' she said. 'So you're going to do something for me.'

'Me?' Lena said. 'What the flame do you think I can do?'

'What you've been trying to do behind my back this whole time: catch Saimon's real killer.'

After everything they'd said before, after all the orders and obstructions, now Maier was on her side? Lena flung her head back and laughed. It was too bitterly absurd.

Clerks turned to stare, then just as quickly turned back to their work, heads down, shoulders up, quills scratching across parchment.

'You want to shift the blame?' Lena said at last. 'How the hells will that help?'

'It's not about blame, it's about justice,' Maier said sharply. 'If someone framed Holy Saimon, then her execution is their fault. We hand over that killer to Everhart, they have the justice they want, and we get left in peace.'

Lena almost laughed again.

'That army didn't come all this way for the sake of a single dead priest. It's an excuse, and they'll find another if they need to.'

Maier had to know that, but she had to put on a performance too. It wasn't a gift Lena had, pretending to believe in something she didn't. She carved her defences from the solid stone of reality, and when it wouldn't take the shape she needed, those defences fell. Maier wove hers from complex threads of fact and fiction, making the world what she needed it to be, reweaving the web every time a strand was severed. She was a deft enough weaver that she could work with blunt tools when she needed to.

'I'll deal with that problem when we come to it,' the councillor said. 'For now, I just want us to survive.' She leaned forward, fingers steepled, light reflecting off the half-empty bag of gold beside her. 'I don't like you, Sturm. You crawled your way to Unteholz to die, just like the monsters in the caves. You can't see that this is a place of life, something we've been carving out of the cold, hard mountainside through generations of struggle. You have no respect for the city or the people in it, and you don't put in the honest work others do. But sometimes we don't need honest work. Sometimes we need a scarred arsehole who strides through life with a butcher's blade.

'So, what will it take to do this? Help from the constables? Time with the high and mighty? More money?'

She pointed at the gold.

'Name your price.'

There it was again, the look that said Lena was just some washed out mercenary, there for whoever could pay enough. She'd seen the people who fought just for money, and she wouldn't give them mercy if a dragon got their guts.

The chair scraped back as she rose like a beast from winter's slumber.

'To hells with your money,' she said. 'And to hells with your pox-ridden town. I'm doing this for the poor woman you had me kill.

'Don't think I won't look your way either. Hunting for a scapegoat doesn't make you any less guilty in my eyes.'

She turned and strode from the room.

Lena was through the antechamber and into the corridor beyond when footsteps came rushing behind her. She spun around, hand on the hilt of her dagger, and glared at a clerk as he skidded to a halt. He was dressed in long black robes with a loose cloth cap and had the expression of a mouse caught in a cat's gaze.

'What does she want now?' Lena snapped. 'I've already said I'd do it.'

'It's not that.' The clerk's head twitched back and forth as he looked up and down the corridor. They were alone amid the wood panels, with no sight or sound of anyone else, but he still lowered his voice to the barest of whispers. 'I need to tell you something about her.'

Lena stepped closer. There was nothing she wanted more right now than to learn Maier's dark secrets.

'Go on.'

The clerk glanced around again, swallowed, and spoke.

'Councillor Maier and Councillor Saimon used to meet once a week,' he said. 'With no one else around, not even a clerk to take notes.'

'I thought they were rivals.'

'They were. They constantly competed for monopolies and trade deals, and they almost always took opposite sides in council meetings.'

'So what were these meetings about?'

'I don't know, but it could be important, couldn't it?'

Lena narrowed her eyes. The man was a little too eager to betray his employer.

'Why are you telling me?' she asked.

'My husband comes from Canvald. He was there when the armies of Father Earth stormed the city. He still wakes up screaming in the night.'

'And what do your boss's secret meetings have to do with that?'

'I think she's right. Our best hope is to prove that the execution was a setup, even if Councillor Maier did it. I'd rather lose my job than see my city burn.'

It was a plausible story, made stronger by the fear written across his pale face.

'Tell me more about these meetings,' Lena said. 'When were they? How long did they last?'

The clerk opened his mouth to speak, but footsteps approached around the corner. His eyes went wide, he shook his head, and then he rushed away without another word.

Lena cursed under her breath. There was more to be learnt here, and now she'd lost her chance.

At least now she knew to look, maybe she could find out more about these meetings. Councillor Maier's web of lies was about to collapse.

Lena dreamed about the execution.

Beatrice Saimon knelt in front of her, head shaved and eyes wide, giving her that sad, desperate look. The crowd cheered and howled, stamping their hooves and flapping their wings, every monster that had ever died under Unteholz now haunting its killing ground. But Saimon's voice cut through the chaos.

'My body,' she said. 'What's wrong with my body?'

The sword fell, the blood sprayed, and Lena jerked upright in bed.

Weak grey daylight oozed through the gap between the shutters. It shone off the longsword hanging from the wall and picked out the battered scales of her wyvern hide armour. But instead of thinking about battle, Lena found her mind stuck on Saimon.

What had been wrong with her body? Nothing that Lena had noticed. There had been no scars that would have made her stand out, no bruises or cuts except where Eljvet had been careless in shaving her scalp. She had walked slowly but surely to her death, arms hanging loose, a little dazed perhaps, but that was hardly surprising for someone being marched to the Weeping Stone.

No tension though. Normally, the guilty party tensed when they saw their executioner. It was inevitable, the most human of reactions to knowing that death had come. In their heart, no-one believed that they would die, and so some part of them prepared to run or fight, even though it was impossible. Some bought a drink from the jailer to ease their passing, but even they flinched when the sword was drawn.

That calm hadn't been right.

Lena cast off the blankets and pulled on her clothes, wincing as her tunic brushed her bruises from the Lucky Dice. It would be a while before they faded.

That thought triggered another. As well as belting on her dagger and slipping the whittling knife into her boot, she picked up a sturdy cudgel that she'd been given to help manage prisoners. In five years of service she'd never once needed it, but that was back when she just doled out punishments; investigating a crime was proving far more dangerous. She would have buckled on her sword if the city's laws let private citizens carry one. Instead, the stick would have to do.

It was late morning by the time she reached the trail to the funeral plateau. A thin rain pattered down, dribbling off the hood of her cloak, and rivulets of water ran down the hillside. High above, Steel Peak loomed like a dark colossus.

She had no idea what she was hoping to find. The wyverns would have stripped the flesh from Holy Saimon's bones days ago, and even the scraps would have been picked off by vultures. But that last moment of the dream kept spinning through her head, pointing her towards something that she couldn't quite reach. She had to head up here, if only to shake it off. Beatrice Saimon would give her no rest.

The plateau opened out in front of her, green grass scattered with white bones, like a field of macabre flowers. Most of the vultures had returned to their nests, leaving only the hungriest to pick at recent offerings. Whoever they worshipped, everybody ended up the same in the end-cold, naked, and exposed for the carrion creatures. Even Moon Cultists wound up here, their flesh feeding the sky.

She reached the corner of the plateau and trudged on up to the high ground beneath the Needle where criminals were interred. A stray humerus rolled from under her foot, and she slipped on the wet grass, but caught herself before she fell face first to the ground.

Curse the rain. It was getting heavier as the day went on, making the ground squelch and streams appear from nowhere across the mountain. Its only advantage was that it might bog down the army's siege train. If a wagon hadn't slipped and broken an axle by now, then she knew nothing about war.

At the top of the slope she looked around, trying to remember exactly where she had put Saimon's body. One of the wyverns had been out that day, but like the vultures they were hiding now, sheltered in their cave mouth. Two of them peered out at her, slitted eyes wide, sniffing the air. They knew the hand that fed them, but they could see that she had nothing to offer. Smarter creatures than her, or than the miners trudging up the distant side of Steel Peak. Humans were constantly straining against the world, but beasts flowed with it. It made them so much easier to deal with.

'Sorry,' she called out. 'I'm just here to look at your leftovers.'

Then she spotted a body, its flesh intact, lying discarded amid the bones.

Lena frowned. No one but her was meant to bring bodies up here. Had one of the wyverns carried it up and set it out of the vultures' reach? Or was someone trying to hide a body?

She strode over to the corpse. Even with the rain pouring down, its stench hit her full in the face, a cross between an outhouse and an abattoir, with a musty, sweet undertone that made it so much worse. A smell she was used to from battlefields, where it could take days to clear the dead, but not from up here.

Why had the wyverns left something to rot?

She fought back the urge to puke and knelt down next to the body. The head was missing, cut off with a clean stroke. What remained was a woman's corpse, someone in middle age and passable shape, discoloured by decay and bloating as gas formed inside.

A few feet away lay the head. The eyes bulged, and the tongue protruded between swollen lips, but there was no mistaking the face that haunted Lena's dreams. This was the body of Beatrice Saimon.

So why in all the hells hadn't the wyverns eaten it?

Curiosity overcame revulsion. Lena pulled her cloak across her nose and leaned in close. With her free hand, she prodded at the corpse. It was cold and wet, a little stiffer than she'd expected, but that made sense at this altitude and in this weather.

Reluctantly, she let go of the cloak and used both hands to roll Saimon over. More gases burst from the body, and she lurched back, gagging at the stench. All her efforts revealed were the blotches of deep purple-red where blood had sunk within the corpse, nothing that should put a wyvern off its dinner.

She folded her arms and stood staring at the remains of Beatrice Saimon.

'I'm doing this for you,' she said. 'The least you could do is show me a clue.'

She prodded the corpse with her toe. In response, something oozed out of the stump of the neck, a trickle of rotting fluids and of something else. Something oily and blue.

Lena crouched on the wet grass and peered more closely at the liquid. Her throat tightened and her stomach churned, but she forced herself to dip a finger in that ooze and hold it up in front of her face. Something glittered in the oily blue liquid and there was a smell, sweet yet sharp, a smell no corpse would make.

Silver dream. Lena had only tried the stuff once, as she had lurched from town to town, leaving behind a broken marriage and a career in arms, two losses that left her robbed of purpose, hollow and exposed. She couldn't escape the tangle of guilt, grief, and anger that came when her own son turned his back and let her walk out the door. Even drinking her way to the bottom of the barrel wouldn't chase that memory away, so she'd accepted an offer from an itinerant alchemist, a small spoonful of a silver-blue liquid that promised to dissolve all her cares.

He had been right. For that one night she didn't refight old arguments with a memory of Jahann, didn't chase through the memories of battlegrounds and burnt cities, didn't berate herself for innocents dead or a marriage destroyed. There was a brief moment of peace.

The next morning, she woke with fresh shame, remembering the clueless, pathetic shell she had become on silver dream. Someone who sat docile in the corner while the barman overcharged her, idiots poured their opinions into her ear, and a cutpurse brazenly stole her coins. The alchemist's elixir added fuel to the fire of her self-loathing. She needed purpose and a place to hide from her past, not just a way to ignore it.

Witnesses at Holy Saimon's trial had talked about her heavy drinking, and many silver dream users drank. But they were the quiet drunks slumped in the corner, wishing the world away. They weren't the angry ones bitterly raging about trouble with their spouses, as Holy Saimon had done, and no silver dream addict could have fired up a crowd of worshippers.

Someone had fed silver dream to Holy Saimon, too much of the potion for her body to absorb it all before she died, so much that it was still in her corpse days later. So much that the wyverns, smart to the strange smell, hadn't touched the poisoned meat.

No wonder Saimon had seemed dazed during the execution. She had been high as an eagle on the wind.

Someone had really wanted Holy Saimon sedated. Not just sedated for the execution-for that they could use booze-but sedated for days, out of her wits while others decided her fate.

They hadn't wanted Saimon talking to Lena about what happened. Now she really needed to know what the woman would have said.

Chapter Thirteen

Sidekick

The atmosphere on Rustbeck was more subdued than the last time Lena had been there. Wagons and messengers still flowed in and out of the gates of the middling merchants, but they went quickly and quietly, as if standing in the street might leave them exposed. The haggling, gossip, and clink of coins that were the audible pulse of trade now took place behind closed doors.

People hurried up the steps of the Temple of the Sundered Rose, hastily casting a few coins into the bowls of the beggars, rather than taking the time to display their largess. Normally, some would have lingered on the temple steps, ostentatiously washing their hands until the last boom of the temple gong. Today, those trembling souls were eager to be indoors, hands raised in prayer to Mother Sky. They had to make good with the gods now death waited beyond the gates.

As the sound of the gong faded, the beggars stayed in place. A man with one leg and a pox-scarred face shook his bowl hopefully, and the woman next to him gave a dramatically consumptive cough, but no one else was coming. Like a ragged and wingless flock of birds, the beggars rose and set out for their next spot.

From an alehouse doorway across the street, Lena watched them depart. The one she had her eye on was among the last still sitting. A short figure, wide around the middle, with a ragged hood covering their face. It wasn't an unusual outfit for a beggar.

It could usefully imply all manner of diseases and disfigurements, to tug at the tender conscience of a temple-goer. It could also hide a beggar's identity from those around them, and she had the distinct suspicion that this one wanted to stay hidden.

The hooded beggar adjusted something in their shoe, then got up, bowl in hand, and headed down an alley between two of the merchants' compounds. Lena swallowed the last of her ale, then set aside her tankard and followed them.

The alley was narrow and grim, less a path between destinations than a place for people to empty their chamber pots. The buildings to either side had no windows facing out on the bottom two floors. It was a good place to go if you didn't want to be seen.

The beggar stopped halfway down the alley and transferred the contents of his bowl into a pouch, which he then slid inside his tunic. He had tipped his hood back, the easier to see his earnings amid the shadows, and in doing so exposed a familiar, guileless face hung around with greasy hair.

To her surprise, Lena found herself smiling.

'Hello, Deppel,' she said.

The lad looked up, clutching his precious coin pouch close. There was a flicker of recognition, a brief smile at seeing her, and then his face went white with fear.

'It weren't what you think,' he said, his voice strained. 'I would have told you I knew those people, only I didn't want you to get rid of me, and the longer I didn't say the more scared I got, and then they turned up and-'

'It's alright, Deppel,' Lena said. 'I'm not angry at you.'

'You ain't?'

'Maybe I was at the start, but that's done. I knew you went begging, and I know what sorts of people beggars meet. It's not like I don't know criminals too.'

'But I-'

'That beating wasn't your fault. I went about things in a stupid way, and I got what I deserved. I'll be smarter next time.'

'Are you…' Deppel took a tentative step towards her. 'Are you alright?'

'All I got was a few bruises.' Lena pointed to the scars on her cheek. 'I've had far worse.'

'You should put fried horse dung on those. Someone told me that once.'

'I'd rather be black and blue than smear my face with pan fried shit.'

They both laughed.

Deppel scratched the back of his head and swung his bowl back and forth. His eyes were downcast, and Lena could almost see him struggling with his thoughts. It was an expression she could sympathise with.

It was tempting to leave him that way, like a hanged man dangling on a rope, but she had work to do.

'Would you like to help me again?' she asked.

'Really?' He looked up at her uncertainly. 'There ain't a lot I can do, you know. I'm not smart or fast or tough.'

'I need someone who knows more about the criminal world than I do. Someone who meets them before they're caught, not after. I thought you might do.'

Deppel nodded.

'I can help with that. What do you want?'

'I want to find out how Holy Saimon ended up full of silver dream, and I plan to start by learning about Jagusia Brodbeck.'

The alarm on Deppel's face almost made her laugh again.

'I'll be ready this time,' she said, showing him the cudgel that hung from her belt. 'And I'll be more discreet. I'm starting to understand this investigating business.'

Deppel looked down at this bowl. The enthusiastic energy he'd had before was gone, and that was for the best. Less annoying chatter, more chance he would focus on what mattered. But it was a shame to see him looking glum.

'Can't we go ask about someone else?' he asked. 'Jagusia, she don't like it when lawmen go poking around the Warrens, never mind when people get into her business.'

'I don't aim to be liked.'

'She's dangerous.'

'Makes her more of a suspect.'

'Once we start asking, she'll soon find out.'

'Not if we're careful.'

Deppel let out a long sigh and looked up at last.

'Alright, then. What do you want to know?'

The doorway of the Woodsman's Arms burst open, and candlelight smashed through the darkness of the street, creating a bright wound in the black flesh of night. A swirling cloud came with it, wood smoke from a fire and sweeter, mustier scents, billowing outward on a waft of warm air, along with the chatter of the revellers within. The streets might be gripped by darkness and a spring chill, but there were always warm, soft spaces to be found in the city.

A man stepped out of the doorway. He was in his early twenties, his black hair slicked back against his head, face painted pale and lips brightened with a touch of madder red. As he stepped laughing into the street, he hitched up the bottom of his embroidered silk robe to keep it from trailing in the dirt.

'That's him,' Deppel whispered to Lena in the darkness next to the tavern. 'Konrad Elmal. One of Jagusia's favourites.'

Lena scrutinised Elmal as he stood in the street, staring up at the stars. He was slim, but not in the emaciated way she was used to seeing, spending her days down in the caves with the sgeir. This was the slender, willowy figure of a man who kept himself boyish, one who lived by his looks.

The door slammed shut, cutting off the flow of warm air and laughter. Elmal shivered and wrapped his arms around himself, then set off down the street.

Pulling a hood up about her face, Lena emerged from the alley and followed Elmal. It was gone midnight in a city that had just seen war arrive, and the streets were deserted, the only sound the scuttling of rats through the gutters. She matched her footsteps to Elmal's and hoped that he was too wasted to notice the echo.

It only took a few minutes to leave the tavern safely out of view. Lena was considering where best to deal with Elmal when he made the decision for her, veering into the narrow gap between two houses. She glanced around, then followed him.

Her eyes took a moment to adjust to the deeper darkness of the alley, where barely a hint of light from the stars and moon shone. This was the darkness in which Jagusia's gang did so much of their work, their cruelty and violence unseen amid the black of night, not the honest horror of battle but the sly work of human parasites. It was also the darkness in which people went for a piss. Elmal stood facing the wall, one hand hitching up his robes.

Lena grabbed him from behind and slammed him against the wall. Elmal squawked a protest, but she pressed her cudgel against his neck, forcing his face against the stone.

'Quiet,' she said, lowering her voice to a deep growl. 'You don't want to get on my bad side.'

'You made me piss myself,' Elmal whimpered.

'I'll do it again unless you tell me what I want to know.'

She almost felt sorry for him. He was barely more than a boy, a kept creature living off his charm. Perhaps he'd had to work hard when he was younger, to stand out from the mass of street kids that roamed Unteholz's poorer districts and the Warrens where the gangs lived. But he'd left that life behind long enough for his skin to grow soft and his muscles to fade. He'd made himself prey to the likes of Brodbeck, and he'd clearly done well out of it, but that made him easy prey for Lena too.

'Do you know who I am?' Elmal hissed, finding some morsel of courage, some remnant of a bright, barbed spirit beneath the makeup and the clothes. There was nothing of substance here, just an empty skin of showmanship, but that facade hadn't quite collapsed yet. 'Do you know who I belong to? She'll have you gutted just for touching me.'

'Do you know who I am?' Lena growled, an inch from his ear. This close, she could smell the ground bone and whale oil that made up his skin whitener. It mingled with the haze of craydragon smoke and perfume that clung to him like another set of robes.

'Of course not,' he said, and she caught the scent of red wine on his breath. 'You're just some disgusting street thug.'

'Then how will your mistress know who to gut?'

Lena pressed harder with the cudgel. She didn't like torture. It was an ugly business that twisted the souls of everyone involved, and the answers it wrenched out were more often desperate lies than treasured truths. But sometimes applying a little pressure helped, a reminder of where the power lay.

'Tell me about your mistress and Holy Saimon. Did Brodbeck sell the priest silver dream?'

'Jagusia doesn't sell drugs,' Elmal said with a hint of mocking laughter.

'Like flame she doesn't.' Lena pressed with the truncheon again. 'She'll sell anything people don't want to be seen buying.'

'I mean she doesn't do the selling. She has people to do that for her.'

'Oh, so you're splitting threads? You think that's a smart idea right now?'

The boy whimpered and writhed. Lena tightened her grip.

'I'm sorry,' he moaned. 'I'm trying to help. Truly I am.'

'Then truly you're not smart. If you want me to let go, you need to tell me something useful.'

'Like what?'

'If I knew that, I wouldn't be asking!'

'Ow! Please, you're making it hard to breathe.'

Lena felt the tension in her arm, realised that she had been pushing harder than she meant to, had let the moment take control. That way lay all the worst mistakes: ill-timed charges, unchecked slaughter, screaming for answers from a loved one who had none to give. She eased off, then took a step back. She didn't need to touch this boy to keep him obedient. He wasn't the sort to rebel.

'Don't move,' she said. 'Don't turn around. Just keep talking.'

'Yes, yes, of course.' Elmal nodded. Lena's eyes had adjusted to the darkness enough to see that he was shaking. 'But please, don't tell anyone I talked to you. Jagusia, when she gets angry, it gets-'

'I'm not going to tell anyone I was pushing painted boys around in an alley. Now tell me what you know about Brodbeck and Holy Saimon.'

'Jagusia goes to the temple every holy day, and some others in between. She's a real believer. She has these books, ones that the council won't let into the city, all about what it means to worship Mother Sky and why it matters. She's always talking about how the Mother smiles on those who find their own way, how the new faith has space in it for the likes of us.'

'She talked about this with Holy Saimon?'

'A little, maybe. I don't think she's comfortable around priests. We always go to the services, always sit near the front row, and always leave the moment it's done. It's not to avoid the collection plate, I've seen her hand over more for one service than she pays some of her people in a month, but she doesn't wait around to socialise like the rest.'

'So her and Holy Saimon never talked?'

'Not that I saw. Not normally.'

'Not normally?'

He hesitated and turned his head uncertainly, on the verge of looking over his shoulder.

'Do I know you?' he asked, his voice tight as a bowstring. 'There's something familiar about your voice.'

'Maybe, maybe not.' She prodded his cheek with the cudgel, turning his face towards the wall.

'But you're one of us, aren't you?'

'What do you think?'

'I think if you were a constable you would have arrested me.'

'Well then.'

She let the implication hang there unspoken, the potential for violence that was a constant threat in this young man's world. A huge part of her wanted to tell him that she was different, that she wouldn't hurt anyone who didn't deserve it, had only ever done that out of ignorance and she wasn't that person any more. But she needed him afraid, so let the weight of violence and deception settle on her and ignored the queasy feeling it brought.

'Well then…' He took a deep breath. 'It happened at the Convocation, a couple of weeks back. Most of the bosses were in the back room already, including Jagusia. We were sitting in the tap room with the rest of their entourages. Big Haust had just arrived, so they were about to close the doors and start the meeting, which meant the bar was about to open for the rest of us.

'Then Holy Beatrice Saimon strides in, with a look of fury on her face. No one knew what to do. We're used to lowlifes trying to gatecrash Convocation, claiming they've got a golden opportunity for the bosses. They get a beating, and they get thrown out, and that's that. But a priest, and not just any priest, but the voice of Mother Sky in Unteholz… I mean, do you know how many of the real people follow the Mother?'

Real people. Lena had heard that phrase before, a way for criminals to distinguish themselves from the law-abiding masses. Convocation was something new, but she could work that out later. Right now, she stood tensed and expectant, eager to hear more.

'Keep going,' she said.

'There's this silence as we all look at each other. We're not on anyone's territory, so none of us can claim to be in charge, and the bosses are all in back. No one knows what to do as Holy Saimon just strides through the middle of us, past Big Haust, into Convocation, and the doors slam shut behind her. It was like a prince had strode into temple and started pissing on the floor. What do you do with that?

'We're all staring at each other, because we know we've screwed up by letting her in and we don't know who's going to take the blame. Then suddenly there's shouting. Jagusia and Saimon, tearing into each other. I couldn't make out what they were saying, but they were really mad.

'This goes on and on. Big Haust's still standing out there with us, looking real uncomfortable. Then suddenly it goes silent. The door opens and Holy Saimon strides back out, red-faced, her eyes all puffy, and she storms away.'

'So what was it all about?'

Elmal shrugged.

'Thundered if I know. The only ones who heard it were the other bosses, and they don't talk to the likes of me. It's bad form to make eyes at another boss's plaything.'

'Jagusia didn't tell you?'

'Hells no! One look at her face when she came out, and I knew better than to ask. First time they've cancelled Convocation in five years, and we all pretend it never happened.'

Lena stood staring at the back of Elmal's head, trying to make sense of what she had heard. She had come here to find out how Holy Saimon wound up full of silver dream. Instead, she'd heard about some secret gang meeting and a stand-up row between a priest and the most dangerous woman in Unteholz. Where did any of that come from? And what did it mean?

'You… you want more?' Elmal asked.

'Have you got more?'

'No.'

'Then we're done. You stay here for a slow count of three hundred. If I see you leave before I'm clear, you're going to regret it, understand?'

'Y-yes.'

'Good.'

Lena strode out of the alley and up the street. She didn't even glance back to see if Elmal emerged. She didn't need to. Long experience had taught her which sorts of people would obey and which sorts would break ranks. This one had all the courage of a sheep turd.

She walked all the way back to the alley by the tavern, where Deppel was waiting.

'You get what you wanted?' he asked.

'I got something. Do you know what Convocation is?'

'Oh yeah. It's this big meeting what's got all the bosses of the gangs in town. They have dinner and make deals and… and… and… And that's all I know, really.'

Just what Lena had expected, but it raised another question.

'How widely known is it? If a beggar like you knows, it can't be much of a secret.'

'Most of the real people know about it, and some of us living around them. But you ain't allowed to tell outsiders.' He hesitated, and when he spoke again, his voice was high with tension. 'You ain't gonna tell them I told you?'

Lena laughed and shook her head.

'No, Deppel, I'm not. And it sounds like the secret's blown, anyway. The question is, who told Holy Saimon about it, and why would she go there?'

'Holy Saimon went to Convocation? Thundering hells, why?'

'Maybe she wasn't as honest as she made out. Or maybe she was really ambitious in her quest to save souls.'

Or maybe there was something else important missing, another piece of the picture than Lena could sense but not quite grasp, its jagged edge protruding into the story she knew.

Maybe it would be clearer once she had a good night's sleep.

'Alright, Deppel, I'm off.' She opened a purse, fished out a shilling, and pressed it into his hand. He'd earned this small part of her gift from Councillor Maier. 'Come find me tomorrow and I'll see what other use I can put you to.'

'Thank you, Headsman.'

She was just about to step out of the alley when a thought crossed her mind. She turned back to where Deppel stood, a grey shape in the darkness.

'Where do you live, Deppel?' she asked.

'Oh, you know, here and there.'

She silently cursed herself for not asking sooner. Of course the boy didn't have family or a place to call his own. He'd been out by himself, begging for charity on the temple steps.

She remembered when her Jekob had been this age. She hadn't seen much of him, too busy fighting wars and paying their keep, but she had enjoyed the moments they had. If she hadn't known that he was safe, warm, and sheltered, she never could have lived with herself. And now, if she left Deppel out on the street, she'd be thinking thoughts like that all night.

'I've a spare blanket if you want it,' she said. 'And a space by the hearth. Just for tonight, you understand?'

'Really?'

'Don't dawdle, I need sleep.'

She strode out of the alley and he rushed after her, chattering excitedly as he went. She groaned inwardly, but let him keep talking.

This was the best thing to do. Not for his sake, of course, but for hers. She needed that good night's sleep.

Chapter Fourteen

Ready for War

It was a dreary morning, clouds dark and heavy as iron ore filling the sky. Dead weather, they called it in Unteholz, the sort of weather where you were just waiting for it to fall.

Lena trudged up the steps to the top of the city walls, Deppel scurrying along behind her. She had put on extra layers beneath her heavy tunic, enough wool to keep her warm without a cloak getting in the way of her sword arm. In spite of her efforts, she was going to need something more soon, not for her, but to stop Deppel's distracting shivers.

A few men and women were walking the walls, a hastily raised militia in moth-eaten tabards dug out of the depths of the citadel. Some of them had bows and one even had a gun, an arquebus with a brass dragon's head around the mouth, a decoration that added weight in the worst place. They looked at Lena as she emerged on the top of the walls, then returned to watching the army beyond.

The Third Host of the Righteous were a more impressive bunch, but Lena didn't envy them. They had already started digging in around the city, with their right flank fixed against the River Seltwasser. It would be a gruelling task in the stony ground, and if this Lord Everhart had any sense, then the infantry would be working with the sappers, to get the ditches dug and the parapets built before Unteholz's troops could sally out to spike the siege guns. There would be a lot of miserable soldiers down there, palms blistered from wielding shovels and chopping down trees.

Lena ran a finger over her own palm, felt the lingering trace of old callouses, and listened to the distant sound of filthy, off-key singing. She smiled. The life hadn't been all bad, even when it was a heap of shit.

The big siege guns were lined up close to the road, so that they could batter the East Gate. It wasn't a bad approach, but she would have dragged them around to the Manden Gate instead, where the terrain was worse but the walls lower and the gates weaker. Good to know that Unteholz wasn't facing a military genius, just a general with an overwhelming advantage in soldiers and resources.

She tapped one of the militia on the shoulder.

'They said that Captain Baumer was up here.'

'Over there.'

The volunteer soldier pointed to one of the town's own artillery emplacements, where a pair of cannons sat behind the battlements of a broad tower. Baumer stood with some of his constables, looking at the same depressing view as her.

He nodded in greeting as Lena approached. His fingers rose to make the sign of the eye, but it was a casual move, unlike the nervous tension with which his constables made the gesture.

'Headsman,' he said. 'Come to fight?'

'I don't do wars. Not anymore.'

'Don't tell me you brought him instead.' Baumer pointed at Deppel.

'I don't do wars neither,' Deppel said. 'I'm a lover, not a fighter.'

'You're an eater, more like.'

Baumer laughed, and his constables with him. Deppel laughed too, the high, nervous laughter of the habitual victim. Lena tensed defensively.

'I've seen the way you look at Maier's fruit bowl,' she said, eyes narrowing as she looked at Baumer. 'You'd sell your right arse cheek for a basket of peaches.'

'Your arse, maybe, if it's not too leathery from years in the saddle.'

'It's still soft as a peach, but that's one fruit you won't be touching.'

'Shame.' Baumer laughed again. 'But you didn't come up here just to disappoint me.'

'I want to talk about Saimon.'

Baumer frowned and folded his armoured arms across his chest. Several of his constables shot dark looks at Lena while others looked away.

'I don't have time for this,' Baumer said. 'We're under attack, remember?'

'Not yet we aren't.'

'Got to ready the defences.'

'You've got your little minions. Get them to run your errands for a bit.'

She waved a hand at the constables. One of them glared and took a step forward.

'Who you calling a little minion?' the constable said, hand reaching purposefully for her sword.

'Stop, Gretta,' Baumer said.

The constable stood stock still, eyes on Lena, hand on her sword hilt. Lena slid one foot back, putting herself side on to the constable, and reached for her own cudgel.

'I said stop.' Baumer glared at them both. 'Gretta, you take this lot to the iron mongers in town. Start requisitioning cauldrons we can use to boil oil and heat sand. Anyone kicks up a fuss, tell them to send the bill to Councillor Maier.'

'Whatever you say, Sor.' Gretta let go of her sword, saluted, and strode away.

The other constables looked at Baumer. He gave a small nod, then they too saluted and followed Gretta towards the stairs.

'Now can we talk?' Lena asked.

She leaned back against the battlements and Deppel joined

her, crossing one leg across the other just like she did.

'Do we have to?' Baumer drummed his fingers against his arm, creating a quiet, ringing rhythm of steel on steel. 'I was looking forward to thinking about war, instead of chasing down cutpurses and con artists.'

'It's Maier's orders. Unless we want this city to burn, I need to find the real Saimon murderer.'

'Real murderer.' Baumer snorted. 'We caught her practically red handed.'

'But not actually red handed. No blood on her.'

'The story's never perfect. That doesn't mean it's not true.'

'This time it does.'

'I don't believe that.'

He placed his hands on the battlements and stared down the mountainside, across the army, the forests, the terraced fields.

'Thundering hells, Soren,' Lena snapped. 'I knew you could be stubborn, but I didn't take you for stupid. So you made a mistake. It happens. Now either we fix it, or we face that whole horde.'

She pointed down into the armed encampment lying just beyond arrow range. Past the tents and the supply wagons, the war beasts were corralled. Manticores, gryphons, wyverns, and worst of all, the curled, slumbering dragons, the smallest of them four times the size of any other beast, bodies steaming in the crisp morning air.

'Have you ever fought monsters?' she asked. 'Because it's a savage business, and without trained beasts of our own it'll be a costly one.'

'So we ignore the truth?'

'It's not the truth.' She grabbed his arm and forced him to face her. 'It's a mess we've got to clean up.'

'Or a mess we're making now.' He leaned in closer. 'Did you think of that?'

'I get it. It hurts to admit when you're wrong. Hurts worse when we killed someone for it. But if I can face that then so can you.'

He took deep, snorting breaths, like a wild beast caught on the end of a chain, unable to break free but unwilling to surrender to its fate. If not for his armour, she could have seen the rise and fall of his chest.

'You don't have to believe me,' Lena said. 'But you take orders from Maier, and she wants us to find another murderer.'

'Fine,' he said through gritted teeth. 'What do you want from me?'

Lena stepped back and steadied herself against a crenellation, taking a moment to gather her thoughts. His resistance, so complete and so unexpected, had thrown her. She'd thought that he would at least be on her side, given everything that was at stake.

'I wanted to ask about the dagger,' she said. 'The one you found at the Saimons' home.'

'The one he was killed with.'

'Seems that way, yes.'

'Oh, so now it's not just the wife I'm wrong on. He was killed with some other Illora dagger, and that one just happened to be in the house. Gods' eyes, Lena, are you trying to make me look stupid?'

'So you did recognise it as an Illora.'

'Yes.' Now it was Baumer's turn to take a step back. He stood with one hand resting on the battlements, looking out across the siege camp. 'What about it?'

'Why didn't you tell Maier?'

'Why didn't you?'

She wanted to say that it hadn't been relevant, but that looked like a poor excuse now. If she was going to tear down Baumer's work, she at least owed him honesty.

'Spite,' she said. 'I liked knowing something Maier didn't.'

Baumer laughed and shook his head.

'Flaming hells, Lena. You'd be a terrible constable.'

'Suits me. But you haven't answered my question.'

He shrugged and turned to her with a disarming smile.

'It didn't seem relevant. We'd got the knife, didn't need to talk about what sort it was.'

'Turns out it might be relevant after all.'

'Oh?' Baumer straightened. 'Why's that?'

'Because I saw another one, in the hands of a priest at the cathedral.'

'At the cathedral?'

'That's what I said.'

He shrugged.

'Doesn't seem like it's got much to do with this. The Merchant Monarchs have given those things out to half the priests and defenders of the faith in the Salt Cities.'

'Defenders of the faith?'

'Soldiers who've done something they can label as righteous. Save a cathedral, keep a prince in power, that sort of work.'

Lena frowned. She had met a few priests who had come north out of the Salt Cities, as well as mercenaries who had come to the Principalities after the Marsh Wars ended. They had left the impression that Illora daggers were a rare and precious symbol of priesthood. But then, how often had they discussed this? Probably just once, a passing conversation she could easily have misunderstood.

She had relied on that half-formed impression in judging Beatrice Saimon, a failing she cursed herself for now. Anyone could plant a bloody knife in the home of a victim, but it had been a priest's knife, a rare knife, and so she had believed it belonged there. Now she knew that there were two in her city, hundreds of miles from the Salt, and that the killing blade might not even have been a priest's.

'Still, it could mean something,' she said, trying to convince herself. 'That Fiete Saimon was killed with one of those knives.'

'Probably means the owner sold it. Tell me you've never pawned your weapons to stay fed through a winter.'

'Never,' Lena said.

There were some places she would never go; however desperate she had been in the early days. She had her pride, and she knew that without a weapon she might not find work in the spring. She had clung to her first sword like she had clung to her child when he came kicking and screaming out of her. She clung to her weapons still, though she had angrily proclaimed that she would never use them again. They had started out as tools, and in time they had become a part of her, as hard to cast away as her own hand. But she knew others who had taken a different path, and she understood. When all you had against the fury of the wind was a threadbare cloak and all you had to eat was a handful of herbs dug out of the snow, then you might give up anything to stay alive. People who thought like that never got to be drachenritters. They were too soft for a life of claws and flames, not devoted enough to bond with a beast. But they were less likely to be found frozen in a ditch, a sad and wilting flower emerging from the snow with the first bluebells.

Lena brought herself back into the moment. Thoughts like that were a distraction. Normally she would wash them away with a drink, but right now she needed to focus. Beatrice Saimon was counting on her.

'Something bothering you?' Baumer asked.

Lena shook her head.

'I was just hoping I could make something of this dagger.'

'There's nothing to be made. Wife kills husband. Old story.'

'No.' Lena shook her head. 'Not this time.'

'Far as I'm concerned, that's a heap of turds, but if you want to get a beer and talk about it, you know where I'll be.'

'Up here, posing in your shiny armour?'

'That's right.' Baumer grinned and thrust his chest out, standing like an icon of a warrior saint. 'Champion of the city.'

Lena laughed. 'It's a good look on you. The sort of thing statues are made of.'

'Statues are for Sky priests and other idolators. I'm going to be an oil painting, one of those grand ones like they paint in

Vacaros, standing over my fallen enemies with the sun behind me like it's shining out of my arse.'

'Would that be a peachy arse or a leathery one?'

They laughed again, and for a moment, Lena almost forgot what a mess she was living through.

Then footsteps came rushing up the steps. Gretta appeared in her constable's uniform and stopped sharply at attention between the two of them.

'Message for you, Headsman,' she said. 'Councillor Maier wants to see you right away.'

Lena groaned and pressed her fingers to her temples.

'Of course she does.'

The scratching of quills and clatter of counting stones once again filled Maier's office. She had even more clerks now, including ones Lena recognised from the entourages of other councillors. It was a commander's privilege to requisition forces for war, and Renate Maier's main weapons had always been the coin chest and the ledger, not the sharp edge of a blade.

As Lena walked in, most of the clerks glanced her way, though three kept their gazes firmly on their parchment: her furtive informant from the other day and the two clerks whose shoulders Maier herself was peering over, a quill in her hand and her brow furrowed.

'This can't be right,' Maier said. 'The foundries have been running without break since the army arrived. We must have more shot.'

'Mistress Maechveld says that she needs Salt City ducats to pay the ore suppliers.'

'Mistress Maechveld has to bear her part of the cost for saving the city. Get down there and tell her the council expects better.'

'Yes, Councillor.' The clerk jumped to his feet and hurried out.

Lena strolled into the room and looked around. Half the storage chests were open, many of them empty. She could accuse Renate Maier of many things - greed, pomposity, shortsightedness - but she was no hypocrite. If she asked others to bear the burden of defence, then she would bear her part, financially as well as administratively.

'How's the war going?' Lena asked.

'Not yet begun,' Maier said, scribbling on a scrap of parchment. 'And I'm going to keep it that way.'

She dropped her quill into an ink pot and turned to face Lena. Even in a time of crisis, she was calmly composed and immaculately dressed, with a jewelled belt around her velvet doublet. If she had brought this crisis down on them, then she wasn't showing it. Lena admired the woman's poise if not her practicality. Maybe a few months under siege would finish straightening out her priorities.

'Violence here would be wasteful,' Maier said. 'This Lord Everhart is smart enough to command an army, and that makes him smart enough not to start a needless fight.'

'You haven't met many generals, have you?' Lena asked.

'I don't see high commanders spending much time with you.'

Lena shrugged and pushed aside the first answer, the one that would have put Maier in her place, and in the same moment given away the part of herself she held close, the part she had come to Unteholz to hide.

'You spend time in an army, you learn how generals think,' she said. 'Plenty of them will fight to prove they can.'

'Then let's hope this Everhart isn't one of those. I've spoken to his herald, and we're going out to negotiate tomorrow.'

That 'we' made Lena stiffen. She folded her arms across her chest, a barrier against whatever demands were coming her way.

'You taking the whole council?' she asked.

'No,' Maier said. 'Just a couple of guards and you.'

There it was, the thing Lena had seen sliding towards her through the conversation, a serpent she must slay before it got her killed.

'No.' She shook her head firmly. 'I'm not going.'

'Yes, you are. I need you to tell them about your investigation, to prove that we're acting on their request.'

'Their demand, you mean.'

'I do, but I won't be phrasing it that way. This moment needs tact and diplomacy.'

'Good reason not to take me.' Lena pointed at one of the fading bruises on her face. 'This is what happens when I try to be tactful.'

'No excuses, Sturm. You're coming.'

'No.' Lena hadn't meant to raise her voice, but she heard the anger in it and saw half the clerks looking up at her in shock. One of them touched a finger to his eye.

She didn't mind doing the city's dirty work, killing off its criminals so that honest citizens could live in peace. She could stand being scorned as badly as the dregs she punished. But she accepted those things because they let her put her old life behind her, a life symbolised by that camp beyond the walls. There was a limit to what she would bear for Unteholz, and Maier had reached it.

'It's not a request,' Maier said, her own voice hard but level. 'You work for the council; you will do as you are told.'

'I'm clearing up the mess you made when you set my blade to the wrong neck. You can deal with this business yourself.'

'You're part of this business.' Maier took a step forward. They were inches apart, the councillor glaring up at Lena. 'You will come along whether you like it or not.'

'And what will you do if I don't? Get me to cut my own head off for treason?'

'No. I will get Baumer to deal with you.'

Lena's fingers dug into her own arm as she fought to keep her temper in check. Of all the people she'd met in this city, she could name perhaps a dozen she wouldn't have fought rather than back down on this. Baumer was one of them. Did Maier know her this well, or had she just got lucky throwing her weight around? It hardly mattered, except in deciding how angry she was.

'If he can find me, maybe I'll come,' she growled.

'Good.' Maier picked up her quill and waved dismissively at Lena. 'Go continue your investigation, Headsman. I'll see you tomorrow.'

Still seething, Lena stormed out of the room.

Chapter Fifteen

The Other Side of the Story

The door of the Saimon house opened, and Jonatan Ottmor looked out. He still wore a black mourning band and his brass steward's chain over his yellow doublet. The mortal world might be done with his master and mistress, but he wasn't.

'Come in, quick,' he said, ushering Lena and Deppel inside. He glanced around the courtyard and the street beyond before he shut the door behind them. 'Does Captain Baumer know you're here?'

'That's not a problem anymore,' Lena said. 'I'm allowed to investigate now that it's about politics, not just right and wrong.'

Ottmor's brow furrowed, and he stroked his neatly kept beard.

'That is… Well, it's something,' he said. 'Do you want to ask more questions?'

'I want to look around. Did your mistress have a private room, somewhere Councillor Saimon didn't go?'

Ottmor's frown deepened.

'What are you saying?'

'I'm saying that everyone has secrets, but you can't embarrass the dead.'

Ottmor was a good servant. The only sign of his anger was a flaring of his nostrils.

'I remind you, Headsman, that this is a house in mourning.'

'I haven't forgotten, but I'm here to pay my respects in truth, not pretty words.'

His steps heavy with reluctance, he turned away from her and started walking up the staircase at the back of the room.

'This way,' he said.

The stairs were flanked by a bannister of intricately carved pine, on which the elaborate imitation of creepers wound around balusters shaped like ancient Laugerin pillars. Twin tapestries hung from the wall, one an image of well-presented travellers on the pilgrim trails, the other a merchant caravan winding its way out of the mountains. Piety and commerce, the pillars around which the lives of the Saimons had wound.

It wasn't all that different from the way she had once lived. Last she'd heard, Jahann was still trading out of the house she'd had built for them, though she assumed that he had taken her trophies down. It had always been good to come back there at the end of a long campaign, to the gryphon's head carved above the doorway, her seat by the fire, and her place at the table. It was never quite the same house as she remembered, from one return to the next. The creak of the stairs changed each winter, the trees grew in the grounds and the mattress gained new lumps. Then there was Jekob, achingly different every time, growing so fast in her absence that she could almost have cried for what she missed. Each spring when she rode away, she did so happily, proud to earn a keep and protect the city she called home, eager to get back into action after months of idleness turned to twitches of frustration and a shortening temper. It was when she came home, when she wrapped herself in the absence she had created, that she felt the loss.

No more of that now. A stone house in a mountainside would never change, and it wouldn't expect her to become someone she wasn't.

At the top of the stairs was a corridor running down the centre of the house. Ottmor stopped at the first door on the right. It opened smoothly on well-oiled hinges.

Beyond lay the Saimons' bedchamber. The far wall held a

window of leaded glass looking out onto the courtyard below. The shutters outside had been hooked back to let the light in. Much of the room was taken up with a four poster bed hung around with yellow drapes and covered in blankets of the same colour. To each side was a small stand for a candle and a large armchair.

'Wow,' Deppel said. 'Even the sheets is in their colours.' He ran a grubby hand over the blankets, to Ottmor's clear distaste. 'That's so soft.'

'Through there.' Ottmor pointed to one of two doors on their left, opposite the bed. This time he didn't lead the way, but stood back to let Lena approach. Just watching her try the handle seemed to set him on edge and he stood, half out in the corridor, back stiff and chin raised.

Through this second doorway was another, smaller room, again lit by sunlight falling through glass. There were chests against the walls and above them robes hanging from hooks. In a display case near the window, a necklace glittered. A jewellery box sat on a small shelf beneath it.

'They never entered each other's robing rooms,' Ottmor said. 'Master Saimon said that it was important to each have a place of their own, not to keep secrets, but to keep from losing themselves.'

Lena walked in and took a deep breath. It smelled of lavender and freshly cleaned cloth. She ran a hand down the grandest of the hanging robes, felt the smoothness of silk, the bumps of embroidered beadwork, a slight ridge where torn cloth had been artfully repaired. Next to it was another, still in Sky priest yellow, but more mundane. The heavy cloth was fading on the shoulders and ragged at the hem, a long-worn and much-loved relic of Holy Saimon's years of service. A single dried rose, its petals pale and fragile, was pinned to the chest with a simple silver broach.

Lena had mementos like these. The armour hanging from the wall of her bed chamber. Another suit, one she didn't care to remember but couldn't let go, hidden away where no one could see it. The outer layers of her past selves, shed like the skin of a growing wyvern, once a part of her life and now a part of her past, cast off to let her become Lena Sturm.

And here she was, about to rifle through another woman's memories, to violate a safe space. She mourned the memory of the innocent woman she had killed, staring at her wide-eyed a moment before the sword fell, then steeled herself to press on.

'Get in here, Deppel.'

When she looked around, he was already there, staring at the necklace in the display case, his fingers reaching for the jewellery box.

'Don't even think about it,' she growled. 'We're here to uphold the law, not break it.'

'I weren't going to!' Deppel protested. 'Just wanna see.'

He cracked open the lid and peered inside.

'Imagine,' he whispered, 'having so much money you can spend it on these. Bet they ate 'til their bellies ached every night.'

'You stop doing that, when you know that food will always come.' She peered over Deppel's shoulder. 'Anything in there but jewellery?'

Deppel rummaged through the bracelets, necklaces, and rings, then shook his head.

'What we looking for?' he asked.

'Bottles or jars. Holy Saimon died full of silver dream. I need to know if she was already enjoying it, or if someone forced it on her.'

They worked their way through the small but crowded room, opening one chest after another, dragging Holy Saimon's life into the light one garment at a time. Cloaks and cassocks, drawers and jerkins, all were pulled out, shaken out, and abandoned in a growing heap.

After a while, Lena looked up to see Ottmor staring sadly in, steadying himself against the bedpost as two strangers tore down the curtain protecting the last of his mistress's privacy. A small black cat leaned against his leg, watching the commotion. Lena smiled and held out a hand, but the cat hissed and rushed away.

'Is she yours?' Lena asked.

'Not my place to own pets,' Ottmor replied. 'I found her for Councillor Saimon. Sometimes, Holy Saimon was very busy with work, especially around high festivals and the deeps of winter. It was good for the master to have company.'

The sad familiarity of the story gave Lena pause. Was this why she felt so committed to Beatrice Saimon, because she had seen a fellow soul in her, someone struggling to be part of a family while staying true to herself? Or was it just that this story happened all the time, couples limping brokenly along, unwilling to put their partnership out of its misery? Perhaps a victim like this had been as likely as one with brown eyes, and Lena was just looking for excuses to explain why she cared.

'Is this where they found the dagger?' she asked, gesturing at the robing room and its growing heap of clothes.

'No, that was under the bed,' Ottmor said. 'On the mistress's side.'

Lena paused, a linen cap in her hand, a small heap of shoes beside her. She looked around at the chests that filled this room. If Holy Saimon had wanted to hide something, then there were a dozen places here better than putting it under the bed. Even if she had been in a rush, this was where she kept her secrets, the place to which instinct would surely have led her footsteps. Perhaps the person who set her up had been in a rush, or perhaps they hadn't known her well.

'Had she had the dagger for long?' she asked.

'I don't know,' Ottmor said. 'I'd never seen it before.'

A valuable dagger, so secret Saimon's steward didn't know about it, and the murderer had found it but not known to put it back in here? The very idea made Lena snort in derision. That weapon hadn't been found in this house. It had been brought here.

'Found something,' Deppel exclaimed. 'But it ain't silver dream.'

He held out an earthenware bottle, short and round, with a black crust around the cork. Its paper label was decorated with sigils, none of which meant anything to Lena, but the colour of the ink and the style of the lettering were familiar.

'Either all alchemists write the same, or this is Pawlitzki's work.'

Lena took the bottle and tugged at the stopper. It came out with the pop of a well-fitted seal, releasing a smell that mixed the sharp and the earthy. In among the other ingredients, she recognised the scent of silphium.

'You knew about this?' she asked, holding it up for Ottmor to see.

He took a step closer but couldn't bring himself through the doorway and into the robing room. The look of puzzlement on his face said all she needed to know.

'What is it?' Deppel asked, leaning in to take a sniff. 'Urgh, it smells like dung!'

Of course these two didn't know what they were looking at, but every woman Lena had ever campaigned with knew silphium and the stomach-churning range of ingredients that alchemists used to increase its potency. Never tasting it again was one advantage of getting older.

'You told me the other day that the Saimons were trying to have a child,' she said, putting the stopper back in the bottle. 'So why was she taking a potion to prevent one?'

'It can't be,' Ottmor said.

'It is.'

'It must be Bessa's. She's the only servant allowed in there.' Ottmor strode across the bedroom and bellowed into the hallway. 'Bessa!'

Footsteps rushed up the stairs. Lena got up, bottle in hand, and stepped out over the heap of clothes.

The serving woman they had seen on their last visit appeared in the hallway.

'What is it, Jonatan?' she asked.

'Is this yours?' Ottmor pointed at the bottle in Lena's hands.

'No.'

'Don't lie to me.' His expression was fierce, eyes bulging.

'I'm not!'

'Then how have we-'

'I have my own.' She glared at him. 'You want me to show you? Because right now, that's the only reason you're coming near my bed.'

Deppel nudged Lena. When she looked down, he waggled his eyebrows and grinned.

She stifled a laugh.

'We should go,' she said. 'But I have another question first.'

Ottmor and Bessa, both red-faced, turned to look at her.

'Of course, Headsman,' Bessa said sweetly. 'Anything I can do to help you.'

Ottmor shuffled his feet and looked down at the floor.

'Your master was having secret meetings every week with Councillor Maier. Do you know anything about them?'

There was an awkward silence, Ottmor still looking at the floorboards, Bessa looking sidelong at him.

'Go on, Jonatan,' she said. 'The mistress's secrets are coming out, why shouldn't the master's?'

Ottmor sighed.

'Secrets won't do them much good now anyway,' he said. 'The master and Councillor Maier were working on a business deal. They bought unicorn parts off the sgeir and stockpiled them, while arguing in council about how unicorns weren't coming to the caves any more. There are only two licences to trade in unicorn horn out of Unteholz, and with a big public shortage, no one wanted to buy them. They were going to get those licences cheap, then sell their stockpile at a high price before anyone realised that the shortage was over.'

'It took weekly meetings to do that?'

'They'd done other deals before. Things where being on opposite sides could profit them both.'

'And for that to work, people had to be convinced that they really were opponents.'

'Exactly.'

Lena smiled, masking her disappointment. She had liked having a reason to blame Maier for the killing, but motive had been all she had. If the arguments between the two councillors had been for show, then that motive vanished like dew in the dawn. She would have to find other ways to punish Maier for meddling in her life.

Meanwhile, she had other suspects to pursue.

The cathedral gong rang out across Saint Lukara's square. Its rich boom filled the air, almost drowning out the jabber of the faithful as they hurried to prayer.

Lena had never seen such a crowd heading for temple. Men, women, and children, rich and poor, old and young, clutching holy disks and prayer beads. She would have bet her sword hand that half of them hadn't been to a service all year, but things changed when an army arrived. Nothing fired people's faith like the fear of death.

The followers of Mother Sky were out in force as well. Around the edges of the square, yellow-robed priests proclaimed the arrival of a reforming storm, the virtue of a renewed and purified faith. They bellowed that the army showed the Mother's strength, but that she could also be the city's shield. Their exhortations drew some of the congregants away, triggering a bitter argument between green and yellow priests. But few people came to Saint Lukara's for its theology, and no other temple in the city could inspire certainty like the dragon-bone cathedral.

Unlike the rest of the crowd, Lena hadn't come to seek Father Earth's protection. She was here to watch people, and one person in particular.

Beside her, Deppel stopped walking, sat down in the dirt, and took off his shoe.

'What are you doing?' Lena asked.

'Something come loose,' Deppel said, carefully adjusting the inside of the shoe.

'Probably just a stone. Shake it out and let's get going.'

'Got it.' He gave a seam one last prod, then slid the shoe back on and got to his feet.

Together, they joined the throng making its way through the great doors, beneath the ribs of the long-dead beast whose hide, and bones formed the building, and into the cavernous interior.

Deppel made the sign of the circle as they entered, along with many of the others.

'I didn't see you as the god-fearing type,' Lena said.

'My grandma taught me to always make the signs,' Deppel said. 'Show respect to gods and the wealthy, she said, 'cause if you don't they might strike you down.'

'Smart lady.'

'She could be crazy sometimes too.' He looked wistfully around. 'I miss her a lot.'

More candles had been lit since the last time Lena was in the cathedral. They hung from wrought iron chandeliers, sat on small shelves, rose on pillars above the torrent of congregants seething towards the front of the building. Their glow was joined by the coloured light shining through the stained glass windows, illuminating thousands of people pressed against each other and against the altar rail.

On the dais beyond, Natalia Kunder stood before the huge lizard scale that formed the high altar. She was dressed in the full green robes of a bishop of Father Earth, with cloth of gold for its trim. Her long blond hair fell loose across her shoulders, fanning out like radiant beams of sunlight. In front of her, lesser clerics kept the crowd at bay or swung censers that filled the air with a sweet and heady smoke. Off to one side, a choir of priests sang the god's praises. Father Earth was a jealous god, and there was no place in his services for the saints. His sister, Mother Sky, had barely been allowed a sign on the altar before her own priesthood raised her up, and Saint Lukara's place of glory was rare. The old faith declared to the world that humans should know their place; divine inspiration could only come from the highest source.

The hubbub of the crowd rebounded upon itself; a cloud of noise that grew as more people came in. Lena found herself pressed from behind. She jabbed back with her elbow, drew a protest and a shove, then shot a glare over her shoulder that stilled the man behind her, even as others barged into him.

At last, the great doors slammed shut. Kunder raised her arms, and the crowd fell silent.

'Blessed citizens of Unteholz,' Kunder called out, her voice filling the chamber. 'Siblings in the one true faith. I welcome you to the house of the gods. May Father Earth grant your spirit strength and your body rest.'

'Praise be to him,' the crowd said in union, following the familiar liturgy. Even Lena, who had long ago chosen another path, felt the words form on her lips. She didn't belong here, and yet the aura of holiness lifted her up, the grandeur of the moment promising the acceptance she craved and the forgiveness that she knew she didn't deserve. If the people praying here knew who she really was, they would drive her out of the cathedral, or worse, and though she would fight back, because she always had to fight back, she would know that every blow was one she deserved.

'I call upon you today to consider the ways of justice,' Kunder said. 'Justice is not a simple thing, nor an easy one. When I was training for the priesthood, I spent many hours studying its nature, trying to comprehend what justice meant to me and to the world. It was not a thing I could hold in my hand, like a coin or a loaf of bread. It was not a song I could sing or a story I could tell. It was, like the great Father himself, a mystery, and like him it was a mystery I could not live without.'

As she spoke, the bishop strode back and forth on the dais,

hands outstretched as if pleading with the crowd. Her gaze ran across them, locking eyes with one congregant after another, promising each one that she was talking to them.

'Again today, I find myself contemplating the mystery of justice, in a world that seems brutal and unfair. For the past ten years, we have suffered through long winters and poor harvests, through the hunger that follows and the disease that rides its tail. Every one of us has suffered. Every one of us has wondered whether the world can be fair.'

There were murmurs of assent from the crowd, but Lena stood silent. This was leading to something, as any speech should. The priest was laying out a trail of breadcrumbs and the congregation was eating it up, but what lay at the end, a wholesome loaf or one riddled with maggots?

'Now an army comes to our doors, saying that they seek justice. Who among us wouldn't want that? Who wouldn't grab hold of the chance for a fairer world?

'But if this is justice, why must they bring it at a sword's point? Why must it be forced upon us, as if justice were not something we craved? Would you reject true justice?' She pointed at a face in the crowd, and then another. 'Would you? Or you? Or you?'

'No!' someone shouted, and others joined in, an angry cry from a thousand lips, echoing back from the bones of the beast in which they gathered while Bishop Kunder basked in the sound.

There it was, not the maggot in the bread but the trail it had left. Lena's stomach clenched as, all around her, faces once desperate with worry transformed into ugly snarls.

Kunder raised her hands and a hush spread across the congregation. Once silence had fallen, she spoke.

'I have warned you before and I will warn you again, this is the way of Mother Sky's people. They tell you that they love what is right: justice, peace, truth. But look more closely and you see that they hold a sham of that thing, a dark version twisted to their selfish ends.

'I remember a time when there was justice in this city. A time when all our bellies were full.

'Then the so-called priests of Mother Sky came, raising our father's sister and servant to his place of glory. They belittled our god and those who place faith in him. Their creed crept through our streets and into our hearts. Their twisted religion spread, catching the righteous with words that sounded good but hid evil.

'If you are here today, then you were strong enough to drive those words back, as I was. But many were not so strong, and now the lies of Mother Sky are inside them, as she seeks to usurp our father's place. Just as the harvests have failed, so has justice in this city. What could more clearly show that than her own priest, Saimon slayer of Saimon? A murderer at the head of a cult.'

Outraged cries echoed around the room, a rising storm of noise. Men and women shook their fists in the air.

Dread settled over Lena. Kunder was stirring up a mob, turning fear into anger, riling these people against their neighbours. Had the city always been like this, and she simply hadn't noticed, or was the bishop seizing this moment to tap into something terrible?

It barely mattered. It was enough to know that Kunder would do this. Anyone who would stir hate in this way was capable of killing her opponent, or of setting her people to the task.

Kunder raised her hands and again silence fell. Many in this crowd had seen her rhetoric before. They knew the ebb and flow, the call and response. They were hers to master.

'Justice calls upon us to deal with the menace in our midst. After all, how can we trust the Sky worshippers among us when their army is at our door? But justice is a mystery, and sometimes a hard one to follow. Now is not the time for rash action. It is the time for watchfulness, the time to wait and to observe. I ask all of you, in the name of justice, to watch for signs of treachery, to gather them and bring them together. For that knowledge is the armour that will protect the innocent against their lies, and only when the truth is revealed will we make our city safe for righteous souls.

'Now, let us pray…'

Lena stood with muscles tensed through the rest of the service, watching the passion in the faces of the congregation, observing the slender difference between righteous fervour and raging hate. Though no one looked at her, she felt them closing in.

At last the service ended. The doors opened, and the faithful poured out, sweeping Lena and Deppel along with them, into the fading light of evening.

'You think they're giving the same sermon at the Sundered Rose?' Deppel asked. 'Except about how Earth worshippers are traitors and can't be trusted?'

'Probably.' Lena rubbed at her temples. An ache was coming on that only drink would chase away.

'Except they can't both be right, can they? That don't make no sense.'

'Very astute.'

'So why do people listen to them both? Shouldn't they just find out who's right and listen to them? Why are they all getting up against each other?'

'Because people are idiots and thugs.'

Heads turned to see who had shouted. Their expressions reminded Lena why she usually kept her thoughts to herself. Nobody liked to hear the truth. They would rather close their ears than face the need to change.

And only an idiot let it get to her.

'Come on,' she said, quickening her pace to escape the milling flock. 'We need to eat.'

Lena took the pan off the grid-iron over the fire, carried it to the table, and pushed the eggs and mutton onto a pair of bread trenchers. The meat was a cheap cut, the bread baked with coarse flour, but the eggs were fresh, and just catching a whiff of food made her mouth water.

She pushed one of the trenchers across the table to Deppel, who sat on a stool she'd dragged out of the pantry, fiddling with the inside of his shoe.

'Something wrong with your feet?' she asked.

'No, nothing,' Deppel said and hastily put the shoe back on. He picked up a knife and spoon and looked eagerly at the food.

'Thank you, Headsman Sturm,' he said.

'Might as well call me Lena,' she said, settling into her own seat.

'Really?'

'Yes, really. Now eat.'

Whoever had smoked the meat had done a lousy job. It was starting to turn, not enough to keep her from eating, but enough to make her wish for something fresher. She realised that she had stopped buying spices, had tolerated bad food when she could easily have remedied it. As she poured them each a watery cup of small beer, she wondered if she should buy some pepper again, to give cooking a little more pleasure. It wasn't as though she couldn't afford it, and if she was going to have guests, then she couldn't keep feeding them like this.

'This is brilliant,' Deppel said, spraying fragments of egg. 'Ain't hardly no one's cooked me dinner that weren't the last smear of stew, not since grandma died.'

'It'll do,' Lena said. 'Hardly exciting.'

'Depends what else you've been eating. Some days, you can't afford nothing but a dry crust from what comes of begging.'

'Can't you save money from the other days?'

'Can't hold onto much when you ain't got nowhere to keep it.'

Lena watched the boy eat. Sometimes he seemed like an idiot, but then he would say something she herself had missed. And what fourteen-year-old wasn't an idiot some days?

From the side of the room, the borrowed portrait of Fiete Saimon watched them eat. Though fixed in paint, his wide smile seemed soft and natural, and blue eyes sparkled from that round, jovial face. Lena could imagine wanting to punch away his smugness, but she couldn't imagine anyone wanting to murder a man like that.

Of course, appearances could be deceptive. She'd taken the heads from plenty of villains who seemed sweet and innocent until their crimes were listed.

Had Fiete Saimon been part of his wife's religious conflict? Sometimes a murder wasn't about the victim but about what they stood for. A wealthy Sky worshipper sitting on the city council, his wife preaching to one half of the city's divided faith, that could have made him a target.

'He looks happy, don't he?' Deppel said. He had finished his eggs and meat and was tearing grease-soaked strips off the trencher, gobbling the gritty bread down with unfeigned enthusiasm. 'I suppose it's easy to be happy when you're rich.'

'You clearly haven't met many rich people.'

'Ain't a lot of them round where I live.'

'That's by Othagate?'

'Near enough, yeah.' Deppel paused to lick crumbs off his fingers. 'It ain't the sort of place honest people stay once they've got money of their own.'

Lena set her spoon down and leaned back in her seat. She had to ask the next question, even if it wasn't one she herself liked to answer. The boy had been following her around for days and she could only ignore what that meant for so long.

'What about your family?' she asked. 'Are they from Othagate?'

Deppel shrank into himself, arms drawing in, his gaze settling on the crumbs that remained of his meal.

'Ain't got family no more,' he mumbled.

'No one at all?'

He shook his head.

Lena closed her eyes and took a deep breath, stifling the wave of sadness that came rushing through her. She had known, really, but she hadn't wanted to look that truth in the eye.

Part of her wanted to rage against it, to scream at Mother Sky and Father Earth, demanding to know what sort of world left a boy like this orphaned. But she knew all too well what sort of world it was - one in which she severed heads for a living, and once upon a lifetime had done far worse. It was a world she helped to make, and whether Deppel's parents had been taken by war or accident or disease, she had played her part in filling the world with Deppels.

'I'm sorry,' she said, opening her eyes and looking over at him.

She could do that. She could mean what she said, despite what she had done. It was a pitiful recompense, but a hard one, and it left her feeling as though she had crossed some great divide.

'It is what it is,' he said in a small voice.

The boy needed a hug. He needed the warmth and the comfort of contact with another human. For a moment, Lena almost went to give it. But if she couldn't be that person to her own family then she really couldn't be them for somebody else's son. Instead she sat in silence, waiting to see if he would talk more, knowing that he should and dreading the possibility that he would. Offering him a meal and a place on the floor to sleep, that was something she could walk away from. But if he poured out his heart, then their lives would become linked. She would lose the isolation that kept her safe from the world, and kept others safe from her. If there was no one in her life, then there was no one she could hurt. Some people might consider that a punishment, but there was comfort in it too.

Deppel rubbed the back of his sleeve across the bottom of his nose, then looked up at her.

'What do we do now?' he asked. 'Question another suspect? Rough someone up for answers?'

'Now we sleep. I'll get some straw and blankets, make a proper bed for you down here. Come the morning, you can help me look for clues.'

'Thank you, um, Lena.'

'That's alright, Deppel.'

It was all going to be alright.

Chapter Sixteen

Into the Warrens

It was a bright, clear morning. A wind whipped up the valley and made the smoke swirl above the foundries, long black trails bleeding from the blunted tips of brick fingers, staining the clear blue sky. Around those chimneys came the clamour of industry: the roar of furnaces, the pounding of hammers, the shouted instructions and the rattle of wagon wheels.

'This ain't a good idea,' Deppel said, shouting to be heard above the racket.

'Then why did you tell me about this place?' Lena snapped.

'Because you asked.'

She wasn't going to protest; if she had help, then she wanted it cooperative. But Deppel had been moaning and predicting disaster the whole way from her home, and it was starting to wear at her nerves. She had to remind herself that he had reason to worry. Their last run-in with Jagusia Brodbeck's gang hadn't ended well, and now they were going into the belly of the beast.

The Warrens were like the Blade Market, a place many people had heard of, but most chose not to learn about. A district of criminals and outcasts living in the shadow of industry, amid the soot and smoke that kept honest citizens and idle lawmen away. It wasn't a healthy place for anyone to go uninvited, and Lena wasn't just anyone, but she had to know what had been happening between Brodbeck and the Saimons. For Beatrice to have confronted the criminal in front of her peers was a dangerous step. There had to be more going on than just pastoral care.

She had woken in the night picturing Beatrice Saimon's face, that slack-jawed expression of loss and bewilderment a moment before the sword fell. The woman had needed help and instead Lena had given her death. If she ever wanted to put this behind her, to wake with the gentle misery of a hangover instead of the stomach-tightening dread of that face, then it was going to be through the one gift she could still offer the dead priest: justice.

Deppel led her down a street between two foundries. Labourers were hurrying back and forth, some of them carrying tools, others barrows full of ore carved from the mountainside and brought down to feed the raging, famished maws of the foundry furnaces. Those furnaces had been blazing away night and day, leaving the air between the buildings hot and dry. Sweat ran down Lena's back and soot stuck to her cheeks.

A pair of labourers stood idle at the end of the street, a man and a woman, both muscular and wearing thick leather aprons, but neither looking as red-faced nor as weary as the rest. As Lena and Deppel approached, the woman nudged the man, who hurried away around the corner.

The woman nodded and Deppel returned the gesture. He was quivering with tension, sweat plastering his lank hair to the sides of his face. Lena would have felt guilty at dragging him into this, but it was going to be good for the boy. Looking into the darkness was the surest way to learn right from wrong.

'Didn't expect to see you, Deppel,' the woman said.

'I, er...' Deppel looked down at the ground.

'He's with me,' Lena said, laying one hand on her cudgel and the other on the dagger at her hip.

'I'm sure the boss will be happy to hear that,' the woman said, looking Lena up and down with a sneer. She lazily tapped the skin just under her eye.

'Are you going to stop us?' Lena asked, nodding down the street behind the foundry.

'Not at all. You go right on in, Headsman. There's plenty of folks will be excited to see you.'

They walked around the corner and along a street between the foundry and storehouses. The air was hot and heavy as anywhere among the foundries, but the noise lessened as they progressed into the gloom between the buildings. Stone closed in on either side.

'Seems people around here know you,' Lena said quietly.

Why was she surprised? Had she thought that Deppel's knowledge came at one remove, fragments dropped into his begging bowl with the coins? Only an idiot would think that way, yet she found herself disappointed.

Deppel had gone quiet.

'Say something,' she snapped.

'Ain't you meant to be meeting Councillor Maier?' Deppel asked. 'To go talk to the other side.'

'This is how we'll get them off our backs-by finding justice, not offering soft words.'

A storehouse doorway hung open ahead of them, a chasm carved from the mountainside. A big man with tattooed arms gestured inside.

'She's expecting you,' he growled.

There had always been a risk to this plan, but now that risk was made concrete, a doorway into darkness. The other side, they would be outnumbered and surrounded by solid stone walls. No easy escape routes if things went wrong. No authorities to rescue them. It was the perfect way to get murdered.

She should have feared that more than she did. The blade in the dark. The club to the back. The shot out of nowhere. For those who could imagine them coming, these were meant to be things of terror. She had fought alongside long-serving soldiers who still shook and sweated at the sight of enemies coming for them, who would have walked through this door with weapons drawn if they walked through it at all. But Lena welcomed the danger that darkness represented. Better women than her had passed through life's final dark portal, many of them at her hands, others at her command, and their loss wasn't even the greatest guilt she carried. She had no right to hide from death.

And she had to know why it had come for Holy Saimon.

Through that forbidding portal, Lena found herself standing in a cavernous warehouse that had been converted into a feasting hall. Trestle tables ran in three long rows down the room, with a scattering of men and women on the benches by them. There were tapestries on the walls, mismatched pieces probably stolen from a dozen different merchants. A wooden gallery overlooked the room and the minstrels upon it sang a lively madrigal full of innuendo. At the far end of the room was a dais on which stood a round table with high-backed armchairs gathered around the far side. At the table sat Konrad Elmal, his slender frame draped elegantly across his chair, white-painted face and pale lips contrasting with his blue silk robe. All the other chairs were empty, with one exception. The central seat held Jagusia Brodbeck.

Lena strode down the room, between the lines of benches, not looking to left or right. From the corners of her eyes she saw women and men make the sign of the eye even as they reached for their weapons. Most people despised and feared her, but these ones offered her their rage, and she appreciated the honesty in that. Out in the city streets, people preferred to pretend that she didn't exist, right up until the moment when they called on her to kill for them. The people here lived with the threat of her every day. They saw friends she had mutilated and remembered those she had killed. They offered her the fiery heat of hatred, not the bitter cold of exclusion.

She braced herself in case that hatred stirred them to action. Scattered as they were, she could deal with any three of them before they became a problem, but there were at least a dozen, and more lurking beside the minstrels, shortbows at the ready.

The minstrels finished their song and her final few footsteps echoed around a silent hall; their rhythm closely followed by the patter of Deppel's feet. At last, she stood looking up at Jagusia Brodbeck.

The crime lord was a woman of points and edges, from her pronounced cheekbones to the steel tips of her exquisitely tailored boots. Necklaces, bracelets, and broaches gleamed in the candlelight, but her fingers were bare of adornment, free for whatever dirty work was needed. Her eyes were narrowed but the pupils wide, and a small alchemical bottle lay next to a goblet of wine on the table. Beside them was a book of saints' lives, ornately decorated in gold and enamel. On the wall behind her, sheets of paper were pinned by blades to a board, lurid pamphlets bearing woodcuts of terrible crimes and warnings against the villains who perpetrated them. Brodbeck held a dagger up between two fingers, a slender thing with a beautifully engraved handle and a simple, practical blade. She let it fall. The tip thudded into the table and stood shuddering while she reached for the wine.

'Thank you for seeing me,' Lena said, more polite than if she was dealing with a merchant or councillor. Those people might have power, but they also recognised the authority of the law. Jagusia Brodbeck would take more persuasion.

'You've got a nerve coming here, Headsman.'

Brodbeck's fingers never strayed to her face. She had no need to ward off evil; she was its incarnation.

'I just want to talk.'

'And I just want to kick your pretty teeth in. Wonder who'll get their way.'

With an effort of will, Lena kept her hands from her weapons. Criminals made threats all the time. If she got riled by everyone, then she'd never make it out of here.

'Seems like you're a good influence on our Deppel, though.' Brodbeck grinned like a cat with a mouse in its sights. Her voice was a little slurred, but it had a hardness underneath the fuzzy edges. 'He must have finally gotten some bones, to come back here after running off on us.'

'So he is yours.' Out of the corner of her eye, Lena saw Deppel hang his head. She would deal with him later. 'It's good that someone looks after the beggars.'

'Oh, Deppel's more than just a beggar, he's one of the real people. We was training him up, wasn't we, Deppel? Teaching him to coax a lock, heft a bludgeon, cut a purse, sell a lie. At least that last bit stuck, eh?'

Deppel shifted from foot to foot, his gaze downcast.

Konrad Elmal sat staring at Lena. It seemed he finally recognised the voice that had accosted him in the dark.

'They're handy, kids,' Brodbeck continued. 'Can get into places others can't. It's not just those little bodies and the slender hands. It's the air of innocence.'

'I didn't want to,' Deppel mumbled.

'What's that, you ungrateful little turd?' Brodbeck leaned forwards in her seat, hands splayed across the table. 'We housed you, fed you, kept you warm in the winters, and now you say you didn't want it? Well piss on you, Deppel.'

Lena took a step forward, placing herself between Deppel and Brodbeck. He'd lied to her by omission, and they would be having words about that later, but she wasn't going to abandon him to this piece of filth.

'We're not here for the boy's sake,' Lena said. 'I was hoping you might talk to me about Beatrice Saimon.'

Brodbeck stared at her in confusion, then burst out laughing. She hammered her fist against the table, shaking with wild laughter. More than humour made her smile.

'God's eyes, but that's good,' Brodbeck said with a snort. 'Ain't you done enough for her?'

A door opened at the side of the hall and a pair of youths came in, both carrying serving trays. Lena recognised Tild, Deppel's former tormentor, but the boy was new to her, a smiling lad with a round face and blue eyes. As Tild headed out around the tables, offering ale to Brodbeck's men, the boy headed up the dais.

'Thank you, Kerl,' Brodbeck said as the boy filled her goblet. 'You got anything else there for me?'

'Yes, Ma.' The lad leaned in and kissed Brodbeck on the cheek.

'Good boy.'

Lena peered at the lad. She could see something of Brodbeck in him: the arc of his nose, the blond of his hair. But there was something else familiar.

'Get on with it,' Brodbeck snapped. 'Say your piece before we kick your hole in.'

'You should just kill her, Jagusia,' Elmal said, touching Brodbeck's hand. 'She doesn't belong here.'

'Don't worry, my flower,' Brodbeck replied, her gaze fixed on Lena. 'You'll get to see blood soon enough.'

Still Lena didn't flinch. This was the posturing of a woman built for violence, no more meaningful than a duellist's goading insults. If an animal threatened you, then it did it with its body, every bristling hair and tensed sinew a sign that the threat was real. This was just words with barbs.

'Holy Saimon came to confront you at Convocation,' Lena said. 'Why would she do that?'

'Priests,' Brodbeck said with a shrug. 'Always meddling.'

'This sounded like it was more personal.'

'She's my priest. It don't get much more personal than saving a soul.'

'I've been to temple. There's nothing personal about salvation.'

'Ain't you heard, there's a storm coming. The gods ain't distant no more, they've sent their saints to show us how to be saved. Holy Saimon saw to it I was cleansed.'

'Moon's shadow she did. Mother Sky frowns on theft and murder just as much as Father Earth does.'

'Salvation ain't easy.' Brodbeck tapped the book lying next to her dagger. 'Saint Taniso taught us that.'

'Saint Taniso turned the bandits out of Soteri. If Holy Saimon was trying to reform you with that story then it wasn't working.'

Brodbeck leaned back and took a long swallow from her wine.

'You're so sure what it weren't between me and her, why don't you tell me what it was?'

Lena's gaze went from Brodbeck to her son and back. What was it about the boy that looked so familiar?

'I'm not here to accuse you of anything,' she said. 'But you have to know that this could look bad. Beatrice embarrassed you in front of your peers, then her husband turned up dead. People might think you tried to get at her through him.'

'Shut your cursed face.' Brodbeck leapt to her feet, knocking over her goblet and spilling red wine across the book. Her chair hit the ground with a thud.

Around the hall, armed criminals rose to their feet.

'You don't know nothing about me,' Brodbeck growled. 'Nothing about who I am or what I done. You're just one more rich shit come to take what's good, 'cause you think people in the gutter only deserved dirt.'

Lena held out her hands, as if she was trying to calm a beast. She had missed something important. She didn't understand what it was, why the relaxed and disdainful crime boss had tipped on that moment into a red-faced pillar of rage, but things she didn't understand could still kill her.

'I'm sorry,' she said. 'I only wanted to talk.'

'We don't talk down here,' Brodbeck said. 'Ain't you heard? We're all thundering killers.'

The scraping of benches across the floor. Footsteps, swift and sudden. A creak as bows were drawn.

'I'm sorry for wasting your time,' Lena said. 'We should go.'

'I don't think so.' Brodbeck's voice was cold and hard as ice.

Lena whirled around, grabbed Deppel by the wrist, and strode towards the door.

A man stood in her way, holding out a matching rapier and sword-breaker dagger, the weapons of a wealthy duellist or a flashy imitator. Down here, he would be the latter.

Lena drew her cudgel and lashed out even before the man's sword was up. Her heavier weapon easily knocked his aside, then came down with a crack on his wrist. He gasped, and both blades clattered to the floor.

She kept moving, past that man and onto the next. No time to hesitate. Keep moving or die, just like she used to be.

She feinted high, swung low, and smashed the man's kneecap. Then she was leaping over him, still dragging Deppel.

An arrow thudded into the table. She ignored it. There was nothing she could do about the archers except hope that fear of hitting their friends threw off their aim. Assuming they even were friends.

A woman with Dunvari facial tattoos blocked her way, an axe in each hand. She swung one in slow, hypnotic loops, while the other drew slowly back, a scorpion's tail waiting to strike.

No time to observe or calculate. Lena let go of Deppel and lunged. Her cudgel caught the raised axe as it came down, knocking the blow safely aside. The other axe came up, the flat of its head thudding against her ribs on the back swing, and she clamped her arm down, pinning the weapon to her side. The woman brought her head forward, but Lena was quicker, and her fist hit the tattooed face. The woman staggered. Lena shot out a leg, caught the woman's ankle, and swept her feet out from under her.

'Quick!' Lena snapped.

She ran for the door, ignoring the throbbing in her side where the axe had hit. Deppel rushed after, panting with exertion and panic. Another arrow hissed past her head.

They dashed out into the shadowy street. A handful of thugs were idling by the door. She raced past while they stood looking confused.

She ran up the street, swinging the cudgel. She was too old for this shit, could feel the strain in her legs already, hear the rasping of her own desperate breath. But she kept running, and Deppel with her.

'After them!' Brodbeck's voice bellowed.

There were more footsteps, the sounds of a criminal posse in pursuit.

They rounded a corner and almost ran straight into the sentries they had met on the way in. Lena slammed into the woman, shoulder first, knocking her back into the man. The two of them fell, cursing and flailing.

Lena and Deppel kept running, the noise of the foundries smothering the sounds of pursuit. Though she couldn't hear them over the clang and roar, Lena knew that Brodbeck's people were still there. She looked around for a twist in the route or some hidden nook that she and Deppel could duck into and lose them, but there was nothing that would do. Entering a foundry would just lead to dead ends and angry labourers. The only way was to keep running.

They burst out into a plaza. Lena grinned. There were half a dozen ways out of here. Take one quick, get out of sight, and their pursuers would have to split up or lose them.

She ran for the nearest exit, but a wagon rolled into the way. She swore, spun around, and headed for the next one, Deppel close behind. This time the way was filled with crates waiting to be loaded onto the same cursed wagon. Her heart raced and sweat crawled down her sides as she looked to see where their best option lay.

It was too late. Brodbeck's gang had appeared. A dozen of them, all armed and dripping with villainy.

'Get out of here, Deppel,' Lena said, raising her cudgel.

'Shouldn't I-'

'No you shouldn't. I'm going to have a hard enough time defending myself.'

Then the gang stopped.

That couldn't be a good thing.

'Let me guess,' Lena shouted above the roar of the foundries. 'You're waiting while your friends get around behind us.'

The reply didn't come from the criminals, but from a familiar voice behind her.

'Not likely,' Soren Baumer said, his plate armour clanking as he approached. 'I've got men back there.'

Half a dozen of Baumer's constables came with him, swords at their sides and halberds in their hands. The blades of the polearms gleamed.

The numbers weren't even, but it looked like a closer fight. She was damn good, and Baumer had bonded armour. His troops' experience and professionalism might not count for so much in these streets, but their chain mail would help.

On the other hand, Brodbeck's people knew the ground. They were street brawlers. This was their fight to lose.

'Alright, folks,' Baumer said. 'No need for anyone to get hurt.'

'Ain't you arresting them?' Deppel asked. 'You're all constables and they're all criminals, you're meant to clap them in chains and chop off their fingers and show people how they's all-'

'Shut up, boy,' Baumer growled.

Slowly, with weapons still raised, the two sides backed away from each other. Once they were far enough apart, Baumer turned and led his group hastily away.

'I don't get it,' Deppel whispered. 'Why didn't they fight?'

'You've got to know your limits,' Lena said. 'Which fights aren't worth risking.'

'But what about law and justice and… and… I don't know, all that stuff what constables are meant to be for?'

'My job's keeping the peace,' Baumer said. 'Justice is a happy accident.'

Lena might not agree, but she understood. If you served long enough, saw enough, then it was easy to lose your ideals. She wouldn't condemn anyone for accepting the inevitable.

'Why were you even there?' she asked.

'Maier needs you, remember? It's diplomacy day.'

For a little while there, amid the tension of confrontation and the thrill of the chase, she had been able to forget. Now it came back, like icy water across her soul.

They walked on through the streets, heading with terrible inevitability towards the east gate. Lena looked down at herself, dressed in a padded woollen tunic and stained leggings. At least she wasn't dressed for diplomacy. That might put them off talking to her.

'You learn anything?' Baumer asked.

'Not much,' Lena admitted. 'Just that Saimon's a sore spot. Oh, and Brodbeck's got a kid.'

'She's got three,' Deppel said. 'Kerl's the oldest. They say she's gonna make him an underboss, once he's got a few more years.'

'You know a lot about them,' Baumer said, looking at Deppel for the first time.

Deppel looked away.

Lena shook her head.

Children. They seemed to be everywhere in this mess. She had one hanging on her coat tails. Brodbeck had one lined up for an heir. Holy Saimon had been avoiding having one, even while she played at grieving with her husband over a childless home. Had he known that he was never going to be a father?

She imagined the man in the portrait, with his sparkling blue eyes and his jolly round face.

And then it hit her so hard she swore out loud.

Fiete Saimon was Kerl's father.

Chapter Seventeen

Peace Talks, War Listens

They marched through the heart of the army's encampment, Councillor Maier in a slashed velvet doublet and embroidered waist-length cape, Lena in her dirty hose and sweat-stained tunic. They had left Baumer working on the defences, but four of his constables had come along as guards, for all the good they could do if this turned into a trap. Those constables stared around warily, hands on sword hilts, twitching at every flap of a lightning bolt banner and every cart horse that snorted as they marched past.

Deppel trailed along behind, there at Lena's insistence, not because she thought he would be much help but because it might annoy Maier. It was hard to tell, with the councillor already wearing her most diplomatic smile, but Lena liked to think it was working. The thought made Deppel's constant questions and comments bearable, even helped her to forget how much she didn't want to be there.

Soldiers stopped to stare at them, some with eyes full of hate, but most of them simply curious, just as she would have been. One stiff-backed young man with his hair cut short raised his lightning bolt amulet, warding off their evil. Another clutched a small book and muttered prayers for their souls, while a third simply drew her sword and glared. Lena held each one's gaze in turn and bared her teeth in a predatory smile.

The soldiers were a mixed lot. More professionals than she had expected, with matching uniforms and gleaming weapons, but that might have just been because they were near the centre of the camp. The rabble and fanatics tended to be forced out to the edges. The perimeter was marked by banners raised on pikes, each one carrying the heraldry of its unit, some of them symbols of saints, others crossed weapons or the emblems of distant towns. One banner pole had a human skeleton hanging from it, the bones strung together with gold-coated wire, emeralds gleaming in the eye sockets. Nothing motivated the righteous like following a real saint into battle.

She could smell the presence of war beasts and hear them growling to each other, but they were out of sight for the most part, hidden by wagons, embankments, and tents. At one point a wyvern reared up, its wings spread and head snaking high, scales glistening as it hissed and flapped and tried to break free of the chains on its collar, but steel was stronger than the beast, and it disappeared from view.

Lena got a better look at the artillery, which had been positioned in two batteries facing the East Gate. A dozen large cannons, a couple of mortars, and a scattering of lighter guns. Enough to breach the walls if they were given a few weeks, or the gates given a day and a good bombardier in charge. She didn't recognise either of the women ordering the gun crews about, but it was a while since she had been among artillerists, and by now there could be skilled bombardiers whose names she had never even heard.

It was strangely reassuring, assessing it all, to see that she had been right. If this turned bloody, they stood almost no chance, but at least she would be able to feel smug while she fought to keep the looters from her door.

Their escorts led them to a large tent made from cloth of gold. Banners flapped from its peak, black with a red tree. Under the entrance awning, a bowl glazed in warm summer yellow sat on a waist-high iron stand, with a jug of water at its base. The front of the tent was open. They stopped outside while a guard announced them.

'The delegation from Unteholz, sir.'

'Let them in, man!' came the booming reply. 'I won't have guests standing out in all weather.'

Maier gestured to the constables.

'Wait here,' she said quietly. She looked at Deppel. 'As for you-'

'He's with us,' Lena said, and relished the way the councillor cringed.

'Fine.'

The guard stepped aside, but Maier didn't walk straight in. Instead, she took off her rings, set them carefully on the edge of the glazed bowl, washed her hands, and dried them on a cloth that hung underneath. As she slid the rings back on, she gave Lena a pointed look.

It wasn't needed. That ritual cleansing was as habitual to Lena as it was awkward and forced to Maier, a set of motions made familiar by years of repetition. Hand over hand, water droplets glistening, a moment of peace before important business.

Deppel, following their lead, studiously washed his hands, then wiped them on his grimy tunic.

Together, the three of them walked in.

The tent was richly appointed, as befitted a general in the armies of Mother Sky. There was a large table with intricately carved legs in the centre, a smaller one off to one side, and a set of plumply upholstered chairs around the edge. A small altar stood in one corner, carved from ebony and decorated with three different shades of gold. Rings of scented candles, currently unlit, hung around the tent's two main poles. There were refreshments on the small table and a map spread out on the larger one, with wooden pieces marking the deployment of troops.

Lena knew that trick. Leave a map out while negotiating with your opponents. If you were in a position of strength, make it accurate. In a position of weakness, make it deceptive. The important thing was to intimidate, presenting a steel gauntlet around the soft hand that offered a drink.

'Would you care for wine?'

The speaker was a tall, broad-shouldered man, dressed from neck to toe in plate armour, his black surcoat embroidered with a red tree. He looked to be about forty, but bearing it well, his dark hair not yet touched by grey.

'That would be most kind,' Maier send. 'Nothing constrains conversation like a dry mouth.'

'And nothing flattens it like an over-watered mind,' the man said, clearly reciting a familiar phrase. 'You've read Saint Nitsini.'

'I try to keep an open mind.'

'Ha! I like that.' The man held out a gauntleted hand. 'Anselm Everhart, General of the Third Host of the Righteous.'

'Renate Maier, Chair of Unteholz City Council.' Maier returned Everhart's handshake. 'And this is Lena Sturm, our Headsman.'

Lena took the commander's hand, the familiar gesture made alien by strained circumstances, a wordless lie of friendliness and equality. He was well kept for a soldier, with only the tiniest of scars showing on one cheek. His armour, with its perfectly fitted plates and engraved pauldrons, was clearly bonded to him, and his movements had the fluid grace of an acrobat despite the solid layers of steel.

'Have we met?' Everhart asked, even as his fingers touched beneath his eye. 'I feel I know you.'

'I doubt it,' Lena said with a sinking feeling. 'Most people don't meet a headsman more than once.'

She had feared that someone here would recognise her, but at least Everhart hadn't worked out who she was yet. If she kept quiet, answered concisely when she had to, and played the role of the gruff headsman, then maybe she could get through this without unearthing the past.

A servant approached with a tray of silver goblets and Lena took the opportunity to turn away, disguising her discomfort in the act of passing Deppel a drink. His eyes widened as he saw the silverware and took a sip of the wine, but for once he had the good sense to stay silent.

'Take a seat,' Everhart said, flinging himself down in one of the chairs. 'I don't think even Father Earth considers comfort a sin, does he?'

Maier sank into the chair next to the general, while Lena sat as far out of his direct gaze as she could. Deppel settled next to her, staring at the gold-embroidered cushions of his seat.

'I don't suppose you've come to surrender, have you, Councillor?' Everhart asked. 'Mother Sky blesses those who save her people from pain.'

'I hope to save us all pain,' Maier said. 'You've come to ensure justice for Holy Saimon, and I wanted to reassure you that we share that goal. Unteholz takes no side in the great debate of our age, but it takes the safety of its citizens very seriously. Headsman Sturm has been working night and day to find out who framed Saimon, and there's no one more committed to justice than Sturm.'

Lena shrank back, but Everhart kept facing Maier as he swirled the wine around his goblet.

'I'm glad to hear it,' he said. 'But I'm sure you understand why we can't leave this to you, a follower of Father Earth.'

'The Council of Unteholz has members of both faiths. We protect the interests of all our citizens.'

'That was what they said at Stromrotter, but the minute the prince turned his back, your people threw down our statues, burned our books, murdered our priests. Gothersrech once preached toleration, and now its citizens can lose a hand for hanging a lightning bolt over their door. Your own Bishop Kunder has overseen burnings of our books.'

'The Bishop does not speak for the city council.'

'But her actions are accepted, and as Saint Esyl said, great sins grow from small, dark seeds. One of our leading priests was killed by an Earth worshipping executioner. How long before the rest of our priests in Unteholz face the sword?'

'Who said I worship Father Earth?' Lena asked, then realised how stupid her words were. She was trying to sell a bigger lie than her religion, who cared if she had been misunderstood?

Now Everhart's attention was on her. His brow crumpled.

'I do know you, don't I?' he said. 'I've seen you in service, years ago. Was that how you got the scars?'

Lena's hand went to her cheek.

'I've fought,' she admitted.

'You see,' Maier said. 'Sturm here understands what is at stake, and she will not rest until–'

'Mother above!' Everhart let out a bark of laughter. 'I do know!'

He turned to his servant.

'Tolder, get the best wine, and some of those fancy sweetmeats.'

Lena felt as if the whole army was tramping across her chest. Years of hiding from her past, taking on pariah's work just to be left in peace, and it had brought her here. Exposed.

'We're in the presence of greatness,' Everhart declared. 'This is General Seeger!'

Lena's cheeks burned with shame. It was years since she had heard that name, but she never went a week without thinking about what it stood for, what she had done and what she had failed at along the way. Not just the fires she had set in other people's lives, but the ashes she had made of her own.

She gulped back the wine, but it had lost its flavour.

'Dragontamer Seeger?' Maier blinked. For once, Lena had surprised her. 'Living in Unteholz?'

Lena bolted to her feet and strode across the tent. A servant cringed as she snatched the wine jug and took a deep swig. A trickle ran down her chin.

'Where did we meet?' she asked, looking down at trampled grass.

'The Faustrech Valley campaign,' Everhart said. 'I was just a squire to old Lady Graulech, but it was an honour to watch you in action. I like to think it made me who I am.'

These were the worst, the ones who saw her as some sort of hero. She'd just been lucky, floating to the top when the rivers of hell burst their banks, flooding the land with blood. It could have happened to any of a hundred commanders in that army, but somehow she had wound up in charge, an idol to idiots bent on destruction. Some had wanted to call her saint after she saved Kirkstat, more had uttered that word after she seized Alvard and her soldiers burned it down, but by then she could feel her convictions slipping away, so that each piece of over-wrought praise became a knife blade slicing at her self-regard. How could she accept the label of saint when she barely believed in the gods? How could she climb to heights of adulation on a ladder of bones? That was why it hadn't been enough to leave the armies, why she had left her home town a hundred leagues behind, and with it, the husband she no longer knew.

'There we go then,' Maier said from behind a stiff mask of poise and calm. 'How can this be an Earth conspiracy with Mother Sky's greatest general involved?'

'There's nothing great about this shit,' Lena growled and took another drink. 'You'd know that if you'd seen an army tear through a city.'

'Quite,' Maier said. 'So, General Everhart, given what we now know, I wonder if-'

'Wait, wait, wait.' Everhart strode to the tent's entrance and bellowed at the camp. 'Somebody fetch the drachenritter colonel!'

He turned back to them, grinning like a child at a feast. When he caught Lena's expression, his confidence cracked for a moment, and she glimpsed a flicker of doubt, but then it vanished beneath the steel-hard armour of a bold voice and a proud stance.

'Wait until he sees who's here,' Everhart said. 'Of all the people to walk into our camp…'

'I'm not here to be exhibited like a head on a spike,' Lena said. 'Let's get this over with.'

The wine was softening the edges of her senses, slowing the

bitter thoughts that chased around her mind. Still she stood stiff, eyes downcast, determined to be done and gone and back to honest anonymity.

She took another swig.

'Councillor Maier, if you can trust General Seeger, then surely you can trust me?' Everhart said. 'Let me into your city, I'll help ensure that justice is done, and then I'll be on my way. All I want is to do Mother Sky's will.'

'And what about your men?' Maier asked. 'Will they go with you?'

'I might leave some for your protection, and to make sure nothing like this happens again. After all, these are troubled times.'

Everhart's smile was warm, but there was a hardness to his words, a tone that betrayed no room for compromise.

'I know what sort of protection foreign armies offer,' Maier said. 'It's not to my tastes.'

'Do your tastes matter here, Councillor?'

'Very well then, let's consider the sentiments of our citizens. Can you guarantee that the temples of Father Earth will be allowed to continue in the old ways, to venerate him above Mother Sky?'

'For as long as they feel the need. I'm sure that many will see the light of reform, once they know it's safe to follow the Mother's path.'

Lena knew the pressures that would fall upon those priests to see that light: the agitation of reformers within their congregations, the stern soldiers coming armed to pray, the wash bowls set up pointedly outside temple doors, with informers watching to see who cleansed themselves. She had left matters of faith to her army's priests, but she wasn't blind to how they acted.

'Of course, there is one exception,' Everhart added. 'The Cage Cathedral of Saint Lukara will be turned over to the true and reformed faith. It's only fitting, given Father Earth's neglect of the saints and their promise for human potential.'

'Your exception is the high temple of our Father's faith in the city, a site of pilgrimage for his followers from across the Saved Lands.'

'An inspiring symbol of faith in action, one man slaying a vast monster to honour the gods. A symbol too of how our faith has become corrupted, the saint's image gone, his story barely told. His shining example should be restored, for the souls of all your citizens, and of the pilgrims who come to his shrine.'

Lena would have loved to see the cathedral turned over to the Sky priests, not for the sake of faith, but for the look on Kunder's face. She imagined the bishop's horror as the place was filled with statues and reliquaries, illuminated scripture replaced by printed copies of the reformed word, the disk of the world lowered to the base of the altar and the lightning bolt raised above it. The place would be stuffed with gold and jewels, its priests dressed up in their most elaborate robes, the melodious choir drowned out by the tuneless enthusiasm of congregational hymns.

And for that exact reason, it was a price Maier could never pay, not just because of her faith, but because it would humiliate Unteholz.

This was futile. The whole trip out through the gate had been a needless risk, time wasted from Lena's real work. Wars ground on, armies marched, cities rose and fell, and none of it had the least to do with right or wrong. It was in the little things that good could be done. She should be in the city, hunting a murderer, not listening to politicians fight with fragments of theology.

Maier and Everhart were into the thick of it now, words darting between them, lines of logic and legality that had nothing to do with the hard facts of politics. They bargained using a pretence of morality, questions of faith and ethics presented like counters on a merchant's board, and the most the councillor could negotiate was false hope. Everhart's army was driven by the brutal bellowing of religious war, not delicate jurisprudence. Lena had sat where he did, and she knew how this ended.

She imagined Unteholz in flames, winged beasts soaring through the sky, cannons pounding at the walls. It left her feeling like one of the creatures in the caves, sad and hurt and hopeless. Unteholz had let her find peace after a life of violent turmoil. She loved the city, for all its flaws, she even loved the purpose an executioner's duty gave her, and now, like everything she loved, it was going to be torn away.

A hand tentatively touched her arm. Deppel stood looking up at her. He swallowed, licked his lips, and finally spoke.

'Say something,' he whispered. 'Maybe he'll listen to you.'

'Why in thunder would he do that?'

'Because I would. And because out here you're a hero.'

She snorted with laughter, but he was right. She was the one thing that made Unteholz different from a dozen other cities this army could have besieged. Dragontamer Seeger, hero of Faustrech, Kirkstat, and Alvard, a general to whom whole cities of Sky worshippers had entrusted their fate, a champion praised by princes and once weighed down with lavish rewards. She had always hated the spectacle of that position, while reluctantly appreciating the power it had. Perhaps the reputation she had fled still counted for something. If she placed her counter on the scales might they tip, just a little, in Unteholz's favour?

One final swig, then she set aside the wine and walked back to the ring of chairs around the map table. She placed one hand on the map and the other on Everhart's shoulder.

'General,' she said, smiling down at him. 'I'm sure that there's space for us to find common ground.'

He looked with wide eyes at the hand on his shoulder, then up at her.

'What do you suggest, General?'

She looked at Maier, shoulders tensed and expression wary. After a moment, the councillor gave her an encouraging nod. An old thrill ran through Lena for the first time in years, the prospect of snatching victory from desperate odds. A narrow trail lay open before them, and it fell on her to guide the city down that path. Her chest with hopeful anticipation.

A figure appeared in the doorway.

'You wanted to see me, General?'

At the sound of that voice, Lena's heart froze. She looked at him, past his wyvern hide armour, past the drachenritter commander's sash, past the longsword and the crude globes of grenades in a leather bandolier, to a face so familiar it hurt.

'Jekob,' she gasped.

The young man looked back at her, so familiar and yet so strange in an adult's body, with a soldier's bearing and a drachenritter's garb. Eyes the same deep green as hers stared into her soul.

'Mother,' he said, and the word fell like lead in the quiet of the tent.

Memories clawed at Lena's heart. Jekob as a child, running down the garden path to greet her when she came home from war. A little older, engrossed in his books, as he grew taller and her time at home shorter. As a teenager, standing stony faced through her victory parade. And lastly the young man who turned her away from the door, told her that there was no place for her in this family anymore, while her own failed apologies and fumbled excuses rang through her hollow heart.

Jekob's hand went to his belt, and for a moment she thought he would draw his sword. Instead, he clutched a small book bound in silver and suede, the lives of the saints written on pages no bigger than an infant's palm. She remembered Jahann buying that book from a trader travelling out of Kirkstat, her husband's eyes shining as he picked out the very first gift their child would receive. She could almost feel the bulging of her belly, their hands resting on it together, full of love and hope for their unborn baby.

Now her son stared at her, his eyes full of hate.

'Isn't this remarkable!' Everhart was on his feet, grinning. He slapped Jekob on the shoulder. 'Old Seeger and young Seeger together at last. A family reunion in the middle of war. A grand omen, eh, councillor?'

Maier sat stiffly in her seat, eyes flitting between Lena and

Jekob, knuckles white as she clasped her hands together. It was a shame she had faced the general in such imbalanced circumstances, because she was clearly smarter than him.

'A symptom of our times, perhaps,' she said.

'Jekob is one of the finest officers I have.' Everhart took a pair of goblets from a servant and held one out for the drachenritter. 'You should be proud, General Seeger. He's taken after you.'

Hope stirred in Lena, like the first beam of sunlight after a storm. Maybe there was something here. If he had followed in her footsteps, he might finally understand.

'Come and sit with us, Colonel,' Everhart said, gesturing towards a chair. 'You can convince your mother of what needs to be done.'

'No.'

One word, and that light of hope was quashed.

Lena looked around for the wine, her head jerking back and forth, but the only drink in reach was Deppel's goblet.

'Colonel Seeger, I asked you to sit down,' Everhart said. 'Don't make me order you.'

'As Mother Sky is my witness, I will not sit with that woman,' Jekob said.

'Jekob, please.' Lena heard her own wheedling voice, so pathetic her cheeks flushed with shame. 'Just sit down for a minute. Talk.'

Now that she was focused on him, she couldn't look away. He had grown up handsome, like his father. Not tall but proud and well-proportioned, every inch the good soldier.

'I have nothing to say to her,' Jekob said, his face stern, his hand trembling as it gripped his silver-bound book. 'And no desire to hear what she says.'

'Please, I'm not here to argue with you again. Let me explain.'

'Enough!' Jekob's voice was a whip lashing out and she stumbled from its sting. 'My childhood was full of your explanations, but now I know them for what they are, lies and excuses.'

'I never lied!'

'You never told the truth.'

'I tried. It was just hard, when your father was so sad, and you were so distant, and everything felt like a weight bearing down on me.'

'So that's what we were to you: a burden.'

'No! See, this is it. I can't find the words. Not in the moment. Not when my head is full of, of, of all this.'

She flung her hands in the air, like she could cast away the hurt and frustration and guilt that welled up inside her, clogging her thoughts, drowning out her last scraps of coherence.

'Who's this?' Jekob pointed past her to Deppel. 'Taken in some stray again, like you used to squires and servants? Found a replacement for me?' He caught Deppel's eye. 'Don't trust her, boy. She'll abandon you soon enough.'

'It's not like that,' Lena said. 'He's just some kid who follows me around.'

'I thought-' Deppel began, but now the words had started pouring out of Lena and she couldn't hold them back.

'How dare you judge me?' she snapped, pointing at Jekob. 'You were the one who turned your back, who closed me out when I came to you.'

'When you finally came to me. Finally got bored of fighting and decided it was our turn to give you validation.'

'It's not… That's not…' The pressure kept building inside her mind. Why couldn't he understand? Why couldn't any of them?

'Maybe this was a mistake,' Everhart said, stepping between them. His voice had lost its rich, smooth confidence, that swagger with which every word had marched from his lips. 'General, why don't we get back to negotiations, eh?'

'Negotiations? Ha!' Here was something she understood, a point she could pierce with all the hard finality of cold steel. 'This isn't a negotiation, it's just siegecraft by words.'

'Excuse me?'

'I've been where you are, General Everhart, and I see what this is. There's no space for compromise. You've decided you'll take us on your terms, and this is a chance to menace us into accepting them, to field sharp words and petty posturing alongside your cannons and dragons. It's pathetic.' She slapped the map table, sending wooden counters flying. 'At least in my day I was honest about it. You've gilded a turd and now you're selling it as gold.'

'Enough, General,' Everhart said, his broken smile slipping into a snarl. His hand went to his sword. 'If we weren't under terms of truce, I'd teach you a lesson in honour.'

'Oh gods, now you think you're a duellist.' Lena shook her head. 'Here's the thing about duels. They just use honour to justify animal instincts, to let us kill and call it civilised. That's what you're trying to do here, to my city. You've dressed conquest up in justice, and you're counting on us all not to call it out, because then we'd have to admit we do the same shit too. But everybody's seen the turd that is my soul, and by the blackness, I won't let you hide yours.'

'Maybe your soul is so tainted that you lost the Mother's light, but we are pure of heart and fired by faith.'

'And I'm the Queen of Dunvar. Drop the charade and get to the point, while we're still young enough to fight.'

Everhart's face was the perfect image of righteous indignation, but Lena knew him for the fraud he was, just one more posturing tyrant.

He turned to Maier.

'I invited you here in good faith, Councillor. I wanted to talk peace with only the gods watching us, in hopes that we might avoid bloodshed. Instead, your city's representatives insult and provoke. As you relish conflict, I will give it to you.'

'I'm sorry to hear that,' Maier said, rising from her seat. 'And I'm sorry if we have pushed you to this. If you wish to talk peace again, I will be ready and waiting.'

Everhart turned to Jekob.

'Colonel Seeger, find the artillery masters. Tell them to ready their guns for a bombardment.'

'Yes, General.' Jekob shot Lena one last bitter glare, then strode away.

Everhart turned back to them.

'You have until the guns are ready to get back inside your walls. I suggest that you hurry; I hired the very best artillerists.'

They rushed out of the tent and through the camp, Lena and Maier striding purposeful and grim-faced, Deppel scurrying along with a fretful look. Their escort of city constables fell in behind them without a word.

The responses of the soldiers they passed had changed. Some must have heard who Lena was, must have known her reputation, because they stared at her wide-eyed and raised their fists in salute. Others had heard the alarm rippling through the camp, the order for war to begin. They jeered, cursed, threatened, spat. Words lashed at the ragtag embassy all the way out of camp and across the open ground towards Unteholz's forbidding walls.

'He was lying,' Lena said, her head spinning with fury. 'He never wanted peace.'

'You think I don't know that?' Maier snapped.

'Then why play along at the end? Why keep begging for scraps like a dog at the feet of a scoundrel?'

'Because any scrap of peace may mean a life saved, a home preserved, a few hours for friends or allies to come.'

'Today changed nothing.'

'You don't know that.'

But she did. She knew men like Everhart. She had cursed near been one of them. Saving herself from that blackness had crushed the last of her joy, then ended her career. Her choice had been simple: become a monster or become lonely forever, and she had chosen loneliness. Everhart lacked the courage for that path, and now his cowardice would kill a whole city.

They reached the gates as the first cannon roared.

Chapter Eighteen

The Past Unveiled

Baumer was waiting behind the East Gate. As the great iron-bound gates slammed shut and the portcullis rattled down, he drew the negotiating party aside in the shelter of the walls. His knowing smile was a terrible contrast to Maier's grim resignation, but Lena took comfort in it. Baumer, like her, had known that this would be a waste, and that meant he had kept preparing.

'Went well, did it?' he asked.

The boom of artillery rolled up the valley like thunder, then came crashing back in a muffled echo from the mountainside. Each blast was followed by the thud of a cannonball hitting the wall or the crashing of a mortar's load through the roof of a house. Dust fell from the wall behind them, a drifting cloud shaken loose by the trembling stones. Birds and wild wyverns took flight and circled above the city, watching warily for the monsters that made this terrible roar.

'As soon as we're done here, get the fire watches ready,' Maier said. 'I'm not having one smashed bakery burn the city down. I'll leave the decision about counter-bombardment to our military commanders.'

'So me?' Baumer said.

'That's the one good thing to come out of this. We now have General Seeger on our side.'

'Dragontamer Seeger? She's one of them.'

'Apparently not.'

'And what forces is she bringing? When will she arrive?' He rubbed his gauntleted hands together in anticipation.

'Oh, she's already here.' Maier pointed at Lena, who took a shuffling step back, hands clasped around her belt, awkward and embarrassed.

'What?' Baumer's face went through confusion to incredulity, and then he laughed out loud. 'Holy thundering blackness, you kept that quiet! And to think you could have been bossing me around this whole time.'

Lena shrugged. An hour before, she had been sure of her place in Unteholz, a position that ensured she was left in peace. Now the expectations of a whole city threatened to haul her out of her comfortable hole.

'I was a different woman back then.'

The initial chorus of artillery fire subsided, giving way to sporadic shots, each gun working at the pace that its crew's skill allowed.

Citizens of Unteholz had emerged onto the streets and stood staring at the walls or at the sky. Unable to defend themselves against those blood-thirsty machines, they were reduced to watching for death, trying to give shape to lives in the path of destruction. Lena knew that by tomorrow it would be business as usual, people trying to pretend there wasn't a war on. For now, let them gawk and gossip.

Some were watching her conversation with Maier and Baumer, waiting expectantly for guidance from the head of the city council. Maier glanced at the gathering crowd, then back to Lena.

'I'll address them once we're done,' she said. 'Keep things calm. But first I need to make sure that we're moving forward as one.

'Captain Baumer, I still expect you to coordinate your men and the levies you raised, but it's clearly in our best interests for the general here to take overall command.'

'What?' Lena stared at the councillor. 'No.'

'We can't have a divided command. Things are chaotic enough already, people need clarity, and that means one person in charge.'

'Fine, leave Baumer in charge.'

'Don't be so stubborn. You have more experience.'

'I told you already, I'm not a soldier anymore.'

Lena took a step back. Her cheeks were flushed, and not just from the wine she'd guzzled to get her through that meeting. Her whole body tensed, shoulders rising, heart pulsing to a faster beat.

She couldn't do it. She wouldn't do it. That was the part of her that had brought ruin, the part she had closed off behind the walls in her mind and a stone in the corner of her house. There was no abandoning the past, but there could be no return to it either. Not without losing herself.

'Few people in this town are soldiers,' Maier said. 'But they'll have to rise to the occasion.'

'I won't do it.'

'That is not a choice you get to make.' Maier's face reddened. 'I am ordering you to take charge.'

'I have a duty to the Saimons.' Lena steadied herself, feet planted square on, voice levelling out from a wail of alarm. 'I'll keep hunting their killer, but I won't lead your war.'

'The Saimons don't matter now!' Maier took two steps forward and stood staring up at Lena, her fist raised. 'You said it yourself, that man out there just wanted to fight. You can't fend him off with legal niceties. It's blades and blood or let our city be sacked.'

Lena listened to the roar of the cannons, like old friends greeting her across a tavern, their boisterous bellow calling her to join in. She thought about the cities she had seen fall, about ash and blood smearing the streets of Unteholz. The attraction of action and repulsion of destruction both drove her toward the same end.

But she hadn't just seen cities fall. She was the one who had cracked their walls and left their people exposed, who had never stopped long enough in pursuit of victory to understand what horror followed. Not until it was too late. She wouldn't become that woman again. She wouldn't do it to herself, or to the world. There was one good thing left for her to do, and it wasn't to fight.

'I'm not hunting a killer for him.' Lena pointed out past Maier, through the walls, to the army encamped beyond. 'I'm doing it for the man who died and the woman I killed. Justice doesn't stop mattering because we're at war.'

'So you'll let others die for lack of your leadership?'

'I told you, I'm not a soldier anymore, and I'm sure as hells not a general.'

Maier stared in incredulity as Lena turned on leaden legs and walked away, through the nervously whispering crowds, towards a safer part of town.

One with a drink in it.

Toblur started pouring ale the moment Lena walked in. The man had a good memory for his regulars and a barman's expertise for keeping them happy. He even had the good sense not to make the sign of the eye, at least not until her back was turned. If he hadn't inherited a shitty drinking hole in a shitty part of town, he might have bought his way up to innkeeper, offering well-kept rooms for rich travellers. Instead, he was standing on three-day-old rushes, selling cheap ale for coins that had been clipped so many times they were barely disks.

Lena took her tankard to a corner table. She felt twitchy, knowing that she should be out there investigating, especially after she'd made an issue of it. Maybe finding the truth would even do some good, giving Maier a sliver of leverage if they ever got real negotiations, unlikely as that was.

But her head was full of other things. Anger, frustration, flashing images of Jekob's face, the words he'd said and the ones that she wished she'd thought of. She relived the confrontation over and again, feeling the blade of his anger slicing her heart, while she tried too late to armour herself with words.

A movement made her look up from the table. Deppel had pulled out the stool across from her and was sitting down. He tugged at his shoe, adjusting something she couldn't see, then looked up with a nervous smile.

Why had she let this urchin start following her around? Why had she given him a roof over his head and food in his belly? Was Jekob's accusation true, that she was looking for a replacement, as if she could make up for the neglect she had shown him?

No. Sentiment had nothing to do with it, any more than her past did. Deppel was a useful contact, someone to use in her investigation. That was why she had taken care of him, so that he could lead her to places she would never have found for herself. Places like Jagusia Brodbeck's lair.

More memories came back, things she had needed to say before politics intervened.

'You're one of the real people,' she said, the words as hard and pointed as a nail.

Deppel's smile faltered. He looked down at his hands, cupping them as if around a drink.

'I was,' he said quietly. 'I'm sorry.'

Lena stared at him in the dim light that Toblur's windows allowed. He looked pathetic, but then he always did. What shifted was her sympathy. It was too rare a commodity to waste on anyone who lied to her face.

'You lied to me,' she said.

'I never!' Deppel snapped, then cringed back in on himself. 'You didn't ask.'

'I didn't ask if you were the archbishop, but I would have expected it to come up.'

'Well I ain't a bishop and you ain't being fair.'

'I'm not fair? You were a trainee criminal taking my food while I tried to uphold the law. For all I know, your boss sent you to watch me, to help hide the truth.'

'That ain't it! They was done with me, and I was done with them. I wanted out, and you gave me the chance. Why wouldn't I take it?'

How dare he take this tone with her? She was a Moon-damned general and deserved some respect. No, she was an executioner, the only person in the whole city who could bear that burden, and no one was going to treat her like dirt for it anymore, especially not some snivelling, self-righteous brat, slinging blame at the woman who fed him because he couldn't accept the hard realities of the world.

'Why should I believe a word you say?' she growled.

''Cause I helped. I took you to Jagusia, didn't I, even though I knew it weren't going to go well for me. And I come with you to all them places, helped find that bottle at Saimon's house.'

'Like I couldn't find that myself.'

'I was helping.'

'I don't want your help.' She slammed her tankard down. 'I don't want some weak-kneed child following me around, begging for bread and attention, demanding that I do things for him and judging me when I fail. I didn't want that before and by the blackness I don't want it now.'

Deppel's lip trembled and there was a gleam of tears at the corner of his eyes. He got to his feet.

'I'll go,' he said. 'I just…'

Whatever he was thinking, it didn't get as far as his mouth. He rubbed a hand across his face and headed for the door, shoulders slumped, as wretched as she had ever seen him.

Guilt grabbed Lena by the heart so hard she almost gasped. He wasn't the one who had hurt her, and she knew it. Gods' eyes, what had she become?

'Wait,' she called out.

Deppel froze halfway through the door. He tilted his head but didn't look back at her.

'I'm…' The words stuck in her throat, but she had to get them out. 'I'm sorry. Come back here.'

Deppel sniffed. 'What if I don't want to?'

'I'll buy you a drink.'

'A proper drink?'

'Doom and dust, boy, you're fourteen years old, of course I'm not buying you a proper drink. This isn't Jagusia Brodbeck's den of delinquents. But you can have a third ale, and we'll share a pie, and then we'll work out what happens next.'

Deppel licked his lips.

'What sort of pie?'

'Rat and dung if you're not careful.'

'There's good eating on a rat.'

He came back to the table and sat across from her. His face was blotchy, but his smile was back, and it widened when she returned from the bar with a tankard for him and two slices of meat pie on a wooden platter.

The pie was greasy, with nearly as much gristle as meat, but the pastry was good, and she was far hungrier than she had realised. The two of them sat in silence until every crumb was gone, then leaned back licking their fingers in satisfaction. Around them, other customers quietly got on with their drinking, without commenting on what they had heard. Lena could almost have felt content, if not for the distant cry of the siege guns.

'I really am sorry I didn't tell you,' Deppel said. 'I was afraid you'd send me away.'

'I might have done. I'm not a good person.'

'I think you are.'

'You don't know the things I've done.'

Deppel shrugged. 'You still do them?'

'No.'

'Then you ain't bad no more.'

It was ridiculous logic: childish, simplistic, untethered from the real world where men and women carried old instincts like coiled snakes in their hearts, waiting to be disturbed. But still, his faith in her brought comfort. She smiled.

'Thank you, Deppel.'

There was a piece of bone in the pie. She sucked the juices from it, raised it between thumb and finger, and held it up to the light. The curve of its outer edge, together with the gouge left by a butcher's cleaver, reminded her of a hunting dog curled in around itself to sleep. She drew the little whittling knife from her boot and started to scratch patterns across the bone.

'Tell me about your time with Brodbeck,' she said. 'I won't judge.'

'You promise?'

'My word is always my promise.'

And she had always kept her promises, in the best way she could. She had loved Jahann with all her heart, even if she couldn't make him happy. She had protected the people of Mother Sky, though in the end she had done it by leaving. She had served justice in Unteholz, and if she had failed Beatrice Saimon, that only made it more important to right the wrong. Now, her word was to Deppel, and what mattered was to listen, like she should have done when Jekob was young.

Deppel licked his lips, then started to talk.

The tale unfurled slowly at first, like a gryphon waking at winter's end. Deppel talked about his parents, a poor couple who had died while he was too young to remember, leaving him in his grandmother's care. She was a weaver, working every day at the loom in their home, making crude cloth for people who couldn't afford better, people like her. Her spare money had gone on feeding him and her spare time on making him happy. When she wasn't weaving, they had played and talked, and when she was busy, she sent him for schooling with the clerk who lived next door. Every night, she and Deppel curled up together in bed, where he lay wrapped up warm in her love, while she told him stories of heroes who brought justice to the world.

Then there had been a fire, as happened all too often in the city. An untended hearth perhaps, or cinders from a foundry, had set the house next door burning. Their whole street of cheaply built timber tenements went up in flames. Neighbours and constables rushed to form a bucket chain, as much to protect the rest of the city as to save the burning homes. But it was too late.

At dawn, Deppel sat amid the steaming ashes, utterly alone. His grandmother and the clerk next door were dead, along with five others. His neighbours had gone away, seeking shelter with relatives. There was no one left for him.

He was seven years old.

Then another child appeared out of the smoke that clung to the streets like the stench of death. A girl around his own age. Tild.

She told him that there was a safe place, somewhere he would be fed and cared for. He just had to come with her.

And so he did.

Thus began Deppel's life of crime. Seven years of living with other children that the gang had taken in, all of them being groomed for a dark sort of work. Their education was quite unlike the one he'd had before. They were taught how to penetrate locked doors, how to create a distraction and then dart away, how to cut a purse with a sliver of bone. Bit by bit, the games by which they learnt became reality, as they were sent out to make money for Jagusia Brodbeck, the matron mother to these poor impoverished youths. It was only fair that their earnings went back to her; after all, they owed her their lives.

A few of the children ran away when they reached adolescence. Deppel didn't know how many of those had succeeded, but he knew the battered ones who were dragged back and promised never to do it again.

Deppel's grandmother's stories had stuck with him. He knew right from wrong. What he didn't know was how to do the right thing and live. He bought himself time by playing the incompetent, failing in lessons where he knew how to succeed. His teachers grew tired of trying to beat learning into him and relegated him to the beggars, the lowest rank in the armies of crime. There he spent his days, bullied and belittled for his failings, but at least doing nothing his grandmother had said was wrong.

Then Lena had come along, and he finally saw a way out. With a heart torn between hope and bitter experience, he grabbed hold of the chance to do something good while getting fed. Even if he only escaped the gutter for a moment, that moment would be one to make his grandmother proud.

By the time Deppel finished his story, Lena's hands lay motionless, clutching the whittling knife and the half-carved bone. Those things had none of her attention. It was all on Deppel.

'Gods' eyes,' she said in a flat voice. 'I'm so sorry.'

Deppel shrugged and gave her a half-hearted smile.

'Ain't no point being sorry,' he said. 'Plenty got it worse than me.'

Lena's hand tightened around the knife. She imagined taking its blade to Jagusia Brodbeck, delivering justice on a woman who used kids. Then instead of the knife she imagined swinging Brute, the executioner's sword heavy in her hands, ending Brodbeck's life the way it should be done, on the Weeping Stone.

If Brodbeck was the killer she sought, maybe it could happen.

'Is Brodbeck usually at that place near the foundries?' she asked, sliding the knife into her boot and setting aside the bone.

'Look at that!' Deppel picked up the pale and half-finished fragment. His eyes lit up as he turned it in his hands. 'It's something sleeping, ain't it? All curled up and that. You gonna make it a dragon?'

'Yes, Deppel, it can be a dragon.' Why not, if that would make him happy.

'Can you show me how to do this?'

'Later, perhaps. I'm not much of a teacher, but I'll do what I can. Now, please, answer my question.'

Deppel looked around nervously, then back at her.

'Jagusia ain't always there,' he said. 'She moves around, especially when there's trouble. Pretty sure what we done before counts as trouble.'

'I need to speak with her again. How can I find her?'

'You can't do that!' Deppel stared at her. 'She'll kill you.'

'She can try.' Lena gripped the edge of the table so hard that the battered wood creaked.

'Why d'you want to talk with her, anyway? You don't think she done for Councillor Saimon, do you?'

She could just tell him what she had noticed at Brodbeck's lair, the boy with a striking resemblance to the dead councillor. Maybe Deppel had worked it out already. Maybe it was common knowledge in the Warrens.

But maybe it was a secret, or a thing left unsaid. That could make the knowledge dangerous.

'I noticed something. It might mean she's behind this, or it might mean something else. I need to look her in the eyes when I ask.'

Lena shifted in her seat, kicked at the rushes, tapped her finger against the battered table top. How in all the hells did she get through to a woman who had tried to have her killed?

Deppel was talking again, going on about how they had got away from Brodbeck before. What started as a warning of the perils the gangster presented turned into an excited account of their escape, with Lena as the hero who saved Deppel's life. He got out of his seat, picked up a bone from the floor, and used it as a cudgel to act the story out. Others in the alehouse started taking an interest, and the story grew for its audience, while Lena shrank into the shadows.

Her toe, still raking through the rushes, caught on another piece of bone.

She needed to send a message that Jagusia Brodbeck could understand, but that people who weren't in the know would miss. A message about Jagusia, and Fiete Saimon, and the boy Kerl.

Deppel reached the end of his story, to a smattering of applause from his listeners. He grinned and bowed.

'Well done, Deppel,' Lena said as he sat back down. 'You're a born entertainer.'

He picked up her half-finished carving and smiled hopefully. 'Can you show me how to do this now?'

There it was, the answer she needed.

She picked up the bone by her foot, a piece of rib the size of her finger. With her knife, she carved a series of crude lines into the bone, just a handful of letters.

'Without putting yourself in danger,' she said, 'could you find someone to pass a message to Brodbeck?'

'Oh yeah,' Deppel said. 'I'll give it to one of the beggar boys.'

'Good.' Lena handed him the bone. 'Tell them to pass on this bone to Brodbeck, with a message-that the Headsman wants to speak with her.'

Deppel's face scrunched up as he stared at the bone.

'F begat K,' he said, reading the letters out loud. 'What's that, something out of one of them holy books?'

'Something like that,' Lena said. 'And if I'm right, it's just the scripture to get your old boss's attention.'

CHAPTER NINETEEN

COMMANDER OF THE DEFENCES

For a week, the artillery of the Third Host of the Righteous had battered the walls of Unteholz. Cannonballs crashed against the defences, filling the air with dust and splinters of rock, until cracks riddled towers that had stood strong for centuries. Mortar stones smashed through rooftops and tore down walls, crushing any poor soul who got in the way. It was only a prelude, but that pounding spoke of the destruction to come.

All that time, Lena had stayed away from the defences, away from Maier and Baumer and anyone else who might force her into fighting their war. She had other business to occupy her.

Except that it didn't. There had been no word from Brodbeck. Perhaps her nudge had been too subtle, the criminal too resistant, or the bone got lost along the way. It didn't matter why. What mattered was that she was left pacing the streets, waiting for a message that never came. The idleness gave memories time to chase each other around her skull, a morbid mixture of bitter arguments and body-littered battlefields. Each day, she started drinking earlier, the simplest way to chase the memories away. Each night, she slept worse. And every morning she woke to the sound of the cannons, the pounding drumbeat behind a song whose crescendo would be the city's fall. Her time was running out.

But there was another way to find Brodbeck, so she strode up the steps to the top of the walls, trying to ignore the stickiness of her skin and the pulsing of a well-earned hangover.

'Will there be bodies up there?' Deppel asked. 'Soldiers what have been killed in the fighting?'

'Soldiers don't die in this part,' Lena said.

'But I seen bodies being taken to the temple.'

'Civilians. That's who a siege hurts. At least until the end.'

'War's mostly just dull and sort of miserable, ain't it? Not like how it was in grandma's stories, with heroes defending their homeland against dragons and evil kings and that.'

'Oh, it'll get exciting,' she said grimly, thinking about what would happen when these walls fell.

The stones shook beneath her feet as she reached the top of the stairs.

Sure enough, Soren Baumer stood at the battlements close to the East Gate, looking out towards the enemy encampment. His armour gleamed in the light of a clear, sunny day, and a banner bearing the city's silver and blue arms flapped defiantly nearby. His chest was thrust out, feet planted wide apart, watching the world with the pose of a warrior saint.

A line of earthworks zigzagged across the open ground towards the walls. It would take the sappers weeks to reach their target, the same weeks it would take the artillery to breach the walls. Arquebusiers and crossbowmen would take shots from those trenches, while soldiers on the wall returned the favour, but by the time any of them were close enough to hit it would barely matter. The breach would come, and men would pour out of the trenches, while war beasts swooped in from above. The streets of Unteholz would be muddy with blood while ashes fell like a summer snow. Lena had seen it too many times to believe in any other end.

'You come to help at last?' Baumer asked as Lena approached.

'What do you think?'

'I think you're a stubborn old monster, and you've found another rock to beat your head against.'

Lena smiled despite herself.

'Do you think there's still a place for old monsters in this world?'

'Of course. That's what Unteholz is for.'

He reached into a pouch on his belt, pulled out two apples, and handed one to her.

'I've been raiding Maier's fruit bowl again.' He glanced at Deppel, rolled his eyes, and dug an orange out from deeper in the pouch. 'Here, one for you.'

Mouth wide, Deppel grabbed the orange and tore it open in a spray of juice.

They stood, eating their fruit and watching the siege works. Lena had never realised how much she missed moments like this, the days of watching, waiting, evaluating, building an understanding of her opponents while they prepared their forces for the fight. The quiet had been part of the work, an empty space for her thoughts to find themselves. She dreaded that empty space now, but once upon a time, it had been a close companion, and just for a moment, chewing on an apple and watching the siege lines, she welcomed that old friend.

Baumer had chosen his spot well. From up here, they would have a better view of the sappers' progress than the enemy general, at least until he sent a spotter up on a wyvern. That wasn't the sort of job anyone would waste a dragon on. Those great beasts would be saving their strength, waiting for their chance to strike.

A shot hit the wall below them. The shock of the impact ran up Lena's body, rattled her teeth, and made the throbbing in her head just a little more intense. Deppel went pale and stared down at the stones in alarm, but Lena took comfort in the familiar sensation, despite her aches. It would take a bigger hit than that to crack the walls of Unteholz, carved by men who lived their whole lives shaping stone. There was nothing to fear today.

'How goes the investigation?' Baumer asked, tossing away his apple core.

Lena folded her arms and stared out across open ground to where smoke trailed from a hidden dragon corral.

'About as well as this,' she said. 'Thought I'd made a breakthrough a week ago, but it turns out I was fooling myself.'

'You giving up, then?'

'I'm a stubborn old monster, remember? That idea made sense at the time, but now I've got another one.'

'Which is?'

'I want you to help me.'

A curious expression crossed Baumer's face. He seemed about to laugh, but instead he shook his head and pointed out towards the assembled army.

'I'm busy, remember?'

'Last I heard, you were still responsible for upholding the law.'

'I told you already-'

'Get your people to arrest Jagusia Brodbeck.'

It all made sense. Brodbeck had got defensive about Fiete Saimon because the two of them were lovers. Maybe she'd killed him in a fit of passion, or maybe one of her rivals had got to him. Just being linked to her created motives for his death, and Lena needed to be sure that the link was there.

This time Baumer did laugh, a sound as bitter as a widow's tears. 'That's all? Arrest Brodbeck?'

'You must suspect her of something, and if I'm right, I can add a murder to the charge. Shake down enough beggars and you'll find her latest lair. I'll do the questioning; you just need to-'

'Stop.' Baumer held up a hand. 'Just stop, Lena. It isn't happening.'

'Why the hells not?' she asked, turning to face him directly.

'Because I need everybody in this city on our side, especially those who know how to fight. I arrest Brodbeck, I might as well fling the gates open, save her people the effort of betraying us.'

'So she gets away with murder?'

Along the walls, sentries turned to see who was shouting.

'Yes, you ridiculous shit, exactly that.'

She clenched her fists and glared at him, but Soren Baumer wasn't going to be stared down. He stood steady, staring right back at her.

Worst of all, he was right. If she had been in his position, she would have made the same call. She should have known that before she even came up here. She'd been so focused on her own obsession, on the face of Beatrice Saimon swirling through her dreams, that she had lost sight of an obvious and terrible reality.

This was it, the dead end. A suspect she couldn't question. A murder she would never solve. She seethed at the injustice of it all, but the blood was on her hands as much as Baumer's. She was the one who had brought Brute down on Saimon's neck, who had chosen not to see the gaps in the priest's story. She had got too comfortable in her role, become complacent, and slipped into the very thing she had promised never to do again. Baumer wasn't the one who deserved her anger, not given her own part in killing an innocent.

'Sorry, Soren,' she said, turning away. 'I've just got caught up in this mess.'

'Happens to us all.' He squeezed her shoulder briefly, the touch comforting despite the cold steel of his gauntlet. 'Just be careful how you throw your words around. I can't have you undermining my authority, especially not when half the city thinks you should take my place.'

He was right again. If she wasn't willing to lead the defence, then she couldn't be seen challenging him, whether or not it was about the fighting. When it came to holding an army together, authority mattered. She might not love it like Baumer did, but she could respect it.

The boom of a cannon was followed by the crash of a shot hitting the wall, further along this time. A distant trembling shook them.

'Are we safe up here?' Deppel asked, peering nervously out around a crenellation. 'Ain't we gonna get shot?'

'You're fine, kid,' Baumer said. 'I've lived through this before.'

Deppel looked at Baumer with a beggar's hard-learnt suspicion. 'Where?' he asked. 'When?'

'Nowhere you'd have heard of.'

'I've heard of lots. Mistress Brodbeck, she had all these pamphlets about the places what people were fighting over, and how Father Earth's people was oppressing Mother Sky's, and they was freeing people in all of them. There was all these battles and sieges and burnings, all over the principalities.'

'This wasn't in the Principalities of Stone.'

Lena had never heard Baumer talk about where he'd fought. She had always assumed it was in the Principalities like her, but apparently not. He didn't talk about ships, and those who'd fought in the Ice War never shut up about them. That left one likely option.

'You fought in the Salt Cities, then,' she said. 'The Marsh Wars, or something later?'

He took a step away, watching her with suspicion.

'Why do you ask?' he said.

'Just curious.' And trying to reassure Deppel, but saying that out loud would defeat the point.

'You like people getting curious about you?' Baumer asked.

'No, but I-'

'Me neither, so quit this shit.'

'Gods' eyes, Soren, I didn't mean anything by it.' Her voice rose and Deppel flinched, but she wasn't going to let anyone talk to her this way. Sure, she had to respect Baumer's authority, but she had her self-respect to consider too. 'I was just asking a question.'

'Like you've been asking questions about Brodbeck and the Saimons?'

'What the thunder are you talking about?'

'This always happens. When they can't find anyone else to blame, it's the mercenaries who get it in the neck. Well, I'm not having you pin this on one of my people.'

'I've seen what mercenaries do, and there's a reason no-one trusts you.'

'I knew it.' Baumer bared his teeth. 'You want help again; you can go find some other idiot.'

He stormed off along the walkway.

Roiling with rage, Lena bit back the urge to shout after him.

What kind of dung heap had she been dealing with all this time, that he'd go off the handle like that?

'Who does he think he is?' she snarled.

Deppel wouldn't meet her eye, but she could see he was itching to speak.

'Spit it out,' she snapped.

'Must be stressful, defending a city.'

'What a brilliant insight. They should put you on the thundering council.'

'I just mean…'

Deppel's words trailed off, fading with the echoes of the last cannon shot.

And in that moment of silence, his meaning sank in. Baumer had broad shoulders, but they had never before carried the weight of a city.

She hadn't deserved to be talked to like that. But then, she hadn't let it go when he asked her to. No, not asked, told her to, and it wasn't his place to boss her around. Except that it was. He was bossing half the city around, and she knew all too well how necessity hardened a commander.

The arguments got tangled in her head like a hissing knot of snakes, guilt and anger snapping at each other's tails with toxic barbs.

And now she had alienated the help she needed for her investigation. Maybe she had been better off just swinging a sword.

Animated by her own annoyance, she stormed off along the walkway that ran the length of the city walls. Militiamen in moth-eaten city colours, mismatched weapons in their hands, jumped out of the way to let her pass. Pathetic, the lot of them, cowering amateurs. If this was all they had, then Unteholz was doomed.

Soon, she was leaving the bombardment behind, the roar of cannons and crack of shot becoming distant and muffled. The only sound accompanying her was the patter of Deppel's footfalls, a hurried echo of her own.

Black shapes wheeled in the sky above: wyverns and crows, both drawn out of their mountain nests by the sounds of war. The city should be trying to tame those wyverns, to have something against the besiegers' beasts when the time came. But who aside from her had a scrap of relevant skill?

Her route took her in a long loop around the boundary of the city. Terraced fields and tamed forests went past to her left, crowded streets to her right. As she came around the loop, the mountain loomed ahead, and she felt peace radiate from its ageless peak.

At last she reached the Manden Gate. There she looked out across the open ground to the Weeping Stone. That arrogant swine Everhart hadn't sent many soldiers this far around, just a smattering of scouts lurking beyond bow range. Not enough to storm the gate, but more than enough to stop a messenger getting through.

She laid her hands on the cold stone of the battlements and looked out at the Weeping Stone. It stood as dark and remorseless as ever, like a blade that would split evil from good.

In her hands, it had missed.

She remembered Holy Saimon's face, the sound of Brute slicing through her neck, the cheer of the crowd echoing across this ground. She felt sick to her core.

'I'm meant to right wrongs,' she said quietly.

'You're going to,' Deppel said, coming to stand beside her. 'You just ain't worked out how yet.'

Beyond the execution ground, a rough trail headed into the woods. That was where she had seen the first scout of the army, on the day she found Pawlitzki driving beasts mad with alchemy.

'I could try the alchemist again,' she said. 'Holy Saimon had been drugged, and he had connections to both victims. If I shake him, maybe something shakes loose.'

'So we gonna question him?'

Lena watched the scouts as they drifted through the forest's edge, watching, waiting, slow and patient, like the wyverns overhead. Both would have their blood in time, but that time was not yet.

'Let's try something else,' Lena said.

Chapter Twenty

Equals in Darkness

The alchemists' street stank just as badly at night as it did during the day. The foundries were still blazing away to one side, billowing smoke as they churned out weapons and armour, and nothing could disguise the stink of the tanneries. But Lena had been through worse.

Was this how it felt to be a mugger, lurking in alleyways under cover of darkness, waiting for a victim to pass? Did they feel the same nervous tension that kept her shifting from foot to foot?

This was easy compared with trailing Pawlitzki during the day, when all he needed to do was turn around and she would be revealed. But that daylight pursuit had revealed nothing with even a whiff of suspicion, no hint at how his potions, whether silver dream or birth control, might connect Fiete Saimon to his killer. If there was dirt on him, then it would have to be found at night.

The door to Pawlitzki's shop opened and a square of light fell across the street. A moment later, the man himself emerged, a bald bag of bones in ill-fitting clothes and a dark cloak. He closed the door, pulled up his hood, and hurried away.

Lena slid out of the alleyway and padded after Pawlitzki. He headed with long, swift strides along the moonlit streets through the tanneries, then into Othagate. Down through the slums he strode, past alehouses still bustling with desperate drinkers, rats skittering away down the gutters at his approach.

Somewhere in the darkness, cats were fighting, their battle cries yowling through the night.

Not far from the Manden Gate, Pawlitzki stopped at the door of a tall building with a misshapen chimney. Lena stopped in another darkened doorway and watched as he knocked on the door.

There was a clack of wood on wood and a voice too quiet for her to make out the words.

'All are touched, or none at all,' Pawlitzki said, the words just audible through the screeching of the cats.

Light spilt across the alchemist. Hood still hiding his face, Pawlitzki walked inside, then the door closed behind him.

Mysterious words and secret meetings. Lena grinned. Here was something worth following the alchemist for. There was nothing like a conspiracy to motivate murder.

She hesitated a few yards from the house, listening for sounds from within. If anyone was talking, then they were keeping it quiet. She would learn nothing out here, so the question was, how best to get inside? It wouldn't be hard to get the shutters open, but sneaking in would only work if there was no one to see her, and someone had been there to answer the door. Barging in would play to her strengths, but it might not get her much information, and the bruises of recent fights were only just starting to fade. That left a different sort of boldness.

She pulled the hood of her cloak up and let the front droop, so that she would be shadowed even when the door opened, then she raised her hand.

Again she hesitated. Could she really pull this off, without knowing what lay inside?

On the other hand, what was the worst that could happen? If she learnt nothing, then she would be no worse off than before. If they got confrontational, then she had a cudgel on her belt and the skill to use it. Better to seize the moment than to waste her life waiting.

She knocked.

A moment later the door opened. A woman was silhouetted

against the light.

'Who is touched by the gods?' the woman asked.

'All are touched, or none at all,' Lena said, repeating the words she had heard Pawlitzki use.

The woman nodded, then tilted her head on one side.

'You're new, aren't you?'

Lena nodded. The fewer words she used, the less likely that she would be caught in a lie.

'From out of town?'

She nodded again.

'You chose a lousy time to come to Unteholz,' the woman said, stepping back to let Lena inside. 'But at least you've found us.'

She closed and bolted the door, then led Lena across a sparsely furnished room to a doorway at the back. The woman looked familiar, and Lena realised that she had seen her at the Blade Market, handing out heretical pamphlets. One of Brother Moon's cultists, preaching revolution for the god of death. The city's world of secrets and lies was smaller than Lena had imagined, and potentially deadly, if Brother Moon was involved. Lena brushed her hand over her cudgel, checking that she could easily grab it if things went wrong.

In the back room, the woman rolled back a worn rug to reveal a trapdoor, which she heaved open. Steps descended into the ground beneath the house, lit by a series of wall-mounted tallow candles, with their trails of greasy, sickly smelling smoke.

'All the way to the bottom,' the woman said. 'You're just in time.'

The stairs were narrow and winding, carved into a natural fissure through the rock. As Lena followed them, the trapdoor slammed shut with a weighty thud, closing her in.

No way back. She gripped the handle of her dagger and stepped on down.

Voices emerged from the darkness ahead, a low chanting of nonsense sounds.

'Arda, varda, kohn,' the voices said. 'Arda, varda, kohn. Arda, varda, kohn.'

With each repetition they grew quieter. By the time Lena emerged into a subterranean cave, they were just a whisper, a rustling of breath as close to silence as the dance of autumn leaves.

The cave was the size of a decent alehouse, with a rough domed ceiling from which stalactites hung. A small crowd filled the space, thirty or forty in total, all with the hoods raised on their cloaks. They faced the centre of the room, where an oak table stood surrounded by empty space. On the table were three skulls: one from a gryphon, huge and beaked; one from a mouse, tiny and pointed; and one between them from a human. Lena shuddered as she stared into eye sockets as black as grief.

The chanting faded into silence. Lena looked back and forth, trying to fathom what any of this meant. She had heard reverent silence before, in the brief moments before a priest began their sermon or a choir began to sing. This one stretched out like a chasm into which her thoughts fell.

Those thoughts weren't about the investigation. Not even Beatrice Saimon's face, the one that haunted her dreams. It was Jekob, her own son, glaring at her from the entrance to Everhart's tent, his eyes filled with hate. That look was like a fist squeezing her chest, crushing the breath from her lungs. She had failed him so badly, and now when the chance had come to reconcile, she had failed again.

She shouldn't be thinking about that. She should be focused on her work and on this place, but the silence and the shame weren't to be denied.

A man stepped into the circle and pushed back his hood.

Pawlitzki.

'I speak as an equal,' he said.

'All speak as equals,' the congregation replied as one. 'None high, none low.'

Pawlitzki licked his lips, laid a hand on the gryphon's skull, and looked up at the ceiling as if he might find wisdom carved there.

'Our city lies trapped between two lies,' he said. 'Two fictions woven from the falsity of priests and the distortions they cast across weak souls.

'On the one hand stands the church of Father Earth, the deception we have always known. A faith of unthinking tradition and unchanging hierarchy, keeping the same families in power from one generation to the next. They tell us to stay grounded, to be steady as the earth. But what they really mean is to stay obedient.

'On the other stands the church of Mother Sky, the new lie. They claim to bring a great reforming storm, shaking off the shackles of tradition and freeing humanity to follow a righteous path. But to them, righteousness is reflected in wealth, money and power are the divine rewards for purity, and to challenge the opulence of our overlords is to challenge the heavens themselves.

'Both would see us put in our place. Both justify poverty and cruelty by saying that the gods will it so.

'But we have felt the truth in our hearts. Not all gods single some out for glory while leaving others to dwindle into death. Brother Moon offers justice, because we are all equal in his eyes.'

His hand ran from the gryphon's skull, across the human, down to the mouse. A chill ran down Lena's spine.

'All are touched,' Pawlitzki said.

'Or none at all,' the congregation chanted back.

And there it was. A secret worth killing for. Pawlitzki was a heretic's heretic. He belonged to Brother Moon.

Lena had met Moon cultists before, though never for long. As a general for the armies of Mother Sky, she had been judge and jury whenever they were revealed, whether hiding in some distant village or burrowed like worms into the flesh of a city. It was one thing to take prisoners from the ranks of Father Earth, rational women and men who might one day find the light. It was another to uncover those who, in their derangement, worshipped the embodiment of death. Such people deserved the flames.

She had continued that work as executioner of Unteholz, and never flinched from the task. She didn't swing the sword for them, with its quick mercy. They faced the noose or the flames, a reminder that there were limits of what even Unteholz would tolerate.

The cold stone and silent cavern closed in around her. She had seen all she needed to. She should get out of here before these savages realised that she wasn't one of them.

She took a step back. Her heel knocked against a protrusion in the floor. She stumbled, flung an arm out to balance herself, and almost collided with a woman in a faded blue dress. Lena's cloak swayed, and the hood fell back, just as the congregation's eyes turned.

The ones who recognised her stepped back, muttering fearfully and making the sign of the eye. Whispers flew around the room, telling them all that the Headsman was among them, turning expressions from confusion to hostility. The most infamous fanatics in the world, bringers and worshippers of death, stared at Lena, and she stared back.

Lena remembered the Moon cultists she had met at the Weeping Stone. They had always seemed disappointingly ordinary, not the scarred killers, dead-eyed conspirators, and pinch-faced schemers their reputation announced, but ordinary looking men and women. It had been easy to conclude that they were the outliers, the weak members of the cult, or that their plainness had been a disguise. But looking at this group, all she saw were ordinary faces, scared and angry perhaps, but not hardened by years of violence or drawn into expressions of perpetual low cunning. She had to remind herself that they worshipped the god of death.

Her hands hovered inches from her weapons. She was badly outnumbered, but none of them looked like soldiers. If she was careful and lucky, then skill and experience might see her through.

'There's no need to worry, Headsman,' Pawlitzki said. 'Nobody here is going to harm you.'

'Tell that to him.' She pointed at the skull on which Pawlitzki's hand rested.

He looked down, then back at her with something approaching a smile.

'You misunderstand, Headsman. This poor soul's demise was none of our doing. He was the first of us in this city, and now he takes a place of honour amid our ceremonies, joining us in prayer into eternity. In another faith, he might be considered a saint, this very skull displayed in a gilded casket for all to praise, but Brother Moon raises none above the rest.'

'Don't lie to me, Pawlitzki. I know who you people are. Lunatics. Fanatics. You brought a plague upon Drescheim. You murdered the Count of Arlesbach. You steal babies while their parents' sleep.'

'Do you see any babies here?' Pawlitzki spread his arms wide. 'Any sign of disease? Even a weapon?'

Lena ran her gaze across the crowd. None of them had drawn arms. No one was making a move towards her.

'So that makes it all go away?' she asked.

'You have listened too well to the rumours about us,' Pawlitzki said. 'It is against our beliefs to harm another person, except in self-defence. All are equally touched by Brother Moon, and so all are equally deserving of life. It is not for us to deprive another of the spark the gods put within them.'

It was such a bald-faced lie, it stopped Lena in her tracks. Everyone knew that Brother Moon's people were killers. It was heresy that they ended up hanging for, but the violence of that heresy was renowned. Everyone knew that they were dangerous.

Then again, everyone in Unteholz considered her cursed. Everyone in the Third Host of the Righteous thought their war worth pursuing. She herself had thought that Alvard deserved to burn. Ignorance was as contagious as any plague.

All she truly knew was the Moon cultists she had executed, people heading to their death for heresy or treason. She had taken their calm as a form of lunacy, the steely demeanour of the fanatic. But what she saw here, now that the shock of her presence had passed, was people watching her with calm detachment, not the panic of criminals exposed or the judgement to which an executioner was treated. Even Pawlitzki seemed strangely content.

Would murderous fanatics wait so peacefully with an intruder in their midst?

'Why should I believe you?' she asked.

'Judge us by our actions. We risk all of our lives if we let you go, knowing that you might lead the city's constables to us. But still, an obligation lies upon us to release you in peace.'

The crowd parted, clearing her way to the foot of the stairs.

'You should be extracting some promise from me,' she said. 'Safe passage in return for silence.'

'No one can be bound by words made under duress. All we can do is pray for mercy.'

She stared at him. This couldn't be real, could it? Everyone fought, when it was that or die. That was human nature. It was how the gods had made them. That was why she had done such terrible things, why it had been so hard to leave it all behind. It was why the beating of the war drums outside the city made her heart stir. One person might, in extremity, set aside the will to defend themselves, but not a whole community. Not if they wanted to live.

No one moved to block her way. No one drew a knife.

'What if someone threatened to reveal your secret?' she asked. 'Someone like Fiete Saimon?'

Pawlitzki raised an eyebrow.

'I'm afraid that you once again misapprehend the situation, Headsman,' he said. 'As you imply, Fiete was well appraised of our secret, but not through some act of chance or skulduggery. He was one of us.'

'No, he worshipped Mother Sky. His wife was her leading priest.'

'Many of us attend her temple. Persecution forces false faces on us all.'

'So why not play at being Earth worshippers, instead of

risking your necks as reformers?'

'In a town this divided? Better that we divide ourselves, hear the gossip of both communities, listen out in case someone hunts us. You of all people know how that could end.'

Pawlitzki seemed happier the more he talked. Around him, the rest of the secret congregation watched Lena with uncanny stillness. She had killed members of this community, mutilated their bodies on the order of a judge. They should have fallen on her in a fury, just like Brodbeck's gang, but instead they watched and waited, blank faced.

She sighed. If what Pawlitzki said was true, then these people didn't deserve to live in dread, and if it wasn't, then they could overcome her with sheer numbers. She took her hands from the hilts of her weapons and folded her arms across her chest.

It was as if the whole cave let out a sigh of relief.

'I'm going to have a lot of questions for you later, Pawlitzki,' she said. 'But just one more now before I go. All this…' She waved a hand, taking in the cave, the congregation, the collection of skulls. 'Was this why the Saimons argued, a matter of faith?'

Pawlitzki shook his head.

'Beatrice was too committed to her own faith. Fiete never dared tell her that his path to freedom had been illuminated by Brother Moon's light.'

'Was it a family thing then? I found a bottle among Holy Saimon's belongings, one from-'

'Please, Headsman,' Pawlitzki said, giving his head a tiny shake as he spoke. 'I can answer all your questions at a later juncture. For now, we have little time left for worship. If you do not intend to betray us to the authorities, might you also grant us the favour of completing our service in peace?'

For a moment, she almost said no. What if she left and then Pawlitzki ran off, robbing her of the chance to learn more? But where would he run to, with the city under siege?

'Don't hide from me,' she said, and waved at the room around her. 'Or I'll smash this secret wide open.'

She headed up the steps, keeping the hollowness of that threat to herself. She didn't care how people prayed, but she cared that they weren't killed for it. Even when she had led Mother Sky's armies, it had never really been about faith. It was politics and all the bloody business that stemmed from it, those days when protecting one town meant attacking another, not because of what the people there believed but out of the cold, hard necessity of war. There was no necessity in seeing Pawlitzki's people put to the sword. She already had too much blood on her hands.

The trapdoor thudded open, and she stepped out into the house above.

'You need to improve your watch words,' she said to the woman on guard as she headed out the door.

It was still dark outside, though past the deepest of night. Bakers' apprentices would be rising to stoke the ovens, servants of merchant houses setting out clothes and fetching water.

Lena walked slowly through the streets, contemplating the complex puzzle of the Saimons' lives. Pawlitzki claimed to have a peaceful faith, but shared secrets could lead to desperate action. Bishop Kunder had battled Beatrice on the field of faith, but would the holy woman stoop to murder? Councillor Maier had seemed to be a political opponent: did business ties negate or exacerbate that? And then there was Jagusia Brodbeck, a known murderer lying in the heart of their lives. All of these people had been invested in the Saimons' fate. Which one of them had cared enough to kill?

She kept walking, letting her feet choose their own path, the peace of the darkness giving her thoughts space to settle. There was none of the noise and bustle of the city or of the artillery beyond its walls. The army needed its sleep too.

That army lay out there to the east, Jekob among them. She wondered if her son thought of her, and if he did, whether it was ever with kindness. Did some memory of love remain, or was there just hate?

If only she could make him understand. She had fought for justice, for security, for the safety of the people she loved. And yes, she had fought for pay, but that pay had fed and sheltered him, had bought him the education she never had, had let him and his father live in comfort. She had tried so hard to do right by him, but he refused to see it, and no matter what she had ever said or done, she could not get through.

Grief and anger, always bitterly twined together, sank their barbs into her heart.

A mewling sound brought her out of her thoughts and into the world. She was on her way through Othagate, back towards her home, as the sky turned from black to grey. A scrawny ginger cat emerged from the mouth of an alley and looked up at her. The creature's legs were tensed, ready to spring away, but it didn't flinch as she bent slowly down.

'Sorry,' she said. 'I don't have any food for you now, and no one else will during a siege. Hells, if this goes on then they'll make a meal of you.'

'Meow?' The cat pressed its head against her outstretched hand, and she tickled it under the chin.

'I could take you home, find you an egg or a scrap of salted goat. How does that sound?'

The cat pressed against her leg and purred. Its fur was matted and hopping with fleas, yet Lena's heart stirred.

A temple gong boomed, then another, and another. A distant shout went up and others joined in, a chain of voices racing through the city.

The cat froze in alarm, head pointed towards the noise. Before Lena could take hold, it slipped through her fingers and raced off into the darkness.

A band of men and women came running down the street. Many wore old chain mail or buff jerkins, the leather armour hanging open in their haste to get moving. They carried arquebuses and halberds, matching weapons drawn from some militia armoury.

'To the walls!' their leader shouted. 'Every armed soul to the walls, we're under attack!'

Lena's hand went to the place on her belt where her sword should be. It was early in the siege to seize the place by assault, but sometimes it was worth increasing the pressure, in hopes of breaking the defenders' will. If she wanted to keep the city strong, then she should head to the walls, to put some steel into the nervous volunteers.

To hells with that. Her wars were behind her.

She turned the other way and headed home.

Chapter Twenty-One

The Go Between

The moment they stepped into the shop, Pawlitzki's apprentice appeared. Her eyes were wider than usual, her skin pale beneath the tiny alchemical scars, and she held a broomstick like she was wielding a blade.

'Oh, it's you.' She sighed and lowered the broom.

'Who were you expecting?' Lena asked. 'Wyverns down off the mountain? Bandits come to steal your pots of over-priced mud?'

She waved dismissively at the shelves full of jars covered in arcane sigils. As on their previous visit, smoke trailed from the back room, this time sweetly scented and blue-grey.

'Everyone knows that when a city falls the soldiers go wild,' the girl said. 'They run around stealing and beating people and… you know…'

Lena grimaced. She wished that she could tell the girl she had nothing to fear, but a victorious army was a terrible thing. It took a will of steel to keep it in check, even if the commander wanted to. True believers like Everhart seldom saw the need.

'You're called Lotta, aren't you?' she asked.

The girl nodded.

'Well Lotta, you don't need to worry, the army hasn't taken the walls yet. These first assaults are testing the city's mettle.'

'How long will that last?'

'Depends on how soon they bring out the dragons.'

The girl went even paler, and the broom trembled in her

hands. So much for Lena's attempt to provide comfort, maybe she could distract the girl instead.

'I've got questions for your master,' Lena said. 'But Deppel wants to learn about all this junk, don't you Deppel?'

'Yeah!' He pointed at a red jar emblazoned with skulls. 'What's that?'

'Rat poison,' the girl said quietly.

'What's it made from?'

'That's a guild secret.' The girl frowned, set her broom down, and went to stop Deppel opening a jar. 'You shouldn't touch these.'

'Alright, then what's this?'

Lena walked quietly past the girl, pushed aside the curtain at the back of the shop, and stepped into Pawlitzki's lair.

Heaped embers in the fireplace gave the room a hellish glow. It shone off the gleaming dome of Pawlitzki's head and through the winding, intricate glassware over which he was hunched. A thick dark liquid was running along the pipes, through sections heated by candles and others cooled by water, before emerging drip by drip into a clay jar. Pawlitzki poured powder from a flask into an alembic at the end of the apparatus, his whole body tensed over that single action.

'Whoever it is, tell them that I can't come out now,' he said without looking up. 'If they wish to retain my services for a custom preparation, then they should arrange an appointment at a mutually beneficial hour.'

'You're sending me away?' Lena asked, folding her arms across her chest. 'That might not be wise.'

Pawlitzki froze. His head gave a jerk, caught between his half-completed work and the inescapable fact of her presence.

'Headsman Sturm.' He licked his lips and tipped the powder a little faster. 'Might I crave a few moments reprieve to complete this endeavour? I don't mean to be dismissive, not at all, not to you, but the outcome of many hours work now depends upon precision and timing.'

Lena walked, slowly and purposefully, across the room and around the table so that she faced Pawlitzki through his bubbling glassware.

'That's alright,' she said. 'We can talk while you work. It won't take much concentration to tell me the truth.'

Pawlitzki laughed uncomfortably.

'Could you perhaps move just a foot to your left, Headsman? I need the light from the fire.'

'Of course.' With a small step, she illuminated the alembic while leaving Pawlitzki's face shrouded in shadow. 'Now, tell me about silver dream.'

'Silver dream?' Pawlitzki's hand shook, and the powder hit the edge of the flask. Some fell into a candle flame and blazed with a purple light. He paused to steady himself before speaking again. 'I thought that you were here about the Saimons.'

'I am. Did you sell any silver dream to Beatrice?'

'All I ever sold her was a contraceptive draft. I realise that I should have told you about that sooner, but it hardly seemed pertinent, and there is a certain discretion that-'

'Do you know why she was taking that potion when they were trying to have kids?'

'No, I never asked. Each of them was unaware of my relationship with the other and I had no desire to risk revealing myself.'

'Then let's get back to silver dream. Who else in the city makes it?'

'I wouldn't like to speculate upon the endeavours of my fellow guildsfolk.' Pawlitzki's hand trembled again. 'We all have our own secrets, our own customers, our own-'

Lena took a sidestep, blocking his light again.

'Please, Headsman, this is a critical juncture!'

'For both of us. Stop blowing fog in my path and answer the question.'

There was a purple flash as more powder missed the alembic.

'No one. No one else here makes silver dream. Now please, please move.'

Lena stepped aside, then laid her hand palm down on the table. 'I get twitchy when I'm impatient, Master Pawlitzki.' She splayed her fingers slowly across the wood. 'It would be a shame if this beautiful glassware got tipped over.'

'I'm sorry! Please, just ask your questions.'

Pawlitzki tipped in the last of the powder, then took a step back. He stared at Lena's hand. His own fingers pressed, white knuckled, against his chin.

'Why only you?' Lena asked. 'Surely others could make silver dream?'

'I'm something of an expert in that potion. The others struggle to compete on quality, and the council charges a high fee for the licence to produce it, so the guild permitted me a five-year monopoly.'

'Why sell through Brodbeck if it's all above board?'

'The council sets a strict limit on how much can be produced and sold, an artificial attempt to keep the masses from enjoying the pleasures of the rich. I found a way to circumvent that restriction, for the greater happiness of all.'

'Or to put it another way, you got rich selling potions off the book.'

'Only for the best of causes. All of my spare money is channelled into my peace potion, to end these ghastly wars and the oppression of those who share my faith. Once it is completed, I will be able to-'

Lena nudged the table. Candle flames wavered and glass pipes clinked. Pawlitzki froze, staring in horror.

'I don't care about your pet project,' Lena said. 'I care about your sales. Did anyone buy a large batch of silver dream around the time of the Saimon murder?'

'Please, Headsman, please be careful,' Pawlitzki whimpered. 'I don't want to be blown up.'

'Blown up?' Cold dread swept through Lena. 'This potion could explode?'

Pawlitzki nodded frantically.

'It's very unstable at this stage.'

Lena stepped swiftly back, planted her boot in the fire, jerked forward again and just missed crashing into the table. She looked from the bubbling concoction to the wide-eyed alchemist.

'Doom and dust, man, why didn't you tell me?' she said, her voice rising.

'I thought you knew.' Pawlitzki shrank back from her, arms clutched tight to his chest. 'I thought that was the point.'

'For Moon's sake!' Lena flung her arms in the air. 'What sort of lunatic would risk blowing themselves up for a few questions?'

But of course the answer was standing in front of her, trembling like ashes in the wind behind his thick leather apron.

The curtain twitched. Deppel and Lotta peered in past the heavy cloth. The boy looked excited, the girl fearful.

'We heard shouting,' Deppel said. 'What's going on?'

Lena took a deep, steadying breath.

'This idiot,' she said, pointing at Pawlitzki, 'is about to tell me about his sales of silver dream, or else I'll be telling the council how he's broken the terms of his monopoly.'

'Yes yes yes!' Pawlitzki said. 'I'll talk, just please, don't wave your arms around so close to the table.'

Lena stepped aside and rolled her shoulders back. Her joints clicked.

'Tell me,' she growled.

'There are a lot of small sales.' Pawlitzki sat on a rickety stool and laid his hands in his lap, one set of fingers drumming against the other. 'Mostly to councillors and other merchants. A few more through the Blade Market, to whoever has coin for it. Regular consignments to Jagusia Brodbeck's people, who sell it through her networks.'

'So if someone wanted a large dose they would go through Brodbeck?'

Pawlitzki made a non-committal noise.

'Not exactly. I sometimes make potions on commission, and someone came to me for such a service just before Councillor Saimon's demise. They wanted a large quantity of silver dream, which is an unusual request, and an awkward one to fulfil given the limits of my licence, but they assured me of their discretion.'

'Assured you how?'

'Their generosity was indicative of a certain quality of character.'

'Because money and integrity always go hand in hand.' Lena shook her head. 'I don't suppose this saint gave you a name, still less their real one?'

'Please, Headsman, I'm no fool. I don't undertake uncertain deals without safeguards. Lotta, tell the Headsman what you saw.'

The apprentice stepped out from behind the curtain.

'I followed him to his house,' she said. 'Out near the East Gate. His real name is Heibar Goreck.'

'And who is this Goreck?'

'No one who matters,' Pawlitzki said. 'The man was but an intermediary, a factotum for some shadowy hand. He referred several times to his employer, as if they were a person of significance.'

'So we find Goreck, and we find them?'

'I believe so, yes.'

Lena felt as though she stood at the door of a treasure house. Just one small shove and she would see what she had been after all this time.

'Come on then, Lotta,' she said. 'I need you to show me this house. Your master will have to blow himself up without you.'

It had been a small but well-kept house, with walls of rough-cut stone and slates for a roof. The house of someone who could afford well-fitted shutters but not glass to go behind them. A house to take pride in, because pride was all the owner had.

Now it was rubble, the roof and half the front wall caved in, beams, tiles, and stones tumbled into the street. The shutters had somehow remained intact, though they had been blown out of their frame and landed in the middle of the road.

Two soldiers from the city militia stood in front of the building, each with a heap of buckets by their feet. They flinched each time a mortar bomb whistled through the air. Neighbours watched them nervously from around window frames.

'Mortar hit about an hour ago,' the calmer of the two soldiers said, running a hand over her close-cropped hair. 'We were sent to stop any fire from breaking out.'

'I don't see smoke,' Lena said.

'We're always to wait a couple of hours, just in case. Sometimes a fire starts deep in the rubble, doesn't get seen for a while.'

Lena approached the building and took a deep breath. There was a faint smell of smoke as if from a cooking fire, but no telltale trail coming out of the ruins.

'You're sure it was this one?' she asked.

Lotta stood between her and Deppel, looking down at the scattered stones and shattered tiles. The fear on the girl's face wasn't the wild panic she had shown when they came to the shop, frenetic and untethered by reality. This was a fear dragged out by facing the real world, as grim and weighty as the mountains themselves. It left her face pale, her hands trembling, her voice a rough whisper.

'Definitely,' she said. 'You think he was inside?'

'Only one way to find out.' Lena turned to the soldiers. 'You two, help us clear this rubble, make sure there's no fire.'

'That's not what we're meant-'

'I'm here on a job for the city, to try to stop this thundering siege. Do you want me to tell Captain Baumer that you wouldn't help?'

Reluctantly, the soldiers abandoned their buckets and came over to the rubble.

It was easy enough to clear the doorway. Lena set up a human chain, her and Lotta picking rubble off the heap and passing it back to the others, who piled it in the middle of the street. It was good to see the girl regain some steadiness, now she had something more than staring to do, and the militia volunteers let go their resentment as they settled into the work. One by one, neighbours came out to watch, and then to join in, despite the thunder of guns pounding the walls a few streets east. A sense of agency energised them, this rare chance to make a difference in a city besieged by forces they couldn't possibly stop. When a mortar's whistle came, everybody leapt for cover, then emerged once the danger passed. There was something strangely comforting for Lena about those moments, a wave of nostalgia for past campaigns and the camaraderie of sheltering together from the artillery's storm.

Once they'd cleared a way to and through the doorway, things became easier. Without a roof, the interior of the house was well lit, showing up the debris within, a litter of splintered planks, fallen stones, and fractured slates. Lena clambered carefully across the detritus, looking for the telltale shape that wouldn't match the rest.

Sure enough, there it was. A pair of legs sticking out from under joists fallen against the back wall.

Her heart sank. She didn't know Heibar Goreck, had no interest in his personal wellbeing. If her conclusions were correct, then he was a conspirator in a murder, a man she would happily have beheaded, but to find out who hired him, she needed to catch him alive.

She clambered over a heap of roof beams, almost fell as a tile slid from under her foot, and righted herself, cursing under her breath. She cursed her own clumsiness; cursed the artillerists who smashed open houses as easily as wyverns cracked bones;

cursed her delay in finding this place. If not for those things, she would have had a suspect to question.

Then she looked around the beams and cursed herself for leaping to conclusions.

A man's body lay against the wall, one arm crushed beneath a fallen joist. Blood lay in a wide puddle beneath him. His tunic was crusted with it, his grey hair darkened and clotted, the floorboards stained a deep red-brown, but none of it came from his crushed arm.

The man's throat had been slit.

Lena worked her way around the beams until she crouched by his head. She brushed away dust and fragments of rubble to touch the floorboards beneath. From the colour of the blood she had known what she was going to find. It was dry.

She hadn't just been a few hours late. It had been days.

There was a clatter as Deppel and Lotta scrambled over the rubble. Lena waved the girl closer, then pointed at the corpse.

'Is that Goreck?' she asked.

The girl blanched and wrapped her arms around herself. She nodded slowly.

'Gods' eyes.' Lena surveyed the rest of the rubble, as if a clue might emerge through some wild act of alchemy, a miraculous intervention to guide her next steps. 'Every time I think I'm getting somewhere; some fresh ox turd falls in my path.'

She climbed back across the rubble in a clatter of falling stones, not caring what she disrupted this time. At the doorway, the two soldiers stood staring.

'No fires,' she said. 'But there's a dead body in the back.'

'Thundering Sky worshippers,' one of the soldiers said with a scowl. 'Throwing bombs at innocent folks.'

Lena shook her head. As if it was that easy, just faith against faith, right against wrong, killers against the innocent. Once, she had fooled herself into those lies, but she wasn't that fool any more.

The sound of artillery had dropped off, probably a false lull while Everhart sent his men against the walls. There were no shouts and screams of battle yet, but they would come soon enough. Meanwhile, the quiet had lured out Goreck's neighbours, come to gape at the ruins.

Lena strode over to the nearest of them, a short woman in a brown woollen dress.

'You know the man who lived there?' Lena asked.

'Master Goreck?' the woman asked. 'Was he in when it hit?'

'Tell me about him.'

'Tell you what?'

Lena waved her arms in exasperation. How hard could it be to get some answers?

'What did he do? What sort of things did he say? What kind of person was he?'

The woman shrugged.

'He never seemed like anything special. Used to be a barge pilot on the river routes down to the Salt Cities, but he got too old for all that travel. Now he cleans and repairs up at the cathedral.'

There it was. Not a turd on the trail but a signpost to the next destination.

'Thank you,' Lena said. 'You've been very helpful.'

'Is he dead then?' The woman peered past Lena towards the broken house.

'Yes.'

'Sky worshippers.' The woman shook her head. 'We'll make them pay for this.'

Behind her, a neighbour tucked a lightning bolt amulet away inside his tunic, then took a step back, hiding himself amid the angry crowd. Win or lose, Unteholz would never be the same.

Chapter Twenty-Two

Trespassing On Holy Ground

The cathedral echoed with voices in pain, the divine harmonies of the choir drowned out by an all too human cacophony. Instead of a congregation standing attentively to hear a sermon, injured women and men lay on crowded pallets and heaps of straw, while priests and attendants bandaged their wounds, handed out bread and goats' milk, or offered spiritual consolation in the looming face of death.

As Lena and Deppel walked in, a novice in a smart green robe greeted them.

'Are you here for aide or to assist?' he asked.

'Neither,' Lena said. 'I'm looking for a friend of mine, Heibar Goreck. Haven't seen him in a few days and I was starting to worry.'

'Holy Angvalt has a list of our patients. You could ask her.'

'Heibar works here, mending and cleaning.'

'Oh, I see!' The novice smiled. 'In that case, you should talk to Holy Lufven, she runs the servants. You'll find her near the high altar, overseeing the volunteers.'

'Thank you.'

Lena made her way down the nave, past the rows of unfortunates laid low by war. The place stank of blood and shit and a desperate attempt to cover it up with incense. On one pallet, a man whimpered and twitched in his sleep, one hand clutched to his bruised head. On another, a woman reached out with the bandaged stump of her wrist, then collapsed into a heap of blankets. It was a sorry sight, and only the beginning of what this siege would bring.

Most of the priests were too busy to pay attention to passers-by. Of those who looked up, a few recognised her well enough to make the sign of the eye, always with a glare. Perhaps they had been here when things turned ugly between her and Bishop Kunder, or maybe they just resented the unholy presence of a Headsman and feared the ill luck she brought.

Close to the altar stood a red-faced priest in well-kept robes, her hair tied tightly back. She held a sheet of paper in one hand and a piece of charcoal in the other. Each time someone approached, she replied with a few brief words, made a mark on her paper, and sent them off on some new task.

Lena stopped, studied the woman's face, then bit back a curse. This was one of the priests she had confronted before, when violence skulked beneath the trembling surface of civility. There was no way she would fail to recognise Lena.

'I need you to talk to her, Deppel,' Lena said. 'Find out who here was close with Goreck.'

Deppel nodded eagerly, then hurried off towards the red-faced priest.

Lena sidled away to the edge of the cathedral, where the shadows of ancient ribs would shelter her from view. She leaned against the wall, its ancient leather rough beneath her hand, and wondered what sort of creature had left its carcass to become this place. Had it really been a dragon, breathing flames the size of fields? It seemed too large to fly. More likely some lumbering beast, not predator but prey, ambling through the valleys in a constant quest to fill its vast belly. Sheer size would have protected it from predators while it was young, but age laid everyone low, from the cats in the alleys to a former general with creaking joints. She raised her fingers to her scarred cheek, a reminder of the steps she had already taken on the slow trail to death.

At the front of the cathedral, candles burned on the huge

scale that was the high altar. Above it, the disk of the world hung from the wall, Father Earth's simple symbol cast in bronze. The earthenware lightning bolt that had once hung beneath it had been removed, leaving a dark silhouette where it had kept light off the partition wall for so many years. Mother Sky was no longer welcome here, not even as Father Earth's inferior, his obedient sister and servant. This was no place for symbols of the reforming storm.

A tugging at her tunic made Lena look down. A middle-aged woman with smooth skin and a bandaged head looked up at her from a pine-framed pallet bed.

'I need more of those herbs,' the woman said. 'To numb the pain.'

Lena crouched beside the woman and squeezed her arm. A set of gold prayer beads lay in her lap, a heady perfume drifting from the holes in their engraved sides. This was not someone used to struggle or to suffering, and Lena had seen how hard it could be to endure that first shock.

'Better to accept the pain if you can,' Lena said. 'It helps you to judge what your body is doing.'

'I give you people a gold florin each month,' the woman said. 'For that, I expect more than just prayers for my soul. Now get me those herbs.'

Lena let go of the woman's arm and rose stiffly to her feet.

'Get them yourself,' she said.

Across the nave, Deppel was talking with Holy Lufven. She smiled and gestured with her charcoal in response to something he said. He spoke again and, despite her stern demeanour, the priest laughed, then pointed to a doorway in the corner of the wooden screen that closed the cathedral off behind the high altar. Deppel laughed, nodded his head, and left Lufven to her volunteers.

Lena slid through the shadows along the side of the room, towards that door. Deppel caught up with her half way.

'She's a nice lady,' he said. 'Said they'd feed me dinner if I help out for a few hours, feed and wash people and that.'

'No time.' Lena scowled. 'What about Goreck?'

'Says he mostly kept to himself, done his job, didn't cause no problems. He weren't close to no one here, spent his spare time with people from his barge pilot days.'

'There can't be many of those in Unteholz. The river's not even navigable for a dozen miles down.'

He shrugged. 'Just what she said. That and he kept a chest in the tool cupboard.'

'Which is through those doors at the back?'

'Yeah.'

'I want to look inside.'

There was a time for sneaking through shadows and a time to be more brazen. Lena strode through the bedlam of priests, patients, and volunteers, took hold of the door handle, and raised the latch.

It wouldn't open.

She cursed quietly and tried it again. Something rattled, but the door stayed firmly shut.

'Locked,' she hissed through gritted teeth. 'Maybe we can find a back way.'

'Or I can open it.'

Deppel glanced around, then sat down on the cold flagstones and took off his shoe. He reached inside, lifted the leather of the insole, and pulled out a pair of slender, tapering metal rods. He grinned proudly as he held them against his sleeve, visible to Lena but no-one else.

'Jagusia's lot taught me lock picking, remember?'

Lena looked down at her assistant. He was so pleased to have brought them this far, so excited to take them further. But they were meant to uphold the law. What would it mean if they broke it?

It would mean that justice mattered more than the laws of gods and humans.

Lena placed herself between Deppel and the rest of the room, trying to look like she was waiting for someone.

'Do it,' she said.

Behind her, Deppel's tools rattled and clicked in the lock. Suddenly, she was very aware of her own body, of her forced attempt not to draw attention. She watched every priest as they strode past in their green robes, every patient who looked her way. Whenever someone came closer she tensed, hand tightening around her belt to keep from gripping her dagger. As each one turned away she relaxed, only to see another coming.

She and Deppel were doing the right thing, but that didn't mean she wanted to explain it.

More clicks were followed by a forceful thunk.

'We're in,' Deppel said.

The door creaked open, and Lena followed him through, closing it firmly but quietly behind her.

The rear rooms of the Cage Cathedral were less grand than the main chamber. Partition walls had been built within the bone and leather frame, some of brick and others of wood, creating a network of cramped passages and small chambers lit by dripping tallow candles. Where the guts of the beast had once lain there were now the guts of a working temple, offices, storerooms, and a scriptorium taking the place of stomach, kidneys, and spleen. The tallow of the candles still gave the air a hint of something dead.

They walked through a robing chamber, where priestly vestments hung from wooden hooks, into a corridor lined with small doors, with a staircase halfway along.

'Which room is it?' Lena asked.

'She joked about Goreck skulking under the stairs,' Deppel said. 'We could try there.'

Sure enough, there was a low door underneath the stairway, sturdily built but without a lock. Taking a candle from one of the corridor brackets, Lena pushed the door open and peered into a small storage room. Tools hung from hooks and pegs all along the walls, a barrel half full of sand sat in a near corner, and behind it was a small, simple chest with a lock worth more than the box itself.

A lock spoke to a need for security, something furtive or valuable or both. Had Goreck thought that it would be more secure around priests than in his own home? Or had he wanted to put some distance between himself and the contents? Lena smiled as she let Deppel past. She would know soon enough.

Once again, there was a click of metal on metal as the lock picks slid in. Lena kept watch up and down the corridor, shoulders tensed, gaze flitting back and forth. Every time she heard footsteps she held her breath and pulled back into the confines of the doorway. Every time the footsteps receded, she breathed easy again.

It wasn't the thought of getting caught that bothered her. It was the thought that she might never get back here again, might miss out on some vital clue, might be haunted by Beatrice Saimon's face for the rest of her days.

A tugging on her tunic made her look around. Deppel held the candle over the open box, its light catching the golden edges of stacks of coins, each pile arranged with the precision of a lunatic or a scribe, or perhaps of a man who could only wonder at the sight of such wealth.

'Just coins?' Lena asked.

'Just coins.'

She sighed and leaned back against the wall; arms folded across her chest. What had she expected? An order for silver dream? A journal confessing Goreck's sins? A bloody knife? She kept doing this to herself, expecting each turn in the road to lead to a grand revelation, then deflating when it didn't. She was smart enough to know better.

Deppel held up one of the coins. The candlelight picked out the image of a pair of towers.

'I never seen a coin like this,' he said. 'You think they're important?'

'Of course you haven't seen one. Nobody gives a Salt City

ducat to a beggar.'

'It is a clue!' Deppel grinned up at her. 'Someone from the Salt Cities paid him loads of money, so it must be someone from there what done all this.'

'Half the continent uses Salt ducats for trade. This tells us nothing.'

'Could mean the murderer's rich.'

'Or desperate. Or that Goreck was a miser who'd been hoarding since his days on the barges.'

'But if he weren't paid for it, why buy all that silver dream?'

And then it hit Lena. The stupidly obvious answer. The one they didn't need to go sneaking around a cathedral to work out.

Heibar Goreck worked for the priests. He could have been working for them when he bought the silver dream.

What in all the blackness was she doing trying to play at investigator when she couldn't even see a thing like that?

'Lock it back up. We should get out of here.'

Once again, footsteps sounded from another corridor. Once again, Lena tensed, then forced herself to relax. No one ever seemed to come this way.

Deppel locked the chest and rose from where he had been crouching, candle in hand. Together, they stepped into the corridor.

The footsteps stopped. Two priests stood at the far end of the corridor. One was Bishop Kunder.

The circle of faith shone on Kunder's chest, a gold medallion catching the candlelight. She narrowed her eyes as she glared at Lena.

'Who gave you permission to be here?' she asked.

'Holy Lufven,' Lena replied, throwing out the first name she knew.

'Holy Lufven knows that I would not allow you here. What is that boy holding?'

Deppel moved the offending hand behind his back, too late to hide the lock picks.

'Burglars,' Kunder cried out, striding down the corridor

towards them. 'Thieves in the house of Father Earth.'

More footsteps hurried towards them. Priests appeared at both ends of the corridor as their leader's voice rose in fury.

'How dare you desecrate this place of faith? A criminal and an executioner within our sanctum!'

'We're not here to steal,' Lena said, squaring up to Kunder.

'Why would I ever believe you, when you've been living a lie? An infamous Sky-bound general, skulking in the shadows of Othagate, refusing to admit even her own name.'

'My past is none of your business. I'm doing the council's work.'

'This is holy ground. Authority here comes from Father Earth, not the city council.' Kunder held her chin high and stared at Lena with disdain. 'I am his messenger, and you are trespassing against him.'

Lena's hand tightened around her cudgel as she surveyed the growing crowd of priests. These weren't soldiers, not even labourers with the strength for a fight. In the confines of the corridor, where their numbers counted for nothing, she could take them as easily as drawing breath.

And then what? She would be known throughout Unteholz as the woman who beat up priests. That was no way to protect her quiet life, or her peace of mind.

'We're going,' she said.

With Deppel at her side, she pushed her way past the priests at the bottom of the stairs, down the corridor, and back the way she had come. There was a rustling of robes as priests stepped aside, then moved to follow her. Candle flames flickered and tallow dripped in the gust of their passing.

Back in the main chamber of the cathedral, she hurried away from the back wall, out between the rows of casualties on their heaps of straw. She could hear the distant boom of the cannons again, could smell incense, blood, and fever sweat, could see scores of faces turn to watch as she strode by, pushing past both priests and layfolk. The ribs of the cathedral itself, a beast dead for centuries, seemed to close in as if letting out one last breath.

'Thieves!' Kunder shouted, her clear voice cutting through the hospital hubbub.

Everyone turned to look at the bishop, standing by the altar with her face full of righteous fury and her arm extended, pointing after Lena and Deppel. Lena quickened her pace, just a fraction short of running, trying to get out before she was hemmed in. She sidestepped around a man holding a child and barged past a pair of priests.

'Thieves!' Kunder shouted again. 'They broke into the back rooms of the cathedral, trespassing on holy ground for their nefarious ends.'

Shocked silence turned into a hubbub of angry voices. A woman stood in the way and Lena shoved her aside, straight into a candle stand.

It was all too familiar. The rising tide of anger. The people closing in. The shocked expressions and the outraged exclamations. But this time it wasn't just priests blocking her way, it was ordinary people, hurt and frightened from the war that had come to their door, helpless to protect themselves against the mortar bombs but given a chance now to act, to protect a place of sanctuary and salvation. They took it.

A mass of bodies surged through the room, stumbling between the improvised straw beds. There was a cry of pain as someone trampled a patient in their rush to get at Lena. Someone else tripped and fell into a candle stand, which landed on a heap of straw. Melted wax spattered and flames leapt through the dry bedding. The patient scrambled back in panic as fire spread. A priest tried to beat the flames out with a blanket, and instead sent strands of burning straw onto nearby beds.

A large man grabbed hold of Deppel, who yelped in panic. Lena bent the man's arm back with a snarl, forcing him to let the boy go, but that gave more people time to close in. She drew her cudgel. She didn't want to do this, but she wasn't going down without a fight.

'Get ready to run,' she said to Deppel.

'Fire!'

The scream went up from the side of the nave. Smoke was spreading, not the sweet smoke of incense but the darker smells of burning straw and wood. Shouts of anger turned to panic.

'Fetch water!' someone yelled.

'Get out while you can!' another cried.

The circle around Lena wavered then broke. She grabbed Deppel by the wrist.

'Now's our chance.'

A priest stumbled towards them, struggling beneath the weight of a heavily bandaged man. Everyone else was too busy to pay her attention, fleeing the fire or rushing to fight it. The priest lost her footing, fell, and almost dropped the patient. She looked up with wide, pleading eyes.

Cursing herself for a fool, Lena lifted the injured man from the priest's arms.

'Out,' she snapped. 'Quick.'

They went with the flow of the crowd, drawn towards the temple doors. Bodies crushed together as hundreds of people tried to escape the spreading flames. Lena shoved with her shoulders and held her arms firm, keeping the man she carried from being crushed. For a moment, they seemed stuck, unable to move for all the people around them. Smoke tickled her throat and dread rose at the thought of being caught in the flames.

Then the crowd surged again, and they were out in the fresh air. People had gathered, drawn by the sounds of panic, and some were forming a bucket chain. Dread and determination filled their faces. No city could survive if it let fire take hold.

Halfway across the square, priests were assembling, gathering patients and checking their wounds. Lena thrust the man she carried at one of them, who took him with trembling arms. Another priest frowned as he recognised Lena.

'You did this,' he hissed.

She could see by the fury on his face that there was no point arguing, and much to lose by staying. There were enough people to save the cathedral from fire, if it could be saved.

This hadn't been her fault. She hadn't knocked the candles, hadn't started the rush of the mob, hadn't been the one to spread the flames, so why did she feel this knot in her guts as the fate of the cathedral hung uncertain on the end of a bucket chain?

'Come on, Deppel,' she said, striding away from the priests. 'We should be gone.'

Chapter Twenty-Three

Lost Love

The stew was cold now as well as greasy, a lumpy mess that clung to Lena's bowl while her spoon clattered against the wood, the only sound in the house.

She stared at the portrait of Fiete Saimon, and he smiled back at her, his happiness mocking her own misery. It was too much. She got up and seized the painting, planning to turn it to face the wall. But when she took hold of the frame, she couldn't bring herself to do it. The man was murdered already, she shouldn't heap more indignity on him.

'I'm trying,' she said. Only a fool would talk to a picture, but there was no one else to hear her thoughts. Deppel had gone to see if the fire was out at the cathedral, and to listen for if they were blaming Lena. He had promised to be careful, to keep his hood raised and not to risk drawing attention, and still she had almost banned him from going. But she needed to know.

'I'm trying,' she said again, 'but it's all going to fire and ash. This town's full of liars, and I can't just shake the truth out of them. I found the man who drugged your wife, or at least paid for it, but now he's dead and I've no way of learning more. Every Earth worshipper in Unteholz will want my hide for today, and I can't do this with half the city after me.'

She took Brute down off the wall, the executioner's sword satisfyingly hefty in her hand, and picked up a whetstone from a shelf near the fireplace. Back at the table, she drew the sword and set to sharpening it, something to keep her hands busy, to settle her mind.

'If someone brings you justice, it won't be me.' She looked up at the painting again, then pointed at the blade. 'But I can be ready for if we catch them.'

That was a big if. The walls around the east side of Unteholz were crumbling beneath Everhart's bombardment. Somewhere out there, Jekob and his drachenritters were preparing their mounts, checking their harness, sharpening their blades. The besieging soldiers would be rested from their march by now, ready for the final assault, and once that moment came, all hope was lost. There was no place for justice in a pillaged city.

The scraping of the whetstone along the blade soothed her. She might make a lousy investigator, but at least there were some things she could do well. Ugly things, but necessary, and if she couldn't be wanted, she could at least be useful.

Sly footsteps approached outside the door. Lena tensed in her seat, drew the dagger from her belt and placed it on the table. Brute was no sort of weapon for a fight, especially not in a space like this.

The door opened and Deppel stepped in, the hood of his cloak pulled low across his face. Lena smiled in relief. Then he pulled the hood back, and she saw the nervous set of his features.

'Brought someone to see you,' Deppel said, stepping to one side.

In came a woman in velvet doublet and hose, her wine-red cloak lined with fur. She pulled back her hood, revealing the short blond hair and sharp features of Jagusia Brodbeck.

Lena leapt to her feet.

'Peace.' Brodbeck held up her hands. 'I ain't here to fight.'

'No, you have people to do that for you.'

'And I left them behind.'

'So what, you've got cocky, or you've got stupid?'

Brodbeck scowled and one of her hands clenched.

'I come to talk with you, Headsman, but you insult me again

and I'll do the talking with my fists.'

'Of course you will.' Lena stepped around the table. 'What makes you think I'll give you the chance?'

Deppel stood between the two women. He was trembling, his skin pale, but he held a hand out towards each of them, as if he could ever have held them back.

'Please, Headsman Sturm,' he said. 'I never saw Mistress Jagusia do nothing like this before. I think you should listen.'

Lena looked down at the lad, so earnest and eager to please, yet somehow standing up to her. His courage took her by surprise.

Reluctantly, she stepped back around the table and sat down, giving herself enough space to leap up if needed.

'Alright,' she said. 'Talk.'

Brodbeck settled into the seat across from Lena. As she did so, her eyes fell on the portrait of Fiete Saimon. A trembling hand went to her lips, and she sat staring, eyes wide, at the image.

'Mother give me strength,' she whispered. 'He was so thundering beautiful.'

Lena snorted.

'Was he still your lover,' she asked, 'after all these years?'

They were cutting words, as hard and pointed as any knife, words that should have been cushioned in soft circumspection for the sake of a woman struck by grief. But Jagusia Brodbeck had earned no mercy from Lena.

Brodbeck took a deep breath and closed her eyes. When she opened them again, her demeanour was restored, hard as bones and cold as a corpse on a winter's night.

'How did you know?' she asked.

'Your son Kerl looks a lot like his father.'

'Aye, he does. That's probably why I'm softer on him than the rest. I didn't care for all their fathers like I do for his, and they've ended up stronger for it. Love makes you soft.'

'And that's a bad thing?'

'You tell me. You're every bit the killer I am.'

Brodbeck tapped a finger against Brute, and the sword let out a low, ringing note.

Lena wondered if she had been too soft on her own son, or too hard perhaps. Would he have stood by her if she had been more like Brodbeck? Would he still speak with her if she had let him have his way? It was a pointless question. The past could not be undone. All she could do was deal with its consequences.

She pulled Brute out of Brodbeck's reach and sheathed it.

'Why are you here?' she asked.

'I want revenge for Fiete,' Brodbeck said, her voice catching on his name. 'And whatever I think about you, whatever you've done to my people, you're the best chance of catching who really killed him.'

'Your support is touching.'

'I ain't here to cheer you on. I'm here to tell you what I know. Or don't that interest you? Are you just going through the motions because you killed the wrong poor arsehole?'

Lena leaned forward, hand gripping the table edge. 'I'm the only reason anyone's even trying to get at the truth.'

Brodbeck laughed bitterly. 'Full of yourself, ain't you, Headsman? Have you forgotten that whole Moon-blighted army outside our doors?'

It stung to be called out by this woman, a thief and a killer, a parasite who sucked the life from the city to keep herself rich. The destruction an army brought was terrible, but it ended when the soldiers marched on. Brodbeck was a knife in the guts of Unteholz, twisting and pressing while the city bled out.

So why did Lena feel a need to justify herself? To say that she had cared about the fate of the Saimons before the army arrived? To make clear that without her, there would be no investigation, no hope of finding the truth? Perhaps she saw some twisted reflection of herself in this woman, or perhaps she was sick of being misunderstood.

She sat back, arms folded.

'Go on, tell me what you know. Maybe we can help each other.'

Brodbeck took a deep breath. She too leaned back in her chair.

'Fiete and me, we go back a long way.' She looked fondly at the portrait. 'We grew up together among the real people. You wouldn't know it to look at him these days, but he was one of the best of us, the kid who could take a penny and turn it into a bag full of florins. He wasn't some pale, foppish creature neither. There was fire in our hearts and knives in our hands and when we hit the sheets, we near shook the house down. Doom and dust, but I would have stolen the stars for him.

'We were both ambitious, but that ain't always a good thing to share. I wanted to lead the real people, but he wanted out. Same night Old Man Rochus fell on his own knife, Fiete up and disappeared. Took me a whole thundering week to find him, when I had better things to occupy my hands, and when I did he was setting up shop as a merchant. Turned out he'd been saving for years, ready to buy his way into an honest trade, and he'd never flaming told me. We argued like we'd never argued before, cold and hard and calculated, hitting each other where we knew we was weak, the sort of argument that leaves love bleeding in the gutter.

'I never even told him why I'd made my move then. He didn't know about the little boy growing inside me.'

She laid a hand on her belly and shook her head, smiling softly. Lena remembered her own pregnancy, that sense of joy and potential at the life growing inside her, and of fear at what the world might do to it. She couldn't say that it had changed her, not after what had followed, but it had made her strive harder than ever before.

'It was because of Kerl that we found that bond again, years later,' Brodbeck said. 'I took him to temple, not knowing Fiete would be there. Fiete and his wife.

'God's eyes, but she were impressive, giving this grand speech about how people had to change, how we all had to find a new redemption. She were the embodiment of the reforming storm, come to save us poor ash-faced sinners, to show us what passion and righteousness could be. I went to speak to her after, to get her blessing on my boy, and there was Fiete. He took one look at Kerl, and I could see he knew.

'He came to me that night, back in places he hadn't set foot in years. We talked for hours, and I wanted more, but he loved Beatrice and he'd grown too honest for the real people.

'We met up again over the next few years, more often as we got to know each other again. It was our secret, something I kept from my own people as well as his. He was safer that way.

'About a year ago, things changed. His marriage was rotting. They'd been trying for kids, but it weren't happening. He was trying not to blame her holiness, but he knew it weren't 'cause of him. He'd got Kerl as proof, even if he couldn't tell her that. I don't know exactly what was happening, but I know she had a foul temper and a taste for drink. He came to me more and more worked up. I offered him a sympathetic shoulder and a few cups of wine, and the old longing stirred between us. Soon we were shaking the house down again.

'I don't know how she found out, but you know what happened then. She walked in on Convocation, made a whole thundering scene, screaming about how I was trying to steal her man. By the blackness, if it had been any other woman I would have gutted her right there. But I couldn't. He still loved her.'

Brodbeck looked across the table at Lena, and there were tears in the corners of her eyes.

'I swear by all the real people, I never hurt neither of them. I couldn't do that. Not to my Fiete.'

Lena gazed at Brodbeck, this fearsome woman, dreaded and respected in equal measure. She had robbed, cheated, and murdered her way to wealth, and yet here she was, talking like the lovelorn author of a cheap romantic poem, her skin salted by tears instead of the blood in which she had long been drenched. Where Fiete Saimon was concerned, she couldn't help herself.

Once, Lena had been like that too, so lost in love she couldn't find the words. And when love had turned sour, frustration had thwarted those words as well. Trying to talk to Jahann had made it worse, because she could never express what she felt. It had been easier to run back to war, to hide from his disappointment, from the dreadful possibility that he might not love her still. But her love had remained, through all the tears and the rage and the distance. She could never have hurt him, could never even have abandoned the corpse of their marriage if he hadn't declared it dead. Love had blazed so bright in her that it burned. She could see that same love in Brodbeck's eyes.

'I believe you,' Lena said. 'Not sure a judge would, but the judge isn't the one hunting a killer.'

'Thank you.' Brodbeck leaned forward, and suddenly she was hard as steel again. 'Anything I can do to help, I'll do it. But you tell anyone about this, I won't be the one missing a head. Understand?'

'Your secret's safe,' Lena said. 'But if you threaten me again, you'll be feeding the wyverns on the mountainside. Understand?'

It wasn't a useful thing to say. It wasn't smart. It didn't bring her any closer to what she wanted. But she would roll in all the ashes of Moon's unholy darkness before she would back down from a threat.

For a long moment, nobody moved. The two of them stared at each other, like dragons fighting over a mate, their muscles tensed, claws barely concealed. Lena watched for any flicker of movement, any sign that Brodbeck's familiar fury had returned.

Instead, Brodbeck laughed.

'You should have been one of us,' she said. 'You're wasted on honest citizens.'

'And now you're wasting my time. Get back to your people so I can get some sleep.'

'Ah, but I've still got something you'll want to know.'

'What?'

Brodbeck stretched out her legs and leaned back. The chair wobbled under her, uneven legs not matching an even rougher floor. Gemstones shone on the jewellery at her neck and wrists.

'My mouth's dry as a cardinal's crack,' she said. 'If this were my place, I'd have offered some wine by now.'

'I've only got ale. Upholding the law doesn't pay as well as breaking it.'

'What's that bit from Saint Botlen's letters to Dunvar? "Hospitality repays itself most richly in the poorest hovel."'

'I never cared much for saints, even when I was fighting for their honour.'

'And I never gave a dead cat's turd for headsmen, but here I am, and I know you'll want to hear me out.'

'You don't know anything about me.'

'It's about your boss, judge of the blood court, the most gracious Councillor Maier.'

That gave Lena pause. Brodbeck was right, now she wanted to hear, whether it led to the killer or not. The thought of scuffing Maier's shiny reputation was hard to resist.

She got up, went into the storage room at the back of the house, and picked up two wooden cups off the shelf, small old things worn smooth by years of use. Then she stooped into the back of the room, rummaging beneath the shelves. Her fingers crossed a rounded slab of rock, two feet across, sealing a hiding place in the wall, and for a moment she hesitated, as she always did when reminded of that nook and the mementos it held. Then her hand moved on, closed around the neck of a bottle, and she headed into the front room once more.

At the sight of the dusty bottle, Brodbeck raised an eyebrow. The stopper came out with a pop and Lena poured two good glugs of amber liquor into each cup, then slid one over to Brodbeck. She sipped at her own, tasting sweet summer fruits while the Marlesan brandy warmed her throat.

Brodbeck sipped, smiled, then knocked the rest of her drink

back in a single gulp.

'Tell me,' Lena said.

'I heard you was looking for a man named Heibar Goreck, used to work the southern rivers, wound up here after he got in some trouble with a Salt City lordling.'

'Go on.' Lena forced herself to sit back, to hide her eagerness at the implication that this troubled man might be linked to Maier.

'The thing about the law is it ain't just two sides, clean and simple. Your councillor hires you to keep up what's good and lawful, but she hires other sorts too. Eyes and ears to spy on her rivals. Wagging tongues to piss on some poor sod's reputation. Thugs when there's real dirty work to do.

'Obviously, I'm an upright citizen, I don't know nothing about that, and you can swear I said so in any court you like. But sometimes I make introductions, one person to another, for business that ain't mine. And one of them introductions was between Goreck and Maier.'

Lena swallowed her whole cup of brandy, sweet, rich, and heady. The cost for a night of ale gone in a single gulp, worth it to mark this moment. Such luxury reminded her of old times, sitting with commanders of the reformed faith, sharing the bounty Mother Sky granted for their righteous work. Sometimes her companions would even be opposing commanders, met under a flag of truce or captured in battle and waiting to be ransomed, sharing fine dinners and discussing their craft. It hadn't all been muddy roads and cold nights around sputtering fires, not by the end.

She refilled her drink, leaned forward, and did the same for Brodbeck. She smiled at the other woman and raised her cup in a toast.

'Here's to those of us who do Maier's dirty work,' she said. 'I'll still kill you, if that's what the job needs, but I'll make it quick.'

'The same to you,' said Brodbeck. 'And, of course, to Councillor Maier.'

The cups clacked against each other. This time, Lena took

the drink slowly, closing her eyes and enjoying the taste of sun-drenched lands, where peaches grew as thick as bones on the mountainside. When she opened her eyes again, Brodbeck was rising from her seat.

'I should go,' Brodbeck said, but she didn't turn to the door. Instead she stood staring at the portrait of Fiete Saimon.

Brandy and nostalgia had melted the sharp edges off Lena's hate. Looking from Brodbeck to the image of Saimon, it almost seemed that they were staring into each other's eyes, a loving couple torn apart by bad luck and big ambitions. Lena knew about love lost and the pain it brought. Maybe it was easier to love a memory than the person behind it, but if that love gave a single soul shelter from life's storm then wasn't that worth something?

'Take it,' she said. 'I don't need it anymore.'

Brodbeck turned a suspicious gaze upon her.

'What do you want in return?' she asked.

'Nothing,' Lena said. 'No, wait, there is something. Tell your people to leave Deppel in peace. He's done with his old life.'

Brodbeck looked at Deppel, who had been standing quietly in the corner.

'That what you want, boy?' she asked.

Deppel nodded. 'Please.'

'Alright, I'll allow it this once.' Brodbeck picked up the painting. She didn't move, barely even seemed to breathe, just stared at the streaks of pigment on canvass, an oil-daubed ghost of lost love. When she spoke, it was softly, like a sinner begging their god's forgiveness. 'Deppel's a good lad, but good lads stumble battered and needy through my door every week. This here is unique. It won't fill the hole he left, but it'll do better than just memories and my fingers in the dark. I owe you, Headsman Sturm.'

With that, she headed out the door and into the night.

Chapter Twenty-Four

Before the Storm

Lena and Deppel strode through the dawn-bronzed streets, past shopkeepers opening their shutters and householders emptying chamber pots into the gutter. A funereal silence hung across the city, the sound of ten thousand held breaths, of people listening for the crash of guns to begin.

A priest in dirty green vestments and a scraggly beard stepped out to block their way, teeth bared, waving an accusatory finger in Lena's face.

'You,' he said. 'You burned down the cathedral. You've cursed us all.'

Lena's fingers clenched around the handle of her cudgel. She didn't have time for this-she needed to find Maier and speak to her before things got any worse.

'I don't want trouble,' she said. 'Just let us pass.'

'We're all going to die now,' the man said, wild-eyed and swaying. 'They'll burn this whole place down, and it's you who has brought the darkness upon us.'

It was nonsense, as anyone with an ounce of sense would know. The cathedral still stood, smoke-blackened but intact. The fire hadn't been her fault, and even if it had, how did that make their lives worse? The army beyond those walls would be happy to see Father Earth's temple disrupted. For all this idiot knew, she had earned them a reprieve. Yet other people were standing in doorways or leaning from windows, calling out their agreement, urging him on.

'Get out of my way,' she said, her patience fading.

'You're on their side, aren't you?' the man said. 'You've fought for those heretics outside the walls. You want us to lose, so your friends can march in and put us to the sword. Everyone knows what you Sky worshippers are like. I bet they promised you a heap of gold and a string of pretty boys for your pleasure.'

'Get out of my way.' Lena drew the cudgel.

'Oh, you'd like that wouldn't you?' the man said with a feral grin. 'A chance to beat the righteous, to show your true colours.'

The words crowded together in Lena's throat, too many to come out coherent, too jagged to make peace even if she wanted to. She raised the cudgel.

Deppel moved between them and smiled up at the priest.

'You should be careful, holy father,' he said. 'Everyone knows its bad luck talking with a headsman. You wanna curse yourself when vultures are circling the city?'

The priest swayed, the hem of his too-long robe dragging in the dirt. His fingers rose slowly toward his eye, remembering too late to ward off bad fortune. Was it reason that held him or the threat of a beating, fear seeping in through the gap in his rant?

A woman emerged from one of the houses, shot Lena a venomous glare, and took the priest by the arm.

'Come on, Holy Kamen,' she said. 'No need for you to get hurt, eh? Someone else will deal with her.'

The priest let her lead him aside, muttering darkly.

Relieved, Lena hung her cudgel from her belt once more. Together, she and Deppel walked on through the silently staring streets.

It was still quiet when they reached the walls. Cold dread

marched up Lena's spine. As long as things stayed the same, a siege was simple: you managed supplies, put out fires, and tried to keep panic from people's minds. It was when things changed that you had to worry, even when that change was silence.

Councillor Maier stood on the battlements close to the East Gate, just as the clerk at her house had said. It was where the city's leaders should be this morning. That was in her favour, at least. A sword hung from her belt, its guard an elaborate and fragile silver filigree set with semi-precious stones, absurd but perhaps the only weapon the councillor owned. She wore a breastplate, well-made but poorly fitted. Lena doubted she had owned it a week before.

Maier stood with Captain Baumer, his deputies, and a nervously twitching clerk, looking out across the land outside the city. Trench lines crept like snakes through open ground and terraced fields, bringing the venomous barbs of twenty thousand soldiers ever closer to Unteholz's throat. The battlements here were battered, crenellations missing, and a chunk of the walkway torn out. Cracks spread between stones where the wall below had shifted. One patch of stonework bore a dark, spattered stain.

There had been a stain like that in Goreck's house. Blood on the floor. One person dead for another's cause. Not a deed Maier would have done herself, but she never needed to dirty her hands, did she? She had people for that. Goreck had been one of them, earning Salt City ducats by buying silver dream and probably more besides. His death could have been Maier's way of ending the employment.

Was Lena one of those people now? She had taken the councillor's silver, knowing that something was expected in return. Perhaps Maier had stronger reason for buying the Headsman's silence than Lena wanted to admit, bound as she was by service to the city and those who ran it. Perhaps Maier was still counting on that bond.

To hells with that. Lena's loyalty wasn't for sale.

Maier and Baumer stood close together, their hands each clad in their own protective metals, hers in gold rings and his in gauntlets of bonded steel. Wealth protected as well as any armour, in the right hands.

'Councillor,' Lena said as she approached, Deppel walking quietly behind her. 'We need to talk.'

'Is this the prelude to the main attack?' Maier asked. 'The captain thinks not, but we would all value your input.'

Baumer glared at Lena. She held his gaze for a long moment, neither backing down nor responding in kind. If he wanted a fight, he could start it himself, she already had enough of other people's nonsense to deal with.

Across the trench lines, chains rattled, and some great beast roared.

'I'm here as a headsman, not a general,' Lena said.

'Still rejecting who you are?' Maier frowned. 'Even when we need you?'

'I know full well who I am, and I'm no soldier.'

'Then you should get off these walls,' Baumer said, flexing his armoured fist. 'Today is for soldiers' work.'

More roaring, louder this time. Half a dozen dragons, some of their voices deep with menace, others young and shrill, all hungry and frustrated from being bound to the earth.

'Are you saying I shouldn't ask my questions, Soren?' Lena asked. 'Some people might find that suspicious.'

Baumer flinched, looked away, looked back at her again. Armoured fingers rubbed at his brow, and when they pulled away, they left the skin deep pink.

'Fine,' he said. 'Ask. Then go.'

'That is not your decision to make, Captain,' Maier snapped. 'We have to-'

A roaring rose from the siege camp, the dragons' voices joining in a single raging cry that washed across Unteholz and echoed back off the mountainside, intertwining with itself in a chorus that shook Lena to her bones. A cloud seemed to rise from the forests as hundreds of birds took flight in alarm, the flutter of their wings an insistent susurration beneath the dragons' hunting cries. They flocked away from Unteholz, a widening ring of darkness with clear sky at its heart.

Into that clear sky, the dragons flew.

There were a dozen of them, the smallest eighty feet long and with a wingspan just as wide, their forelegs stretched out so that their claws caught the sunlight. They seemed to rise slowly from the rear of the siege camp, but Lena knew how deceptive that was, how the wind snatched at a drachenritter as they rode into the air, the vast muscles of their beast pulsing beneath them, scales sliding back and forth beneath the harness.

'They're amazing,' Deppel said, eyes wide. 'Like the biggest birds I ever saw, only shiny, all them glittering scales.'

Fire flared from the mouth of the lead dragon, offering a warning and a promise. Lena remembered landing amid charred remains, ashes swirling around her feet, letting her beast dig through the ruin for the bodies its breath had cooked. The smells of smoke and roasted flesh. The terrible wet sound of the creature chewing.

Once, it had just been part of the job, and she had cared more about her beasts than the people they devoured. Then the march of years had become a cavalcade of faces, the dead and the dying, real people lost on both sides. She had learnt how rarely war's victims were the soldiers, how much rarer still it was for them to deserve death. Satisfaction became acceptance, then became a horror that she couldn't face any more. Unteholz had been a safe place to hide from that feeling, until now. Today, the body might be Deppel, the charred ruins her own home.

'Get every gun and bow you can,' she said. 'Pikes too, for when they fly in low. Get buckets to the wells and every spare soul there to carry them.'

The others all stood frozen, watching the dragons as they

spiralled higher.

'You heard the general,' Maier snapped. 'Get to it!'

Soldiers raised their fists, uncertain who to salute, but Lena was already gone, dashing down the stairs, followed by a confused and fearful looking Deppel.

'Where are you going?' Maier shouted after her.

'I'm not a general anymore,' Lena shouted back, 'but I can still fight monsters.'

Chapter Twenty-Five

Dragontamer

Lena yanked clothes and blankets out of the chest, scattering them across her bedroom floor. Doublets, drawers, a ruff; broadcloth, cotton cloth, and fur: all were flung heedless into a heap as she searched for the one thing she needed. At last her fingers closed around an old armouring jerkin, patched and faded but still well padded. She tore off her tunic, pulled the jerkin on, and yanked the laces tight down the front.

In the streets, people were screaming. The dragons hadn't reached the walls yet, but panic was setting in. Most people in Unteholz had led safe lives, sheltered from the ravages of war by their city's carefully nurtured neutrality, but they had all seen monsters. Everyone had heard of a friend of a friend who had got in the way of some dying beast on the mountainside, had recounted in grisly detail what followed, the horror of it adding to the thrill as they told the tale in the safety of an alehouse. Now those monsters were coming for them, and the beasts weren't here to die.

Lena grabbed her wyvern hide armour off the wall. The leather was stiff beneath the scales, left untended for too long. She cursed herself for not seeing that this day must come. It didn't matter that she had hidden from the wars and destruction. The past was a relentless hunter that always found its prey.

Footfalls rushed up the stairs and Deppel came panting into the room, sweat plastering his hair to the sides of his red face.

'What can I-' he got out, then had to stop to catch his breath. 'What can I do?'

Lena pulled the armour over her head. Its familiar weight settled onto her shoulders. She smelled old leather and a hint of the oil with which she used to treat it, soft smells that brought back nights around the campfire, singing and telling tall tales while they fixed their war gear.

A roar rattled the shutters. The dragons were at the walls.

'Help me buckle this up,' she said, raising her arms.

With nimble fingers, Deppel worked his way down the small buckles on her left side, joining together the front and back of the armour. She turned so he could do the same on the right.

'Should I...' He waved his hands in the air. 'Do I need armour?'

'Do you know how to fight?'

'No.'

'Then there's your answer.'

She took down the longsword in its scabbard and fastened it at her waist. The sword belt took much of the weight of the armour, freeing the movement of her shoulders. She rolled her neck and grimaced as it clicked, then swung her arms in familiar movements, loosening the muscles for what was to come.

'Are you gonna fight them?' Deppel asked, wide-eyed. 'The dragons?'

'I'll do my best.'

She drew the longsword. After years of wielding nothing more elegant than Brute, it was a delight to hold something so precise, so perfectly balanced. She spun the sword, a showy and useless move, but one that made her grin.

She still had what it took.

'I call him Tomas,' she said, holding the blade out for Deppel to see.

'Like the saint?'

Lena laughed. 'Like a lover I had once, but don't tell the priests that.'

She sheathed Tomas and headed down the stairs, an old spring back in her step. The immediacy of action swept away doubts, leaving her mind clear for the first time in years.

She bounded out of the house and down to the end of the street. Here among the mountain-carved houses, she had a good view across the city. Fires were blazing in a dozen different places already, while the dragons soared overhead, vast wings catching the updrafts, long necks twisting as they looked for likely food. The drachenritters clung tight in the harness on their backs, bringing them together for their next attack.

The smell of smoke and shrieks of panic came to her on a rising wind. Clouds were approaching out of the southeast, darkly pregnant with rain, a promise of mercy for a burning town. But the wind that brought them in fanned the flames, spreading destruction.

Maier and Baumer had done their work, gathering soldiers with pikes, guns, and bows to fight off the dragons. Speartips gleamed on tower tops and arrows buzzed like gnats at the vast winged shapes above. All of them were in the richer districts, and Lena cursed the city's leaders for the same shortsighted tactics as so many before them. Did they really thinking that an inferno lit in the tinder of a poor district would hold back from burning the whole city down?

The drachenritters were led by a competent commander. Would it really be her Jekob? Doom and dust, she hoped not. Whoever it was, they had seen the concentration of defenders, seen where the city was vulnerable, and now they were sweeping towards Othagate.

Of course it was Othagate. War might touch the rich and powerful, might trim their numbers or whittle at their wealth, but the poor it trampled underfoot, crushing whole communities, leaving not even a record of their passing. This time, it was coming for the people who let an executioner live among them, who didn't mean it when they made the sign of the eye, who drank with Lena around alehouse fires on cold winter nights. People who had made space for her to hide from her past self. The fight was to control the rest of the city; Othagate was just its battleground.

But not to Lena.

'What do I do?' Deppel asked, staring open-mouthed as the leading dragon gave a short belch of fire, a signal to the rest.

'Follow behind me,' Lena said. 'Hammer on every door you see. Tell them to get buckets and fight the fire, or if they've children, then to get into the caves. No other way to stay safe through this.'

Then she ran, sprinting down the hill, heedless of the unmanageable momentum she was building. Better to arrive in a heap sprawled on bruising cobbles than to arrive too late.

She ran down the street, looking ahead for a high spot close to where the dragons circled. She slipped on something, almost fell, flung her foot forward and found her balance again, running on with Tomas bouncing off her hip. A building stood out among the rest, tall with a misshapen chimney, and she realised that she knew it: the house where Pawlitzki and his Moon cult had met. A fitting spot for her to rejoin a religious war.

The dragons were descending, sweeping over the roofs in a preliminary dive. Barrels fell from their flanks, released by the drachenritters. They shattered on the rooftops, coating them in a thick and sticky oil that filled the air with an acrid stench. Then the dragons rose and circled back around, ready for the real attack.

Lena reached the house. The door was locked, so she took a step back and kicked it close to the latch. Her knee twinged as it twisted, but the door gave on the second blow, bursting in.

The doorkeeper was there, eyes wide with terror, two children clutched close.

'Get to the thundering caves,' Lena shouted as she ran up a rickety flight of stairs.

She didn't stop to see what was on each floor, just kept running, up and up until she reached a trapdoor into the eves.

It was dark in there. Outside, there was a roar and a thud of wingbeats, then the whoosh of sudden flames. Not close enough to burn this place, but close enough for her to feel the heat.

Lena felt along the underside of the roof until she found a weak slat, then heaved until it snapped. Slates slid down the outside of the roof and she knocked more out with her elbow, until there was a gap she could squeeze through.

Othagate was burning. People ran screaming as the smaller dragons swept in low, chasing them with gusts of flame. Small was relative, and eighty feet of clawed, fire-breathing lizard was still a nightmare beyond the imagining of most people.

But that wasn't the real threat. The real threat was the large beasts, some a hundred and fifty feet long, breathing fire as they soared across the rooftops, igniting the alchemical oil as it seeped through rafters and dripped down walls. The slightest ember was all it took to ignite that oil, turning homes into blazing pyres that spat sparks into the wind, spreading the inferno.

The dragons were pulling up again, circling around for another attack. In the street, people looked up in relief, thinking that they were safe.

'Buckets or caves, you thundering idiots!' Lena yelled down at them. 'Get buckets or get to the caves!'

Some of them ran back into their houses. Didn't they understand what was happening here? That there would be no safe space within these streets once the fire took hold?

A wind was rising as the flames sucked in air. A roof crashed in, and blazing timbers tumbled onto screaming men and women.

The thud of wing beats. The dragons were coming back around.

Lena watched their course, looking for a likely target. One of the smaller ones was coming her way, set to fly past on the other side of the house.

She scrambled up the roof, slates sliding from beneath her feet, and swung a leg across the peak. The dragon was rushing in, chasing people along the street, fire flaring from its maw.

Lena waited a heartbeat as the beast came closer, then let go of the peak and slid down the roof. Tiles broke loose under her, slid clattering towards a fall and destruction. Her teeth rattled against each other. Then she hit the edge of the roof and pushed off with her feet. Momentum carried her into the air above the street, and she laughed out loud at the sheer stupidity of what she was doing, things she hadn't done since the crazy days of youth, before parenthood and generalship and running off to hide in the mountains. Back when she was willing to risk her life on her own reflexes and split second timing.

Then she was falling, the dragon was sweeping in along the street below her, and she slammed down onto its back.

She slid again, across the warm smoothness of scales, towards another fall and death below. Her feet flailed over nothingness as the wind whipped her face. One hand snatched at the spines that lay flat against the beast's back, but they were smooth, and her hand kept slipping. Instead she snatched at a strap that had once held alchemical barrels, and kept hold long enough to bring her other hand around. Once she had a firm grip, she swung a leg up over the ridge of the dragon's back.

The dragon's body was seven feet wide, tapering to a long neck at one end and a longer tail at the other. Lena bent her legs as though she was crouching on the ground, like her first riding master had told her, using her knees and lower legs to form a grip on the creature's flanks. Vast muscles pulsed beneath her, and she breathed the sweet, sulphurous smell of the dragon.

The drachenritter sat buckled into a saddle by thick leather straps, just behind the dragon's shoulders. She wore wyvern hide armour and a black helmet of boiled leather. Her attention was on the city below, oblivious to the woman behind her.

Lena spread her hand across the dragon's scales, closed her eyes, and reached out with her mind. This would been easier on the ground, face to face with the dragon, but she hadn't earned the nickname Dragontamer by doing what was easy. She forced herself to ignore the screams, the smoke, the crash of falling buildings, to put all her attention on the dragon.

Their minds touched.

There was hunger here. Hunger for food, the sort that commanders fostered by starving their beasts for days before a battle. The sort that drove hunting instinct to wild frenzy, a destructive force for the drachenritter to channel. But there was a deeper hunger too, a yearning for freedom that told her how young this beast was, how recently tamed. It had not learnt to love its captors yet, that cruel trick of the mind that made older beasts more pliable. It had not forgotten what it was born to be.

Lena slid in on that thought. She showed the dragon the trapped beast she had been, yearning for freedom from the responsibilities that piled up on her, as a commander, as a mother, as a wife. The resentment she had denied because she loved the people who depended upon her, but that had only hardened like steel beneath the hammer of her denial, had become the cage in which she was trapped. The images meant nothing to the dragon, but it knew the emotion. It recognised itself in her.

At a nudge from Lena, the dragon rose, leaving behind the terrified citizens and blazing streets, soaring into the open air. Another mind stirred, one bound to the dragon in ambition and aggression. The drachenritter tried to steer the dragon but felt something pulling against her.

Lena opened her eyes. The drachenritter was looking back, the domed helmet turning her features into those of a menacing black insect.

Swaying with the movements of the dragon, Lena rose to a crouch, one hand still clinging to a strap, the other drawing her dagger.

The drachenritter started unfastening her straps, twisting in her seat as she tried to free herself.

The dragon swung into the thermals above the Othagate blaze. It flattened out to catch the heat beneath its wings.

Warm satisfaction flowed into Lena's mind.

Lena let go of the strap and dashed along the dragon's back.

The drachenritter twisted, still half tied into her seat, drew her sword and swung it into Lena's path.

The dagger was too short to parry with. Lena lurched back, almost lost her footing, and the sword swung past an inch from her thighs. She fought for balance, desperately trying not to think about the ground a hundred yards below.

The drachenritter fumbled one-handed with another buckle.

Lena slid a foot back and steadied herself. The drachenritter's sword had come around, but not far enough to make a proper swing, not while she was twisted about like that.

Lena lunged. The sword came up. She flung her arm out, felt the dull pain of a clumsy blow bouncing off her armour. Then she grabbed hold of the drachenritter's helmet, yanked up the lower edge, and slammed her dagger into the woman's throat.

Blood sprayed across the saddle and up Lena's arm. The dragon jolted as one of the voices in its head became a flash of pain. Lena was flung from her feet, clung on by dagger and helmet, crashed to her knees on the dragon's back. She closed her eyes and reached out with her mind, forcing herself to be calm despite the height and the pain and the blood pulsing over her fingers. The dragon felt that calm, felt the pain vanish into death, and it settled to a steady flight again.

Lena took a deep breath. Her whole body was shaking, threatening to shatter that illusion of calm. She drew her dagger from the drachenritter's neck, cut the last straps holding the body in place, and pushed it out of its seat. It went tumbling through the air, towards the flames below.

Lena settled into the saddle.

The dragon's mind reached out for hers, already craving the closeness that older warbeasts came to rely on, that bound them to their humans despite all the pain of war. Her mind intertwined with the dragon's until she felt its yearnings, its pains, its every desire, from the scratching of a buckle under its belly to the fire in its throat. Youthful excitement burned bright in the beast, like it had in Calebek, who she had ridden to victory at Faustrech Valley, or Goldfeather, the gryphon on whose back she had first flown. Her own body was weary, her enthusiasm long burned away, but the touch of the dragon's heart made her feel young again, and her presence made it feel safe.

It was a long a time since she had felt this closeness, more total and dependant even than love. And now, for the sake of the city below, she would betray it.

At her urging, the dragon turned towards the flames of Othagate.

The district was an inferno, a blazing nightmare that sucked the air from the surrounding streets and spat back embers, threatening to cast the conflagration across the city. Around the edges were people, tiny figures from this height, like ants crawling in front of a fireplace. Some were forming bucket chains, the smarter ones targeting buildings that had not yet caught light, that might be saved if the flames were kept from taking hold. It was far too late for those blocks of buildings already touched by flames.

There were other people too, trying to get clear of the blaze. Some carried their worldly goods with them, hoping to save more than just their lives. As Lena swept low, she saw flames closing in from both sides of a street down which people were running. The front of a building crashed down, crushing some and trapping others. Their screams were almost lost amid the flames and wind. Lena gripped the dragon's harness so tight it bit into the flesh of her fingers. There was nothing she could do to help.

The last of the runners were nearing the end of the street and with it the hope of safety. One man had arms full of cloth, sheets trailing behind him. He struggled against the growing back draft as air was sucked down the street. It snatched the sheets from his arms, and they danced for a moment on the wind before being consumed in fierce flashes of flame. Then the wind took him too, heaving him off his feet and into the onrushing inferno.

Lena's legs shook against the dragon's sides. She had used dragons in battle, had set them to burn garrisons and defences, but she would never have done this. The innocent always died in war, but that was no excuse for making them the target.

She drew Tomas and swept down towards a square past the edge of the blaze. A larger dragon had landed there, cutting off a crowd of people fleeing the flames. It reared up, wings spread wide, teeth bared, rider raising his sword in the air.

She flew straight at the beast, urging her own steed ever faster, letting her rage flow. The creature was confused, finding itself up against one of its own flight. Its instinct was to fall into line beside its larger kin, to bare its neck in subservience, but Lena was in the beast's mind, stirring up old memories and ancient instincts. She marked the city as their territory, the other dragon as a rival for all the food here. The stink of burning flesh, together with the dragon's hunger, added to the power of the illusion. Everhart's drachenritters had primed their beasts for aggression. All Lena had to do was tip those instincts her way.

The beast beneath her roared, spread its claws wide, and opened its mouth as it rushed upon its rival.

At the last moment, the other dragon saw what was coming. It started to lift off, but it was too late. Lena's beast slammed into it, teeth grasping at its neck, claws raking its flank. She leapt clear as the two of them crashed into the buildings behind, rending and tearing, spraying fire and blood.

She landed hard on the cobbles by a well, rolled, and came to her feet, sword raised, shaking the dizziness from her head. The other drachenritter lay sprawled on the ground, limbs twisted, head tipped back, bones shattered beyond repair when his steed had rolled over him.

Another dragon was coming down towards them, drawn by the crash and cries of its brethren fighting.

'Quick!' Lena waved to the people in the square. 'Get out of here, now!'

They all ran, some towards safety, others towards the well with buckets in their hands. Among them was Deppel.

'Faster,' he shouted. 'We can still save Wetwillow Street.'

'Run, you idiots.' Lena pointed at the sky with her sword. 'Get out before that thing arrives.'

The would-be firefighters looked up to see the dragon almost upon them. With curses and screams, they turned and ran.

Deppel stood frozen at the well, his bucket shaking.

'I don't wanna die,' he whimpered. 'Oh gods, I don't wanna die.'

The dragon soared down. Fire shot from its mouth.

Lena dropped Tomas, leapt, and tackled Deppel around the waist. Heat blasted her back as they went tumbling across the ground. There was pain in her arm and a stench of burnt hair.

The dragon landed on the far side of the square.

Lena got to her knees over the prone Deppel.

'Are you alright?' she asked.

He pulled himself up, pale and trembling, mouth hanging open.

'Answer me.' She had to get through to him, had to get him moving.

He pointed at her shoulder. The fire had badly charred her armour and heated the buckle holding it in place, which glowed as it scorched the wyvern hide. Lena cursed and started fumbling with the fastenings as the heat of the metal reached through the leather to her flesh. Her clumsy fingers couldn't operate the smaller buckles, so she drew her dagger, sliced through the straps, and let the smouldering ruin of her armour fall to the floor.

The dragon turned towards them. It was the largest of the pack, vast but not lumbering, powerfully muscled and perfectly balanced. Behind it, the other two were fighting, crashing through buildings as they tore at one another, tails whipping back and forth, flames flashing and claws rending.

Lena dashed towards her abandoned sword. Fire flared, she dived, and the flames whooshed past her heels. She came to her knees, closed her fingers around Tomas's well-worn grip, then rose to her full height.

Even without her armour, she stood proud and strong with the blade in her hand, ready to face the world. She was a warrior. She was a leader. She was a monster slayer. She was a towering figure of legend who would carve a ragged path through anyone who threatened her people.

Then she looked up at the dragon.

'Surrender, mother,' the rider shouted from the beast's back.

His face was hidden by a helmet of hardened red leather, but those two words told her all she needed to know.

Her heart fell in on itself, a knot of anguish. Of course Jekob was leading the drachenritters.

She couldn't fight her own son.

She couldn't let the drachenritters run riot through the poor people of Othagate.

She had sunk into a darkness and there was no path back to the light, only a choice between the blackened tunnels her life had become.

'I don't want to hurt you,' she shouted back at him.

'Your old lies are your best lies,' he said.

Deppel was on his knees, staring up at Jekob.

'Please,' he cried, holding out his hands. 'We're just poor people here. We ain't standing in your way. Please don't hurt us no more.'

'Pathetic.' Jekob brought the dragon's head lower and Lena could see the hungry gleam in its yellow eyes.

'Don't you hurt him, Jekob.' Lena stepped in front of Deppel.

'You people brought this on yourselves. You could have surrendered, but instead you force us to fight.'

'You're making choices, just like us.'

'And you're making the wrong choices.'

'I won't let you hurt these people.' She raised her sword and stared into the dragon's eyes. She could almost see Jekob looking out through them.

'You always were a stubborn shit.'

'And you were a quarrelsome brat.'

The words shot from her like dragon's breath, hot and hurtful. She was no dragon, and she regretted them the moment they were out, but that moment was too late.

'I thought this would be hard,' Jekob said, 'but you've made it all too easy.'

He placed his hand against the dragon's neck. The beast drew its head back, taking in a deep breath. Lena could smell the sulphur, almost feel the flames to come.

Most people would have run away, but it was too late for that. However far she ran now, the dragon would reach her.

So she ran forwards.

The dragon brought its head down to snap at her. She had seen the way it pulled back, noted the shifting of muscles in its neck, knew how each move would limit it. With its neck curled in, it was slower to the attack than it could have been. Just a fraction of a moment, but enough.

She lurched left, like a drunk running loose-limbed from the alehouse. The dragon turned its head, its neck contorted, struggling to bring its teeth to bear. She lunged right, past its cheek, feeling the heat as it summoned fire from within.

Both hands gripped Tomas as she brought the blade up, then down on the dragon's neck.

It was an executioner's blow, a single stroke driven by all her strength. It sliced through scales and sinew, severed flesh and struck deep into bone.

The dragon screeched and heaved its head back, blood and fire pouring from the wound in a scorching red steam. It staggered sideways, crashed into a building, and its left legs gave way under it. Jekob disappeared into a heap of tumbling timbers. The dragon fell, wings collapsing around it, and its head flopped to the cobbles.

The beast was still breathing, a terrible, ragged rasp through the charred and steaming hole in its throat, air bubbling through the pouring blood. Its lips drew back, and its eyelids trembled as it struggled against the pain.

Lena laid her hand on its brow and opened herself up, just a little. She accepted its pain, one more layer upon her own, and soothed its fears. She had done what she must, but this beast didn't deserve what had happened to it. There was no justice in the bond of humans and beasts, but there could be kindness. There could be mercy.

'It's going to be alright,' she whispered, tears forming at the corners of her eyes. She remembered soaring high above a sunny mountainside many years before, looking down on the goats running fat and vulnerable below. That memory was her gift to the dragon. Its eyes grew distant, and it gave a satisfied snort.

She pointed her sword at one of those eyes, the weakest place in the dragon's skull, and drew back for a thrust.

'Wait.' Jekob emerged from the rubble. His helmet was gone, his face dusty, blood trickling from a corner of his mouth. He held himself up on one leg, the other twisted awkwardly beneath him, and leaned against the dragon's neck for support. He almost had to hop to move towards her, and yet, absurdly, he clutched his sword, unrelenting to the last.

'She's mine, and I'm hers,' he said, looking not at Lena but at the dragon. 'I should be the one to end this.'

Lena stepped back to let Jekob approach the beast. He hid his grief well, but she could hear it in the stiffness of his words, could see it in the way he looked at the dragon. Lena had known moments like this, the death of a creature she had raised, trained, shared her thoughts and her feelings with. Jekob wasn't just losing a beast of burden, he was losing a loved one. He was losing a part of himself.

He limped forward, forcing himself to stay upright even as he winced in pain. He had grown handsome like his father, strong and lean limbed, but he held himself like her, defiant even in defeat.

Deppel stepped up beside Jekob, wordlessly offering his shoulder. For a moment, Jekob stood statue still and stony-faced, but then he let out a deep breath and leaned into Deppel. Together, they approached the dragon's head, Deppel's face full of fear, Jekob's masking his sorrow.

With Deppel still holding him up, Jekob laid his free hand against the dragon's scales. They glittered like a field of emeralds, rippled like grass in the wind. The beast's eye turned to him, widened, and it almost seemed to smile.

'Thank you, old girl,' he said. 'For all our time together.'

He thrust his blade through the dragon's eye. She twitched, let out a last sulphurous gasp, and lay still.

Jekob closed his eyes and hung his head. His shoulders shook. Then he straightened, drew out his blood-stained blade, and turned to Lena.

'Thank you, Mother,' he said, and for those three words his tone was soft, accepting. Then a wall rose between them as the old stiffness returned. 'You must be pleased with yourself.' He cast the sword down with a clang. 'I am clearly your prisoner.'

She wanted to tell him that nothing could please her less than this, to make her own son powerless in his moment of grief, to be reunited on such terrible terms. But she couldn't even find the words that would catch in her throat, that would come out clumsy, ill-phrased, misunderstood. Death and dragon-slaying, those were easy things compared with family.

People were coming back into the square. Locals with buckets, come to fight the conflagration. Militiamen with bows and pikes, to deal with the wounded beasts fighting in the rubble. They wouldn't need to kill them, not after the battering they had taken, just steer them out of the streets and let the dying caves call to them. Nothing in Unteholz was as inevitable as death.

Overhead, the surviving dragons were flying away, across the walls and back towards the siege camp, smoke staining the sky black behind them. The wind had turned, driving the storm clouds south while the fires raged on.

'Did we win?' Deppel asked.

'No,' Lena replied. 'But we survived.'

Chapter Twenty-Six

Guilt By Candlelight

The fires were still burning as dusk fell across Unteholz. The whole city stank of ash and ruin. The streets were filled with the wails of the dying and the lost, people grieving for families, homes, and the lives slipping slowly from their bodies. Every temple was a hospital, every free pair of hands part of a bucket chain. But while those efforts had contained the fire, they weren't the ones killing it. The fire was eating itself, burning through its fuel, suffering the same slow death as a bleeding soldier.

There had been no assault on the walls. Lena hadn't expected one. Fear was a poison, one General Everhart had poured into the city's veins, and now he needed it to spread, to weaken both body and spirit, to make a cripple of Unteholz before he went for the killing blow.

All of that was as clear to Lena as the pain in her shoulder and the cold breeze against the right side of her head, where the hair had shrivelled in the heat of a dragon's breath and crumbled to dust. She hadn't even felt that when it happened, had been caught by the acrid stink of it in the aftermath, by the lightness on that side.

There were worse things to lose than hair, and time was one of them. Time spent fighting the dragons. Time spent fighting the fire. Time spent letting Deppel tend her wounds. Time lost while an injustice stood, and its consequences kept piling on towards their terrible conclusion.

The thrill of the fight only made it worse, left her slumped and weary in its aftermath, plagued by the terrible contrast between her excitement and the ruin around her. But she couldn't let the weariness win. Now the fighting was done. Now duty took hold. Now she strode, smoke-drenched and soot-stained, up the streets to Hochfel.

Heibar Goreck had been one of Maier's minions. He had bought the silver dream with which Holy Saimon had been drugged, then been killed in his turn. The world wasn't big enough for that to be a coincidence. The councillor had played Lena for a fool while the city burned around them, and she was cursed if she would let that stand.

There were no constables here tonight to question her presence or turn back undesirables from the gates of the powerful. She couldn't even see the frightened eyes peering out at her through shutters in bolted doors, though she knew they would be there. Her footsteps echoed from the walls of wealth, a lonely rhythm.

The front gates of Councillor Maier's mansion were closed but not bolted. Lena shoved them open and strode through, up a paved driveway, past storehouses shuttered against the world and stables in which horses whinnied nervously.

Despite herself, Lena couldn't walk past that sound. The horses were stomping at the ground, swishing their tails, calling for attention from the staff who had abandoned them. One stood frozen, staring at Lena across the door to its stall, its only movement the desperate flicking back and forth of its ears.

'It's alright,' Lena said, holding her hand out. 'You'll be safe in the end.'

Her words would be nothing to the horse, but her tone held a promise, and the creature responded, leaning its head forward, seeking comfort. She ran her fingers up its face, between its ears, through the coarse hair of its main. She felt its warmth and its shivers of fear at a world shattered by the cries of monsters, the stink of smoke, and the panic of its human companions.

Lena closed her eyes and, just for a moment, thought of a better place, running down a mountain valley with the wind in her hair. That thought flowed from her into the horse, whose stance softened. It let out a gentle snort.

But that promise of safety and happiness was a lie. This place was about to be torn apart, and the people the horse trusted had abandoned it, retreating for their own safety. They wouldn't even notice that betrayal, because to them this was just a dumb animal. Lena jerked her hand back before her bitterness could taint the feelings she had shared. The horse blinked in confusion, but there was no time for this. Cursing herself for another traitor, Lena turned her back on the beast.

In front of the main house, a statue of a gryphon spat water into a marble-walled pool. Lena strode past it and hammered on the door. Thin strips of candlelight fell across her through closed shutters above, slicing her body into patches of darkness.

The door opened, revealing a servant in pressed livery and polished boots. He looked Lena up and down, practised neutrality giving way to a disdainful sneer.

'Headsman,' he said, two fingers touching the spot beneath his eye. 'You're at the wrong door.'

Lena barged past him, into a large receiving hall with a floor of terracotta tiles beneath whitewashed walls and ceiling. A tapestry of hunters in a forest faced a grand, sweeping staircase. It was lit by sweet-smelling beeswax candles, not the rank grease of tallow.

'Here, you can't do that!' the servant said.

Voices drifted from a doorway at the left side of the room, through which brighter light emerged. That was where she had to go.

'Help!' the servant shouted. 'Intruder!'

More servants emerged. Two of them, big bastards with red faces and close-cropped hair, rushed to intercept Lena on her way across the room. She kicked one in the crotch, and he curled over with a rasping wheeze. The other tried to grab her from behind, but she slammed her elbow into his throat, left him stunned and gasping.

Then she was through the door.

In the centre of the room was an oak table, highly polished and with legs carved to imitate intertwining vines. Maier sat in a high-backed chair at the far end, dressed in a gold-buttoned doublet, a wine glass halfway to her lips. A plain-faced man Lena recognised as Maier's husband sat at the near end of the table, and between them four children, one the little girl she had met once before. All looked up from their platters to see who was intruding on their dinner.

Servants, one of them carrying a carving knife, emerged from around the room, closing on Lena with stony visages. She laid her hand on Tomas's pommel.

'Headsman,' Maier said, as calmly as if they were meeting in her study. She gave a small wave, and the servants backed away. 'What an unexpected pleasure. Perhaps Phillipe could find you some refreshment in my study and we can talk once dinner is done.'

Lena stalked around the table.

'Why not talk here?' she said. 'Have you got something to hide?'

'Some conversations are not for the dinner table.' Maier's gaze flickered across her children. She set down her wine and folded her fingers together. 'Give me a few minutes.'

'Here's what I think to your few minutes.' Lena flicked ash and crusted blood from the front of her shirt onto the table. Maier's husband shifted in his seat. 'You've been lying to me and now people are dying because of it.'

'You're clearly unsettled, Headsman.' Maier pushed back her chair. 'I'll see you to the study myself.'

'You're thundering right I'm disturbed.' Lena drew Tomas, then slammed the sword down on the table. Cutlery bounced across the wood. One of the children started to cry. 'People have been out there all day, fighting and dying for this city, and you're sitting up here sipping wine and nibbling on lamb like it's just another day in Hochfel. Doom and dust, but I'm disturbed, as anyone with eyes should be.'

Maier stood. Her expression had barely changed, yet it seemed colder, harder, every line fixed in place.

'Caleb, please take the children to the parlour. I need a private conversation with Headsman Sturm.'

The man ushered the children out and the servants followed. The last one closed the door behind her, leaving the two of them alone.

Fast as a duelist's thrust, Maier slapped Lena across the face, the blow given an extra sting by her row of gold rings. Lena froze in place, one hand on her cheek, struggling to believe that the blow had been real.

'How dare you,' Maier said, her voice as quiet and menacing as a snake sliding through long grass. 'Forcing your way into my home, covered in blood, talking death and ruin in front of my children. I should have you whipped in the street.'

Lena's hand formed a fist. No one struck her without getting struck back. There would be consequences, but to Brother Moon with them, and with everything Maier represented, this cold and corrupt life lived safely behind iron gates while the rest of the world burned.

A memory of a sound crossed her thoughts, heard moments before but only now seeping into her consciousness. Heida, the little girl she had met outside Maier's office, whimpering in fear as Tomas crashed down on the table. Just because Maier deserved this didn't mean that her children did.

'You should have kept them in here,' Lena said, tightening her grip on Tomas. 'Then I might have had cause for restraint.'

'Your actions so far say otherwise. But you have my attention now, so say what you must and then get out of my house.'

Lena lifted the sword and held it between them, the edge gleaming like fire in the candlelight. It would probably be justice just to do this now, while there was no one to stop her. The general turned executioner could become a physician, cutting a cancer from the heart of Unteholz before its corruption killed the whole body. No better time for it.

But probably wasn't enough. Innocent people had died when she relied on the certainty that came from within, whole cities left in ruins for a cause that was no better than what it opposed. This time, she needed proof beyond herself. It wasn't enough to be righteous any more, she had seen too much of the world for that. Before she spilt blood, she had to be right.

'Heibar Goreck,' she said, scrutinising Maier's face. 'You know the name?'

Not even a twitch changed Maier's expression.

'If you're asking, then you know the answer,' she said.

'Why did you hire him?'

'Sometimes I need tasks done discreetly, without anyone knowing the hand behind them.'

'Like in your deal with Councillor Saimon.'

'Exactly.'

'Like buying a massive dose of silver dream.'

'I have no need for drugs, Headsman.' Maier picked up her wine glass. 'Family and home are all the comforts I require.'

'That's what they all say.' Lena took the glass from Maier's hand and swallowed its contents in a single gulp. 'Then the truth comes out.'

Silence held sway as the two women stood staring at each other. The sounds of the city came faintly through the leaded glass and shutters. A crash as a burnt-out building collapsed. A shout for help. A scream, abruptly cut off.

In the room, candlelight gleamed off silver plates and glasses of fine wine.

'You're unstable,' Maier said. 'Charging around the city, bursting into homes, menacing honest citizens. I won't have it.'

'If you were honest, I wouldn't be here.'

Lena twirled the wineglass between her fingers. How much

was something like this worth? Every item in her kitchen? The contents of her larder too? More? She herself had owned these things once, had thought that they made her a better mother, a better wife, a better provider. That they made her a better person. One more lie she had told herself to justify doing what she wanted.

She cast the glass aside. It hit the flagstone floor and exploded into shards that caught the light, glowing like jagged candle flames.

'This is over,' Maier said. 'You're not protecting the city anymore, you're a menace to it. Your complete disregard for status and civility risks everything that holds Unteholz together. I'll find someone else to seek out the truth.'

'Someone who'll accept your story, you mean.'

'Someone who doesn't wave swords around in front of children,' Maier snapped. 'I swear by all the gods, if I hear one word of you harassing our citizens, whether it's a councillor or an alchemist or the bishop herself, the next tongue cut out at the Weeping Stone will be yours.'

'You'd like that, wouldn't you? To silence my investigation. To stop me finding out what you've been doing.'

'Your investigation is over already, Sturm. Now get the hells out of my house.'

Tomas shone in Lena's hand. There was guilt here. She could smell it as surely as the wine and the varnish of the table. Guilt she could end.

Beatrice Saimon's face floated into view, that memory of the poor priest's last moments. Lena had been sure of her guilt too.

She lowered Tomas, her eyes still on Maier, and slid the blade away in its scabbard.

'All this,' she said, waving a hand at the room around them. 'The big house, the fine meals, the loving family. When they bring you to me for the last time, it'll all go away.'

'You're pathetic. You broke your own family, so now you want to break mine.'

Anger flashed, hot as dragon fire, through Lena's veins. She bared her teeth and drew back her fist.

'Philippe!' Maier shouted.

The door burst open, and a servant appeared, a loaded crossbow levelled at Lena. Her whole body clenched, locked in a moment of frozen fury.

'The Headsman is leaving,' Maier said. 'She won't be coming back.'

The point of the crossbow quarrel gleamed.

Lena forced herself to lower her fist, then turned and strode from the room. The door clicked shut behind her, leaving Maier in the safety of her dining hall.

Chapter Twenty-Seven

Amid the Ashes

Lena swung her axe in swift, fierce strokes, imagining that the blood-slicked dragon bone was Councillor Maier's face.

The sgeir had already cut away the hide and flesh from the beast's legs, leaving her to do the hard, satisfying work at which she excelled. Now they were working on the main body, skinning knives sliding swiftly back and forth, peeling away the layers of a once mighty beast. Everything came to this in the end. The holy books talked of sinners ending their days in the blackness, nothing but ashes blown on a cold wind, but Lena had seen the truth. Sinner or saint, human or beast, all were rendered down to meat.

She chopped and chopped; each blow powered by muscles tense as a bowstring. With each blow, she let go of just a little of her anger, but she was a long way from finding peace.

A dozen sgeir had come to the square to help her process the dragon's corpse. Ragged as they were, they almost fitted in now in Othagate. Like her, they belonged in a place made of ash and ruin.

As dawn crept in, tense and fearful residents emerged, some come to recover what remained of their belongings, others clutching buckets with which they had fought fires through the night. They watched the new arrivals through eyes narrowed in suspicion. There was no sight more unsettling to the dispossessed than their social inferiors, a reminder of where they could soon be.

A beast this big would provide a fine harvest for the sgeir

and fine profits for the city's merchants, if their businesses survived the siege. That size made it tough work to butcher, and there was a satisfying ache in Lena's arms from a night's work chopping at the legs, neck, and tail. She had given up on trying to fit lengths of bone onto her cart. The sgeir could take what she didn't: they needed it more than her.

'Brought you some breakfast.' Deppel appeared at her side, holding an earthenware jug and something wrapped in cloth.

Lena set down the axe, wiped her brow with the back of her sleeve, and accepted the offering. She didn't recognise the jug, or the hunk of bread and thick slice of ham inside the cloth.

'This isn't from my stores,' she said.

'I passed Toblur's on the way. He's grateful for you stopping the dragons. Says you saved his alehouse.'

A twinge of guilt caught Lena. She hadn't thought to check on Toblur or any of her other acquaintances in Othagate. Who still lived? Who needed help? Who would never even make it to the funeral plateau?

It was too hard to consider the welfare of all those people now. If she tried to care for so many, then she would sink beneath the weight of senseless destruction. Better to care for who she could.

'Did you sleep?' she asked.

'Like a baby,' Deppel replied.

Lena shook her head and swallowed a mouthful of ale. She hadn't known how tired she was, but now she felt her energy returning with each bite of food.

'Babies sleep terribly,' she said. 'Little sods wake you up at all hours of the night.'

'Like a cat, then,' Deppel said. 'They'll sleep anywhere, just lie down and ignore the world.'

The ham was good, by Othagate standards, the bread not too stale. It was one of the better breakfasts Lena had eaten in times of war. Nothing fancy, but she didn't have to pick out the maggots or scrape off the mould.

'You really think Councillor Maier killed Councillor Saimon?' Deppel asked, leaning in close so that the sgeir wouldn't hear.

Lena shrugged. That small movement shifted the bandage on the blistered skin of her shoulder in a way that the steady rhythm of chopping hadn't. It wasn't a deep pain, and the wound would heal easily enough, but with so much else on her mind it caught her by surprise.

She'd vented her furious theory of Maier's guilt at Deppel the night before, while she was fetching the axe and cart from her home. It still made the best sense of Goreck's death, but it left other things unexplained, and the bright light of dawn illuminated her complete lack of evidence.

'If not, then she's got something else buried away,' Lena said. 'The problem will be digging it up.'

'You could talk to Captain Baumer. He must see what goes on with the council.'

'Soren and I aren't exactly on the best of terms.'

Looking into this murder had caused a lot of wounds in her life. Her relationship with Soren Baumer was one she wanted to leave alone, in hopes that it would heal over. She didn't have many people she might call friends, and she could just about admit that she wanted to keep the ones she had.

If only events had left her with another option.

Somewhere nearby, people were praying. Ringing gongs and rhythmic chanting drifted through the streets. Many people used faith to hold them together in a crisis, but Lena needed something more. She needed to act upon the world.

She ate the last of the bread and brushed crumbs from her sweat-stained shirt.

'How long until the ribs are clear?' she asked the nearest sgeir.

'Not until noon, at least,' he said. 'Got to be careful with the organs. It's hard to harvest a heart that size without damaging it, and the bowels are going to be real messy.'

Lena pulled on her scorched arming tunic, taking care as it settled on her shoulder, and buckled her sword belt in place.

'I'm going to the citadel,' she said. After a night like this, Baumer would likely be there, getting some rest and food while he could. That they kept prisoners there too was neither here nor there. 'I'll try to be back in time to finish this job.'

She stepped away, leaving her axe leaning against the cart, and was about to head down Rinnling Lane when her attention was caught by the sound of gongs and a choir's voices lifted in praise. A column of priests were processing up the street towards the ruins of Othagate, circular amulets hanging heavy on their green robes, prayer breads dangling between their fingers. They sang a complex melody whose tones and rhythms spoke to the deep and comforting power of faith, a comfort given by the chosen few to anyone willing to kneel down and obey. In the lead was Bishop Kunder, her silk robes immaculate despite the ashes drifting in the street.

Father Earth's people had come out to preach.

The priests paraded into the square, a mass of curious onlookers and pious devotees spilling in behind them. They approached the vast carcass of the dragon as if it were another bone cage cathedral in the making, then stopped, their gongs and voices falling silent. An expectant quiet settled across the square.

'We have come to lead you in prayer,' Holy Kunder called out, raising her arms wide, turning to take in the battered and soot-stained survivors. 'To seek Father Earth's blessing for the safety of the city.'

'It's a bit late for that,' Lena said.

She had meant the comment for Deppel's ears, but her frustration gave her voice volume. Not five feet from Kunder, a woman sniggered.

Kunder's cheeks flushed, and she glared at Lena with wide, hate-filled eyes.

'You!' the bishop proclaimed, shaking a finger at Lena. 'You broke into the cathedral, set the holy house on fire, and now you openly mock the chosen of the gods!'

The crowd that had followed Kunder through town followed her into anger. Muttered discontent morphed into a seething hiss of hatred.

'I didn't burn your corpse cathedral down,' Lena said. 'That was an accident.'

'A famed follower of Mother Sky set Father Earth's temple ablaze, while her army batters our walls, and you call it accident? Do you take us for idiots?'

'Heretic,' someone shouted.

'Traitor.'

'Get out of our city!'

'See how she doesn't deny the rest,' Kunder continued. 'Burglar. Idolator. Heathen.'

'I saved this place from ruin yesterday,' Lena snapped. Her body vibrated with anger, a bitter struggle to keep from lashing out.

'You brought this ruin upon us, you and all your kind.'

It was more than Lena could stand. The day before, she had come within inches of death while saving these people and their city, and now they wanted to blame her for their religious wars? To hells with that. She grabbed Kunder by her vestments and swung her towards the corpse of the dragon.

'Listen to me, you ungrateful turd,' she snarled. 'I don't give a dead rat's breath which way people pray, but I'll be damned if-'

'Let go of the bishop.' A meaty hand settled on Lena's shoulder.

She swung back and her fist hit a thick-set priest with piggy eyes. Bone cracked, her knuckles stung, and he staggered back, clutching his cheek.

There were gasps and angry shouts. Another priest advanced on her and the crowd followed him. Some picked up rocks and broken timbers.

Lena flung Kunder on the floor. She had been a fool to grab

hold of the bishop, a bigger fool to strike a priest. But they had deserved it, both of them. It felt good.

'It doesn't have to be like this,' she shouted over the noise of the crowd. 'We're meant to be on the same side.'

A rock hurtled past her head and thudded off the dragon's corpse. Another bounced off her shoulder and fell to the cobbles with a clatter. She raised her fists and braced herself. The oncoming attackers slowed and spread out, moving to surround her. Behind them, the crowd cheered.

Deppel appeared at Lena's side, holding a timber of his own. 'Get out of the way, lad,' Lena said. 'You don't know how to fight.'

'I'll work it out.'

'Idiot,' she said, but she didn't try to push him back. For the first time in years, she stood side by side with someone she trusted, ready to face a fight, and in that moment, the world made sense.

A man swung at Lena with a splintered floorboard. She caught the wood with one hand and punched him with the other. He howled and staggered back, but his friends had closed in, and now their blows came. She dodged a couple, blocked a punch, struck back, but she was outnumbered and surrounded, and it could never go well. A fist caught her in the ribs, and another hit the back of her burnt shoulder, making her howl.

The blood pumped faster in Lena's veins, and she grinned, as fierce as any dragon. This was what she needed. It was worth the pain to have a chance to fight back. It was worth losing for what she would gain.

She fought wildly, punching and kicking, barging and gouging. Street fighting wasn't about poise or elegance, no matter what the wrestling masters claimed. It was about luck and improvisation and the willingness to stick your fingers where they weren't wanted.

Deppel yelped. Lena turned towards him, but ran straight into another fist. The world spun around her, and she sank to her knees.

The attacks seemed to slow, even though the mob had her at their mercy. Maybe the blow to her head had messed with her sense of time. It had certainly made the world louder, with more shouting and scuffling of feet.

Hands grabbed her under the armpits. She shook one off, but the other heaved, forcing her to her feet, and then stepped back before she could respond.

Instead of a crowd of fists and fury, she found that she was standing alone on a patch of bare ground. Her assailants stood back warily, fists and crude weapons raised, shouting and gesticulating.

What the hells was happening?

She looked over her shoulder to see a different crowd close behind her, a mixture of sgeir and citizens of Othagate. One of the sgeir still held her arm. All of them were shouting and gesticulating at the Earth worshippers, each side as angry as the other.

Kunder was back on her feet, standing safely among the priests, her face an icon of cold, frustrated fury.

Lena's grin widened. What could be more perfect. Her people against Kunder's. The battered poor against power wrapped in the pretensions of prayer. A fight not against monsters or nameless soldiers, but against the people who killed the city day by day with their divisiveness and stupidity.

She was ready to charge in and let her fists settle her fate. Not just ready, but eager. Then she caught a glimpse of Deppel, his cheek grazed and blood dripping from his nose, a rock clutched in a hand that trembled with fear.

What in Moon's name was she doing?

'Back off,' she shouted to her supporters. 'Let them go!'

They did as she urged, pulling back around the half-butchered dragon, opening up a space between the two sides.

'See how they flee,' Kunder called out. 'See the cowardice of the heretics.'

Lena clenched her teeth. A conflict raged inside her, between the wild warrior who threw herself into fights and the general who knew which battles to pick. As long as she remembered that struggle, the general would win.

When Lena didn't rise to the bait, Kunder started backing off too. She wasn't so keen for a confrontation now that the sides were even. With taunts and thrown stones, her mob followed her across the square and back down Rinnling Lane.

Those who remained, the sgeir and the poor folks of Othagate, cheered as if they had driven the army from the walls. Lena shook their hands and offered warm words of gratitude; they'd saved her from a beating, at the very least.

Beneath the smile, she didn't feel any triumph. If people acted like this while the enemy was at the gate, then Unteholz was in even more trouble than she thought.

Through cold bars of heavy iron, Lena looked in at the cell where her son was held. Jekob sat on a pile of straw that rustled when he moved and sometimes when he didn't. Light came through a small, barred window high in the wall and the oil lantern that Eljvet the jailer had lent to Lena-for a small fee, of course. The cells had always been a wretched place, whether they held suspects awaiting trial or convicts waiting for the Weeping Stone. They seemed even more pitiful now.

Jekob sat up straight, back against the wall, reading a battered pamphlet with an engraving of Saint Lukara on the front. One of his legs was wrapped in bandages and clay, splinted on either side by wooden rods.

'What do you want, Mother?' he asked.

How could a word showing kinship cut so deeply? It was as if he had taken their past and sharpened it day after day on a whetstone, while he waited for the chance to wound.

'Are you well?' she asked. He could hurt her, even through these bars, but she didn't have to let him know. 'Has someone seen to your wounds?'

'I'm bandaged and fed.' He nudged a wooden bowl with his injured foot. 'After all, I'm too valuable for you to neglect now.'

'If it was my choice, you wouldn't be down here, but I'm not in charge.'

'So you can choose not to put your generalship first? You just didn't choose that when we needed you.'

'There's no need to be a brat. I came to make you comfortable, if I can.'

'How motherly of you. No wonder that fat whelp follows you around.'

The bar of the cell was rough and unyielding beneath her tightening fingers.

'Don't you talk about Deppel like that. He's a good lad. Unlike some, he knows how to show respect.'

'Ah, respect, the foundation of any good family.' Jekob kicked the bowl. It rolled across the flagstones, clattering over bumps and dips, and came to rest against the base of the bars. 'I thought it was love, but more fool me.'

'You could have love, but you're too busy hating everything.'

'I do have love.' Jekob stood. He limped over to the bars and looked out at Lena, so close she could have brushed the dirt from his face as she had when he was young. 'When this campaign is over, I'm going back to him. We'll eat together, talk together, fall asleep in each other's arms for the rest of our lives. And he is never, ever coming near you.'

The old grief from which Lena had hidden in Unteholz burst across her like rain from a thundercloud. She stumbled back across the dungeon, only stopping when her back pressed against cold, damp stone.

'If you hate me so much, why did you follow in my footsteps?'

she asked. 'Why are you a drachenritter?'

Jekob snorted.

'What else would I have become? I grew up around beasts - feeding dragons, petting wyverns, clearing away feathers when the gryphons malted. They were never too busy for me, never told me to leave them in peace or wait until later. They were happy to be loved.

'Those beasts were what I knew, what I was passionate about. I wasn't going to give them up just because you brought them into my life.'

He pressed his face into the gap between the bars.

'This isn't about you,' he said. 'Nothing in my life is.'

The words were everything that Lena had feared, everything she had fled. Cold. Hard. Deadly. A rejection of the love that still stirred whenever she thought of him. Pikes and muskets and dragons' claws were nothing by comparison.

She turned away, unable to face him, and trudged up the dungeon steps, the borrowed oil lamp swaying in the dark.

'That's it,' Jekob shrieked after her. 'Run like you always do!'

She stopped at the top of the stairs and leaned against the stone wall. Her body heaved, and she fought to take long breaths, to slow the racing of her heart and the swirling impulses in her head. The desire to shout, to fight, to scream, to flail madly at the world and everything in it.

'You done with that?' Eljvet asked. The jailer stood with his buck teeth exposed, one crooked finger pointing at the lamp. 'Don't want to waste good oil.'

She shoved the lamp into his hands then strode past him, into the courtyard of the citadel.

The yard was like a rat's nest exposed to the light, a place of frantic, rushing activity, of dirt and snarls and vicious edges. Grinding stones sparked and hammers fell as battered armour and weapons were repaired. Drawn and dark-eyed soldiers huddled around a stew pot or slumped exhausted against the walls. Clerks and commanders strode back and forth, giving orders, demanding information, doing anything to prise order from the crumpled aftermath of battle.

And this was only the beginning.

Despite its grim implications, there was something comforting about it all. Just as Jekob's anger could hurt her because it was so familiar, these sights and sounds could comfort her because she knew them. She knew where she stood in a military camp. She knew what everything meant and what needed to be done. Life had purpose.

Baumer sat on an upturned barrel in the centre of the throng. He had taken his armour off one arm, the first time she had seen him in less than the full suit, and was polishing the vambrace, wiping away soot and blood with a soft cloth. Gretta, his faithful second, stood behind him, cleaning his backplate. She was in plate armour too, but not bonded, and she had taken off her gauntlets to work. They hung from her belt, either side of an Illora dagger.

Lena stared at the dagger. How many of these things were there in Unteholz?

'Nice knife,' she said.

Gretta looked up, then down at the dagger's handle. She frowned. 'Reward for services rendered,' Gretta said stiffly.

'I get it,' Lena said, leaning into the bond between soldiers, looking for a connection to anchor her storm-tossed heart. 'Plenty of times I got given a medal or some ornament. Surest sign my employers were out of gold.'

Gretta snorted and half smiled. 'True enough.'

'I used to think those daggers were rare and precious,' Lena said. 'Now they're turning up all over.'

'Nothing's ever as rare of a merchant says it is.'

Gretta returned to her work, cleaning the soot of the burnt city from Baumer's back.

'Come to see your kid, have you?' Baumer asked, glancing

at Lena. She was relieved to see that his hostility had abated, though his expression was far from friendly.

She weighed her words, trying to decide what would be best. Flattery, honesty, confrontation? If her judgement on these things was any good, she wouldn't be where she was, soul stricken and weighed down with regrets.

'Him and you,' she said, deciding that honest was just easier. 'I want to ask you about Maier.'

Baumer set his cloth aside and slid his arm into the tarnished vambrace.

'Gretta, you go get some food,' he said. 'The Headsman and I need to talk.'

'Whatever you say, Sor.' Gretta gave a casual salute then walked away.

The cannons boomed and shot smashed against the distant walls, a rhythm steady as a human pulse. The heartbeat of war drummed as fiercely as ever, but Lena knew that it would soon die. The walls were close to crumbling. A few days at most and some part would come crashing down, letting the enemy in.

She had all but given up on preventing that now. The best she could do was find justice for Beatrice Saimon before it was too late. One last righteous act before the carnage that followed.

'Out with it,' Baumer said, fingers drumming against the barrel top.

'Did you know that Maier hires people to do secret errands for her?'

'Of course she does. You don't get rich and powerful without secrets.'

'Are some of them criminals?'

'People who work in secret usually are.'

'Did you know one called Heibar Goreck?'

Baumer's eyes narrowed, and he raised his hand to his mouth. Several days' worth of stubble rasped against the ridged iron of his gauntlet.

'I don't think so, but you can never be too sure.' His eyes darted back and forth, as if checking the people around them, and he leaned forward, gesturing for Lena to come closer. 'You know who might have known? Fiete Saimon.'

'Because they were secretly working together?'

'So you know about that.' Baumer leaned back. 'Could be a part of it, but it's not what I mean. Saimon was a great hoarder of secrets. That's part of how he was such a successful merchant: he knew things and he knew when to act on them. One time, the council had me look into breaches of trade monopolies, and the trail took me to Saimon's door. When I presented my case, he just laughed, told me I wouldn't be arresting him. He said he knew a secret about someone powerful in Unteholz, and that secret would keep him safe.'

'Someone like Maier?'

Baumer held up his hands.

'I didn't say that, but can you think of anyone better?'

Lena contemplated the other councillors. Most took their turns as judges, but Maier had enough power to take any case she wanted, to ensure her friends were never found guilty. The running of the city lay in her hands. And yet…

'I don't see it,' Lena said. 'Maier's always talking about upholding law and order. She wouldn't throw a case.'

Baumer laughed.

'You're far too trusting for a killer.'

'You've seen Maier corrupt a trial?'

'Let's just say that not all evidence makes it to court.'

Lena's head throbbed. She needed a drink to deal with this mess, and then another couple to prepare her for what came next.

All this time chasing around the city, hunting for whoever had killed one Saimon and set up the other, and the culprit had been in front of her all along. No wonder Maier had wanted her to let it go, or just to find someone and get it over with. The councillor had pretended it was about pragmatism or power, but the truth went deeper. Lena had been working for a murderer.

It was the solution the city needed. If Lena had found her killer in the church or the crime gangs, Everhart might have found a reason to disbelieve her, to keep up the siege and conquer Unteholz. But if she handed over the woman who led the city's struggle, if she ended this regime and allowed a new one to rise, that could be a win for Everhart. It might just give him a reason to end the siege.

Maybe there was a chance to save the city. All she needed was proof.

Chapter Twenty-Eight

Fallen Defences

The square in front of the cathedral was a maelstrom of competing voices. There were the groans and screams of the injured, brought here from the walls or the burnt out districts, sheltering under canvas awnings now that they were too many to fit inside the temple. There were the prayers of the desperate and the fervently faithful, joining in a ceremony that spilt from the great front steps down between those awnings, a throng of faces turned up expectantly to their priests, seeking salvation in this world or the next. Then there were the soldiers hurrying from the citadel or the foundries, feet pounding the earth as they rushed towards the sound of the cannons and the confrontation that must come. It didn't take a seer to read the omens.

Bishop Kunder stood behind a carved lectern at the top of the steps, framed by the soot-stained doorway of the cathedral. Her arms were spread wide as she proclaimed a sermon, but her voice was lost amid the noise of the crowd. With her blond hair flowing loose across her emerald gown she looked magnificent, a bright blazing prophet from the days before the Sundering, when the gods had torn the world in two. It seemed as though she could reach out and tear storm clouds from a clear sky.

Kunder raised her hands, holding up the lightning bolt of ancient clay that had hung above the altar in the cathedral, for centuries the symbol of Father Earth's most loyal helper. Kunder's congregation watched in confusion, and then anger, as she raised up the symbol of Mother Sky, shouting words that Lena couldn't hear.

Then Kunder's arms came down, and she flung the lightning bolt onto the steps below her. It shattered, and the crowd surged forward, stamping on the pieces, grinding Mother Sky's holy icon to dust. It was only clay, ancient dirt in a shape that no longer meant anything to Lena, but the sight sent a shudder down her spine.

Even if they survived this war, there would be no peace in Unteholz.

Lena took a deep breath and started walking through the crowd, straight towards the bishop.

Heibar Goreck, the dead man in the rubble, had become the key to the killing, and with it the last hope of peace. He had worked for Maier, but he had worked for the church too. Lena had to be sure, before she did what was needed, how Kunder was tied into all of this.

She had hoped to deal with it less dramatically, and with less risk. She had written a note for Deppel to deliver, but he was nowhere to be found, and there was no one else she trusted with the task. So here she was, walking into the wyvern's nest. Mother Sky's most famous general facing a crowd that had just stamped her sign into the dirt.

As she walked, the tone of the noise around her changed. People across the square responded to her presence, pointing, calling out to each other and to her. She tightened her grip around the pommel of Tomas, readying herself to face the wrath of Father Earth's followers.

'It's the dragontamer!' someone shouted, and others took up the cry.

A man grabbed Lena by the arm. She shook him off and raised her fist, but instead of hostility saw gratitude in his eyes.

'You saved us from the dragons,' he said, and she realised that she knew his face, a cheap cobbler from the upper end of

Othagate. 'Bless you, General Seeger.'

'I don't use that name anymore,' she said.

'Then bless you Headsman Sturm!' he shouted, and others joined in.

Her confidence growing with the cheers, Lena walked on across the square. Some people still looked at her with hostility, more of them the closer to the cathedral she got, and there were booing and curses in among the cheers. But she wasn't alone, and some of these people didn't even make the sign of the eye. That thought made her stand a little straighter, hold her head a little higher, approach her destination with a confident grin.

The crowd parted as she reached the base of the cathedral steps. Perhaps they sensed some menace coming off of her. Perhaps they wanted to see her put in her place. Perhaps they just wanted to witness what came next.

Fragments of the ancient lightning bolt crunched beneath her feet. She stopped to pick up a piece of broken clay. Such a stupid thing to die for. Such a wretched thing to kill for. She could be better than this. Perhaps they all could.

Or perhaps people were petty and cruel, and this was the way everything went in the end.

She held up the piece of clay between her fingertips and the crowd held its breath.

'They should make it out of something tougher next time.' She dropped it, just another piece of dirt. There were gasps and chuckles and nervous whispers rippling out to those who hadn't heard. Soon, those words would reach the other side of this divide. How would they receive them: as an offering of hope, a sign of disrespect, or in the way Lena meant, a joke and a plea for calm? There was no way of knowing, no way of controlling, because people would take the world as they wanted to. She couldn't command obedience any more, couldn't line people up and order them to listen. This way was better. This way she had to think about the consequences of her words, to accept the uncertainties and press on.

Kunder looked down from her lectern. The disdain on her face did nothing to detract from how bright and alive she seemed, illuminated by the morning sun. Behind her, the Cage Cathedral of Saint Lukara loomed like the shadow of death, its frame of ancient ribs and walls of centuries-old hide looking more like a corpse than ever.

Lena strode up the steps until she stood beside the lectern, eyes locked with the bishop. Nearby priests looked uncertainly from the crowd to Kunder, waiting for some signal.

Less than a mile away, the cannons continued their relentless roar.

'Shouldn't you be at the walls, Headsman?' Kunder asked, facing Lena but raising her voice so that it carried across the square. She touched the skin beneath her eye. 'I hear that you're good for fighting, if nothing else.'

'I'd like one last conversation about Holy Saimon,' Lena said, firmly and quietly.

'Ask away. I have nothing to hide from my congregation.'

'Really?' Lena moved closer to the lectern. 'You don't think anything I might have learnt about you could sound bad?'

Kunder glanced at the expectant crowd. Her expression only faltered for a moment; a flicker of a frown that departed as fast as it arrived.

'My good friends,' Kunder called out. 'Duty calls me away, but Holy Lufven will lead you in prayers for all our salvation.'

She stepped down from the lectern and walked with solemn poise through the shadowed doorway of the cathedral, into its vestibule. A handful of junior priests were there, hauling burnt furnishings out of the building, and they hurried to offer their service to the bishop. She waved them all away, then turned her attention to Lena.

'Why did you hire Goreck?' Lena asked.

She had hoped to throw Kunder with the unexpected question, to gain some insight or revelation to hook her next question on. Instead, the bishop looked blank.

'Hired who?'

'Goreck. Your dead handyman.'

'I'm the bishop of the greatest cathedral in all the Principalities of Stone. I don't deal with handymen.'

'Like ash you don't. Maier asked you to give him a job, didn't she? Some trade of favours, part of being on the same side against the Saimons.'

'Councillor Maier and I have often collaborated to limit the church of Mother Sky, for the good of the city and all its souls. But I never hired a handyman, at her request or anyone else's. Now if we're done, I should get back to-'

'You knew she wanted the Saimons dead, didn't you?'

'What?' Kunder exclaimed, incredulous. 'Certainly not. I needed the Saimons alive.'

'They were your greatest opponents in the city.'

'Exactly.'

Lena took a step back and looked at the bishop, trying to make sense of her response. Had she misheard?

Kunder pointed out into the square, where the crowd was listening to Holy Lufven pray. Half of them were lost in the moment, the same prayer on their own lips, leaning into the hope of salvation. Every one of them wore simple clothes with prayer beads hanging from their belts, their very dress expressing the will of Father Earth.

'When I took up this post, religion was dying in this city,' Kunder said. 'People came to the cathedral from habit, not faith. Attendance was lacklustre, morality collapsing beneath the greed of merchants and criminals. I have fought heart and soul to bring passion back into these people, to make them truly, fervently believe. Nothing fuels that faith like an enemy they can see.'

'Of course.' Lena rolled her shoulders back and pressed her hands to her face. A joint clicked as it moved. 'You need that fight to build up your power.'

'I need it to save souls. Most people are ignorant. My words fall on deaf ears when I rage against an abstraction. Against a real woman, with all her failings, I have someone they can hate. Her marriage to a councillor, her arrogance, her preaching as belligerent as my own: the gods may never give me an opponent like Holy Saimon again.'

'They've got a whole army of them outside the walls.'

Kunder hung her head. 'That is too much.'

For the first time, Lena noticed that the bishop's hands were trembling. Well they might. If Mother Sky's army seized the city, fired up with religious zeal, then they would do far worse than knock over a few candles in the cathedral.

Kunder drew something from her belt: an eating knife, but sharpened to a wicked edge.

'I've never known real pain,' she whispered. 'I couldn't endure it.' The blade shook. A beam of sunlight, stained red by the windows' coloured glass, danced across its edge. 'But I don't know if I have the courage, or if I'll freeze in the moment. Maybe I should stop waiting. We don't have long now, do we?'

Pity, that most wretched of sentiments, crawled from the depths of Lena's heart and moved her to take hold of the knife hand. It was no way to view another person, to see them only in weakness and loss, but it was the kindest she had ever felt towards the bishop.

Kunder's skin was warm and soft, full of life, not like the cold corpses Lena carried up to the burial field. But if she didn't do something then this woman, and thousands more of Unteholz's citizens, would soon be feeding the wyverns.

'There's no need for this,' she said. 'It's not over yet.'

As if scheduled by some malign god, a crash sounded out across the city. Lena rushed from the cathedral, Kunder beside her, and looked towards the sound.

Dust was rising from the walls close to the east gate. Part of the defences had given way, a great mass of stone collapsing into rubble, leaving a deep V-shaped hole.

Some of the people in the square screamed. Others ran. Many stood, staring in mute horror as their world was smashed open.

Kunder laughed bitterly.

'Father Earth may not have heard you, Headsman,' she said, looking down at her knife, 'but it seems that Brother Moon did.'

Lena snatched the blade from the bishop's hand and cast it to the ground.

'Gods' eyes,' she hissed. 'Don't you dare give up. Not when you've made these people need you.'

She strode to the top of the steps, dragging Kunder beside her. But when she reached the lectern, there was only dread in the bishop's eyes, not the hope her people needed.

Cursing under her breath, Lena climbed the three wooden steps into the lectern.

'Listen to me!' she bellowed in a voice practised across army camps and battlefields. 'Listen to me you shower of turds, if any of you want to live!'

They turned to face her, as they always had. Expectant, hopeful, laying their fates on her shoulders. There was a reason she had given this up, and there was a reason she had done it from the start. Both were the same. For better or for worse, she was damn good at this.

'They won't attack yet,' she announced, projecting as loudly as she could. More voices fell quiet, more faces turned to look. 'The breach is too narrow. They'll keep battering to widen it. But make no mistake, they're coming, and we've only got a few hours.

'If you're willing to fight, then grab a weapon and get to the walls. The constables will tell you what to do.

'If you don't know how to fight, or if you've got kids or old folk counting on you, then you need to go. Holy Kunder will lead you up out of the city, to the funeral fields. You'll be safe from the fighting and from the sack. Take food, take water, but don't take your time, because there's precious little left.'

The crowd stood still, watching her, waiting for those last few rousing words, something to give them courage or comfort or hope. She wished that she could give them what they wanted, that she could wipe away their fear of destruction, fear she had caused in so many other towns. That would be some kind of justice at least, some tiny recompense for all the harm she had done. But it had been too many years and too many drinks for her to find those words again.

'Move, by the blackness! All of you, go!'

Then she was down off the lectern, face to face with Kunder again.

'You see them safe, Holy Kunder,' she said. 'Or I'll be coming for you, and you won't need that knife anymore.'

Hours left. It wasn't enough time. The assault was coming no matter what, and dragging Fiete Saimon's murderer into the light couldn't change that. But the memory of Beatrice Saimon haunted Lena: that lost, slack expression, those innocent eyes. A woman robbed of her partner, of her senses, and finally of her life. Lena had to set right what she had done wrong, while she still had the chance.

Fiete Saimon had known secrets about Maier, not just their shared business but other things, dark truths that could threaten the councillor. And Maier had employed Goreck, the man with the silver dream, the connection between Pawlitzki's potions and a dazed priest at the funeral stone. It was all coming together, but Lena needed to understand why: only then could she see justice done.

She ran through the streets, fighting against the flow of refugees fleeing for the mountain and the rush of volunteers charging to the walls. She shoved them aside without care for who they were or where they were going.

Beyond the walls, the cannons still roared. If anything, they had grown faster and more merciless in their pounding. She remembered the bombardiers she had known, the excitement on their faces when they saw a great edifice about to fall, the renewed bustle as they set to deliver the killing blow. That would be happening out there, as it had happened every time she ordered a city breached. It was only justice that she was on the other side now, but she was one among thousands, and they didn't deserve what was coming for her.

The streets of Hochfel were empty still, gates barred, and windows shuttered. Through an arrow slit high on one building, a musket's muzzle mimicked her path, following her until she rounded a bend, and that house was out of sight.

The gates to the Maier mansion compound were closed. Lena shoved, but of course they were barred, and a chain rattled as she shook them.

The gateposts were made of square cut stone, but wind and rain had worn at the edges of those blocks, leaving a slender gap just above Lena's head. She hooked her fingertips into it, pushed off with her feet, and heaved herself up. Muscles strained and her toes scrabbled for a hold. She shifted her weight, swung her other arm, stretched, and just managed to grab the top of the post. She hung for a moment, took a breath, caught a hold in a crack with her toes, and pushed herself up.

A moment later, she landed in a crouch inside the walls. Her footfalls were soft against the paving stones as she passed the stables with their nervous whinnying, rounded the gryphon-shaped fountain with its tinkling water, and approached the front door.

'Maier, you snake!' She pounded on the door with her fist until the boom of the blows resounded around her. 'Get out here.'

No response. She could hear movement inside and the muffled murmur of an urgent conversation.

She hammered on the door again.

'Answer me, Maier!'

Still no response.

If no one would open the door, then she would go in the window. Except that, now she looked, all those on the ground floor were too small, nothing more than loopholes, designed to let a little light in and a musket shot out. The dining room faced onto an inner courtyard. Maier's office, with its large leaded windows, was on the next floor up, and trying to force the shutters while hanging off the wall would be pure futility.

'Maier!' She pounded on the door again. 'Answer me!'

'Is that you, Headsman Sturm?' Maier's voice emerged muted through the heavy wood.

'Who the hells else would it be?'

'Someone who has forgotten my rank, or their own.'

'Doom and dust, the city's falling and you're whining about titles?'

'It's about authority. I would expect you to understand that, General Seeger.'

Her old name again, like a goad pressing sharply on her mind. She raised her fist to beat at the door, caught herself, and took a long breath while she considered her words.

'Councillor Maier,' she said through gritted teeth. 'Please let me in.'

'I'm sorry, Headsman, but this house is full. I have to consider our supplies and all the mouths here to feed. You'll have to find somewhere else to sit out the sack.'

So that was it. Maier had seen the way the crows were circling and decided to take care of herself. The city's leader sitting safe behind her own walls, fending off looters while the rest of Unteholz burned, waiting until it was safe. The other councillors would doubtless be doing the same. All the fortified manor houses of Hochfel would still stand when this was over, their inhabitants ready to emerge into the ashes and bones, ready to be leaders again. Princes of a graveyard.

There was no getting at the councillor, but maybe Lena could stir the consciences of other people inside.

'I know you did it, Maier,' she said, raising her voice so that everyone inside the house would hear. 'I know you killed the

Saimons.'

'Don't be absurd. I paid you to find the killer.'

'To find a scapegoat, you mean. Fiete knew that you'd been dealing with lowlifes, and he could ruin you. You stabbed him during one of your secret meetings and left the corpse for his wife to find. Then you had her arrested and drugged so she couldn't put up a defence.'

'I don't know how you dreamed up these libels, but you will stop them at once.' Still only Maier responding, her tone sharp.

'I found the man who bought all that silver dream for you. Or rather, I found his corpse. Did you think I wouldn't find Goreck, or that I wouldn't connect him to you?'

For a long moment, there was just the pounding of the cannons and the beating of Lena's own heart. She pressed against the door, testing its toughness and the strength of the hinges. Stronger than her, that much was certain.

'Heibar Goreck?' Maier asked. There was an edge to her voice, as if she were straining at something. 'Used to work on the southern barges?'

'You probably knew him from back then, didn't you? From shipping your goods up and down the rivers. Then he turned up here, one of those anonymous connections Brodbeck provided, someone you could trust with a sensitive task. Except you didn't trust him that much, or you wouldn't have needed to slit his throat.'

Another pause. No whispered conversations from behind the door anymore, but no one opening a shutter either, to let Lena in and let justice be done. She had been too optimistic. Loyalty beat principles in the house of Maier.

'You have it wrong, Headsman,' the councillor said. 'It wasn't me.'

'Oh really? Then who? Spin me another story. Use your silver tongue to talk the blood off your hands.'

'Are the constables still at the walls?'

'Of course. They'll be dying soon enough, thanks to your secret.'

'Then maybe there's a chance. Maybe when this is over I can tell you the truth.'

'You don't even know how, do you? It's all just a way to make people do your bidding.'

'Go fight for our city, Headsman. Afterwards, we can talk.'

Footsteps were just audible through the door, disappearing across a tiled hallway and deeper into the manor.

Lena looked around. Still no way in. Still no sympathetic face.

'I'm not fighting for you, Councillor,' she muttered. 'And this isn't done.'

She stalked back across the courtyard, past the absurdly gurgling fountain, a tamed, clawless imitation of the real majesty and savagery that was a gryphon. Using the bar and chains that secured the gate, she climbed up its back and swung one leg over.

A crash resounded across the city. Lena stared east, towards the gates. There was a second V-shaped breach in the wall, not far from the first, two great gouges as if a beast the size of a mountain had attacked Unteholz with its claws. Dust billowed from the second breach. Above it, the first of the drachenritters had returned to the sky, the dragon's wings spread wide as it watched the destruction below.

Lena shuddered. A few more good hits and the wall between those breaches would collapse, letting Everhart's army in. So little time left before the life she had built here was brought to ruin. No more safe, quiet space for her to hide from the world she had made. No final years of peace.

She dropped into the street, knees protesting as they absorbed the impact. Then she was running again, past the sanctuaries of the rich, heading for home.

Chapter Twenty-Nine

Armoured in Righteousness

Deppel was waiting for Lena as she ran into her home, chest aching and drenched with sweat. He stood rigidly by the table, wearing a nervous grin, arms straining as he held out a sack.

'I got you something,' he said.

'I don't have time.'

Lena pushed past him, heading for the store room.

'But I got it for you.' His voice wavered, then dwindled to a lost whimper. 'It's important. For fighting.'

She stopped in the doorway, caught by that plaintive tone. She had always treated it as a sign of weakness, begging for someone else's approval. But she had seen so much hurt over the past few days, it would have been impossible not to recognise it now.

If Beatrice Saimon still mattered when the walls were falling, if Fiete Saimon mattered as the dragons mustered overhead, then surely Deppel mattered enough for her to share a few moments before it was too late. Mattered enough to show him that she was grateful.

'I'm sorry.' She reached into the sack and pulled out a thick leather jerkin with arm harness attached by moulded pauldrons. The pieces were mismatched, some of them better made than others, but they all looked like a good fit for her.

'I know it ain't the same as your wyvern armour,' Deppel said, 'but I didn't want you getting killed, so I went around all the

347

places I could think of and found all the bits you'd need.'

Lena stared at the armour. It was the kindest thing anyone had done for her in years. It might be mismatched, some of the pieces battered, but it would still have cost money she knew Deppel did not have.

A deep breath stirred within her chest, equal parts gratitude and grief.

'How did you afford this?' she asked.

Deppel shrugged and started unfastening the front of the jerkin.

'I owe a few people favours now, is all.'

'Big favours?'

'It won't matter much if the city's destroyed.'

Lena laid the armour carefully down on the table and placed a hand on Deppel's shoulder. He looked at her, confused.

'Don't you need to-'

'Thank you, Deppel.'

She wrapped her arms around the boy and drew him into a hug. His own arms went around her, and the hard, blood-stained world briefly faded away.

'I'm scared,' Deppel mumbled into her chest. He was shaking.

'It's going to be fine,' Lena said. The boy didn't need the bitter truth, he needed something to see him through. She did too. This small moment, the warmth of the boy against her, those arms clinging for comfort and support, it gave her something more to fight for than a place where she could let herself dwindle into death. If gave her hope that there was something good to be found within her still. It gave her life.

He disentangled himself, wiped his eyes with the back of his sleeve, and reached for the armour.

'I'm scared for you. I've got a place to hide, but you ain't gonna do that, are you?'

'This city was my place to hide. Now it's more than that.'

'So you will need this.'

'No, Deppel. It's a fine present, but I have something else.'

She led him into the storeroom, a cool and shadowed space as deep into the mountain rock as her home went. At the back, she took hold of a stone disk resting against the wall and pushed. It hadn't moved in a long time, and seemed so settled in place that it refused to budge. But she put her shoulder into it and heaved. With a scraping that set her teeth on edge, the stone rolled aside.

In the darkness behind lay a sack made from oiled canvas, its seams stitched with a heavy thread. Lena dragged it into the kitchen, the contents clanking over bumps in the floor, then drew the whittling knife from her boot, sliced the stitches open along two sides, and peeled back the canvas.

It was the first time in five years that she had set eyes on her bonded armour. Her body responded to the sight like she was seeing an old lover, even as her heart sank at the bitter memories it brought. The tips of her fingers tingled, and a warmth spread through her chest as she looked at those polished plates, each one engraved with prayers to Mother Sky, while in her mind's eye she saw ruined cities, lost lives, and her husband closing the door.

'Where'd you get that?' Deppel asked, his eyes wide.

'I was given it by a prince,' she said. 'A reward meant to manage me. As long as I was wearing it, I couldn't connect to our war beasts, so I wouldn't ride into the fight. He could have his general safely on the ground, commanding soldiers instead of leading them.'

Had that been the beginning of the end, the change that gave her enough distance to see what she really was? Perhaps. But perhaps that was an excuse, a way to make someone else responsible for her enlightenment, and with it her downfall. It was comforting to believe that insight had been thrust upon her, that it had been out of reach until then. But wasn't it better to believe that she had been capable of understanding all along, that she was responsible for her own redemption, even if that made her responsible for her own atrocities too. If she was bound for the hells when her end came, then at least her damnation would be built on her own choices.

She set the knife down, kicked off her boots, and took the leg harness from the pile. Choices. Actions. Without them, thought was a waste, however noble its shape.

'Help me get into this, quickly.'

Instinct took over as she started donning the plate. She didn't even have to think about what connected where, how best to get into each piece, where she could fasten the buckles and where she needed to direct Deppel's nimble fingers. Each plate slid on as easily as if she had been wearing it every day of her life. As the enchanted metal wrapped around her flesh, she felt revitalised, renewed by the bond between them. The lingering pain in her shoulder vanished. Aches in her muscles faded away.

She slid on the last gauntlet and flexed her fingers. It was as though the armour wasn't even there. She could sense the air against her skin. When she ran a finger across the table top, she could feel every ridge and groove of the wood.

The worst of it was that it took no effort. To bond with a beast took a gift, carefully nurtured and refined over time. It took empathy and understanding. To bond with armour, all you needed was the money to buy the right suit.

Dragging the armour back into the light felt both wonderful and wretched, and there was no time to settle the storm of feelings inside her.

She fastened her sword belt around the outside, slung Brute in its heavy sheath over her shoulder, and on instinct picked up her whittling knife. There was no boot top to stick it in, and it had no place in a battle, but it hurt to set it aside. This was something of her that wasn't warlike, a tool of whimsy instead of bloodshed, a reminder of who she was now. She thrust it through the back of her belt, fastening its sheath in place with a piece of cord.

Last of all, she picked up the visored helm, the only piece remaining. Slitted eyes stared back at her, blank and menacing.

'I need you to do something, Deppel,' she said. 'Before you go to your hiding place.'

'Is there time?' He glanced out the door, as if expecting to see soldiers come charging at them. 'I wanna help, but…'

'I can't make promises about time, but doing this might just save the city, or at least let more people get out. Will you do it?'

He took a deep breath and looked up at her. His face was pale beneath the trailing strands of greasy hair and his lower lip quivered, but he nodded.

'For you,' he said.

'Thank you, Deppel.' She laid a hand on his shoulder. 'You're a brave lad. Now, I need you to take two messages, one to the alchemist Pawlitzki, the other to Jagusia Brodbeck…'

Lena took a run up and leapt toward the gates of Maier's manor. Strengthened by the bonded armour, she bounded through the air and grabbed the top of the gates. The edges of the wood splintered beneath gauntleted fingers as she hauled herself up and over, before landing with a thud on the paved ground beyond. One of the flagstones cracked beneath her feet.

She strode past the fountain straight to the front door. Tomas hung in his scabbard on one hip, her helmet on the other. She drew Brute from the scabbard across her back, the heavy blade feeling light as ash.

All of this would catch up with her when she took the armour off. If she survived that long.

Five years of practice had given her a perfect grasp of Brute's weight and balance. With both hands on the grip, she swung the sword straight at the front door of the mansion. Normally, it would have taken a logging axe to break through a door like this, but there was nothing normal about the combination of bonded armour and an executioner's blade borne by a soldier who knew how to use both. Splinters flew, and the door creaked as it strained against its hinges.

There were cries of alarm from inside. Good. Let them fear her. Let them know that this was what happened if you stood in the way of justice.

Another blow. A crack ran down one of the planks. The shouting inside grew more shrill.

She swung Brute back and flexed her fingers around the grip, preparing to strike again.

This was good. This was the way it should end.

'Wait!'

There was a thud of a bar being drawn aside, the clack of a bolt, and the battered door swung open.

Maier stood in the entrance to her home. She wore leather leggings, and a beautifully enamelled breastplate just a little too large. Her hair was bound back. The elaborate guard of a jewel-encrusted sword and the engraved pommel of a pistol protruded from her belt.

She held up her hands.

'Please, Headsman,' she said in a calm, steady voice. 'My family will need this door to keep them safe when the city falls.'

'Then you'd best come out and face me.'

Lena took long steps back, making space around the door.

The councillor turned her head to look at someone out of sight.

'Bar the door behind me,' she said. 'I won't be long.' And then, after a moment's hesitation, 'I love you all.'

She emerged, blinking, into the bright light of day and stood facing Lena. Behind her, the door swung shut with a thud that echoed around the courtyard. There was a frightened whinny from the stables. In the distance, the pounding of cannons continued.

'I suppose you want me to draw this,' Maier said, tapping the pommel of her sword. 'Make it into a fair fight.'

Lena shook her head. 'I'm an executioner, not a duellist.'

Maier sighed and stepped away from the door. A single silver shilling danced between the fingers of her left hand.

'I didn't do it,' she said. 'But I know who did. Just wait until the siege is over, then I'll explain.'

'When the constables are free, and you can find an excuse to lock me up?' Lena shook her head.

'What evidence do you even have against me?'

'Beatrice Saimon was drugged with silver dream, which Heibar Goreck bought from the alchemist Pawlitzki. Goreck worked for you, that's how a church handyman had a stash of Salt City ducats.'

'I had no reason to kill the Saimons. You know that I worked with Fiete.'

'Fiete Saimon knew that you'd been corrupting court cases. He was your secret business partner, but now he'd become a threat. You needed to destroy him before he destroyed you. I doubt you did the killing yourself, but you made sure someone did for Goreck as well, so that there would be no trail. Three dead, and all the blood's on your hands.'

'It's quite a story, Headsman, but it's simply not true. You have the pieces, but you've put them together wrong.'

'Enough lies. Get on your knees.'

Maier looked sadly back at the door. She let out a soft sigh, then sank to her knees and let the shilling roll away across the cobbles.

'You're making a mistake, Headsman.'

She pulled her hair across her shoulder, exposing her neck, and knelt stiff-backed, proud as ever.

'Many say that.' Lena walked around behind her and raised Brute, ready for the swing.

'If Beatrice Saimon had said it, would you have listened?'

Lena froze. She imagined that face again, wide-eyed and bewildered. She had been so sure that Beatrice was guilty.

Maier had made a murderer of her. Had lined up the victim

and presented the evidence to make sure she swung her sword. She had made Lena complicit in covering up her crime, spilling an innocent's blood so no one would know that she was a murderer. The evidence showed it, evidence Lena had fought for as tenaciously as a beast on the hunt. Evidence she knew to be true.

As she had known before.

'If not you, then who?' she asked.

'Promise me that you won't act on this until the siege is over.'

'I'm not making promises to a murderer.'

'Then I can't tell you yet. Not until he has done what he has to. Not until the city is safe.'

Maier looked to the door again. Tears were running down her cheeks, but she didn't move, didn't even let her feelings touch her voice. She was as steady as the mountain itself. Was that a sign of innocence, or one of guilt?

Then the meaning of her words sank in. A man who was keeping the city safe, who had to be kept in place until the siege was done. Many men had taken to the walls, but few mattered beyond their ability to fill a gap and hold a spear.

'Baumer?' Lena asked, incredulous. 'You're saying that Baumer did it?'

Maier looked back over her shoulder, a flicker of frustration darting across her face. Then she faced forward, hands on her knees, head held high.

'No,' she said. 'It was me. I've been trying to delay the inevitable, but that can't last. Do your work and end this.'

A confession. What more proof could there be? Lena tensed her muscles, ready to swing.

But it was Baumer who had told her that Maier hired Goreck. If Baumer was the killer, that would be an easy way to throw her off the scent, to send her after someone he knew she disliked.

Baumer and his men had found Fiete Saimon's body, hadn't they? Easy to do if you were the killers.

Baumer's men had Illora daggers. Had Baumer had one once,

until he left it as a clue at Saimon's home?

She lowered Brute.

'Why?' she asked. 'Why would Baumer kill Saimon?'

'He didn't. It was me. Now deliver your justice.'

The dull and rounded end of Brute's blade, no good for a fighting sword, rested on cold stone. Beyond the gates and down the hill, a dragon swooped low over the warehouse district, smoke rising in its wake.

'Wrap your lie in the truth,' Lena said. 'It's the easiest way to sell a story. Baumer told me that Fiete Saimon knew someone's secret, made me think it was yours. But it was Baumer's, wasn't it?'

Like shards of stained glass in a temple window, individual pieces, previously unconnected, came together to form a picture in her mind. Baumer and his constables, all veterans, with that easy camaraderie that came from years of service. She had assumed that they met here, but that didn't have to be true. Plenty of mercenary companies moved on together when a campaign was done.

'Maybe it's not just his secret,' she said. 'It's theirs. Something he's hiding to protect his comrades in arms.'

'Enough!' Maier leapt to her feet, drew her sword, and stood facing Lena. 'It was me. My dirty secrets. I'll kill you here and now, take your body down to the walls, pretend you were one more casualty of war, because justice is just a tool to people like me.'

Lena looked at the sword. Despite the determination on Maier's face, the tip of the blade trembled like a firefly in the air. It was almost noble, how far this woman would go to protect her family.

'You couldn't kill me if you tried,' Lena said. 'And I'm not going to be pushed into killing you. You must be desperate, because all this posturing, it's just proving my point. Now tell me the thundering truth, or I will smash your door down, rip your gates open, and leave everything you love exposed.'

'You wouldn't.'

'Try me.'

Maier lunged, the sword heading straight for Lena's face. Lena swung up her arm, batted the blow aside with a clang of steel against steel, grabbed the blade with her gauntleted hand, and twisted. Maier winced as the sword was torn from her grip.

'Tell me.'

Lena flung the sword away, and it clattered down near the stables. Maier looked at her, face red with rage, hair hanging wild and loose. She looked at the door, one plank already splintered, and sighed.

'Did you ever hear of the Slaughter of Saints?' she asked.

'When someone wipes out a monastery, word gets around. Some of the Salt Cities still offer bounties on the soldiers who did it.'

'Baumer and his people were those soldiers. They came here not long before you did, pretending to be just one more mercenary band looking for work, but they were sweating desperation, and it didn't take me long to work out why. I knew that the war would come our way sooner or later, and that we would need protection, so I offered them a deal, a place to hide and their secret kept safe, as long as they stayed loyal.

'It was all working fine until this winter, when Fiete worked out who they were. He didn't know that I knew, so he went to Baumer and tried to blackmail him into spying on me. But Baumer knew where his loyalties lay. He told me all about it.

'Baumer was feeding Fiete false information. For a while, Fiete tried to use it against me, and of course he always failed. But the past month he stopped trying. Looking back, perhaps he knew what was going on.'

A wyvern screeched as it flew past overhead, high enough to avoid the dragons. It turned its head, watching the city below. It would smell the blood and smoke, hear the screams, and drool in anticipation of the feast to come.

'If Baumer betrayed you, you'd give away his secret,' Lena said. 'If he didn't betray you, Saimon would give him away. He needed a way out.'

'When Fiete died, I thought that Baumer had got lucky. But when I realised that he was lying to you, trying to set me up, I saw that he was making his own luck.'

'Was he the one who drugged Holy Saimon too, kept her sedated so she couldn't offer a coherent defence?'

'You think I would know?'

'She was held in the citadel. It would be easy for him to get access.'

'If you say so.'

'You seriously want me to believe that you never suspected?'

Maier hung her head. 'Maybe I didn't let myself see it. I was too focused on the good he did, maintaining order and protecting the city. There were so many other dangers, we needed him.'

Metal clinked against metal as Lena clenched her fist. She shook her head slowly, her movements heavy with the weight of reluctant acceptance. Of all the people in the city, Baumer was one of the few she liked, trusted even. The one she felt something in common with.

But that common ground came from both being killers. She still killed, though her wars were behind her. Was it so hard to believe that he would?

'I can't arrest him,' she said. 'Not with all the constables on his side.'

'Once the siege is over, we'll deal with this together.' Maier held out her hand, palm open, the skin red where Lena had ripped the sword from it.

'We could die. He could escape in the chaos. I can't risk that.'

Lena sheathed Brute and headed for the gates. Maier grabbed her arm, only to be dragged along in her wake.

'You can't do this,' Maier said. 'We need Baumer and his people. Without their leadership, the city will fall.'

'Without justice, the city isn't worth saving.'

'You self-righteous, hypocritical heap of ash!'

Maier's hand shot up, slapping Lena across the face. The shock made her stop and stare.

'You chose not to fight,' Maier snapped. 'A veteran general, and you chose not to protect this city. Now you want to kill the man who stepped up when you wouldn't, and you're pretending like you're doing the right thing? You're going to doom us all, you petty wretch.'

'I should beat you senseless for that,' Lena snarled, feeling the heat and the sting of her cheek.

'That's who you really are, isn't it? Just one more killer, using the law as a cover. You don't give a gust of ash for anyone but yourself.'

Lena grabbed Maier's wrist and twisted. Maier whimpered in pain.

The sound made Lena freeze. She remembered a whimper like that from Deppel, hurt and scared, trapped by a gang of bullies in a back street. No safety, no justice, just someone throwing their strength around because they could, because no one was there to stop them. Until she came.

She let go.

'I was too set on escaping my past,' Lena said. 'I should have thought about what I have now. Should have done what was needed.'

Maier rubbed at her wrist. She straightened and offered Lena a soft smile.

'Come in and have a drink,' she said. 'Help keep my house safe. If Baumer lives through this, then we'll deal with him.'

She reached for Lena's arm. In the distance, the cannons roared.

'You were right, but so was I,' Lena said. 'The city needs protecting, and it needs justice too.' She shrugged off Maier. 'I'm going after Baumer, and I'm going to save the city.'

'How?' Maier screeched, flinging her hands in the air. 'What can you do that can possibly make up for killing our war leader?'

'I have a plan.' Lena said.

'You have a plan? A thundering plan? You can't be serious!'

Lena leapt, the bonded armour lending her strength, grabbed the top of the gate and swung herself up.

'Headsman Sturm,' Maier yelled, 'as the head of the city council, I am ordering you to come back here right now!'

Lena dropped into the street, boots clanging against cobbles. Then she ran, up towards the slopes at the back of the city and their great gaping cave mouths.

Chapter Thirty

Into the Breach

Hundreds of people were streaming out of Unteholz and up the mountain slopes, fear driving them towards the caves and the bone fields. Some pushed barrows full of their belongings or carried heavy sacks. Others had only the shirts on their backs. Many looked back in dread at the city they had left behind, its walls bleeding smoke and dust, dragons circling overhead with their claws spread wide.

Where there was space, Lena ran off the path, leaping up rock-scattered slopes to work her way around the crowds, letting the bonded armour lift her up. Its strength became her strength, its surface her skin. She felt every jagged rock and every hard landing, not as pain but as information, heightening her awareness of the world.

Pawlitzki's apprentice, Lotta, was waiting by the mouth of the first cave. As Lena approached, she held out a huge clay jar, stoppered with a chunk of cork.

'Master said to give you this,' she said.

Lena grabbed the girl by the arm and dragged her into the cave. She ignored Lotta's protests, and those of the refugees she pushed aside. They would thank her later, if they lived that long.

'Where are we going?' Lotta asked. 'You're hurting me!'

Past the frightened crowd, the tunnels ran down into the mountain, away from sunlight and clear air. The way was lit by earthenware lanterns burning cheap oil, all the illumination most cavern dwellers could afford.

The further they went, the more the smells of smoke and humanity were left behind, replaced by blood, rot, and fur. The tunnel opened into a wide cavern, the first of the dying caves.

The sgeir were gathered at the near end of the cavern, a ragged band of families and loners, clutching tight to the tools of butchery.

Beyond them lay the dying beasts. Lena had never seen so many in here. Some had come crawling across the principalities to die: gryphons, unicorns, manticores, every manner of monsters. Others were local wyverns, bleeding and broken, creatures that had got too close to the besieging army and fallen victim to its monsters or to its guns. There were even a few from that army: a gryphon with a broken wing, one more with crossbow quarrels buried in its flank, and a weary, battered dragon.

Lena knew the dragon. It should have looked at her with hatred. She had betrayed it, forced it to fight one of its own then abandoned it so that she could confront Jekob. Its teeth should have been bared the moment it saw her, fire flaring from its maw. Instead, it lumbered over with one leg trailing, leaving footprints of blood and pus, and lowered its neck to nuzzle at her. She was part of its flight now.

Lena laid a hand on the beast's head. Even through her armour, she could feel its sadness. The sensation was distant, like the last dying echo of a friend's voice bouncing off a valley side. Her bond with the armour was too strong for her mind to merge with the dragon, leaving her unable to sooth its pain. But it still pushed closer, drawing its wings in to enter this narrow end of the cave, pushing at her as it let out a plaintive whine.

She ran a hand across its brow, felt the rounded edges of scales and the warmth of the body beneath.

'You remind me of an old friend,' she said softly. 'His name was Calebek, and he nearly killed me the first time I rode him, but by the end I was his favourite person in the world. He never made it to the caves, but he died for me too. I'm sorry I couldn't do better for either of you.'

She closed her eyes for a moment and let an old grief take her, but there was no time for mourning. The living needed her help.

'Open the jar,' she said, raising her voice.

Lotta stood frozen, staring at the monster. The adult sgeir pushed their children back and raised their weapons.

'Open the thundering jar,' Lena said, her voice soft but menacing, 'before this one gets hungry.'

Lotta gave a frantic nod, put the jar down, and levered the lid out with a knife. A smell of cloves, sage, and sulphur emerged. Spirit salve. A balm Lena used to use on her own beasts' wounds.

Lena dipped her hand in the jar. The salve was warm from its brewing, thick and greasy. When she took her hand out, the gauntlet gleamed. The dragon drew a deep breath and looked excitedly at her.

'Not yet,' Lena said.

She walked down the dragon's flank until she reached a ragged claw mark, three thick scabs between the protruding edges of broken scales. Slowly, carefully, she ran her hand down each wound in turn, coating them with the salve.

The dragon gave a deep, base hum. Its eyes brightened.

The injured leg was worse, mangled and twisted, infected gouges oozing putrid yellow filth. With one hand, Lena scraped away the worst of the pus, feeling the dragon tremble as she ran iron fingers over raw ends of flesh. With the other hand, she rubbed spirit salve into the wound.

The dragon shuddered, then steadied itself. It leaned back, putting weight on the injured leg again, and twitched its tail. Wings strained against the confines of the cavern, one of them too torn and tattered to fly.

Lena reached into the jar once more and held up her hand. The dragon's tongue flickered out, a pointed purple worm that ran across her gauntlet, licking up every drop of the oily medicine. It pawed at the ground and then nuzzled against Lena once more, snorting excitedly.

It would have grown into a magnificent beast, bold, strong, and adventurous. The thought almost broke Lena's heart.

'I'm sorry,' she said, laying her hand on its brow again. 'For what I did to you before, and for what I'm going to do now.'

That sorrow wasn't enough to stop her. Not with everything else at stake.

She turned to Lotta and the sgeir.

'All of you, take the salve, do what I did with the other beasts. The city's counting on you.'

One of the sgeir stood up and raised a cleaver.

'To hells with the city,' she said. 'Those people treat us like dirt. We should get to butchering the beasts, so we have something to offer the other side when they win.'

Murmurs of assent swelled like breath in the chest of a waking beast. Lotta took a trembling step away from the sgeir.

'You know me,' Lena said. 'Do you know any of those soldiers out there, past the walls?'

More murmurs and the shaking of heads. The sgeir weren't people who spoke up, who proclaimed their will loudly or fought for what they believed. They were poor, downtrodden, unheard, their voices reduced to murmurs and muttering. Lena almost wished that they were stronger: strong enough to argue back, to give her something to push against, a better sign of whether she was getting through.

'Trust me when I say that my plan will give you more beasts,' she said. 'And that a battered city will need you more than before, while a triumphant army will just see enemies to stamp on.'

The sgeir looked at each other. Whispers ran through the group like the footfalls of a hundred insects. Then they came forward and, one by one, reached into the jar.

The sgeir moved confidently among the injured beasts. They knew from long and deadly experience how to avoid catching a wyvern's gaze, where was safest from a manticore's sting, how to sooth a unicorn. Knowledge passed down through generations, used to get in close and finish the dying monsters off, now served a different purpose as they tended to wounds.

The rustle of feet on stone and hands across fur was the only sound. The roar of the cannons was gone. When had that happened, Lena wondered. Could she just not hear the noise down here, or was it too late? Was the city falling, making a mockery of her last desperate gambit?

Gods, but she wanted a drink.

The dragon's head shot up. It sniffed the air, eyes wide, tail tapping the ground.

'Get back,' Lena said to Lotta, who stood with the empty jar in her hands, peering at the dragon's scales.

The girl didn't need telling twice. A wave of excitement was running through the beasts, sending the sgeir scurrying back against the walls. Claws scraped against stone. Howls and hisses filled the air.

'What's happening?' Lotta asked, eyes wide.

'They smell the other potion,' Lena said. 'The one your master is brewing.'

Lena took hold of the dragon's shoulder and flung herself onto its back, where a scuffed saddle was still bound in place. It felt uncanny to sit there in such a state of detachment, her thoughts separate from those of her steed, their feelings severed by the barrier of her armour. This second skin protected her from the world by deadening all pain. It made her isolated among others, cold and hard and self-contained. Once, it had felt like a sort of safety. Now it felt like a self-inflicted punishment, like being the executioner of a distant mountain town.

The beast barely noticed her presence. All its attention was turned towards the cave mouth.

'That's it,' Lena said, laying a hand against its neck. 'Follow that smell.'

Setting one paw in front of the other, the dragon prowled down the widening cave, leaving the humans and their healing behind. Other beasts followed, slowly at first, but accelerating with each passing moment as a distant alchemical smell filled them with an unquenchable hunger. Lena could feel it in the air as she was carried down the cave and out onto the mountainside, bouncing in the saddle as the dragon reached a gallop.

She unhooked her helmet from her belt and pulled it on. Like everything about this suit, it was a masterpiece of the armourer's art, the slit in the visor granting her an almost perfect view of the world. She knew that she couldn't feel the wind against her skin, but her bond to the armour made the illusion feel real.

They emerged from a cave mouth above the southwest edge of the city, close to the Manden Gate. From here, Unteholz spread across the mountainside below, a mad clutter of mismatched buildings, the creation of humanity's eager, unconsidered expansion. The towering keep of the citadel and the vertebrae spire of the cathedral stood above the rest, one black as night, the other a pale tower of bleached bone.

Beyond the cathedral, the walls had fallen. A span of stone hundreds of meters wide, running clockwise from the East Gate, had been reduced to rubble. Buildings blocked Lena's view of the fighting, but she could hear the clamour of arms and voices, could see dust and dragons filling the air.

She pressed her heels to the dragon's flanks, but there was no need. The smell of Pawlitzki's concoction, though still far away, was irresistible to the beast. It spread its wings and tried to take flight, but they were too torn to catch the wind. Instead, it went crashing and sliding down the precipitous slope that led to the execution ground.

The other beasts came with it, a disparate herd of monsters, things with feathers, scales, and fur, with twisted legs and broken wings, splintered talons and rotten teeth. They howled and screeched as they raced down the mountainside, the strong shoving the weak aside. A unicorn fell, slid, and was trampled underfoot, reduced to a mangled corpse amid the bloody trail of hooves and claws.

Lena was flung about in the saddle as the dragon ran and leapt, trying to stay ahead of the pack. Her teeth rattled against each other, and her thighs clenched as she held herself in place, but she grinned and whooped and joined in the noise of the beasts, rediscovering the fierce joy that she had lost.

Her plan was working. Their pain deadened and their spirits briefly revived, the dying monsters were heading for where she had told Pawlitzki to throw his potion, the open ground outside the East Gate.

Stones rattled down with them as they reached the flat ground around the Weeping Stone. The sound of their passing echoed back like thunder from the city walls.

Lena had ridden out of the cave on a wave of pure exhilaration, but now that was fading. They still had a long way to go, while the city's soldiers fought desperately for their lives. If the enemy got a good force through the walls, then it would be too late. If Baumer failed, then all her efforts would come to nothing.

And if he succeeded, then she was coming for him.

Someone was watching them from the battlements of the city, a tall, bearded man with a shabby cloak pulled up around his ears. As Lena looked up, he waved the stump of one hand, then vanished from view.

If Deppel had got through and if his message had been taken in - neither certainty in this moment- that wave meant Brodbeck's people were heading for the fighting, ready to hit at the same time Lena did. She pushed aside the thought of what would happen if Deppel hadn't got through. Galloping towards danger on the back of a dying dragon was no time for doubts.

They ran around the outside of Unteholz, trampling through terraced fields of cabbages and grain, the monsters spreading out to fill the space between the city and the forest, between humanity and the wild. A wave of hot and howling flesh, stinking and seeping with rot and death, rushing towards oblivion.

The siege camp came into view. Barricades of earth and freshly felled timber. Tents and wagons, supply heaps and corrals. Rows of siege cannons and mortars. Trench lines zigzagging towards the walls.

Their attention already taken by the assault; it took the artillerists a minute to notice what was coming. Then the more attentive started shouting at the others, yelling and pointing at the onrushing monstrous horde. With more haste than coordination, they turned the guns and started reloading.

It was too late. The closest cannon had just finished turning when the beasts hit. These were the outliers, the weakest and worst injured creatures pushed to the edge of the pack, but they were more than strong enough to deal with the artillerists. Screams and growls and the crunching of bones joined the pounding of claws and hooves.

Lena's dragon kept moving, utterly intent on what lay ahead. She clung on tight as it leapt across the snaking trench lines, the spines on its neck rising in excitement.

Around the curve of the wall, the breach came into view. Blocks of stone had fallen out as well as in, creating an uneven slope of broken pieces and awkward angles up which the assault party was advancing. More infantry emerged from the trenches to press behind them, pikes raised, swords drawn, muskets at the ready, eager for their chance to enter the fight.

Past them, a scene of sheer chaos was playing out. The monsters of Everhart's army had caught the same scent that was driving Lena's beasts into a frenzy. They had descended upon the ground outside the gates, where Pawlitzki had poured his potion from the battlements above. Dozens of monsters were trying to lap the potion from the ground, tearing at each other if they got in the way. They turned the space between the road and the river into a frenzy of wild fighting, a whirling maelstrom of fur and scales, teeth and claws. Their screeches and howls cut through the war cries and the clash of weapons.

It was a testament to Everhart's confidence that he pushed on, even with his own beasts fighting on his flank. Pikemen and drachenritters held back the terrible brawl, desperately trying to keep wild nature in its place.

Lena's injured beasts didn't care about the army in front of them or the fallen walls. They would go over or through anything in their way. They would do whatever it took to reach the potion. Even as blades turned to face them, they charged up the rubble and into the crush of soldiers. Lena swung one leg over the saddle and jumped as the dragon slammed into the side of a musketeer regiment, crushing them beneath its clawed feet and low-hanging belly.

She couldn't have leapt clear of the beasts on her own. The dragon's wings alone would have knocked her down in the rubble. But she leapt with strength and grace accentuated by the bonded armour, flying past a beat of the dragon's torn wing and landing on a block of fallen masonry halfway up the breach.

The army had been thrown into chaos. Some soldiers were fighting the beasts. Others were fleeing. Many milled around in confusion, looking for someone to take command. None knew how to react to the arrival of an unknown knight in their midst.

Lena strode up the rubble, ignoring any woman or man with the sense to get out of her way. The captain of a halberd company, sporting a thick plume of red and black feathers, demanded to know who she was. She grabbed him by the arm and flung him aside.

At the top of the slope, between the shattered ends of the city walls, the stones were littered with bodies and slippery with blood. The defenders had tried to make a stand here, with the advantage of high ground, but had been driven back by weight of numbers and the fear such moments brought. They had retreated into the streets below, still trying to contain the attack, to save the city from loss and slaughter. It was a desperate battle, the push and shove, stab and gouge of close quarters fighting with both sides tightly packed, no room to dodge or to manoeuvre, just to swing a blade or stab with a spear, to kill the warrior you faced before they killed you. Lines five and six soldiers deep swayed back and forth.

The sound of the battle, the smell of blood and smoke, the cool solidity of the armour around her, it brought back the memory of a hundred moments like this and of how she had dominated them all. This was who she had always been. How could she ever have let it go?

Lena stood at the centre of the breach, her armour shining in the sunlight, watching, waiting, judging the combat.

The monstrous melee she had unleashed had stopped the stream of soldiers into the breach. Some were caught in desperate fights against the beasts while others had retreated. The assault had stalled. But so many had already made it through that the city, with its small band of constables and its inexperienced militia, still seemed on the verge of falling. The line was crumbling on the left, bodies falling in front of a determined pike block, the attackers about to break out into the streets.

Then she saw Soren Baumer. He stood in the centre of the line, swinging a double-handed sword. His once gleaming armour was plastered with blood and dust, dented in a dozen places, the remnants of a city constable's tabard hanging tattered and gore-stained around his neck. His movements were swift and decisive. He smashed his blade into a soldier's chest, almost carving her in two, kicked her into her comrades, and pushed forward to hack at them. It was a bold example and a terrifying threat for the enemy to face, but it was not enough. However hard he tried; no man could win a war on his own.

Then Brodbeck's followers came. A column of men and women in uncoordinated armour and mismatched weapons, filling the avenue that ran down from the cathedral. They howled and screamed as they ran, professional killers of a very different sort.

They streamed in around Baumer, lending his line a new vitality. The invaders faltered and everything hung in the balance.

In the darkness of her helmet, Lena grinned. Ignoring the dead weight of Brute across her back, she drew Tomas and strode into the fray.

She would have pitied the first few she killed, if pity was ever her way. They never saw her coming. She charged them from behind, bounding down the rubble with Tomas swinging in her hand, ending lives as easily as she drew breath. She didn't need her enemies to face her for a fair fight. War had never been fair.

A woman turned, halberd in hand, eyes wide with alarm. Too slow. Lena ran her through, drew Tomas out, and flung the corpse aside.

That soldier's alarm was reflected in the faces of others as they turned towards Lena. A musketeer raised his weapon, the slow match smoldering in the lock. She beat the weapon aside before he could pull the trigger, slashed her blade across his throat, and turned away as he sank gurgling to the ground.

All sense of order collapsed as Brodbeck's gang broke through the invaders' ranks and Lena tore them apart from behind. There were no lines anymore, just battling bodies, small clusters of friends fighting together, individuals caught on their own, men and women hacking, stabbing, battering, rolling on the ground with their hands around each others' throats. Real war.

Lena fought her way towards Baumer. He was in the heart of the fighting, his constables advancing around him, their spirits renewed by the ragged reinforcements. Their glee at the slaughter was a sickness, one that had Lena in its grasp.

Someone hit her from behind. The clang of metal against her helmet set up a ringing that made her ears ache as she stumbled, trying to shake the sudden dizziness and to find her balance. She turned, saw a halberd swinging at her chest, and knocked the blow aside. By the time the man had raised his blade she had her footing again and it was too late for him. She drove Tomas through his chest.

She wrenched the blade free. Her head was spinning from the blow, and that had churned her stomach. She wrenched up her visor and vomited across the body. The sharp taste of bile cut through the chaos of sensations, and she steadied herself, forcing the world into focus.

With a bitter laugh, she raised her blade.

A familiar face leapt out at her from the gang of armed criminals swarming around Baumer. Deppel was there, a mace in his hand, his attacks uncertain and uncoordinated.

The breath caught in Lena's throat. What was he doing here? He was meant to take a message and then run. He was meant to be safe.

A sword swung at Deppel. He raised his mace to block the obvious feint and the real attack went in. The tip of the blade plunged into Deppel's shoulder. Blood streamed across his chest. The mace fell from his hand.

Lena ran through the melee, barging both sides away, swinging Tomas at anyone who tried to block her path.

Deppel sank to his knees. His face was pale.

The sword rose to the top of an arc that would bring it down into Deppel's neck.

A scream burst from Lena; a wail deranged by dread. She was too far away. She wouldn't get there in time.

But Jagusia Brodbeck did. The gang lord appeared at the swordsman's side, driving a shortsword in through his armpit. His weapon fell from his grasp and then he fell with it.

Lena reached Deppel and crouched beside him. With one gauntleted hand she stroked his pale cheek, while with the other she tried to staunch his wound.

'What are you doing here, you idiot?' she hissed.

'I come to help,' he said, tears in his eyes. 'Oh gods, I don't wanna die.'

The blood ran through Lena's fingers, coated her armour,

dripped into the dirt.

'Don't worry,' Lena said, wrapping her arm around his shoulders. 'I'll take care of you.'

'No.' Brodbeck's tone was sharp as any blade. 'You have a bigger task here.'

'I'm not leaving him to die,' Lena snapped.

'I brought my people here on your promise. They're risking their lives to save this city.'

'They're risking their lives because I promised no executions for past crimes.'

'And your promise is worth nothing if you don't do what you said. Save this city. I'll save the kid.'

Reluctantly, Lena pressed Deppel's own hand to the wound, then drew hers away.

'If you let him die then I'll-'

'For Moon's sake, get on with it!' Brodbeck pointed toward the breach, beyond which half an army still waited. 'They'll be here soon.'

Lena clenched her jaw, fighting the instinct to argue back. There was already enough fighting to be had.

'The plan's changed,' she said. 'It was Baumer, not Maier.'

'Piss and poison. Like this business isn't ugly enough.'

'If you need to-'

'My people know to back you. Just get on with it while we're still breathing.'

Lena turned, tightened her grip on Tomas, and strode towards Baumer. The fighting throng parted like flesh beneath a blade. No one wanted to confront the strange soldier who had appeared in their midst, swift and strong and armoured from head to toe in gleaming mail. They had risked enough.

Baumer grinned as she approached.

'I should have known you'd come in the end,' he said. 'No one really leaves this behind.'

His grin shifted to a look of alarm as she swung Tomas. His

sword came up, parrying the blow just in time, and he staggered beneath the force of her fury.

'What the hells, Sturm?' he bellowed.

With cries of alarm, Baumer's constables broke from the line and made for Lena. But Brodbeck's people were in the way, weapons bared and faces fierce as they stood against the lawmen who had hunted down so many of their friends. The two sides faced off in a ring around Lena and Baumer, shouting and waving their weapons, the constables trying to make sense of this sudden shift of sides.

'It was you,' Lena said as she faced Baumer, her voice shaking with fury. 'You killed the Saimons.'

'We're under attack, you lunatic!' Baumer pointed his sword towards the broken walls. 'Whatever you think you've learnt, save it until we've saved the thundering city.'

Lena shook her head. She had trusted him, liked him even. She had thought she had a friend in this stupid city.

'You brought this down on us,' she said. 'You gave them an excuse, just so you could avoid the consequences of your actions.'

Baumer opened his mouth, then hesitated. His expression shifted, defiance becoming resignation.

'Not just mine,' he said. 'I had people counting on me.'

'People like the Saimons, who thought you were here to uphold the law?'

'People who came here with me, who fought beside me for years. Old loyalties come first.'

'Self-serving dung. You were protecting your own hide.'

'You dare criticise me for hiding from the past? I know who you are, General Seeger. There's as much blood on your hands as mine.'

Lena held up her fist. Red streaks ran across its engravings.

'More,' she said. 'But there's a difference between war and murder.'

'No innocent ever died because of you?'

'I can't give justice for a war, but I can give it for a crime.'

She lunged, the tip of her blade darting towards his face. Baumer batted the blow aside, then swept his sword around. The two of them slashed and stabbed, parried and dodged, their swords shifting with speed and precision, a game as deadly as the law.

This was war the way the storytellers dreamed of it. Soldier against soldier, a test of skill and strength, old instincts guiding her blows before she could even think. The clang of their blades cut through the screams and roars all around.

Lena fought with all her strength, pressing at Baumer with a flurry of attacks. Her sword was lighter and faster than his, her style more fluid. If she could get a hit in somewhere vulnerable or throw him off balance, then she might win.

Her muscles ached already. It had been too long since she fought like this. Her movements were slowing, her edge fading, while Baumer found some fresh well of vitality. He swung his sword overhead in a long, deadly arc that she was too slow to block.

His blade clanged against her shoulder, sending a flash of pain from her burnt skin and a shudder down her arm. Tomas slipped through numb fingers and almost fell from her grip. Another blow knocked him flying from her hand.

'You couldn't leave it alone, could you?' Baumer growled. 'All you had to do was crawl back into your drunken pit and keep rotting away like your sgeir friends.'

Lena took a step back, stumbled over a piece of rubble, found her footing again. She reached over her shoulder for Brute, not a good fighting weapon, but what she had left. Even before she could draw it, Baumer lashed out, forcing her back. Every time she raised her arm to grab for Brute, she was stopped by a swing of his blade.

'You made me a murderer,' she said.

'That's what it's really about, isn't it?' Baumer grinned like a dragon descending on a sheep field. 'Revenge.'

'It's about justice.'

He lunged suddenly. Lena leapt aside, landed on loose rocks, and the rubble rolled away beneath her foot. She crashed to the ground.

Cursing her own clumsiness, she rolled onto her back. There was blood in her mouth and something pressing against the base of her spine. Baumer towered over her, deadly in his determination.

This was it. A fitting death for a general turned drunk, lying sprawled in the dirt as her city fell.

Baumer's blade rose, shining as it caught the sunlight.

Lena remembered Beatrice Saimon's face as the blade had come for her. She wished that she could have made up for that moment, but a death could never be undone.

Then she realised what was pressing against her back. She reached behind her and took a grip on her whittling knife.

Baumer's blade came flashing down, a blow full of strength and fury.

Lena flung herself aside. The blade hit the rubble. She twisted, jumped to her feet, and leapt at Baumer.

Their bodies collided, armour clashing in a cacophony that echoed around her head. Baumer grabbed her left arm and wrenched it up. Twisted muscles sent a silent scream of pain through her body.

'Just give up and die, you pickled grey-haired has-been,' Baumer hissed, raising his sword.

Lena's fist shot up, plunging the whittling knife through the gap in the armour beneath his arm. He grunted, grimaced, stared at her in confusion. His sword clattered to the ground.

With a twist of her wrist, Lena pulled the knife out. Blood was streaming from the wound. Not enough to kill him, if he could find a physician, but she had severed muscles he needed to wield that damn greatsword and probably punctured his lung. His face spoke of dreadful pain.

'You win,' he whispered. For a moment he laughed, but then the pain of his shaking chest cut that short. 'Finish it.'

He slumped against her. She dropped the knife and slid her arm around him.

'What are you doing?' Baumer asked.

'Ending this.'

She led him up the rubble, towards the breach in the wall. The fighting was done on this side, the scattered invaders forced into retreat. Brodbeck's gang had disarmed Baumer's constables and a weary calm prevailed. But the howls and screeches of the monsters outside the walls were almost over. Soon fresh troops would be ordered into the gap. Soon the assault would start again.

She only had moments.

They staggered up the heap of rubble, Baumer's blood running between them, staining both suits of bonded armour.

'It looks good on you,' he mumbled.

'The blood?'

'The armour. It suits you.'

At the peak of the rubble she stopped and lowered him to his knees.

Beyond the walls, the ground was littered with the bodies of monsters and of soldiers, blank eyes staring at the sky between twitching tangles of lost life. Wounded beasts still hissed and bared their claws outside the city gates, but Everhart's pikemen were closing in, finishing off one wounded monster at a time. Lena saw the dragon she had ridden lying dead, its hide torn in a hundred places, its neck twisted and limp. She allowed herself a moment of sorrow at the sight, but not the guilt that rode with it. She had done what had to be done.

Soldiers were gathering outside the siege camp. Fresh units in orderly columns, ready to advance. Survivors of the previous fighting, some tending their wounds, others preparing to return to the fray. They watched her uncertainly.

Smoke burst from a musket. The shot flew wide of Lena and struck splinters of stone from the wall. She half expected a volley to follow. When it didn't come, she took off her helmet, then Baumer's, and dropped them at her feet.

'My name is Corin Seeger,' she shouted. 'This is Captain Soren Baumer, commander of the defences of Unteholz. We've come to parley with General Everhart.'

Confused conversation ran through the assembled army. Baumer didn't look like a man come for a parley.

A gryphon screeched and spread its wings, trying to escape the carnage around the gate. Muskets fired, and it collapsed, torn feathers fluttering on the breeze.

Everhart appeared from around a block of halberdiers, dressed in his gleaming plate armour and red and black surcoat. One hand rested on the pommel of his longsword. The other held his helmet. He walked out in front of the army, flanked by armoured bodyguards, and stopped halfway to the walls.

'General Seeger.' He raised a fist in salute. Lena almost wished he had made the sign of the eye instead. 'Have you come to surrender?'

'I've come to give you what you came for: justice.'

She reached across her shoulder and drew Brute. Everhart's guards stiffened.

'We can take that for ourselves,' Everhart said, unmoving.

'Perhaps.' Lena turned her head, ostentatiously scanning the army and the blood-soaked ground in front of it, making sure they both saw the damage she had done. 'But that's not your job.'

She pointed at Baumer, who knelt with one hand on his thigh, the other pressed to his wound, trying to staunch the flow.

'Soren Baumer murdered Fiete Saimon, to hide the sins of his own past. He framed Beatrice Saimon, to the same end. The punishment for these crimes is death.

'As city executioner of Unteholz, it is my duty to carry out this sentence, no one else's. Do you want to stand in my way?'

Everhart looked from her to his army. His beasts were gone, all dead or dying. His ranks were depleted, wounded soldiers being dragged from the field. More would desert after the shock of how this day had gone.

Was he as good at this as her? Did he see that he could still win this battle, but would leave his army too broken to win any more, vulnerable to whatever forces his opponents gathered? Or was he so blinded by the immediacy of victory that he would not see the looming shadow of defeat?

He looked back at her, and Lena saw in his eyes that she had won, if this mess of blood and destruction could be called winning.

'All I have ever sought is that which Mother Sky demands: justice,' Everhart called out, his voice deep and clear. 'Seeing that sword in the hand of her greatest general, I know that it will come. We are all blessed to be here this day.'

No one spoke on either side of the walls. There were only the growls of dying monsters and the cries of the vultures overhead.

Lena turned to Baumer. From the corners of her eyes, she saw both attackers and defenders watching her, but her attention was on him. A friend, an enemy, a dark reflection of who she had been. She wasn't grieving for the man in front of her, but for the one she had imagined him to be. That man had been killed by the truth. For this one, the duty was hers.

'Soren Baumer, you have been found guilty of the murders of Fiete and Beatrice Saimon,' she declared, raising her voice so that both crowds could hear. 'By the judgement of the Blood Court of Unteholz, you are to die this day. Do you wish the consolation of a priest, that your soul might find mercy in the beyond?'

Baumer laughed. Blood trickled from his lips.

'Moon take all of you,' he said.

Lena nodded. The world moved slowly as both her hands took a firm grip on Brute. She looked at Baumer, hoping to find some shred of guilt, some glimmer of shame, but he wouldn't offer her that comfort.

She shifted her foot back, found her point of perfect balance, and swung the sword.

Chapter Thirty-One

One Final Deal

Lena stood by the gates, a sealed roll of parchment in one hand, arms folded across her chest. She kept gazing toward the citadel, wanting to see if Jekob was coming yet, then looking away, unable to stand the pressure of waiting.

It seemed absurd to be standing here, with the gates barred shut against the outside world, when the wall lay in ruins only thirty feet away, a gaping wound in Unteholz's skin. It would be easy to storm through that gap now, with the rubble cleared in preparation for rebuilding, but this was how politics worked: harsh realities were less important than symbols, truth less important than letting people feel like normal life had returned.

She rolled her shoulders beneath her leather tunic and felt as much as heard the clicking from within. She had plenty of new aches and pains to deal with, but that didn't mean that the old ones had gone. The cuts and bruises would fade, leaving pale scars and a body feeling its age. After all, that was her truth.

At last, Jekob appeared. He was dressed in his drachenritter armour, the dirt cleaned off and the surcoat washed by some citadel servant. He limped along on a wooden crutch, Eljvet hovering by his side, eager to please now that his prisoner was a free man.

Jekob scowled as he caught Lena's eye. Imagining his arrival had been enough to make her look away, but the reality held her attention, skewering her with a bitter mixture of anticipation and dread. She wanted to talk with him, to hug him, to feel his love again, but she knew that wasn't what would happen. It would be guarded looks and barbed words on both sides, a struggle to keep from reopening old wounds. Perhaps, if she was lucky, it might be worth the pain.

'You have something for me?' he snapped.

Lena held out the parchment.

'This is for Lord Everhart,' she said. 'A formal record of Baumer's crimes and execution, signed and sealed by the city council.'

He took the parchment and slid it into a pouch on his belt.

'I hear that you killed your own city's commander, so that you could make peace.' He looked down at the pouch as he fastened its strings. 'I'd expected you to fight to the last.'

'I can compromise, Jekob,' she said, fighting the urge to reach out and touch him. 'I can be reasoned with. I'm sorry if I failed in that when you were young.'

His hands left the pouch and clenched tight around the crutch, as if it might spring away at any moment and drop him in the dirt.

'I never meant to hurt you,' she said. 'Somewhere along the way, I lost the ability to talk with your father, and somehow that spread to me and you. That's my failure, and I'm sorry.'

Jekob dragged his gaze up from the ground and met her eye.

'Maybe you're right,' he said. 'Maybe it was a failure to communicate. Or maybe you're just a shit, like I always thought you were. In the end, it doesn't matter. Having you in my life hurts too much.'

Lena nodded sadly. She had a terrible feeling that it was true for her too. Once upon a time, this had been about who was to blame, now it was just a matter of what pain she could bear.

With a creaking of hinges and a scraping of wood against dirt, the gates of Unteholz opened. Outside, a delegation of Everhart's soldiers waited.

'Goodbye, Mother.'

'Goodbye, Jekob.'

As the gates closed behind him, Lena looked back at the shattered city wall. Some things could be mended, but some couldn't. Perhaps she could make peace with that.

A clerk scurried out of Councillor Maier's office just as Lena was walking in. He kept his head down over his bundle of papers, not meeting her eye, not giving her the chance to show a sign of recognition. No one wanted their boss to know that they had been spilling secrets.

Inside the office, desks were still lined up beneath the window, littered with the papers on which a campaign of resistance had been planned. Through those windows, the charred peaks of Othagate's ruins were just visible beyond the foundries and artisans' houses. The broken stretch of wall was out of sight, but Lena was confident of what she would see there: the city's inhabitants beginning to rebuild, the army outside packing its wagons and preparing to move on.

Maier sat behind her desk in a red fitted doublet, a silk cap holding in her hair. Gold rings flashed on her fingers as she scribbled a note with a goose-quill pen.

'Headsman Sturm,' she said, without looking up. 'Or General Seeger. Which would you prefer?'

'Headsman,' Lena said. 'Always Headsman.'

A padded chair faced Maier across the desk. The councillor didn't offer Lena a seat, but she took it anyway.

'I sent for you hours ago,' Maier said.

'I was sleeping.'

'For eighteen hours?'

'You try fighting in bonded armour. It catches up with you in the end.'

There was a bottle of wine on the table and a goblet beside it. The temptation was hard to resist, but Lena had pushed her luck with the chair, and she could see Maier tensing, ready to reassert her dominance. They could fight it out now, a battle of wills in which Lena might emerge on top or might just alienate the most powerful woman in the city. Or she could accept that the war was over and return to who she had been.

She rolled her shoulders, felt the ache of weary muscles, and settled lower in the chair.

'What did you call me here for?' she asked. 'I've earned a rest.'

Maier picked up a cloth, wiped the ink from her quill, and set both down.

'You made a deal with Brodbeck,' she said, scowling. 'Immunity from the law for her people.'

'I said I wouldn't execute them for past crimes, as long as they came to fight.'

'You had no right to make a deal on behalf of the city.'

'I didn't. I made a deal for me. You find someone else to swing the sword and you can chop off all the heads you want.'

'You have undermined the foundations of justice in Unteholz.'

Lena crossed her arms.

'How many crimes more than a month old does anyone get convicted for here?' she asked. 'I could count those since I arrived on one hand. They've been let off a punishment they were never going to get.'

'That's not the point. I should sack you for this.'

Lena laughed. 'You couldn't sack me before. What makes you think you can do it when I'm the hero of the city? You should throw me a thundering parade.'

'Oh, we plan to.'

Lena's stomach tightened. She glared at Maier. The corner of the councillor's mouth twitched up, the tiniest hint of a smile.

'That's not funny,' Lena said.

'I'm not joking. A lot of people want to throw a victory parade, with you at the head. Once the army's out of sight, of course, and we can pretend that we've achieved something.'

There had been victory parades for Lena once, back when the religious wars were young, when faith, glory, and righteousness seemed like real things. Before she understood who she had become. She had come here to escape all that, to find a quiet corner where no one tried to praise her for atrocities or blame her for doing what duty demanded. She couldn't face those crowds again.

'I won't do it,' she said.

'The people want it.'

'The people can shove it. I've done enough for them.'

'You're a hero in a city that needs them. An example to be held up. It would take quite an effort to stop this.'

'Then make the effort!'

'I could, if you promise to stick to the straight path from now on.' Maier leaned forwards, fingers steepled in front of her. 'No more deals with criminals, no more investigations without permission. You do as you're told, when you're told, or we'll have the biggest parade the Principalities have ever seen and invite the whole world to come celebrate General Seeger.'

'I don't like being blackmailed,' Lena growled.

'And I don't like disobedience.' Maier leaned back in her chair. 'Do we have a deal?'

Lena sighed. It could have been worse, and she would have liked to just accept it, but she needed to make sure everything was done, all the loose ends tied off so she could leave this cursed business behind.

'I need some other things from the city,' she said.

'Really?' Maier raised an eyebrow.

'Master Pawlitzki the alchemist is owed two dragons' hearts, at the council's expense. You can't just demand them off the sgeir, you've got to pay them proper rates.'

'An expensive gift by most standards,' Maier said, picking up her quill to make a note. 'But cheap compared with rebuilding the walls, and we have the dead dragons. What else?'

'Baumer's constables, the ones that came with him.'

'You want them exiled?'

Lena had considered it. After all, they might come at her for vengeance. But they had fought to keep this city safe, and if they still wanted what shelter it could offer, didn't they deserve that just as much as her? Besides, it was easier to watch an enemy if you knew where they were.

'I want you to send a clerk to them,' she said. 'Get their account of the Slaughter of Saints. If they want to pin the blame on Baumer now he's dead, let them. Then send that account down to the Salt Cities and let their princes decide whether justice has been done.'

Maier stared at Lena, her quill hovering over the paper.

'Are you trying to start another siege?' she asked.

'The truth is out, and sooner or later it will reach the people who care. Wouldn't you rather control how that happens?'

Maier sighed and made another note.

'You're right, Headsman. Better to lance the boil than to let it fester.'

'Then I think we're done.'

Lena stood. The chair scraped across the floor behind her.

'One last thing.' Maier picked up a pouch the size of her fist and threw it to Lena. Coins pressed, hard and heavy, through the soft leather. 'You might not want a parade, but the council has to give you some reward. After all, you saved the city.'

'Not everything is a business,' Lena said. 'Sometimes we do what we do because it's right.'

'Then call this an act of justice, good things for those who do good. And now you're dismissed; I have work to do.'

Lena hefted the pouch. It felt good. Not the value of the coins, but the people they represented, the ones who looked at her with gratitude as she passed in the street. It wasn't always so bad to have her achievements recognised, as long as there was no thundering parade.

She stopped halfway to the door. The weight of the coins and the talk of rewards had reminded her of something else. Like the fragments of a broken mosaic pushed back together, the pieces fell into place and a previously unseen picture emerged.

'I have one more thing,' she said.

Maier looked up from her next document, one eyebrow raised. 'Go on.'

'I'm taking on an apprentice. The city will need to buy him a uniform and provide a stipend for his food and lodging.'

'It's about time, but do you really think that boy Deppel can swing an executioner's sword?'

Of course the councillor had seen through what Lena was thinking, had made her feel predictable and foolish, had raised that sharp spike of anger that made her want to say something different, to deny that she had ever meant it to be Deppel.

None of that stopped it being the right thing to do. Deppel needed a safe place to live and a craft to keep him from a life of crime. He had earned his reward from the city, and if she enjoyed having some company while she worked, that was just because any job became easier when it was shared.

'He'll learn,' Lena said.

Outside the window, a gryphon screeched as it flew over the city, feathers falling from ragged wings. An old and battered creature on its last flight, heading for the caves above Unteholz. An ageing warrior heading home to die.

Acknowledgements

Huge thanks to David Knighton and Ben Moxon, whose feedback once again sharpened the blade of my prose.

To Milena Buchs, for all the support and encouragement.

To Amy, James, and Ted at Northodox for taking on my story. In particular, thanks to Amy for the edits and to James for the stunning cover.

To Charlotte, Megan, and Lucy at the Breaking the Glass Slipper podcast, always a big influence on my writing but particularly so this time.

And lastly, a thank you to someone I've never met. This story was partly inspired by Joel F. Harrington's book The Faithful Executioner, which I found by chance while working on something else. If you'd like a peak into the strange reality of a sixteenth-century executioner, it's a fascinating read.

NORTHODOX PRESS

FIND US ON SOCIAL MEDIA

@northodoxpress

@northodoxpressofficial

@northodoxpress

@northodoxpress

www.northodox.co.uk

NORTHODOX PRESS

SUBMISSIONS

CONTEMPORARY
CRIME & THRILLER
FANTASY
LGBTQ+
ROMANCE
YOUNG ADULT
SCI-FI & HORROR
HISTORICAL
LITERARY

SUBMISSIONS@NORTHODOX.CO.UK

Made in United States
North Haven, CT
25 April 2025

68304127R00240